# THE KARASIK CONSPIRACY

# THE KARASIK CONSPIRACY

## KENIN M. SPIVAK & JULIE CHRYSTYN

PHOENIX BOOKS

Copyright ©2005 Spivak Management Inc.

ISBN: 1-59777-519-3

Library of Congress Cataloging-In-Publication Data Available

Book Design by Sonia Fiore and Phil Oster

Printed in the United States of America

Phoenix Books
9465 Wilshire Boulevard, Suite 315
Beverly Hills, CA  90212

*www.karasikconspiracy.com*

10  9  8  7  6  5  4  3  2  1

*In loving memory of my father.*
*— Julie Chrystyn*

# FOREWORD

International alliances were once the exclusive province of great nations. The emergence of expansive multi-national corporations added a great many considerations and players to the equation. Now, cross-border terrorism, religious fundamentalism, ethnic cleansing and rapidly evolving capabilities in once developing nations have dramatically shifted the paradigm. A conventional army is no longer a pre-requisite for projecting power. Nations, corporations and even terrorists become allies one day and enemies the next.

This book is a fictional thriller based upon very real battles being fought in the United States and Eastern Europe by nations, corporations and terrorists. Our playing field begins with America's pharmaceutical distribution capability, itself the site of two pitched battles.

The first pits one of America's largest global businesses, the pharmaceuticals industry, against consumers.

The second pits America's law enforcement and intelligence communities against committed and proficient terrorists who many believe are preparing to launch an attack using adulterated medicines distributed to unsuspecting customers of Canadian web sites.

Though these battles at first seem unrelated, they have become part of a single war—a war in which the pharmaceuticals industry gleefully hypes all manner of potential attacks on Americans as a justification for limiting consumers' access to Canadian distributors. The result not only keeps the prices of prescriptions in America 20% to 100% above the cost of the same drugs in Canada, but it also illuminates a road map for terrorists.

The result is the worst of all worlds. The risk of a terrorist attack on large numbers of Americans becomes all the more real, and already high prescription prices skyrocket as American consumers are deprived of the benefits of free market competition.

Congress stepped into this mess in 2000, when in typical fashion it passed and President Clinton signed into law the Medicine Equity and Drug Safety Act. That law opened the door for Canadian and other foreign drug manufacturers to enter the U.S. market, but only if the U.S. Secretary of Health and Human Services certified that implementation would not reduce the safety of U.S. pharmaceuticals.

To this day, the Secretary has not done so. As a result, consumer groups have advocated that Congress fix the loophole by eliminating the required certification. Legislation is working its way through committee and may come up for a vote by the end of 2005, or early 2006.

The pharmaceuticals industry is doing everything it can to hold the line, including funding and cooperating with numerous studies that paint a scary picture. Its lobbyists hammer away at the theme that we take for granted the safety of our medicines. They assert that allowing importation of drugs from Canada will lead to a significant increase in counterfeit, adulterated, and diverted medicines, and greatly magnify the risk of terrorist attack, posing an unbearable threat to the safety of U.S. citizens.

As described in the Afterword at the end of this book, *The Karasik Conspiracy* started its life as part of that effort when a consultant for the industry proposed funding a novel that would scare the American public into supporting its efforts to preserve restrictions on imported drugs.

We were asked to view the industry as heroic, to assume that women are interested chiefly in fluff, and to change our manuscript to make fundamentalist Muslims the terrorists and greed their motive. In the end, our book does none of this. In a multi-layered world where 150 North American Muslim organizations and leaders joined in July 2005 in a fatwa against terrorism, and the industry's principal lobbying group, Pharmaceutical Research and Manufacturers of America (PhRMA), considers covertly funding novels to make its case, even our fiction should be more nuanced than that. In the end, this novel is a more balanced exposé of the dangers we confront in a perilous and confusing world.

The consultant for PhRMA even tried to buy us off for $100,000. The contract he unsuccessfully insisted we sign is reprinted in the Afterword at the end of the book. Its most interesting provision would have deprived Julie Chrystyn, our publisher Michael Viner and me of our right to express opinions—forever—*in public or in private*, if our opinions were critical "in any manner" of the lawyer, the pharmaceuticals industry, or PhRMA.

When the story hit *The Washington Post*, the *New York Daily News* and National Public Radio in October 2005, a spokesperson for PhRMA confirmed what had occurred, but blamed PhRMA's involvement on an outside consultant and a "yo-yo" at PhRMA.

Extensive materials regarding PhRMAs role in the publication of this book can be found at *www.karasikconspiracy.com*. A password may be required to access certain content on the site. Please see the Afterword at the end of this book for additional information.

No doubt PhRMA is more pleased with a 2003 report from Global Options Inc., a risk management firm based in New York City that sounded the warnings advocated by the industry. The report, entitled "An Analysis of Terrorist Threats to the American Medicine Supply," observed:

> "Contrary to conventional wisdom, many terrorist organizations have extensive knowledge in medicine and biology. As terrorists plot novel and more deadly strikes, officials fear they may mount an attack against the United States using pharmaceuticals laced with poisons or pathogens....

> "The...most frightening threat is a terrorist attack using drugs adulterated with poisons or pathogens. While explosives are the weapon of choice for terrorists in the current climate, terror organizations are turning increasingly to chemical weapon attacks... As chemical attacks become more frequent, the threat of a terrorist strike using adulterated medicines increases. Such a strike...could be...devastating to...Americans....

> "A terrorist organization, with limited technical skills, could set up an online pharmacy, generate a customer base, and then deliver tainted goods to unwitting customers from virtually anywhere in the world. Terrorists could employ the same tactics used today by fraudulent Internet pharmacies...."

> "While the threat to the medicine supply system is currently low, the consequences of such an attack could be deadly. Step by step, terror groups are

gaining expertise to produce and distribute fake drugs.... Terrorism involving the medicine supply is a growing threat to the United States that requires immediate attention."

In its report, Global Options described the frightening speed with which al-Qaeda, Hezbollah, Hamas and other terrorist cells could master all of the skills necessary to launch a deadly attack in the United States. Then, Global Options advanced the pharmaceutical industry's central claim in opposition to legislation that would facilitate the importation of drugs from Canada:

"Current legislative proposals to allow the importation of drugs from Canada would create new, lucrative opportunities for terrorists in Canada seeking to generate funds from drug counterfeiting. Legalizing the importation of drugs would also facilitate a terrorist attack on the medicine supply. Instead of smuggling drugs across the border, a strike could be launched by sending tainted drugs through the mail system or by adulterating drugs bound for the U.S."

Just recently, on July 7, 2005, PhRMA announced "an advertising campaign to broaden the reach of the industry's efforts to educate consumers, especially America's seniors, about the safety risks of importing prescription drugs from foreign countries...."

Annually, an estimated two million Americans purchase medicine from Canadian pharmacies, creating an inviting target for terrorists and a powerful economic incentive for one of the world's largest industries to take strong action to protect its multi-billion dollar profits.

Those pharmaceutical companies are truly huge. The five largest publicly traded pharmaceutical companies have a combined market capitalization of more than $650 billion, combined revenues exceeding $175 billion and cash flow of more than $90 billion. Few industries come close.

Who has the most to gain from a terror attack on our medicine supply? Muslim fundamentalists? Far right extremists? The pharmaceutical industry itself?

These questions form the premise of this book. While the pharmaceutical industry continues to spend billions of dollars to market its products, deliver its protectionist message to you, and keep opposing views at bay, just how far will it go to preserve the industry's incredible profit margins and all the power, influence and perks those profits can buy?

By the way, Operation Cyber Chase described in the book is real, though the date of the press conference has been changed for literary convenience. All of the drugs are also real, except for cyprofaxin, nermycin and other drugs sold by C3. Finally, the history in the Balkans is accurately described through 2004, though again for literary convenience, from only one perspective. Ivan Maslac, Viktor Dzogan and more recent events are fictional. There is no C3 Group or PharmCorp — or is there?

We hope you enjoy our contribution to the dialogue.

*Kenin M. Spivak*
*Beverly Hills, California*
*October 2005*

# PROLOGUE

Lori and Ed Lasman and their nine-year-old son Ron planned to spend Thanksgiving with Aunt Tessie and Uncle Lou in Queens. The usual half-hour drive on the Belt Parkway from their modest home in the Sheepshead Bay neighborhood of Brooklyn would stretch to an hour with the holiday traffic. Who would care once the turkey, stuffing, cranberry sauce and pumpkin pie came their way?

They never made it to Queens. Instead of a joyous holiday with their family, Lori was weeping silently as she sat on a worn armchair in a children's ward of Coney Island Hospital. She stared at Ron, hooked up to a multitude of drips, and a tube that augmented his shallow breathing. The fourth grader at P.S. 194 had just won the math contest. He had never even been sick before. When the unexpected pneumonia hit, the doctors said he would rapidly recover. Until just a few days ago, he seemed to be getting better.

At about the same time Ron was slipping into a coma, some 1,100 miles away, Teddy Watler was being admitted to Children's Mercy Hospital in Kansas City. Children's Mercy specialized in pulmonary problems, which was exactly what Mary and Ted senior needed to save their son. Like Ron Lasman, eight-year-old Teddy had never been sick. True, he'd had the odd cold now and then, and a mild staph infection a few months ago. The doctors told them not to worry about the staph infection and they wrote out two prescriptions for drugs they said would cure it. Ted and Mary ordered the drugs from their usual web site, and within a few weeks the infection started to improve. Then, quite suddenly, Teddy developed an aggressive pneumonia. His parents hoped the best hospital in Kansas City would cure him, but they were worried.

Clear across the country, Dale and Cheryl Bolen said good-bye to Cheryl's mother, Estelle. No one at Los Angeles Metropolitan Medical Center could explain what happened. One moment Estelle had been happy and active, the next she was dead. More precisely, along with several of the other volunteers at St. Vincent de Paul's food bank and homeless shelter, Estelle had developed a staph infection. Though the shelter had no doctor on staff, it had a nurse. She suggested some drugs that could combat a staph infection. Because Estelle had only limited medical insurance, Dale, who delivered furniture for a major chain store, and Cheryl, who worked as a receptionist at a retirement home near their house, simply followed the nurse's advice. They looked up the drugs on the Internet, and found a web site from Canada that did not require prescriptions. Everything worked out just fine, and within a few weeks Estelle was feeling much better. The infection was clearing up.

Other than the staph infection, Estelle had been a remarkably healthy 67-year-old woman. Then, two weeks ago, when Cheryl came home from work, she got a call from her mother saying that she wasn't feeling well. Cheryl arrived at Estelle's apartment to find her running a fever of 102. Estelle could barely move and she was having trouble breathing. Panicked, Cheryl called Dale. When Dale got there, Estelle's fever was up to 103. Together, they rushed Estelle to the hospital, where Estelle's Medicare would cover much of the cost. After a wait of more than an hour, Estelle was examined by an emergency room physician. He took blood and a chest x-ray. He diagnosed the problem as pneumonia and told Dale and Cheryl that Estelle should be admitted to the hospital for a few days so she could be given intravenous drugs. He assured them that Estelle would recover.

Instead, Estelle's condition worsened. Her breathing became labored, her skin looked waxy, and no amount of drugs seemed to make any difference. The doctors were very sorry. The nurses were very sorry. Although everyone was sorry, their only explanation was that occasionally these things happened.

Over the next month, an unusually large number of Americans contracted pneumonia. Many of them died, including both Ron and Teddy.

William Bowne completed the program that would irretrievably fragment the segregated partition of his hard drive. The executive vice president of special projects for PharmCorp, one of the world's largest pharmaceutical conglomerates, wanted to be very certain that no investigation could find a connection between PharmCorp and his latest project.

Bowne sat deeply back in his cushioned leather chair as he thought about the risks and the deaths that likely would result. Each time he did the calculations, he came out the same way. It was unfortunate, but it was necessary.

A distinguished looking man in his mid 50s carefully parked his dark blue sedan in the underground lot at the Fashion Center shopping mall in Pentagon City. The upscale shopping center was down the block from the Ritz-Carlton Hotel and just a mile from the Pentagon. But, that wasn't why he selected that mall. After checking that he had not been followed, he took the escalator to the street level and exited on the West side of the building. There, he took a down escalator, extracted an electronic ticket from his wallet, walked down a flight of stairs and after a brief moment, boarded the Blue Line subway, headed toward Franconia – Springfield. He took it just one stop to Crystal City. There, he climbed a flight of stairs and then took yet another escalator. When he reached street level, he turned southwest, and headed for the Marriott.

Once in the Marriot, he located the pay phones just off the main lobby. Carefully counting out the change, he deposited five dollars. He punched in 13 numbers, the prefix telling him that he was calling Thailand. After five rings, a voice said simply "Yes." There was a slight echo, indicative of the connection to Bangkok and the additional locations to which the signal had no doubt been bounced before being answered. "It's me," the distinguished looking silver-haired man replied. "Good. What are you hearing?" a slightly accented voice echoed across the thousands of miles of repeaters.

"Not very good news, I'm afraid. The FBI is proceeding with the investigation. They are getting close to Project Sky and the Centers for Disease Control has detected a pattern with all these deaths. There is no doubt that someone with access to your plans has been advising them. The time has come to issue your demands and end the leaks. Permanently."

After disconnecting, the distinguished looking man carefully reversed his steps, took the subway back to Pentagon City and headed back to the parking lot underneath Fashion Center. After again surveying the area for telltale signs of surveillance and again detecting none, he opened his car using the remote, got inside and very carefully drove out of the Fashion Center mall within the two-hour free parking period. About 45 minutes later he was back at his desk, getting ready for his meeting with the President's National Security Advisor.


Viktor Dzogan turned to his three colleagues and gave the "go" signal. With that, the four Serbians sped into Srebrenica in two jeeps. They came to a stop at the red brick elementary school. Quickly, teams of two each got into position at the front doors. Dzogan again signaled. They burst inside and opened fire. Within 30 seconds, the guards were dead, along with two other adults, probably teachers. As first screams and then pandemonium erupted; they fired their Colt M3 carbines on fully automatic. The large .45 caliber rounds ripped through dozens of students. With military precision, they followed up with fragmentation grenades that killed another 50 students and four teachers. By then the melee was in full eruption, with screams everywhere. Students and teachers were jumping from windows, and shouts could be heard from nearby residences. As the four continued to fire into the defenseless students, Dzogan took out a whistle and blew three short blasts. With that, the four Serbian terrorists withdrew to their jeeps and headed out of Bosnian territory. In less than four minutes, 130 students, eight teachers, the principal and the security guards were dead and another 70 students were seriously wounded.


"That bastard Maslac has to be stopped," Petar Raic declared. "Words. All we get from the United States are words. Milosevic will never pay. Maslac will never pay. And what are we doing about it?"


Sitting in his well-appointed office, behind his ornate desk, Ken Karasik placed the secure phone back on its cradle. The time had come. Three years of planning were over. His vast resources in

Europe, Asia and North America were fully engaged. Many hundreds of thousands of Americans might now die if the government lacked the will to act. If so, those deaths would not be his fault. He picked up another phone and punched in the numbers that would forever change the future for his people.

*"The West is neither corrupted nor degenerate. It is strong, well educated and organized. Their schools are better than ours. The level of respect for human rights in the West is higher, and the care for the poor and less capable is better organized. Westerners are usually responsible and accurate in their words. Instead of hating the West, let us proclaim cooperation instead of confrontation."*

Alija Izetbegovic
President, Bosnia and Herzegovina, 1990 - 2000

*"Today we pay tribute to the victims of a terrible crime—the worst on European soil since the Second World War. Throughout the world this date is marked as a grim reminder of man's inhumanity to man.*

*"Our first duty is to uncover and confront the full truth about what happened. We can say—and it is true—that great nations failed to respond adequately.... We made serious errors of judgment.... The tragedy of Srebrenica will haunt our history forever.*

*"Yet our quest for justice remains incomplete... Those charged with being the main architects of this massacre—Ratko Mladic and Radovan Karadzic—are still at large... The world must equip itself to act collectively against genocide, ethnic cleansing and crimes against humanity. The responsibility to protect must be given tangible meaning, not just rhetorical support."*

Kofi Annan,
United Nations Secretary General
Srebrenica, July 11, 2005
Ceremony marking the 10th anniversary
of the Srebrenica massacre

*"The pharmaceutical industry has used scare tactics to try and stop real prescription drug legislation from passing in Congress. One of its most deceitful and shameless claims is that real reform will somehow stifle research and development and make their business unprofitable. However, the industry is pocketing the largest profit margin of any industry in the nation, with these profits far outweighing their spending on research and development. Make no mistake about it, there is a direct connection between the drug companies' massive profits and Americans being charged the highest prices for prescription drugs in the world. It is my belief that Congress needs to stop working to protect the billions in drug company profits and start working to protect Americans from being ripped off on the price of their medications."*

Bernard Sanders
Member of the United States Congress
(Independent – Vermont)

# PART I

*"Any power must be an enemy of mankind which enslaves the individual by terror and force, whether it arises under the Fascist or the Communist flag. All that is valuable in human society depends upon the opportunity for development accorded to the individual."*

Albert Einstein
(1879 – 1955)

# ONE

*T*HEY WORE MILITARY-STYLE uniforms, but without unit insignia or rank. Weeks of planning and reconnaissance behind them, they had selected a night with a quarter moon. Just enough light to find their way without night vision equipment.

Ivan Maslac's heavily-armed and well-trained unit traveled in five jeeps. They left separately from their bases, taking various routes to Tuzla, the third largest city in Bosnia and Herzegovina. The ubiquitous jeeps attracted no attention in the war-weary region. Each had a canvas tarp covering its upper frame, providing cover from prying eyes and making it unlikely their weapons would be observed.

Kevlar assault vests and weapons were stacked in the back. Their arsenal included Beretta 9mm automatics and the same assault weapons favored by NATO and U.S. Special Forces—the Mossberg 500 ATP-8 12-gauge shotgun with pistol grip, its compact size and eight shots perfect for ballistic breaching and antipersonnel action in close quarters; the Colt M4-A1 carbine, notable for its fully automatic firing mode, reduced size and integrated M203 40mm grenade launcher; and the 5.56mm Colt Commando with 30-round magazines, an older but always reliable fully-automatic assault weapon for close-in fighting.

They had an ample supply of magazines for the M4s and Colt Commanders, cartridges for the Mossbergs, incendiary, antipersonnel, and CS tear gas grenades, blocks of C4 explosives, detonators, gas masks and first aid kits. Prior to departing, each of their assault vests had been filled with just the right ordinance.

Though they had cell phones, Maslac selected commercially available Motorola digital walkie-talkies for their communications. The six-ounce radios clipped to their belts and a standard earpiece fit snugly in their ears. The audio was enhanced by the noise insulation provided by their gas masks.

Maslac timed their approach to reach Tuzla's main police precinct on Skenderija just before the evening shift change, when as many as 100 policemen might be in the building. With the element of surprise on their side, all 100 could be dead in less than five minutes. Then, the unit would simply melt away into the surrounding towns.

The mission was the first in a series of strikes that would torment the Slavic Muslims and prove that none were safe in the Balkans. As his jeep headed alongside the deceptively calm Jala River, Maslac again concluded there were no holes in the plan for the deadly retribution he was about to exact. Three weeks of reconnaissance had given the Serbs a comprehensive understanding of the objective. Greater Serbia soon would be pure.

The precinct was a two-story, 20-year-old brick building located in the middle of the block. South-facing double-doors led from Skenderija into the lobby, where a desk officer controlled access to the remainder of the building. A wall of bulletproof glass shielded the ground floor and a wide staircase that led up to the second floor and down to a full basement.

Another entrance faced the parking lot located at the building's east end. A rear door located at the northwest corner of the ground floor exited into a narrow alley. An adjacent stairway ran down to the basement; only the main stairs off the lobby reached the second floor.

There were surveillance cameras at each of the exterior doors. A buzzer system allowed the desk officer to screen visitors at all three entrances.

The station's top floor included squad and conference rooms and the communications center. The lobby, storage, holding cells, interrogation chambers and a booking area comprised the ground floor. Lockers, a gym, an armory and utilities were located in the basement.

A printing company abutted the station to the west. Two-story shops facing the next street backed onto the far side of the rear alley. Small factories faced the police station from the south side of Skenderija.


The Serbs approached the precinct at 7:50 pm. By then, the stores and factories were empty, and officers on the day shift were streaming into the building for the 8:00 pm briefing and hand-off to the night shift. Maslac smiled. It was his destiny to complete what Milosevic had left undone.

At precisely 7:53, Slavisa Popovic parked his jeep one block north of the police station. He and his partner Srecko Andric pulled on their assault vests, quickly tightening the Velcro straps. Each checked his earpiece. Popovic placed his gas mask on his head, but left it propped up on his forehead. Andric would not be going inside and had no need for a gas mask.

Andric grabbed his M4 carbine with attached grenade launcher and one of the duffels. He headed to the side of a bakery that backed onto the alley behind the police station, locating a window they had previously identified in their reconnaissance. The window had been selected because it could not be seen from the street and had no alarm. Andric smashed the window with the butt of his carbine, cleared out the glass and crawled through. Once inside, he used his flashlight to illuminate the way to the bakery's rear staircase and up to the roof. He moved to the edge closest to the alley, where he had a perfect view of the back of the police station, including the rear door and second floor, rear-facing windows. No windows faced the alley on the ground floor. After carefully unpacking his duffel, he organized the grenades in a predetermined order and waited for Maslac's signal.

Popovic placed his Mossberg shotgun and Colt Commando on the passenger seat along with a small duffel containing C4 explosives and CS gas canisters. He returned to the jeep and quietly drove around to the side street, positioning his vehicle just inside the east end of the alley that ran behind the police station. *It's payback time,* he thought, recalling how NATO jets had leveled his house back in 1999, killing his parents and little sisters. *Yeah, six-year-old girls are a deadly threat,* Popovic thought as he, too, waited for Maslac's signal.

While Andric was making his way to the bakery's roof, Teodor Lucic drove his jeep from a side street into the alley behind the buildings located across Skenderija from the police station. He parked behind the factory that was located directly across from the precinct. There, Lucic and his partner, Jovan Tesla, slipped on their assault vests and checked their weapons. Neither would be entering the station, so they too had no gas masks. Using glass cutters, they efficiently removed a window pane in the men's room. As was too often true in Tuzla, the alarm hadn't worked in years. They pushed open the latch, raised the window and quickly scrambled inside.

Lucic used his flashlight to head for the roof. He had a perfect view of the front of the police station, including the main entrance and the windows on both the ground and second levels.

Tesla remained on the ground floor and headed for the front of the factory. Once there, he quietly used the glass cutters to remove panes from two windows that faced the police station. He too had a perfect view of the front of the building. Once in position, Lucic and Tesla unpacked their duffels, organizing their grenades much as Andric was doing on the bakery's roof at the far side of the police station. It was 7:55.

The third jeep pulled into the alley, just beside Popovic. There, Maslac and Vlade Subic put on their vests and gas masks, checked their weapons and selected the appropriate duffels. Subic remained behind with Popovic, while Maslac drove the jeep around the corner to Skenderija, parking about 150 feet west of the police station's main entrance.

Two other teams followed a similar procedure. Viktor Dzogan, Maslac's second-in-command, and his partner Dejan Jovanovic parked about 150 feet east of the police station, just beyond the edge of the parking lot. Rudjer and Jovan Pupin, brothers who always worked together, parked about 30 feet east of Dzogan.

At 8:01 pm, Maslac used his walkie-talkie for the first time. "Ready," he said in Croatian. By 8:02, each member of the unit had responded with a one-word answer: "Yes." Those who would enter the building pulled their gas masks into position. Andric, Lucic and Tesla prepared to fire. Maslac gunned his engine and drove to the front door of the police station, where he met Dzogan and Jovanovic, who arrived at the same time from the opposite direction. The Pupin brothers pulled ahead, taking over Dzogan's position just beyond the parking lot and silently got out of their jeep. It was 8:03.

Maslac raised his walkie-talkie and yelled "Go!" Then all hell broke loose.

With one blast from his Mossberg, Maslac splintered the main doors of the police station. He, Dzogan and Jovanovic were inside before the desk officer understood what was happening. With his M4 set for three-shot bursts, Dzogan killed him instantly, a mangled mess where his chest used to be. Maslac and Jovanovic sprayed the other officers who were unfortunate enough to be in the lobby, instantly killing three of them. At the same time, Maslac lobbed a grenade at the officers, killing another four. In less than 10 seconds, eight police officers were dead. None of them had even drawn a weapon.

Their hearing already gone from the loud explosions and automatic weapons fire, Maslac and Dzogan reached into their duffels for the C4. Stepping around the lifeless bodies, each made his way to a door located in the bulletproof glass, placing a bar of C4 near the lock and inserting a detonator. They set the timers for three seconds, giving them just enough time to move away from the blast. The powerful explosions destroyed the doors and shattered the glass wall. Alarms sounded throughout the police station, as officers began to react to the maelstrom that surrounded them.

At the exact moment that Dzogan killed the desk officer, Andric, Lucic and Tesla used their M4s to blow out windows in the police station. Each then launched an explosive grenade through those windows, killing any officers within 10 feet of the blast and taking out large chunks of the exterior wall, making it unnecessary to waste precious seconds with pinpoint aiming.

Andric targeted the rear windows on the second floor, making certain the first grenades hit the communications center. Lucic fired into the front windows of the second floor, and Tesla took aim at the far right and left front windows on the ground floor, both of which accessed parts of the floor beyond the lobby and inside the protection of the glass wall. The three killers launched volley after volley of fragmentation and CS gas grenades from their positions in the bakery behind the station and the factory across the street.

Occasionally, they fired additional explosive charges, keeping the officers off-guard, and destroying the station's internal walls.

Within seconds, screams could be heard from throughout the building as razor-sharp shrapnel ripped into unprotected flesh and the CS gas induced blindness and vomiting. By the time the bullet-proof glass shattered some 30 seconds after the attack had begun, the ground floor was filling with the shrieks and moans of dying and wounded officers.

The situation on the second floor was even worse. The upper level consisted of just a few large rooms and it was under attack from both the front and the back.

Breathing for the besieged officers became an exercise in agony as highly concentrated CS gas rapidly filled the area. Choking and gagging, the officers desperately sought to escape the onslaught. Momentarily triumphant, they forced open the side exit and tried to rush into the parking lot. As they did, Rudjer and Jovan opened fire with their M203 grenade launchers, each sending an antiper-sonnel fragmentation grenade into the crowd. They immediately followed up with pinpoint three-shot bursts. In just seconds, they killed 14 officers and the doors closed. Before the screams died down, police in the parking lot returned fire with their sidearms. Rudjer and Jovan methodically cut them down, killing three and critically wounding two.

The Pupins advanced on the station. It was not yet 8:04.

The instant Maslac said "Go!" Subic and Popovic roared down the alley, reaching the rear entrance just as Andric's grenades started exploding on the second floor. Using a bar of C4, Subic blew the rear door off its hinges. They fired two blasts from their Mossbergs, killing or wounding officers trying to flee through the rear entrance. Before any of the trapped police could return fire, they headed down to the basement. Exiting the staircase, they each fired two more blasts with their Mossbergs, before switching to their Colt Commanders. They fired on full automatic, immediately emptying their clips. As they reloaded, police returned fire, using both sidearms and automatic weapons. Pinned down, Subic and Popovic lobbed CS canisters across the basement and then fragmentation grenades. They were gratified by the screams that followed the explosions. Within seconds, additional gas began to filter down the main staircase from the first floor. They also heard gunfire from the front of the basement. It was 8:04.

Even before Subic and Popovic reached the basement, Maslac, Dzogan and Jovanovic were through the shattered glass. After waiting just a few seconds for Tesla to complete his initial attack, they moved forward. Dzogan and Jovanovic indiscriminately killed officers and civilians, while Maslac lobbed CS canisters into the first floor, and then down the main staircase into the basement. When they felt more than heard the Mossberg blasts from the back of the building, they knew Subic and Popovic were on their way to the basement. Because the CS was making breathing all but impossible for the officers, their defense was sporadic and nearly pointless.

Not one officer made it down the stairs from the second floor. Both Tesla and Lucic targeted that level, with Tesla launching additional antipersonnel grenades into the front windows and Lucic firing his M4 in three-shot bursts at any moving target.

As Subic and Popovic reached the basement, the Pupins reached the side door. Rudjer affixed C4 to the hinges and set the timer for just three seconds. As they moved aside, the explosion rocked the parking lot, blowing the door into the building, instantly killing five wounded officers. The sounds of death were terrible, as gunfire and explosions combined with screams and wails. It was about to get worse.

Andric and Lucic switched to incendiary grenades, exhausting their supply into the second floor. There were multiple explosions as the CS gas and the incendiary grenades combusted. Flames came out of both the front and the rear windows. As officers tried to escape by running down the main staircase, Maslac, Dzogan and Jovanovic cut them down. As soon as Rudjer and Jovan entered, they launched grenades toward the rear of the first floor. Rudjer followed with repeated blasts from his Mossberg, while Jovan used two-shot bursts against any moving target. Andric picked off the handful of officers who attempted to flee through the rear door.

With the Pupins cleaning up the ground floor and a raging fire on the second floor, Maslac, Dzogan and Jovanovic headed to the basement to give assistance to Subic and Popovic, emptying clip after clip as they did so. It was coming up on 8:05.

Maslac and Jovanovic stepped from the landing into the basement. The sound of automatic gunfire reverberated through the confined space. Jovanovic crumpled, half his head blown away by a well-placed shot. Dzogan screamed and grabbed his right side, thick blood oozing between his fingers. Maslac dove for cover just as an explosion ripped across the basement and flames erupted around him.

From just inside the parking lot entrance, Rudjer lobbed an incendiary grenade into the back of the ground floor. As it exploded, Jovan cried out. A Slav firing an old Soviet-era Kalashnikov AK-47 had emptied the entire magazine, severing Jovan's right leg above the knee and cutting deeply into his left leg. As he fell, Rudjer knew his brother would bleed out within minutes. Seconds later, flames engulfed the area near the door. It was 8:06.

With the building ablaze and resistance dwindling, Maslac signaled their withdrawal. Subic and Popovic exited through the rear door. With covering fire from Andric, they peeled out of the alley. After stopping for him in front of the bakery, they headed out of

Tuzla, taking a course that would initially put them deeper into Bosnian territory.

Rudjer dragged Jovan back toward their jeep. As he carried his already dead brother across the parking lot, one of the wounded officers opened fire, hitting Rudjer in the leg. Rather than return fire, Rudjer continued dragging his brother's body. As he reached the street, the wounded policeman took careful aim, hitting Rudjer in the head. His last thought before he died was that he would soon be with his brother.

Dzogan's injury wasn't as bad as it first appeared. The bullet had passed straight through. While he needed medical attention he would live. Gingerly, he helped Maslac drag Jovanivic's body out of the blood-soaked building. Lucic and Tesla provided cover for the sporadic resistance still coming from within the precinct. Once Maslac and Dzogan dragged Jovanivic's body into a jeep, Lucic and Tesla quickly made their way out of the back of the factory and sped off.

Less than four minutes after the attack began, 90 Bosnian police officers, 10 visitors and eight prisoners were dead or dying, along with three of the Serbian attackers. Just five officers and three visitors survived, all badly wounded. The seven Serbian killers who escaped were very pleased with the first strike in their renewed campaign of terror.

Yugoslavia was the product of incompatible religious and ethnic groups that had been cobbled together into a single kingdom in 1918 from the rubble of World War I. After years of violence, these resolutely antagonistic sects were ruled with an iron fist by Josip Broz Tito as a satellite of the Soviet Union from 1946 until his death.

The Serbs had long memories. With Tito's death in 1980, the porous truce imposed during his unyielding rule evaporated, and the

Serbs who had started World War I by assassinating Archduke Ferdinand in Sarajevo on June 28, 1914—exactly 525 years to the day after Serbia's loss to the Ottoman Empire—resumed the genocide.

At 45, Maslac was the proud product of this endless cycle of violence—an unbridled ferocity that only grew worse when Communist hardliner Slobodan Milosevic came to power in 1988. With a purposefulness and sophistication reminiscent of Hitler's final solution, Milosevic systematically exterminated the Slavic Muslims who had been engaged for centuries in bloody conflict with the Christians they lived among in the Balkans.

Maslac had been trained by the best. Until NATO stopped them, Milosevic's notorious generals, such as Ratko Mladic, Radovan Karadzic, Nebojsa Pavkovic and Vladimir Lazarevic, had systematically plundered Muslim towns, savaging the men, raping the women, and forcibly relocating hundreds of thousands. The lucky ones were sent to more "suitable" locations elsewhere in the war-torn region, the rest, to slavery and death camps.

The killing had become so bad that in 1995 the United States forced a final break-up of Yugoslavia. The so-called Dayton Accords were dictated by Ambassador Richard Holbrooke and General Wesley Clarke at an air force base in Ohio. The alternatives were made clear to all—agree to a partition that gives Bosnia and Herzegovina independence, or the U.S. would impose it through military means. The Dayton Accords assigned NATO the thankless task of keeping the peace.

But the Dayton Accords did not end the violence. By 1999, the genocide in Kosovo had so shocked the world that NATO launched airstrikes against Milosevic's pompously renamed Federal Republic of Yugoslavia, and the War Crimes Tribunal in The Hague indicted him on 27 counts of crimes against humanity. Though pushed from the presidency, he remained at large until 2001, when he was finally arrested. His trial in The Hague began in 2002, with no end in sight.

Despite Milosevic's fall, the violence continued. In December 2004, the new European Union Army (EUFOR) replaced NATO as the region's so-called peacemakers. Instead of peace, the Serbs and the Slavs adapted, using the peacekeepers' reluctance to use force as cover for continued brutality.

Maslac would now rebuild the nationalist Serbian forces and complete the job of ethnic cleansing Milosevic had begun. He had participated in so many missions over the prior 30 years that he had lost count. He was proud to have personally slaughtered many hundreds of Muslims, burned to the ground many thousands of homes and sent tens of thousands to the death camps. No U.S.- or European-imposed partition, nor any Serb politician seeking to appease the United Nations, could change the fact that the Slavs were polluting Greater Serbia and the only solution was their complete eradication.

The attack in Tuzla was barely a beginning. The next strike was only weeks away and it would shake the world.


The following day, the *Times* ran a half-page story about the slaughter in Tuzla written by Stuart King, one of its top correspondents. Not one other major newspaper devoted more than a few lines to the atrocities. Within a week, no one outside of the Balkans even cared.

# Two

**A**DARK SKY WITH serene sparkling stars blanketed Hillcrest Valley on this Thanksgiving night. The branches of the tall, picture-perfect palm trees appeared to mingle with the clouds. The town was so quiet it was hard to believe that many celebrations were ongoing behind the high walls and perfectly manicured lawns of its many monied estates.

The subtle shades of sunset yellow reflected off Tuscan walls surrounding the estate on Bolero Road. The solid stone walls and hunter green iron gates easily exceeded the 12-foot limit permitted by the town's code. The locals, however, were accustomed to turning a blind eye to the peculiarities of its most prominent residents.

Even in wealthy Hillcrest Valley, the spread on Bolero Road was an object of curiosity among the neighbors who had endured a five-year construction ordeal. It had been reported that it was the state's most expensive residence, at a cost in excess of $30 million.

Tonight, the estate was transformed into a magical place, for the most important accomplishment of Ken Karasik's life was to be celebrated—the birth of his only son, Kenan Joseph Anton Karasik IV.

At 47, billionaire oil tycoon and global businessman extraordinâire, Ken Karasik was an intense-looking man. He stood just over six feet, with broad shoulders and a barrel chest. His dark hair was perpetually combed straight back, exposing his prominent forehead and emphasizing the sharp stare from his intense brown eyes. His stare penetrated anyone in his presence and often unnerved those who lacked sufficient self-confidence.

As befitted his wealth, Ken's wife, Nely Gonzalez Karasik, 34, was a former Miss Mexico. Her striking tan face with its impeccable chin, pouty lips and jade green eyes, framed by rich dark golden blonde hair, was hardly typical of her Mexican heritage. Her slim figure with its alluring cleavage and 22-inch waist created a regal Grace Kelly poise and a perfect ornament for Ken's arm.

In the adjoining town of Paradise Cove, Nely's best friend, Alexa Bart, was consumed with the tasks at hand. The oldest community in New Mexico, Paradise Cove once possessed an upper middle class glory, but had decayed with time as newer and better neighborhoods emerged. In 1986, Nicolas Bart moved there from Brooklyn with his 18-year-old niece Alexa, and his college-aged nephew Marcus. Alexa, who had been orphaned when she was eight, and her cousin Marcus, who had too often come to the attention of local authorities, had emigrated from Eastern Europe some years earlier. Nicolas officially became guardian to both and tried his best to give them a better life.

Now 37, Alexa was a successful fundraiser for universities and other non-profits. She had recently moved back from New York to care for her beloved 'Grandpa' Nico, who had suffered a serious stroke.

Drying off the last dish, she glanced at the clock and sighed as she realized that it was nearly 6:00 pm. She wished that she could just luxuriate in the bath and skip the party, even though it was the most coveted ticket in town. The Karasiks had moved a few years ago into their newly built 32,000 square-foot mansion with its 14 bathrooms from an 8,000 square-foot estate a few miles away, where they lived during construction. Their parties were frequented by an eclectic set of international guests associated with Ken Karasik, Nely's old friends and family, and her new best friend Alexa. Alexa had been introduced to Nely about a year ago by an old associate of Ken's from Switzerland. Nely often wondered about Alexa's background, but each time she asked, Alexa deftly avoided the specifics. Nely realized that she would have to respect the boundaries set by Alexa, who had otherwise become a warm and generous confidante.

Given her profession, Alexa was no stranger to high society functions. She quickly dressed in a sage green Dior gown, selected a pair of stylish shoes, and checked her hair.

"Grandpa, I'll be out this evening but Marie is here to keep you company, ok?"

"Where are you going?" he asked, looking abandoned and confused.

"I'm off to dinner at Nely's, Grandpa. Ken is home and they're celebrating the baby's birth and baptism tonight. Marie will serve you dinner. We'll celebrate Thanksgiving tomorrow, ok?" She spoke slowly and lovingly as she might to a child. She kissed his cheek and ran out the kitchen door.

Alexa got into her silver Mini Cooper convertible and headed down Happy Valley Road, turned right on Quail Run Trail and then onto the shortcut to Bolero Road. She drove fast, with the top down, arriving quickly at a private entrance where she punched in the security code. After a few beeps, the gate opened and she drove onto the estate. She parked near the blooming garden of white vine roses and oleanders, got out of her car and headed down the red brick walkway and into the house.

While the guests arrived and were ushered into the estate's ballroom right next to the formal dining room, a few of the old guard hovered in the sitting area off the kitchen. Alexa walked in confidently and spotted Ben Opperman. He stood apart from the crowd, holding a drink in his hand and observing the scene as if making a permanent record of the moment. His gaze caught Alexa's. Both laughed happily as they greeted properly with kisses on both cheeks.

Alexa walked over to Ken, who held court among the most distinguished of his guests. "I'm pleased to see you again, Alexa," he replied. "Welcome to our home and Happy Thanksgiving, my dear."

Alexa warmly smiled. "Thank you for having me."

Ken briefly introduced Alexa to his other guests and she greeted them with a refined ease and familiarity. After a few minutes of polite conversation, Alexa excused herself to locate Nely.

"You made it!" she exclaimed, knowing that Alexa's responsibilities to her grandfather often affected her plans. "I'm so happy you're here."

"I wouldn't have missed it for the world," Alexa responded, giving her firend a quick hug and a warm smile. Nely and Alexa chatted until the butler signaled that it was time for the guests to move into the exquisite dining room for dinner.

The seven-course banquet was indulgent by any standards—corn tortilla soup, walnut and chestnut stuffed turkey with all the fixings, salad and sorbet—topped off by a chocolate and hazelnut mousse dome covered by an edible sheet of pure 22-carat gold. As coffee and liqueurs were served all around, Ken thanked their family and friends for sharing in the celebration and officially presented and toasted his son Kenan as he was carried into the room by Nely.

The orchestra played La Paloma as the guests danced beneath chandeliers rumored to have once hung from the ceilings of the Palace of Versailles. In a rare public display of her exceptional talent, Nely's sister Sonia stood before the orchestra and sang "O mio bab-bino caro" from Madame Butterfly. The mesmerized guests broke into applause, for the haunting rendition that had taken them to a faraway place.

Drawing nearly everyone into the celebration, Sonia led the guests to join in an a cappella sing-along. The orchestra briefly swelled behind the singing, before transitioning to a lively waltz. Ken and Nely danced expertly across the vast floor and then other guests joined in. When the waltz was over, the orchestra continued with an evening of favorites. Ken remained briefly with Nely before he kissed his wife on the cheek and maneuvered through the ballroom and into the library. A few of his associates discreetly followed.

The music could be faintly heard in the background as the men once again offered their congratulations to Ken and relaxed in the impressive library. A butler brought in whisky and assorted liqueurs; the Cuban cigars were already on the table. As Ken set his glass of whisky on the massive desk, the butler discreetly left the room, closing the double doors behind him.

Ken's mood instantly changed. "I have relied on each of you, and you have done your jobs superbly. For that, I am grateful and I hope each of you knows that you have my utmost respect. Of all of my associates, you are the most diligent and trustworthy. You are my most cherished friends."

The men listened intently and sat motionless, for they knew that a man like Ken Karasik did not offer compliments and it was all leading to something else.

They were an unusual and diverse group.

First among them, at least in Ken's heart, was Petar Raic, Ken's closest friend from childhood. Like Ken, Petar was born in Bosnia in 1958 and immigrated to the United States. After becoming a citizen, Petar served in the U.S. Army, where he refined his considerable skills as a killer. A devout Muslim, Petar now lived in London with his wife, where he served as chief operations officer of Karasik's C3 Group.

Ben Opperman, 72, was a dapper security systems manufacturer born in Russia. Like many Russian Jews, Ben immigrated to Israel. After his family was killed in the Yom Kippur war in 1973, Ben moved on to Paris. Ben had become the one man whose advice Ken might take, even when he disagreed.

The most eccentric among them was Stuart King. The 43-year-old journalist and nephew of former Prime Minister Margaret Thatcher enjoyed the finer things in life—exotic travel, a great party, the best wines and beautiful women—preferably at someone else's expense. King possessed no great convictions. He was dedicated to the full enjoyment life had to offer. King lived with the "in" crowd, loved the "it" girls, and played with the rich boys—however they got their fortune. Raised in the Church of England, he believed in neither Allah nor God, nor much else. His usefulness was a product of his indifference rather than his commitments.

Melvin Darwin Bottner III, 55, was the closest to Karasik's equal among the four of them. The third generation heir to the billion-dollar MDB Corporation fortune, Bottner was a former hell-raiser, a one-time diplomat, and a church-going Episcopalian. He had been born with a platinum spoon in his mouth, a cigar between his fingers and a little black book in his pocket. Surprisingly, Bottner had developed a conscience; a commitment to personal freedom that was perfectly mated to his addiction to danger with the covert and sometimes violent activities of the five men present in that library on Bolero Road—a group that had come to refer to itself as the Karasik Commission.

Karasik chomped on his fine Cuban cigar. He was a man accustomed to controlling his environment, but tonight he was pensive. He fixed his laser gaze on each of the four men in front of him.

"C3 has been subpoenaed by the Justice Department," he started, referring to the C3 Group, through which he controlled his worldwide business activities. "I am under investigation here and in Europe. It seemed a mere nuisance when Interpol began to examine my private business affairs four years ago. Now, their findings have been turned over to the FBI and there is a real risk of arrest warrants being issued for Mel and for me. So far, they don't seem to know about our private activities, although it won't be long before Petar also becomes a target."

The men were unsettled by the news but not entirely shocked. They began to protest until Ken raised his hands and everyone went quiet. Firmly, Ken set the agenda. "Gentlemen, we will meet again in the morning. We must devise a plan to get these gnats off my back. They will *not* interfere in our plans."

All understood. The difficult work would come the next day when they gathered on Ken's houseboat, nearly 100 miles from the Bolero Road estate.

As they rejoined the party, the festivities were in full swing. The debonair, strong and silent Ben, who always had an eye for the ladies, approached Alexa and led her to the balcony beneath the starlit desert sky. They tenderly danced to *Chanson d'Amour* without speaking a word.

The last of the guests didn't leave until nearly 3:30 am. By then, Ken had been asleep well over an hour.

Alexa parked the Mini on the driveway near Grandpa's house. She quietly let herself in, and immediately checked on Grandpa. He lay there with his eyes closed and mouth hanging open. She looked at him sadly but lovingly when he quietly spoke, "How was the party?"

"I thought you were asleep," she said.

"Who can sleep day and night," he replied, now fully awake.

"It's very late Grandpa, go to sleep now," Alexa spoke softly as she pulled the covers to his chin. She maintained a regal posture but fought back the tears that were welling up in her eyes. Nico had been the only parent she had ever really known. Sometimes the pain of seeing him like this was so great she would weep alone in silence until the well went dry.

# THREE

**B**Y EIGHT THE next morning, Petar Raic, Ben Opperman, Mel Bottner and Stuart King returned to the Karasiks' opulent mansion in Hillcrest Valley from the posh Royal Palms Resort less than a mile away. After breakfast, Karasik and his four colleagues were driven for two hours in three black Mercedes jeeps through the barren desert to a private man-made lake. There, Karasik anchored a houseboat—his preferred getaway for peace, quiet and privacy.

There was never enough time for them to say everything, but on this trip, all were quiet. Only Ken talked non-stop on his cell phone to associates across the globe, shifting from one language to another.

At the houseboat, a small crew had prepared coffee and assorted delicacies in the spacious kitchen, long Ken's favorite room aboard the 3,500 square-foot vessel. Almost immediately, the staff dispersed and Ken cut to the chase. "The FBI is getting close to Project Sky. Even the Swiss authorities are helping. They are investigating C3 Pharmaceuticals in Zurich."

Though Ken saw consternation on his friends' faces, he continued. "It gets worse. Interpol and the FBI are trying to manufacture a case that Mel and I are involved in everything from extortion to murder here and in Europe. Why? Because we're rich? Because we have our own opinions? They know full well we haven't done a thing. To top it off, that damn Barry Weiner tried to freeze my accounts." Ken's voice rose when he thought of Weiner, the FBI Special Agent in charge of the investigation.

"They have nothing," Petar said, trying to calm Ken down.

"It doesn't matter," Ken replied. "They're out to destroy me."

Mel thought for a moment and wondered for whom Ken was making this speech. They all knew the truth. Was Ken afraid of being overheard? Even here, where his security team swept for listening devices and the most sophisticated electronic jammers ensured that not even a laser bounced off the houseboat's triple-layered windows could decipher what was being said inside? Or, maybe Ken no longer trusted one of them…

"The most important things we need to do right now are to keep the money flowing and keep Project Sky on track," Ken continued. Each of the four nodded, well aware that the legal costs, already $3 million a month would likely grow, but fully in agreement that nothing was more important than the success of Project Sky.

After a moment for reflection, Ben Opperman, the eldest among them, turned to Ken. "This isn't the best time to bring it up, but there's something else you should know," he said.

"Tuzla was just an appetizer. Maslac intends to step up his attacks and he now has the financing, weapons and troops to do it. Ethnic cleansing is about to resume and this time Greater Serbia might become a bloody reality after all!"

Petar interrupted. "The U.S. and the E.U. pay lip service to protecting our brothers. But NATO has abandoned the Balkans and EUFOR's troops never move from their barracks. It's a joke!" he practically spat.

Ken seldom failed, and never without first exhausting every alternative. Maslac's growing power and ruthlessness produced a visceral response from the man who had devoted his life and half his fortune to defeating the Serbs. "This time America will have no choice. We will make all that has gone before child's play. While America expends itself in Iraq on a fool's mission to bring democracy to people who can't even read, we will show how weak it has become at home. When 50,000 or 100,000 Americans die, President Bush will understand what it feels like to awaken each day in fear. He will have no choice. Then, *we* will direct the military might of the United States and our brothers in the Balkans will finally have real peace and real security."

Ken paused for a moment, and smiled for the first time that day. "It is ironic that the United States will be the instrument of our success," he declared.

Thoughts of his childhood in Bosnia and Herzegovina flashed before him. He vividly saw its mountainous terrain, herds of livestock and tobacco fields. He recalled the huge almond tree in front of his grandmother's stone house and how he loved to climb it. He also recalled the economic hardships of those poor people and their struggle for survival.

Once again calm, Ken put it simply, "Project Sky must succeed, and Maslac must not."

This would not be the first time the five members of the Karasik Commission had put their unique talents to work solving a problem by whatever means were needed. Although their identities and the precise nature of the Karasik Commission were unknown to the U.S. government, as was clear from the FBI's investigation, their efforts had not gone completely unnoticed. Ken had accomplished a great deal for himself and for all of them. It had become all too evident of late that there was a leak, a leak that Ken had been unable or *unwilling* to stop. Most assumed it was Nely, though Ken vehemently denied it. Whatever the source, the rumors had hit their mark, and now Karasik and C3 were under investigation.

When the Karasik Commission met the day after Thanksgiving on Ken's luxurious houseboat just beyond Hillcrest Valley, its members were bound together by years of friendship, shared danger and profits. More importantly, they were bound by a common belief that the Soviet Communist state and its successors, Serbia and the Russian Federation, had to be stopped. The oppressed Muslims in the Balkans and elsewhere in Eastern Europe had a right to be free and secure. They were also bound together by their bitterness at America's failure to do what was necessary, pathological quests for wealth and utter indifference to human life. They had come to that indifference by different paths, but they had arrived at substantially the same place.

Petar and Ken were childhood friends. Nearly 25 years earlier, Petar had saved Mel from almost certain death in Rome. Mel had given Ken his first job. Ben was the one man whose advice Ken gave weight equal to his own instincts. Though only Ken and Petar were from Bosnia, and the five men differed by ethnicity and religion, they shared common experiences and a revulsion toward the atrocities to which the long-suffering Slavs had been subjected for so many years.

Despite their bonds, Ken didn't share everything with his four closest colleagues. He had never told any of them about the sixth member of their intimate group.

When the intensified FBI investigation of Karasik mandated this meeting, the five members of the Karasik Commission present that day were prepared and ready to act. Unknown to all of them except Ken, so was a sixth member. And so too was a Judas. He or she had already created problems for them. They hoped the spy wasn't one of them. Maybe there had been a slip-up in their security. Maybe it was Nely. But not one of them. They could not be paralyzed. Too much was at stake.

They now had three issues to deal with: the investigation of Karasik, Maslac's growing threat in the Balkans, and their ultimate objective—Project Sky. The first shipments had already reached the United States and the next phase would begin by early February. By then, hundreds already would be dead and it would be time for their demands to be made on a very vulnerable United States.

Ken took one last sip of his coffee. Though he usually preferred the serenity of the two-hour desert drive, this time speed was more important. He called the captain to request his helicopter. As was their custom, the other four remained behind to develop their recommendations.

As Ken helicoptered back from the secluded houseboat to his Hillcrest Valley estate, he thought about how much had changed since his childhood in Bosnia. He was worth well over one billion dollars, and that included only the investments and accounts he acknowledged. He lived in luxury. Private jets. Private yachts. Homes in the exclusive and remote Hillcrest Valley, a posh Fifth Avenue penthouse in New York City and a permanent suite at the Lanesborough in London. His own security team. Unsurpassed access to leaders in business, finance and government.

Yet, all of that was a façade. Ken masterfully hid his true nature from even those who knew him best. Except for the members of the Karasik Commission, not one business associate or friend in Hillcrest Valley, New York, or London knew he had been born a

Muslim. He thought about the traditions he had forsaken—the five daily prayers and readings from the Qur'an. From the time he immigrated to America some 30 years earlier, he had been the good Roman Catholic. Unlike Petar, he no longer considered himself a Muslim, though he remained sensitive to their struggles.

It was all for a purpose. By working from inside, Ken could accomplish so much more than he ever could from the outside. That was the problem with al-Qaeda, Hamas, Hezbollah and all the Arab terrorists. They had such a vague and broad agenda, and they came head on, accomplishing very little for all their wailing. And for what reason? The Arab Muslims governed vast, rich countries. In truth, they gave Muslims a bad name. Their complaints were annoying.

Ken Karasik would show them all. With one master stroke he would change forever the balance of power in the Balkans, and with it the prospects for oppressed Muslims throughout the former Soviet Union.

Ken was pleased with his life's journey. Though he had his problems—none greater than the investigation now underway—he knew that in the end he, his lawyers, his contacts, and if need be, the secret Karasik Commission would resolve the situation. Sure, he would pay a fine. He thought the fees and fines might cost him $20 or $30 million, or even $50 million by the time the investigation died down. He smiled. He would use the deductions to avoid a tax on the profit he would no doubt make when, as part of a so-called settlement, he was also "forced" to sell off one of his many companies!

In short, Ken had just about everything he wanted, except peace and freedom for his brothers in Eastern Europe. Soon, he would have that too. And he would actually become richer in the process.

Ken's life in America was a lie. As the purpose of the lie reached its culmination, the lie would continue and Ken Karasik and the Karasik Commission would manipulate events for purposes all their own. He smiled again as he thought that very soon, their plan would be revealed as the deadliest and most insidious attack the world had ever seen.

# FOUR

**K**EN KARASIK WAS born on May 15, 1958 in the rural town of Bihac, later to become part of the sovereign nation of Bosnia and Herzogovina. During Ken's childhood, however, Bihac was part of Yugoslavia, an artificial amalgam of traditional enemies forged into an "independent" Communist state by Josip Broz Tito beginning in 1946.

Under Communism, all land was owned by the State, but the people cultivated the land and were occasionally permitted to sell or barter its produce. Though all citizens were technically equal, Ken was better off than many. His family had a 200-year-old ancestral home, the right to till a large vineyard, and an extended family that worked long and hard to produce enough crops to pocket a few extra kuna. All things being relative, the Karasiks could have been called middle class.

Ken was a helpful and astute child. His brother Slavko, a shy and gentle boy, was three years older and his energetic brother Nikola was two years younger. His twin sisters, with their blonde curls, were the babies of the family.

In the early 1960s, Bihac was a primitive place. The horse and buggy was still the main form of transportation on its dirt roads. Islam was their center. There was but one Allah and Muhammad was his Prophet. Through all of his family's hardships, they waited, keeping the faith and renewing their resolve to achieve the victory that Allah promised to the true believer. Unlike some others, however, Ken's parents instilled in their children a tolerance for other religions. Ken never feared the Greek Orthodox or the Roman Catholics. His animus was reserved for the Soviet Communists and their Serbian henchmen.

Both of Ken's grandfathers and many of his relatives had been violently tortured and killed. They were prey to the Serbians who despised them for no reason other than their ethnicity or religion. Seven of his aunts and uncles died cruel deaths as a result of disease and starvation. The military looted their homes and then gathered up the men and marched them away at gunpoint, before returning to rape or beat the women.

Still worse was inflicted on the imam of their cherished mosque. The soldiers stormed the mosque that had served generations of locals. Capturing the imam during the holy month of Ramadan, they dragged him outside for all to see, cut open his chest, tore out his heart, wrapped a rosary around it, shoved it back in his chest and left him to die. The soldiers hollered and hooted as if breaking open a piñata at a great celebration.

Ken internalized all of the injustices. He learned early on that it was dangerous to speak out. When his third grade cousin was falsely accused by a class bully of spilling ink on his classmate's notebook, the Party-faithful teacher saw it as an opportunity to set the Slavic boy straight by hitting him over the head with a metal bar. A month later, the boy died. No complaint. No charges. No problem.

Ken persevered and gave it his all. He always looked ahead. Then the unthinkable happened. When he was just 10 years old, both of his sisters died in a flu epidemic that swept through much of Eastern Europe. The State had simply run out of vaccines. Though the illness may have started with God, that vaccines were only for Party members was just another of the indignities of a worker's paradise that cared only for its political elite.

He got through this ordeal with the help of his closest friend, the wiry Petar Raic. The two shared all confidences, goals and dreams, and an insatiable desire to win. Ken was fond of Petar's family and they adored the boy in return.

One windy afternoon, Ken accompanied Petar home after school. Something was wrong. Petar's mother sat in her tiny kitchen, sobbing silently. Six days earlier, Petar's father had disappeared. That very day, his mother had learned that her husband had been captured and led away, brutally butchered and buried in a shallow ditch. His only offense had been his ethnicity—a Slav in a Serbian-controlled town. Petar's mother was warned that any effort to seek justice would only bring harm to her and her children.

Ken was devastated. Later, when Petar's unsuspecting brother fell victim to a well-connected black marketeer, Ken's anger turned into an indescribable rage. Ken's parents were all too aware of the harsh realities of life in Yugoslavia. Only the Serbians seemed to have it somewhat better.

They hoped against all odds that like Ken's great uncle Tomislav, somehow they would find a way for Ken to have a life elsewhere in the world, free from Communism. Some years earlier, Tomislav had managed to flee on foot across the Italian border. He found his way to Germany, where he labored for more than a year before he earned the fare and the bogus papers for New York. A few months later, the United States granted him political asylum.

To prepare for Ken's eventual escape, his parents made certain that he applied himself to the Russian language classes that were mandatory in Yugoslavian schools. They also took great risks to arrange for Ken to learn English. By the time he was in high school, Ken spoke almost unaccented American English.

Petar too wished to leave. Unlike Ken, whose family enjoyed a small measure of stability, Petar's life, which had never been easy, had become particularly harsh since his father's death. Petar's mother had no hopes of changing their circumstances.

Petar was able to put into motion his escape shortly after he and Ken graduated from high school in June 1976. He had been selected to represent Yugoslavia in an international soccer competition in Rome. The plan was for Petar to slip away during a break. The two friends wished each other well and naively promised to reunite in America within the year. Though Petar's plan worked flawlessly, that was the last time Ken and Petar would see each other for almost six years. During that time, Petar became part of the Bosnian Muslim underground in Rome.


Tomislav had pursued every means to bring Ken to America. Finally, just a few months after Petar's escape, there was a firm knock on the door. Two men arrived to take Ken on a long journey, first by foot, then by train to a town near the border. After using forged papers for the dangerous crossing into Austria, Ken boarded another train for Frankfurt. There, Ken received new papers with his real name and nationality, a small amount of American currency, and tickets to New York.

On October 15, 1976, Ken deplaned at the international terminal of New York's John F. Kennedy Airport, ready to start a new life in America, free of Tito's harsh rule. He found his way onto the pavement and into his great uncle's Chevrolet. It was bittersweet, however, because his parents and brothers had chosen to remain behind. Ken hoped the day would come when he would see them again. He never would.

At first, Ken stayed with Tomislav in his already cramped apartment in Queens. Ken's plan was to go to college and then into business. Fortunately, he was oblivious to the harsh realities of his ambitions.

With the sponsorship of his great uncle, Ken received a resident visa. Tomislav had only one condition for his help: Ken must forsake Islam to become an American. To Tomislav, that meant adopting either the Greek Orthodox or Roman Catholic Church. Since New York was home to many millions of Roman Catholics, Tomislav urged Ken to adopt the Church of Rome as his new religion. Ultimately, Ken acquiesced.

He eagerly explored New York, and with his excellent English, befriended some of the regulars at a local café. One of them was a professor at New York's prestigious Columbia University, one of the eight select members of the Ivy League. He was taken with the unusually bright and optimistic young man and promised to help Ken apply to Columbia. Ken knew that the students and professors he could meet at Columbia would benefit him for years to come. He also knew that a degree from Columbia could open doors that few émigrés could ever hope to pass through. Through the sheer force of his hard work and willpower and to his complete amazement, Ken was admitted.

In September 1977, 19-year-old Ken Karasik traveled to Morningside Heights where he became one of 754 men in the Columbia Class of '81. Founded in 1754 by royal charter of King George II of England, Columbia was the only all-male school remaining in the Ivy League. Its all-female sister school, Barnard, was just across the street. Though raised a Muslim, Ken saw no reason for this separation. Otherwise, he was honored and awed to enroll at a college that boasted, among others, John Marshall, the first chief justice of the United States; Alexander Hamilton, the first secretary of the treasury; and authors of the U.S. Declaration of Independence and U.S. Constitution, not to mention presidents of the United States and many other nations. Now, Ken saw Columbia as his first step to a new life.

While at Columbia, Ken consecrated his conversion to the Roman Catholic Church. Tomislav was right; Muslims were not well treated in the United States. Though he converted, he would never forget who he was. By working within the system Ken believed that he could effectuate change. He did not yet know how he would do so, but only that he would.

Three years later, May 1980 marked three major milestones in Ken's life. On May 4, 1980, Josip Tito died. Just one week later, Ken received his degree from Columbia. He had graduated in just three years, maintaining an almost perfect "A" average. In the process, he transformed himself from a poor Bosnian Muslim to a member of the American academic elite.

Ken decided to complete his education with an MBA. He had applied to several of the top schools and selected the University of Pennsylvania's prestigious Wharton School of Business. Generally perceived as the best school for finance, Wharton would later gain great notoriety as the alma mater of junk-bond king Michael Milken and many of the more controversial investment bankers of the '80s and '90s.

Most importantly, May 1980 marked the first time in four years that Ken had managed to locate his best friend's whereabouts. Though he only got as far as "someplace near Rome," he knew that it was only a matter of months before he would finally find Petar. Perseverance paid off, and five years after they last shook hands, the two close friends spoke by telephone. Ken reminded Petar of their plans to re-unite, and he convinced Petar to join him in the United

States. In December 1981, almost six years after they had last seen each other in Yugoslavia, they were finally again together.

Ken made all the arrangements, including finding Petar a place to stay and the required visas. Then, using contacts he had made while at Columbia, Ken wrangled Petar, still only a high school graduate, a spot at the City University of New York. CUNY's low tuition and tradition of equal access had provided a road to success for many a New Yorker.

Though separated for a year by the 90-minute train ride between Wharton in Philadelphia and CUNY in New York, Ken and Petar found many opportunities to renew their friendship. Ken helped Petar become American, and Petar reminded his old friend that even Tito's death had not ended the suffering of the Slavs. Instead, as Yugoslavia disintegrated, the Serbs grew ever stronger and in the chaos, the situation was deteriorating. The friends resolved that they would find a way to continue the fight Petar had waged while he was living in Italy.

In June 1982, 24-year-old Ken Karasik became a U.S. citizen. That same month, he received his hard-earned MBA from Wharton and accepted a position in New York as an analyst for MDB Corporation, one of the world's leading oil and chemicals conglomerates. Ken was assigned to a strategic planning team led by Mel Bottner, scion of the Bottner family.

Handsome, athletic and 31 years of age at the time, Melvin Darwin Bottner III had spent his youth breaking every rule he could, first at Andover and then at Yale. Despite his best efforts, he graduated with honors. Nobody was more surprised than his mother. His father expected and demanded that he attend law school (Harvard, Yale or Columbia), join a white shoe New York law firm, preferably Cravath, Sullivan & Cromwell, or one of the other firms to which MDB paid $5 or $10 million a year in fees, and then, after a few years, join the family business as a vice president. Instead, angry at the war in Vietnam, angry at the Establishment of which he was very much a part, and angry at his own wealth, Bottner joined the Peace Corps.

After almost 10 years of finding himself, first in the Peace Corps and then as a minor diplomat in places like Cambodia, Yugoslavia and Italy, Mel finally joined the family business. Ken found Mel a fascinating mentor. Despite his great wealth, Bottner had spent time in some of the most dangerous spots on the planet trying to improve the plight of oppressed people. He understood the need for force. And, he had no aversion to making money.

Mel and Ken grew close. In 1983, when Ken saw an opportunity to expand MDB's energy business in Eastern Europe, he pitched it to Mel. Mel liked what he heard and asked the wunderkind to lead a team to the Soviet Union.

Mel had high hopes and low expectations. Yet, in less than a year, Ken pulled off a coup that would bring MDB more than $3 billion. A few months before completing the deal, Ken had asked for some unusual money transfers totaling nearly $1 million. Though Mel's father had questioned the purpose, Mel had faith in Ken.

Just six months later, with the million dollars carefully distributed to the right people, MDB had a deal to be the key partner for the Soviet Union's State-owned oil producer and distributor. Within another three months every piece of the puzzle fell into place. Mel's father rewarded him with the company's presidency. Yet, despite his utmost efforts to keep Ken, including an offer to promote the 26-year-old to vice president, Ken left to form his own company. When he departed in 1984, he did so with Mel's gratitude and friendship.

# FIVE

**A**T AGE 26, Ken Karasik founded C3 Energy. C3 referred to his then-girlfriend whose first, last and middle names each began with a C. Long after their relationship ended, C3 Energy and later the C3 Group remained happy reminders of their time together.

From the outset, Ken had two goals: to make as much money as possible, and to help establish a free and secure Bosnia as a safe haven for Muslims and other Slavs who had been too long oppressed. Ken realized that his ability to do the latter was very much dependent on his ability to do the former. At first, he focused on energy deals in Europe, the Middle East and the United States.

C3's first venture involved a distribution deal in Eastern Europe, a subject about which Ken had become expert while he was employed by MDB. Rather than compete with his mentor, Ken cut MDB in for 25% of the deal, in return, of course, for 100% of the cost. With the other 75%, Ken funded his new company and its rapid expansion began.

Within two years, C3 had a cash flow of more than $30 million a year. Ken plowed most of that back into operations. With the balance, he began to acquire other businesses, including stakes in technology companies in the United States and drug and chemical companies in Europe. Ken played by the rules. In the United States, that meant strict compliance with every state and federal law. In Europe, particularly Eastern Europe, that meant back-room deals, pay-offs, and threats.

More and more, Ken also allied with freedom fighters throughout the Balkans and the former Soviet Union. It's not that he supported the global anti-Western views of Muslim fundamentalists; rather, he supported the right to self-determination of those oppressed by the atheist Communists in the Soviet Union, and their successors in the C.I.S. and the Russian Federation. He supported efforts in Azerbaijan, Chechnya and neighboring states with funding, and occasionally with access to intelligence information he obtained from his many contacts.

In both Ken's business efforts and his covert activities in the Balkans and elsewhere, Mel could be counted on to share the costs and to use MDB's vast global resources to achieve success. With Ken's commitment to fight Soviet oppression generally, and Serbian aggression specifically, Mel finally found an outlet for his very private and personal faith. In the Peace Corps and as a diplomat, Mel had been looking for one thing—a way to make a difference. Ken found a way for Mel to do just that.

While Ken was focused on C3 Energy, Petar pursued a different course. After graduating from CUNY in 1985, he volunteered to serve in the United States Army. Because of his language skills—Croatian, Russian, Italian and English—he was assigned to military intelligence. His willingness to kill and his ability to plan served him well. After four years, he re-upped for another four, spending much of his time on covert missions with the CIA. When he was discharged in late 1993, he took a brief vacation and re-united with Ken, joining Karasik Capital as the so-called "director of special projects."

In 1988, C3 made a small investment in Gutedrogen, a troubled Zurich company that developed and marketed drugs for the European market. By co-developing products with MDB Pharmaceuticals, also based in Zurich, Ken turned Gutedrogen around. In late 1989, C3 acquired complete control of Gutedrogen, which it renamed C3 Pharmaceuticals. Though Ken didn't know it at the time, that acquisition would mark a turning point in his life.

During the early 1990s, C3 and MDB jointly developed a drug they called Raphlen. The drug was based on formulas provided by Carl Horst, an accomplished chemist who lived in Zurich. Horst had been one of the most prodigious inventors of new drugs in Europe throughout the 1980s and 1990s. Except for a brief period during which he had taken in a young relative, the chemist had no family and few interests beyond his work.

Initially, Horst's single-minded intensity had worked to C3's advantage. Raphlen seemed to offer an outstanding opportunity to treat heart disease. All of the tests were positive, for a while. Then Horst detected an anomaly. After another series of tests that took almost a year, he concluded that Raphlen had serious side effects. By then, C3 had already started marketing the drug. When Horst demanded that C3 cease distribution, there was no possibility of compliance. Karasik's executives tried to explain the reality to Horst, but the middle-aged chemist threatened to go to the Swiss officials.

Ken turned to Petar, who had recently joined Karasik Capital. Unfortunately for the chemist, Petar discovered that Horst had already reported his claims of fraud to the authorities in Zurich. While Petar could personally handle the chemist, he needed assistance to manage the Swiss government.

That's where Ben Opperman came in. Ben had been introduced to Ken two years earlier. They had taken an immediate liking to each other, though the Raphlen mess was the first time they had worked together.

First, Petar paid an unannounced visit to the chemist. He was quite persuasive. Fortunately, the chemist had no immediate need for his left hand. As Petar suspected, the problem would be the officials to whom Horst had squealed. Since the chemist had a use for his right hand, he willingly shared with Petar the name and phone number of the official to whom he had given a full report. It took about a week, but with a few after-hours visits, Ben's team was able to determine the full extent of those who knew about Horst's allegations. Petar was particularly pleased to see that Ben had selected Mike Mihalic to lead his team. The Croatian-American was a former CIA agent Petar had befriended during his military service.

It turned out that Horst's information had reached a total of six government functionaries. Ben's team learned everything they could about each of them. Speed was critical so that the problem could be contained. Fortunately, Ben's team was able to learn what they needed to know in just a few days as to five of the six. Two had mistresses, one had accepted bribes, one had serious financial difficulties, and one was looking for employment in the private sector. So far, they had learned little of value about the sixth person, a 50ish woman who was the executive secretary to one of the other five, the head of the Swiss unit investigating Horst's report.

The team went to work. For the two with mistresses, pictures were taken and emailed. For the one who had accepted bribes, copies of bank transfers were made and delivered. It was soon clear to the three civil servants that they had far more pressing tasks than to worry about a drug that could help so many. The job searcher was surprised to receive an unsolicited offer at almost twice what he was earning. Within two weeks, he was gone, the problems of a potentially dangerous drug behind him. Then, like manna from Heaven, a loan was suddenly offered to a man with debts about to crush him.

The terms too good to be true. The only condition, that he forget about a recently crippled chemist's concerns, easy to accept.

Just as Ben and Petar considered more extreme measures for the efficient executive secretary, Mihalic reported a covert rendezvous. The executive secretary and her boss had a regular appointment every Friday afternoon at the local *skihütte*, though not a ski was ever in sight. It didn't take long to convince her that silence had its own rewards.

Ben's fee of $1 million plus expenses was just a small fraction of what Karasik would eventually earn by selling Raphlen in Canada from where it would find its way into the United States, bypassing the FDA.

Over the next few years, Karasik would call on Ben whenever he had a particularly difficult problem. Increasingly, he also called on Ben for advice. The two became trusted friends. Though 25 years apart in age and of different religions, they shared a hatred for Soviet Communism and a peculiar amorality alien to most.

Raphlen was an example of the duality in Ken's business ethics. He had decided early on that he did not want to be a major player in the pharmaceuticals business in the United States. The FDA was just too tough. Only after repeated trials and tests supposedly proving beyond all doubt that a drug was safe could there be any chance of obtaining FDA approval. In fact, whom you knew was often as important as what the test results showed. Too often the FDA examiners cozied up to the major pharmaceutical companies and approved their latest drugs, while stretching the process to the breaking point for newcomers like C3 Pharmaceuticals. It was all part of the revolving door game in Washington, D.C. and no newcomer was going to get an invitation to that party.

It was not unusual for the FDA to force an outsider like C3 to spend $100 million and 10 years to obtain the necessary approvals. At the end, there was no guarantee of success. That may have made for one of the safest medical systems in the world, but it also deprived Americans of advances in medicine available elsewhere and it created a de facto monopoly for those in the "Club." As it was intended to do, the process sapped the profits of newcomers, often pushing them completely out of the U.S. market. Hence, C3 Pharmaceuticals focused on Eastern Europe, the Middle East, Africa and even Western Europe, where the requirements were much easier. Some of C3's drugs were far more effective than drugs approved by the FDA. On the other hand, C3 occasionally ran the gauntlet when it had a particularly innovative drug whose potential for profit in the U.S. clearly outweighed the exorbitant costs of obtaining the FDA's approval.

As early as 1990, there was a mail order business between Canada and the United States that serviced Americans interested in procuring unapproved drugs they could not obtain at home.

C3 took advantage of this back door to the United States market. The goal was profits, pure and simple. C3's drugs, many of which never passed a single FDA test, and some of which could never have come close to doing so, were sold into Canada. From Canada they were sold into the United States. Until the advent of the Internet, this process required a Canadian intermediary willing to take the risks and bear considerable marketing and sales expenses.

By 1995, C3 was cash flowing more than $125 million a year, and Ken's stake was worth well more than $350 million. He was 37 years old.

The growth of the C3 Group accelerated with acquisitions in energy, technology, and manufacturing. Meanwhile, the situation in

Eastern Europe was deteriorating. More and more, Ken enlisted Mel Bottner, Petar Raic and Ben Opperman to deliver arms and financial support to Muslims in the Balkans and the rapidly dissolving Soviet Union. Their efforts were costly, but Ken didn't care. He was prepared to dedicate a substantial portion of his net worth to supporting his ideals.

In July 1995, Srebrenica, the world's first UN Safe Area, was the site of the worst genocide in Europe since World War II. The UN Protection Force failed to act, permitting Serbian Army General Ratko Mladic to brutally occupy the small, intimate Bosnian spa town and its surrounding region. Over a period of five days, the Serb soldiers separated families and massacred more than 7,000 Muslim men and boys, while torturing, raping, and killing many of the women and children.

The atrocities—and the failure of the West to stop them—shook Petar. Even Ken, who had forsaken Islam for the Roman Catholic Church, was outraged. The friends rededicated themselves to the security of the Slavs and the destruction of Serbian aggressors.

In 1996, Ken named Petar chief operations officer of the entire C3 Group, third behind only Ken, the Group's chairman and chief executive officer and Steve Maier, its president. It was a good arrangement—Petar was in position to support all of Ken's efforts, while Maier was never aware of, let alone involved in, any of the less savory activities.

Ken, Petar, Mel and Ben began to operate together as what they later dubbed the "Karasik Commission." By the end of 1997, Stuart King became the fifth member of what was, in effect, a well-financed, highly organized terrorist cell. Its amorality was apparent in its dual purposes—using extortion and violence to protect Slavs and oppressed minorities in the former Soviet Union, and to advance C3's business goals in Europe and Asia. While the first goal may have been laudable, the same could not be said about their means or their second purpose.

Like many others who supported the Slavs, the members of the Karasik Commission rejoiced when the United States and its NATO allies finally took strong measures against Milosevic in 1999 and 2001. Milosevic's atrocities had become so great that by the end of 1999, the United States and Europe finally bombed him into submission, though he remained free for more than a year, until what was left of Yugoslavia finally turned him over to the United Nations Criminal Tribunal.

On the day Milosevic was arrested in April 2001, Ken and Petar thought the worst was over and the Slavs in the Balkans finally could move forward in a strong independent state. Their joy was short-lived, however, when they discovered that during his waning days in power, Milosevic's thugs had killed virtually every man, woman and child remaining in Bihac, and then burned to the ground the town where they had been raised. Ken and Petar tried desperately to find out the fate of Ken's parents and brothers, as well as the fates of other relatives each had left behind. When the normal channels were inadequate, the Karasik Commission went to work.

Using special permissions obtained through NATO, Stuart King, Petar and his old friend Mike Mihalic, who by then worked for C3 as chief of security, flew into Dubrovnik. They secured local transportation arranged by Mel Bottner. Together, with one of Ben Opperman's local agents, they proceeded to what had once been a vibrant town.

To Petar's horror, virtually every building had been destroyed. At the edge of what had once been the town square, Petar and Mike found a mass grave. It was useless to look for anyone in that orgy of decaying bodies. Though NATO would eventually attempt to identify bodies through DNA testing, Petar and Mike had no intention of waiting. They scoured the area for survivors who might be able to tell them about Petar's or Ken's mothers.

Finally, they had some "luck," but only if that word is truly without meaning. They located a neighbor who had fled just as the Serbian forces had begun to burn the town. Anna Skoko told them how three unkempt and brutal men, none older than 18, had pulled Ken's parents and brothers, and their wives and children from their house, put a bullet through each of their heads, and left them piled on the street. Anna had no idea what had become of the bodies.

Nothing further could be learned of Petar's mother or Ken's family. After a week, Petar and Mike returned to London, each feeling a profound emptiness and great anger.

About six months later, Stuart obtained copies of the NATO analysis. Ken's entire family and Petar's mother and cousins were in the mass grave. Though his parents and brothers had repeatedly refused to emigrate, Ken blamed himself. Even more strongly, he blamed the United States and Europe for failing to act until it was too late. He resolved that Bosnia would be free—and he would manage the circumstances so that the United States itself became the instrument of that change.


The year 2001 became one of momentous events for Yugoslavia, the Karasik Commission and the world. It started with Slobodan Milosevic's arrest on April 1, 2001, continued with al-Qaeda's September 11, 2001 attack on the World Trade Center and Pentagon, and ended with Operation Enduring Freedom, the U.S.-led invasion of Afghanistan on October 7, 2001 that toppled the Taliban and sent Osama bin Laden into hiding.

Bolstered by Ken's financial resources and their passion, the Karasik Commission would respond to those events and America's continuing failure to safeguard the Slavs and other oppressed minorities in Eastern Europe with the deadliest terrorist attack ever launched against the United States.

# Six

THE WEEK AFTER Thanksgiving, a chronic chaos was in full swing around Nely Gonzales Karasik as Alexa arrived at the estate. Brunch was about to be served.

"Finally, she shows up!" Nely shouted in Alexa's direction as she greeted her with a hug.

"What's up?" Alexa asked, as Nely pulled her aside.

"I don't know, but Ken's not been himself. We spend so little time together—just a few days a month—and now that he's here, he seems a million miles away."

"I'm so sorry, Nely," Alexa tried to console her friend. "But you knew what you were getting into when you married him. You could have anything that money can buy, but you would have very little of your husband."

"That's not entirely fair," Nely sadly answered.

Alexa was about to say something more, when Nely's housekeeper, Isabella, called out urgently.

"Alexa! Marie is on the phone. She's been looking for you. Your grandfather is very sick. He's been taken by ambulance to Paradise Cove Memorial."

Suddenly, all went dim. Alexa flew out of the house and drove in complete silence to the hospital. She quickly reached the parking lot, jumped out of her car and rushed into the lobby of the emergency room and through the wide doors that led to the treatment area. She looked from one bed to another until a nurse approached her.

"May I help you?" the nurse curtly inquired.

"Nicolas Bart. I'm looking for my grandfather."

"Oh yes, thank goodness you're here. The doctor has been looking for someone to consent..."

"Consent to what?" Alexa shot back nervously.

Suddenly, there was Grandpa Nico right before her eyes, pale as death, trembling, grumbling and shaking uncontrollably.

"What's going on with him?" she demanded.

"I'm Dr. Goldblatt," a small, bald man who had been standing nearby introduced himself. "It would appear that he is suffering from some sort of neurological disturbance. Further testing is required before we can determine what is wrong with him and whether he should be treated here or at Marlowe Neurological Center over at St. Joseph's."

"Marlowe!" Alexa knew all too well that was the place for desperate cases. "Is it another stroke?"

"It doesn't look like it, Ms. Bart. But we want to keep a very close eye on him."

"Ok," Alexa spoke softly but authoritatively. "How much longer will he stay here?"

"We're making arrangements right now to move him to a special critical care unit on the third floor, with round-the-clock monitoring. I need you to sign some consent forms and then you can stay a while with him if you wish, but I'd advise you to go home and get some rest. He is sedated now and will most likely sleep for a long time."

Alexa stood above Grandpa Nico and stared into his face. She looked down at his still manly body and back up to his closed eyes. She wanted to touch him, but didn't. She walked over to the nurses' station and awaited the consent forms. Without fully realizing what was before her, Alexa signed one document after another, and then stood motionless off to the side as Grandpa was wheeled away to his room. She followed slowly behind.

Once Nico was settled in his room, Alexa stared out of the hospital window for hours until the sky turned from a pale blue to sunset orange and, finally, darkness began to descend. At last, she decided to leave.

A nurse observed Alexa from a distance. When she was out of sight, the nurse picked up a phone. "All's clear. She never left his room," she said.

A few minutes later, several physicians entered Nico's room. "We have been instructed to monitor him closely and do labs on the hour. In the morning, he is to be transferred to the Marlowe ICU at St. Joseph's," explained a no-nonsense middle-aged internist. The other doctors stood there and observed without understanding what was happening to Nico. But they knew that his was not an isolated incident. Elderly patients with the same unusual symptoms had been coming into emergency rooms in at least seven locations in California, Nevada, New Mexico, Arizona and Utah.

Alexa's drive home seemed an eternity. She drove with the sounds of traffic and nature, the wind whipping her hair about her face. She walked up to the side door, turned the key in the lock and stepped inside the small kitchen. The place seemed hauntingly quiet and foreign.

Alexa placed the keys by a row of tea boxes on the top shelf and poured herself a glass of water. She brought the glass to her lips, paused and put it down on the counter without taking a sip. She walked into the living room where Grandpa's wheelchair, walker and folding tray stood abandoned. She looked through the door into his bedroom and felt its emptiness attack the pit of her stomach.

The television remote sat on top of a beige sofa. She turned on the TV, attempted to shake herself into the present moment and returned to the kitchen to boil water for a pot of tea. She slipped into a sweat suit and a pair of thick cotton socks and placed a pair of Nikes near the door, in case she needed to leave quickly.

Alexa leaned back on a stack of pillows and bunched up the red paisley blanket underneath her left arm. She took the remote and selected CNN. Wolf Blitzer was reporting live: "Our topic tonight is dangerous medicine. Should we be allowed to buy cheaper prescription drugs from Canada and Mexico? Congress is considering legislation to expand the rights of American consumers to do so. We want to understand what it's all about."

"We have with us live from Washington, D.C., Cathy Lee, a spokesperson for PharmCorp, one of the world's largest pharmaceutical companies. Thank you for joining us, Ms. Lee. Can you tell our viewers, just what are your concerns regarding the proposed legislation?"

"Wolf, every American needs to know that opening our borders as required under this legislation would increase the likelihood that the shelves of pharmacies in towns and communities across the nation would include counterfeit drugs, cheap foreign copies of

FDA-approved drugs, expired drugs, contaminated drugs, and drugs stored under inappropriate and unsafe conditions," Lee responded.

"Not exactly fair or balanced," Alexa murmured under her breath as she flipped the switch to Turner Classic Movies. Katherine Hepburn and Cary Grant were at each other's throats in "Bringing Up Baby."

Half way through the film, she fell into a deep sleep.

Instead of peaceful slumber, hideous dreams wreaked havoc on Alexa's overburdened psyche. A night of restless sleep came to an abrupt end with the incessant ringing of her bedside phone. It was just past 8:00 am as Alexa picked up the line. It was a report from the hospital on Grandpa's condition. He was not improving.

After a quick shower and a change of clothes, she headed back to Paradise Cove Memorial. Alexa entered Grandpa's room and found it empty. The bed appeared to be freshly made. Quickly, she ran to the nurses' station and asked anxiously about Grandpa's whereabouts.

"Let me see," a young woman said as she glanced at the papers in front of her. "308...that would be Nicolas Bart. Right?"

Alexa gritted her teeth. "That's right. Where is he?"

"He's been transferred to St. Joseph's. Left about 30 minutes ago," the girl said.

Alexa ran down the hall towards the elevators. She drove nervously through the morning traffic for nearly two hours. With each moment, she grew more emotional. Arriving at her destination, she took a deep breath before prying her shaking hands from the steering wheel. She had to get herself under control.

A professional-looking assistant led her to the Intensive Care Unit where Grandpa Nico lay in a single small room, hooked up to a life support system. There was a tube disappearing into his throat and wires, more tubes and rhythmic noises everywhere. A sweet young nurse sat patiently at his side and monitored Grandpa's every bodily function.

"Hi, I'm Samantha," she said, adding, "He's stable now."

The assistant who brought Alexa to the ICU stood at the door and told her that the doctor wanted to see her.

Alexa took one more mental picture of the man she would always think of as her grandfather and stepped into the hallway. She followed the woman without saying a word. A handsome and compassionate-looking man in a white lab coat politely extended his hand, introduced himself as Dr. Michael O'Donnell. He asked her to join him in a conference room. Alexa quietly complied.

"I'm so sorry about your grandfather. We need to talk about his situation. He's in very grave condition. I don't know how long he can remain like this, but short of a miracle, I don't think he will last long. His body is simply shutting down."

A huge lump lodged itself in Alexa's throat. She fought with great effort to maintain her composure. She inhaled slowly and deeply. "Doctor," she said, "I have faith in you."

The doctor was visibly moved. He spoke softly, "Alexa, you don't understand…" but she cut him off and repeated twice more, "I have faith in you, doctor. I have faith in you…"

Dr. O'Donnell looked down and sighed. Finally, he looked her straight in the eye and promised, "All right, I will do my best…we will all do our very best to keep him going."

"Thank you. Is there anything else?"

"No. You can visit him any time, but he can't hear you and he won't know that you're there. So I recommend that you take good care of yourself and do what you'd normally do and just know that he's in very good hands here."

She smiled sweetly through her anguish, "I'll come by every morning and every afternoon. But you'll call me if there's any news, right?"

"Absolutely."

# SEVEN

ALEXA TURNED UP the volume on the television. A distraught young mother in a Chicago suburb was inconsolable. Her five-year-old daughter was one of three kindergarten classmates who had suffered seizures. Each had fallen into a coma. Authorities were looking for environmental causes or possible food contamination.

With her emotions raw, Alexa felt the mother's pain. Tears streamed down her face. The story continued, but she couldn't bear to watch. It's a sign of the times, Alexa thought, when school officials offer no comment and retain the town's leading legal eagles to speak on their behalf before any discovery is made. Alexa flipped the station to Fox. Bill O'Reilly was harping, yet again, on the subject of prescription drug importation. That woman from PharmCorp, Cathy Lee, was on again.

"Welcome, Ms. Lee," O'Reilly said after introducing her.

"Thank you for having me."

"Let's get right into this. During a year in which there was so much talk of sacrifice in the national interest, drug companies increased their astounding profits by hiking prescription prices. Is that fair?"

"Mr. O'Reilly, the industry spends hundreds of billions of dollars on research. Without revenues, how would we fund that research? We are proud of our contribution to the best medical system in the world."

"But, isn't it true that a U.S. prescription drug can cost as much as 87% more than the same drug in Canada?"

"While that may be true in certain instances, it is not a fair comparison. Moreover, Canada has a socialized system. That means that while prices for medical care may be lower, the tax burden supporting that system is much higher."

"Bottom line, isn't it true that the top seven pharmaceutical companies took in more profit last year than the top seven auto companies, the top seven oil companies, the top seven airline companies, or top seven media companies?"

"I would need to see those numbers to be able to comment with any specificity. However, I am certain that in any given year some industries are up and some are down."

Alexa heard enough. She already knew more about pharmaceutical companies than she cared to admit. She switched to the E! Channel.

The following morning was bright and crisp. Although it looked like it was going to be an exceptionally mild winter day, Alexa felt cold and alone. She arrived at the Marlowe wing of St. Joseph's just before visiting hours. When she reached the waiting room outside the ICU, there was great commotion. She took a seat in a row of beige plastic chairs against the wall. Suddenly, heart-wrenching cries for help from a boy being rushed through the corridor on a gurney made everyone freeze.

It was only seconds but it seemed an eternity before a seasoned nurse with watering eyes softly whispered into his ear, "We're taking care of you. We'll stop your pain real soon, honey. Just hang on." A woman ran behind the boy, weeping uncontrollably. As they disappeared behind double doors, the woman's screams echoed in the corridor. "My baby, my poor baby…"

Shaken, Alexa approached the security guard. "I'm here to see Nico Bart, please."

Without bothering to look up, he asked, "Are you family?"

Alexa nodded. Still not looking up, the guard automatically replied, "Have a good day, Miss," as he pushed a button that opened the door to the ICU.

Alexa tried not to look in all the rooms as she walked toward her grandpa at the other end, but it was hard to resist. She was horrified as she observed rooms filled with young children in zoo-like metal cribs that stood on spindly legs. There were babies in nothing but diapers and tubes and toddlers strapped down to their cribs, hooked up to all manner of life-saving machines and monitors.

"What's wrong with them?" Alexa inquired.

"Not sure. Seems to be some sort of pneumonia. We're monitoring them very closely."

"In babies?"

"It's unusual, but it happens."

Alexa turned to Grandpa Nico. "He looks the same."

"He's been stable but he's still listed in critical condition," the nurse replied.

Alexa stared at him with the weight of the world on her shoulders. "Will he make it?"

"I've seen worse," the nurse tried to be reassuring, "and I've seen them pull through somehow," she smiled. "I'll leave you alone for a few minutes."

Alexa sat at his side and looked into his closed eyes. "I know that you can hear me, Grandpa," she began, "and I know there is much you wish to tell me. But everything is going to be just fine and we'll be home together in no time."

After a few minutes, the nurse returned. "Thank you so much for taking care of him. I have to go for a while. I'll see you later," Alexa told her.

As she was leaving, Alexa's pain rose to the surface. Tears rolled down her usually stoic face. Another child was being settled into a room, the hallway marked with vomit. Alexa carried it outside with her footprints. She unlocked her car and just sat in it, staring into space. The sunshine seemed an intrusion. She sobbed quietly for a few minutes. Finally, she steadied herself and drove purposefully to Nely's and a large serving of Isabella's Dutch apple pancakes.

"Are you eating again?" Nely's piercing voice resonated as Alexa ate a mouthful of the pancake.

"Every chance I get!" Alexa said, with forced enthusiasm.

"Listen, what are you doing next week?" Nely asked.

"I have an event I've been organizing in London. I have to go for about a week, but with Grandpa like this, I don't know what I'll do."

"I think it's good that you have something else to do. Why don't you talk to the doctors? If Grandpa's stable, there's nothing that you can do to help him right now, is there?" Nely asked, trying to be helpful.

"I guess you're right," Alexa hesitated, "but it still doesn't feel right."

"Alexa, would your grandfather want you to go and get the job done?"

"He would…"

"Then that settles it," Nely concluded.

"Let me think about it," was all Alexa said. There was no way she would tell Nely the real reason for her trip.

# EIGHT

**A**LEXA HEADED OUT early to spend time with Grandpa, once again arriving before visiting hours. While she sipped a cup of black coffee and glanced around the now-familiar waiting room, she noted faces she hadn't seen before. One man seemed especially pensive. He had a perpetual frown and kept muttering to himself, "It's all my fault...." For some reason, Alexa decided to try to console him, perhaps to divert herself from her own feelings of helplessness. She learned that the man's son was very ill. Apparently his illness had something to do with drugs from Mexico. Beyond that, the man was nearly incoherent.

Finally, the security guard let her in to see Grandpa. When she got to his room, things were much the same as yesterday. "Oh Grandpa, you're all I have," Alexa whispered to him, as he slowly breathed, assisted by the respirator. Though the doctor had told her that Grandpa couldn't hear her, she refused to believe him. After a few hours, she headed out for a break and to make some business calls that were long overdue. She hoped Grandpa wouldn't blame her for the latter.

When she walked out to the parking lot, she encountered a crowd of cameras and reporters. News vehicles were parked everywhere and some were just circling around. Satellite dishes were mounted on the parking lot and across the street. She placed the key in the ignition and pulled out of the parking lot. As the news came on her radio, the local anchor reported, "Some dozen very ill third and fourth graders were rushed today to St. Joseph's Hospital from a local elementary school. The children had sudden seizures that led to a loss of consciousness in five of them. There is no word on the cause of these seizures, but the cafeteria food and vending machines are being closely scrutinized for possible contamination. One school nurse suggested that the symptoms seemed like severe pneumonia. Although unusual, local physicians contacted by Newsradio told us that small epidemics of bacterial pneumonia among children in the same school do occur from time to time..."

*No more bad news...* She turned the station to some music and slowly drove around the town. Finally, she pulled over to a local coffee shop where she made a series of calls to catch up on the fundraiser she was organizing the following week. When she completed her work, she headed back to St. Joseph's. Grandpa's condition was unchanged. She stayed with him until midnight when, exhausted, she finally returned home.


As Alexa pulled into Grandpa Nico's driveway, there was her cousin Marcus, sitting in the open carport. He startled her. "Lexi, it's me! Don't be so jumpy."

"What are you doing here?" she quizzed him.

"I've been worried about Grandpa..." he trailed off.

"Yeah? You could have fooled me."

"That's not fair," he protested. "You know I've been overwhelmed with work and all... Anything I can do to help—I'm here, Lex."

"I know," she replied, aware that he was willing, but not emotionally able.

"Actually," she continued, "you can do something for both of us this weekend."

"You name it."

"Grandpa is resting. I'm told he should be stable for at least the next week. Could you stay with him a few days? I need to go to London for business…"

"Say no more! I'll be right here to take the pressure off you," he reassured her.

"I really appreciate that. I'll be off Friday around noon, but you'll be able to reach me on email and cell at any time if anything happens…"

"Don't worry, Lex, I'll take care of everything."

She was actually relieved. Marcus could never know all of the reasons for her trip to London. It was true that she had business there; indeed, her affairs there were long overdue.

She yawned like a lion. "I need some sleep," she muttered.

"Me too. Ok Lexi, I'll see you Friday morning before you leave."


Sleep was a good idea if not a reality. There was just too much to think about for restful slumber. Pinky, her chubby gray cat, nuzzled at Alexa's rib cage as if she knew something and offered comfort. Alexa rubbed Pinky's belly and the cat contentedly purred. Alexa's thoughts drifted to diamonds, drugs and a certain very wealthy man in London. She also thought about Ken Karasik and Ben Opperman. For the first time in weeks, she smiled. The London trip was indeed overdue. Pinky stretched out alongside Alexa as both succumbed to utter exhaustion.

# NINE

*F*OR MONTHS, ALEXA had been coordinating a fundraiser to be held in London by one of New Mexico's larger universities for its European alumni. Though Alexa had considered remaining home, Nely was right about one thing—Grandpa's condition was stable and a few days away would do her some good. After all, England felt more like home to her than any place in America.

After a rushed visit to the hospital, Alexa headed to Santa Fe for a flight to Chicago. Her client would reimburse economy class travel to London, four nights in the Swallow Hotel in South Kensington, and taxi fare. The university's officers would have been very surprised to learn that Alexa had the means to supplement the reimbursable expenses.

Though Alexa flew coach to Chicago, once there, she boarded British Airways for the eight-hour red-eye to Heathrow. Since she knew her first class seat fully reclined into a private bed, she didn't really mind. Within an hour after departure, she was asleep.

As her flight neared Heathrow, she dreamed about the first time she had met Faisal Ayoub. He had bested Ken Karasik, which meant she had bested Ken Karasik. It had been delightful payback. The first time, but certainly not the last. Poor Nely, so unaware.

Except for Grandpa, she had been alone for a long time, now. She had grown as a person, but she had also ignored who she really was, or who she had been.

Something terrible happened to everyone she loved. So she decided early on to remain isolated and self-sufficient. That was the master plan, the secret to her success.


She awoke just before landing. By the time she cleared customs and retrieved her bags, it was nearly 9:00 am local time. A black Mercedes was waiting to take her into the city. The university and most of her friends would have been surprised that Alexa greeted its driver, Khalid, as an old friend. The two clearly knew each other.

The next surprise was only 45 minutes later, when instead of bringing her to the economy class Swallow Hotel, Khalid delivered her to the Dorchester on Park Lane in the exclusive Mayfair district of London. Most unlike the Swallow, the Dorchester had long been one of London's premier five-star hotels.

"Welcome back, Ms. Bart," the receptionist exclaimed. "We have your usual suite reserved."

"Thank you, Tony," she responded to another of her longtime acquaintances, before heading up to the £680-a-day suite. At nearly $1,200 per night, it was considerably nicer than the £75-a-day room the university was providing.

For many, a trip to London would be meaningless without a visit to Harrods, London's world-renown up-scale shopping oasis. Alexa had her own reasons to visit Harrods. Within an hour after checking in, she had showered, changed and headed back out. As Khalid negotiated London's lunchtime traffic, Alexa relaxed. For the moment, life was good.

On the top floor of Harrods, Faisal Ayoub, its latest billionaire owner, had just completed reading an article about the profits being made by the C3 Group. He angrily slammed the *Times of London* on his impressive desk.

"Bloody hell!" he shouted.

His assistant looked at him but didn't speak a word.

Livid, Faisal stalked out of the office. When he got upset Faisal often wandered into the security section to observe the dozens of live feeds from throughout the massive department store. It made him feel better to see how the crème of London's society worshipped in his temple.

Suddenly, he glimpsed a familiar profile. He asked one of the security technicians to rewind and freeze the shot of the attractive redhead. He had the frame enlarged and refocused. He looked stunned. "I'll be damned!" he said not believing his eyes.

"Sir?" the technician asked.

"I'll-be-damned…" he repeated slowly.

"Send that picture to Hutter," Faisal ordered, referring to his security chief. "I want to know what she's doing in London."

"Yes, sir," the technician replied, used to Faisal's unusual requests.

After a few hours of wandering around Harrods, Alexa was confident that she'd been noticed. The two poorly dressed men who had remained at a discreet distance for the last two hours were all the proof she required. Certain her mission had been a successful one, she returned to the Dorchester. Tomorrow, she would meet with the alumni officers at the Swallow Hotel and then work 12- and 14-hour days to make certain the fundraiser proceeded without a hitch. No one had to know any more about her private life than they knew at home, and, at least as it related to her client, no one did.

Thanks in no small part to Alexa's efforts, the event was a huge success, raising almost $1 million in donations and pledges.

With her charitable work complete, Alexa "checked out" of the Swallow Hotel, and regained her privacy at the Dorchester.

While Nely remained in Hillcrest Valley, Ken was supposedly away on business. At that moment, Ken's business was a lithe, attractive and multi-talented dark-haired young woman named Christine Liu. Sexy and beautiful in her own right, Christine, unlike Nely, was unconcerned with clothes, jewelry, or making all the right impressions on all the right people. Christine's favorite look consisted of blue jeans and a well-worn sweatshirt. When she dressed up, Christine swapped the sweatshirt for a white crisp cotton shirt. Her hair flew freely in the wind, and except for tinted lip gloss, she wasn't much for makeup.

However, Christine was a woman capable of deep passion, single-minded devotion and endearing kindness. Her natural curiosity and fine-tuned intellect appealed to Ken in a way that others might find surprising. Sure, she possessed technical skills and had the energy to make any man beg for mercy, but that wasn't Ken's primary requirement when it came to Christine. Despite his polished appearance, he had always been awkward when it came to women. Nevertheless, what he lacked in poise and Ben's natural lady-killer charm, he more than made up with confidence and the ability to make any woman who tasted the fruit come back for more.

Christine saw herself as something special, even magical in Ken's life. Sure, she knew about his wife and children and privately referred to Nely as "that ridiculous creature," but she also felt down deep inside that she had struck a chord with Ken that made him need her more than want her. She knew they had a bond that could not easily be broken and she worked attentively to be an asset to him in ways that would make her indispensable.

For such devotion, Ken rewarded her with a glimpse into a posh world that she would never manage under other circumstances. He showered her with expensive gifts and privileges that she pretended didn't matter to her, albeit secretly they made her feel very special and treasured by him. On occasion, he flew her first class to five-star hotels and indulged her in all the amenities the location had to offer. A just and fair girl, what more could she offer him in return? Ken had some ideas.

Ken had met Christine about a year ago at The Four Seasons Hotel in Los Angeles where she was attending a bridal shower for a close friend. A small bladder and a large appetite sent her to the ladies room where she literally ran into him as he was exiting the men's room.

"Wooooooooow..." he exclaimed as he grabbed her by the elbows in order to avoid a head-on collision. They locked eyes and grinned mischievously.

"I'm so sorry, sir," she said demurely and proceeded to walk into the ladies room.

Ken grinned and went about his way. But then mid-way, he stopped, turned around and walked back to the scene of the crime. When Christine came out, he was waiting for her.

"Hi," he simply said.

"Do I know you?" she asked.

"Yes, we just met."

She let out an infectious laugh and he smiled at the carefree spirit in that laugh.

"My name is Ken Karasik," he extended his hand.

"Christine Liu."

"Do you have time for a drink?" he offered.

"No. I'm at my friend's bridal shower over there," she pointed ahead.

Ken put his hand inside his coat jacket and pulled out a card. He took out a pen and jotted something on the back of the card before handing it to her.

"If you tell me you'll call me, will you keep your word?" he asked, his tone very serious.

"Scout's honor," she raised her hand.

He smiled right at her. She couldn't resist and grinned from ear to ear herself. Ken was very pleased; their meeting had been no accident. It would prove to be valuable in more ways than one.


Though Alexa was eager to get back home so she could see how Grandpa Nico was doing, she had one other item on her agenda in London she had to attend to first. About two hours later, she received the call she was waiting for.

"Alexa," a deep and heavily accented male voice spoke.

"In your suite in 30 minutes?" she replied.

"I'll be waiting," he said and hung up.

Her luggage was taken by the porter and placed in storage for her return to New Mexico. But first she hopped into a taxi and headed towards the Connaught, just a few blocks from the Dorchester. This was not a trip she wanted Khalid to know about.

Upon arrival, she went directly to the caller's suite, knocked on the door twice, waited a moment and knocked twice more. The door opened and shut behind her as she melted into his arms.

She knew what the stirring sounds of the Bolero meant in the background and this afternoon was no exception. There was no need for small talk. Alexa's secret romance played itself out only when time and circumstances permitted. Occasionally time and circumstances were on her side, though often they were not. She met the man in Switzerland some years ago when she was on holiday visiting her aunt, a travel agent, and her uncle, a scientist.

Although he always assumed that he had bumped into the curvaceous redhead quite by accident when she smiled sweetly in his direction at a local restaurant, that wasn't exactly how it happened. However, Alexa always believed that everything should be *his* idea. And the idea that this was a real love affair was just that—a figment of his egotistical male imagination. At that very moment, his imagination was playing itself out in a very real way.

He kissed her passionately as his hands went underneath her jacket and removed any barriers that kept her flesh from his. The bedroom wasn't always a necessary part of their love-making and that afternoon was no exception. In a passionate embrace, they descended onto the floor before her legs wrapped around his middle. It wasn't long before he got what he wanted, and for a job well done, she bought more time for another future encounter.

They lay on the rug, snuggled closely and sipped cognac for a couple of hours. Alexa's lover trusted her with the concerns that occupied his mind. She listened intently and offered moral support and occasionally, anxiety-busting witty humor. He always appreciated her big heart, wicked wit and steady head. What a rare woman she was. She understood that this man could offer her knowledge, wisdom and a direction that she longed for.

At last, she rose to her feet and put herself back together. He clung to her as if for dear life itself.

# TEN

**A**S THE NEW YEAR approached, Alexa once again diligently headed to St. Joseph's and hoped and prayed that Grandpa's condition had somehow improved. It was one of those beautiful desert winter days that attracted the "snow birds" to New Mexico from colder parts of the country. Alexa parked in the lot and walked in the sunshine towards the hospital's main entrance. As she passed the newspaper vending machines near the entry, she gasped. She walked over and stared at the front page of *The New Mexico Republic.* "It's him!" she said out loud, as she recognized the man on the front cover as the man in the Marlowe waiting room who had been blaming himself for his son's illness.

Alexa dug into her handbag and pulled out some coins. She grabbed the paper and read the story that accompanied the big bold headline: MAN COMMITS SUICIDE OVER SON'S DEATH.

According to the story, Phil Truman worked for PharmCorp as a regional manager in Mexico. Apparently, he had been involved in helping PharmCorp save money by purchasing one of its brands from an unlicensed manufacturer there. When Truman's son became ill, his physician prescribed that drug. Truman believed the pharmacy had filled the prescription with substandard product manufactured at the Mexican plant he had helped select. Because the drugs taken by his son lacked the expected potency, his son's condition deteriorated.

Shortly after being admitted to St. Joseph's, the boy died. Truman left a suicide note in which he explained his role in the scheme and begged his family for forgiveness.

Alexa shook with nervous tension as she quickly walked through the glass sliding doors and into the lobby. She sped towards the ICU. By now the staff recognized her and opened the secure doors as they saw her approaching. Since Marcus hadn't left any messages, she was confident that Grandpa was as well as could be expected.

Grandpa's respirator was still doing most of the breathing for him. She looked at him carefully. His nails had grown and his hair was greasy. The color was gone from his face and his muscles were losing tone. Needles and tubes seemed to be inserted in every artery and organ. Alexa wondered if any part of him was functioning on its own.

"Hello Alexa," Dr. O'Donnell said with a forced optimism in his voice. "Marcus said you were away for a bit. He was here a few days ago but we haven't seen him since."

Alexa turned sharply towards the doctor. "You mean he wasn't here daily?"

Dr. O'Donnell shook his head.

She was furious with herself for trusting Marcus in a time of crisis.

"Alexa, I'm sorry to tell you that your grandfather has pneumonia and that fluid is building up in his lungs. He's going to require surgery."

"Is there anything else?" she asked, expecting yet more bad news.

"He's just not showing any signs of improvement. We're not going to be able to keep him here much longer," he said. "You will need to look into a nursing facility if he doesn't start responding to treatment."

This was the final blow. "How long can he remain like this?"

"He could die any minute or he could last another five or six years," Dr. O'Donnell explained, as he began pre-op arrangements for Nico's surgery.

After the surgery, Grandpa's monitoring equipment was starting to make noises like the primitive computers in old movies. The doctors warned Alexa that the anesthetic was the most dangerous part of the procedure.

Suddenly, she screamed as something grabbed her arm. A resident and a nurse ran to Nico's unit. Alexa shook and trembled as she realized that Grandpa had opened his eyes, grabbed her arm and was staring right at her.

She spoke carefully, "Grandpa, it's me, Alexa. Can you hear me, Grandpa?" He just stared back and then closed his eyes again. The grip went limp almost as quickly as it had attacked her. Alexa tried to communicate with Nico but he was not responding. The nurse rushed to get the doctor. When everyone cleared the room, Alexa parked a small plastic chair in front of Grandpa's respirator and imagined it rising higher and higher. *Breathe, breathe, breathe…breathe Grandpa, c'mon, you can breathe all on your own…just breathe.*

Hours passed. Alexa fell asleep on a lounge chair that was brought to her by a nurse's aide. The following morning, the technician made his usual daily round.

"He's breathing at 80% on his own!"

"Yes?" she replied anxiously.

"If he can get up to 90%, I can disconnect the respirator," he explained.

A great wave of relief came over Alexa as she jumped to her feet and hugged the technician.

"Do you think he can make it?" she asked excitedly.

"I don't know...but we'll keep a close eye on him. Why don't you go home and get some rest?" the technician gently prodded. At first, Alexa shook her head—if Grandpa opened his eyes again, she wanted to be there for him, but after several hours with no change, Alexa finally headed home.

She drove back to St. Joseph's the following morning. Weary, she entered Grandpa's unit. Something was different but she couldn't figure out immediately just what it was.

"Good morning!" said an aide Alexa hadn't seen before.

"Good morning," she replied politely.

At that very moment, Karen, the regular morning nurse came into the room.

"Hello Alexa!" she said jovially. "Can you believe it?"

"Believe what?"

"He's no longer on a respirator and if he starts eating on his own, we'll soon take out the feeding tube."

"Oh my God!" she exclaimed. "Is he conscious?"

"Yup!" Karen said. "He's just sleeping now on his own. There are a lot of meds in him, but he definitely came back to life early this morning."

Tears of joy filled Alexa's eyes. She sat next to him and was flooded with loving thoughts and a hopeful future. Less than an hour later, Grandpa awoke and began to speak. This would be the best New Year ever!

"What happened?" Grandpa wanted to know.

Alexa told him all she could without alarming him. She assured him that he was completely on the mend and would be going home soon.

"Who is Dr. Sun?" Grandpa asked out of the blue.

"Who?" she replied.

"Dr. Sun. Who is Dr. Sun?" he asked again.

"I don't know. Why do you ask?"

"Dr. Sun came in here every day and talked a lot. What kind of doctor is he?" Grandpa wanted to know.

"Grandpa, I know all of your doctors and there is no Dr. Sun. However, I will ask Dr. O'Donnell, who is your chief physician, and perhaps he can tell me," she replied.

Later that afternoon, Alexa bumped into Dr. O'Donnell in the corridor. He nodded a greeting in her direction. She walked a little faster toward him.

"Hi…got a sec?" she asked in a friendly tone, implying it wasn't business.

"Sure. How you doin'?" he asked.

"Not too bad," she replied. "Say, has a Dr. Sun ever consulted or treated my grandfather?"

He thought for a moment, "No."

"Are you absolutely certain?"

"I'm quite sure. Why do you ask?"

"Grandpa says that he recalls a Dr. Sun talking a lot in his room." Then she smiled wickedly, "And he said he didn't like him all that much."

Dr. O'Donnell's mind raced. "No. There's no Dr. Sun at Marlowe or anywhere else at St. Joseph's," he adamantly insisted. "It was probably just hallucinations caused by all the sedatives."

As they separated, Dr. O'Donnell sped to his office. He grabbed a blue phone and punched three digits without sitting down. "I need to see you immediately," he spoke urgently into the phone.

He slammed down the receiver, removed his lab coat and dashed to the adjoining administrative building. Harlan Pullman, St. Joseph's President and CEO, was waiting. Dr. O'Donnell was profoundly anxious for the first time in his long and distinguished medical career. Ignoring Pullman's executive secretary, he entered the president's posh office, shut the door behind him, and took a seat. Pullman just stared at him.

"We have a problem," Dr. O'Donnell said.

With a renewed sense of hope, Alexa headed out for lunch and then to Bolero Road to see Nely and the kids. Alexa gave her friend the good news about Grandpa and Nely was genuinely happy for her, though she also understood the continuing burden that lay ahead. Nely respected Alexa's loyalty and devotion, but usually did not hesitate to tell her that she was wasting the prime of her life while caring for Grandpa. Alexa understood this all too well but knew there was no other option. She had to do the *right thing*.

That afternoon, Alexa returned to Marlowe a renewed person. She would make plans for Grandpa's recovery and get on with her life. When she arrived at Grandpa's unit, it was empty. Her first thought was that he finally was getting a change of scene.

"Is Grandpa getting a spa treatment?" she jokingly asked Joe, one of the afternoon shift nurses.

Joe dropped what he was doing and looked right at her. "Haven't you been notified?" he asked.

"Notified of what?"

"Just wait right here, ok?" he said hurriedly, as he rushed down the corridor.

Alexa looked puzzled but waited patiently.

Dr. O'Donnell's colleague, Dr. Susan Morris, followed Joe back to Alexa.

"Hello Alexa," she said in a deadpan professional voice. "Will you please come with me for a minute?"

Alexa followed, suspecting they would discuss the next steps of Grandpa's treatment.

They stopped at a private little office just around the corner from the ICU rooms. Dr. Morris sat down, waiving Alexa to take a seat as well.

"Alexa, what I have to tell you isn't easy. So I'll just say it…and you know that we're all here for you if you ever need anything, ok?"

"Ok," Alexa nodded cautiously.

"Just over an hour ago, your grandfather went into cardiac arrest. We did everything we could, but we couldn't save him," she said.

Alexa went into shock. "Noooo!" She screamed from the top of her lungs. She slumped into the chair and wept before getting up and punching the office wall with all of her might. Eventually, Alexa's cries subsided into a running of silent tears.

"Where is he?" she finally asked.

"I'm not sure. He may already have been moved to the hospital morgue," Dr. Morris softly replied.

"Is there going to be an autopsy?"

"Well, considering how many medical complications your grandfather had, an autopsy is not required by the state," Dr. Morris answered.

Sobbing, Alexa ran out into the corridor. Joe called out to her and she stopped. "I'm so sorry Alexa. I know how much you loved your grandfather."

"Thank you, Joe. I really appreciate all that you and the staff did for him."

"Don't mention it. That's what we're here for." He waved his hand, "Listen, I have his belongings back in his room. Will you wait a minute and I'll bring them to you?"

"Of course. Thank you."

Alexa looked around. The place seemed strange and foreign. She was heartbroken at how many children were occupying the ward. She observed parents who had the same grief and anguish she had felt not so long ago. And now this was the end of the journey.

Joe came rushing back with a large clear plastic bag that contained the few personal items that Grandpa had left behind. She thanked him once again and they said their final good-byes.

Back at Grandpa's house, the little house that Alexa had called home for so many years, the feeling was one of vast emptiness, an aloneness that could not be expressed by mere words. Emotionally drained, Alexa felt a surge of manic energy. She jumped up from the sofa, rolled up her sleeves, got a box of large outdoor garbage bags and began to fill them with everything that did not need to remain in the house. The first to go to the alley dumpster was all of Grandpa's medical equipment. She did not want to see or own a single thing that reminded her of anything unpleasant about life with Grandpa Nico.

Finally, she opened the clear plastic bag.

Gingerly, one by one, she removed every single item: his dentures, his comb, his electric shaver, the tranquility room spray that Alexa used every day...and a yellow sticky note that had one word written on it—NERMYCIN.

# PART II

*"The greed of gain has no time or limit to its capaciousness.
Its one object is to produce and consume. It has pity neither for
beautiful nature nor for living human beings. It is ruthlessly ready
without a moment's hesitation to crush beauty and life."*

Rabindranath Tagore
(1861 - 1941)

# ELEVEN

*I*N 2000, THE U.S. had enacted legislation making certain direct sales of prescription drugs from Canada into the United States legal, but only with the approval of the U.S. Secretary of Health and Human Services. With that legislation, the floodgates opened and C3 created "*antidote.com*." This web site, owned by an indirect subsidiary of the C3 Group, eliminated the Canadian middleman. For the first time, this put a C3 Group company directly into the business of potentially violating U.S. law.

That potential was realized almost immediately when *antidote.com*, like many other Canadian web sites, started taking orders, even though the Secretary refused to approve of the implementing regulations. Ken preferred to sell effective and safe medicine on *antidote.com*, but given the barriers created by the cozy relationship between the FDA and the major pharmaceutical companies, he decided that if C3 could only make profits in the United States by cutting corners, then so be it. If the pharmaceutical industry and the U.S. government partnered to keep companies like C3 out of the United States, C3 could not be held responsible for the steps it took to overcome the manifestly unfair barriers.

Within the year, the Internet exploded and the United States became an important market for C3 Pharmaceuticals and other offshore drug companies. The business was extremely profitable and the risks remote.

Like other offshore drug companies that sought profits in the U.S. market without having to comply with the FDA's rigorous testing protocols, C3 was turning to low cost—and low quality—manufacturing operations in India, China and developing nations. Though the generic drugs manufactured for C3 were seldom deadly, they were often so adulterated or so ineffective that they were just as harmful. As C3 and others, including major drug companies, took advantage of the gaps in FDA enforcement, many hundreds or even thousands of Americans surely died—deprived of the potency or formulations they needed.

When the momentous events of 2001 occurred, Ken Karasik had been in the United States for 25 years. In that time, he had risen from a virtual political refugee to an international business titan with a disclosed net worth of well over one billion dollars, even after giving nearly that sum to his efforts in Eastern Europe. He achieved that near miracle because of his intelligence, his timing and his ruthlessness. He also had achieved his success by never making a serious mistake. That was about to change.

With the death of his family at the hands of Serbian thugs, Ken decided the time had come for all-out war against those who for too long had oppressed his people merely because of their ethnicity or their religious beliefs, or who stood by doing nothing to stop that oppression.

"The United States failed to act. America talked the talk but left it to the wimps in Europe to do something," Ken told Petar. "Even when the United States finally acted, it permitted Europe to set the tone, and then abdicated its leadership to the mandarins who run what passes for foreign policy in the European Union," he added.

Ken continued his diatribe. "As a result of America's inaction, Milosevic escaped any real consequences for his atrocities. No one in the Balkans is safe and our families are dead."

Petar incited him further, reminding Ken, "The United States did nothing for oppressed Muslims seeking their freedom in Chechnya, Azerbaijan, or other former Soviet satellites. So much for protecting freedom and democracy and those who need help!"

As a precursor to far deadlier action, early in 2002, Ken decided that C3 Pharmaceuticals would step up its production of counterfeit drugs and would more aggressively ignore U.S. regulations. Shortly thereafter, the CEO of *antidote.com* received new instructions from Irfan Pradeep, his boss in India. "No more prescriptions. From now on, you are to deliver whatever medicines your customers want. As you exhaust your current supplies, any further orders will be filled through a new distributor, Inversiones y Distribución Médicas de Las Producciones S.A. I'll get you the contact information."

Pradeep saw no reason to tell the Canadian CEO that Inversiones y Distribución Médicas de Las Producciones S.A. would obtain its supplies from India, China and other developing nations that could manufacture counterfeit drugs at a fraction of the cost of the real thing. Though the orders were delivered by Pradeep, he was only passing on instructions he had received from a woman in China. What he didn't know is that she had received her directions from a lawyer in Zurich. He received his instructions from Petar Raic and Raic received his directly from C3's chief executive officer, Ken Karasik.

C3 stepped up its production and sale of both counterfeit generic drugs and questionable new drugs. *Antidote.com* offered generic versions of every drug imaginable. From Cipro to Zoloft to

Nexium to Ritalin to Viagra, the list went on and on. *Antidote.com* also sold all the feel-good addictive drugs like painkillers and anti-depressants, ranging from Valium to Vicodin, as well as birth control pills, AIDS remedies, and every drug any American could want or need. Significantly, *antidote.com* featured the full range of C3 Pharmaceuticals' branded and patented drugs, including Raphlen, and newer medications for fevers, viral infections and heart disease, some of which, like Nermycin-X, Barontin and Emarin, had actually been approved by the FDA for sale in the United States.

"We have any number of choices about how to proceed. But none of them has the potential for death on the same scale," Ken explained to Mel and Ben, defending his decision on their means of attack.

"Bombs, fuel trucks, or poison gas released in a subway or a stadium might kill a few thousand, but only a nuclear weapon could achieve devastation at anywhere near the same level of what I have selected. With my plan, we can also end the attack if the United States does as we ask. Even if we could develop a nuclear device, we would lose that option."

"Ken, that's true, but we have no idea how long it would take to develop a viable agent," Mel observed.

"Then you better get started now," Ken concluded before dis-connecting their teleconference.

C3 Pharmaceuticals had several research facilities in Europe. All but one were indistinguishable from similar facilities around the world operated by other pharmaceutical companies such as GlaxoSmithKline, Pfizer, Merck or PharmCorp. Men and women in white lab coats and blue scrubs quietly worked in clean, orderly air conditioned laboratories developing, improving and testing new formulas intended to alleviate or even cure illnesses.

After extensive testing on animals, those few drugs that were deemed safe and effective were sent on to a series of outpatient clinics also owned by C3. In these comfortable and subdued environments, willing volunteers participated in double blind studies to assess the proposed medicines. C3 would seek regulatory approvals and begin marketing only those products that delivered real benefits with no more than acceptable side effects.

C3 also maintained one very private facility. Nestled in a secluded area near the Rhine River about 36 kilometers from Zurich, outside the village of Schaffhausen, a converted asylum was the site of C3's special research. It was here that C3 doctored the results of its testing for Raphlen and it was here that Petar and Ben visited in May 2002 to discuss the possibilities of infecting medicines with a virus or some other pathogen.

The drive from Zurich to Schaffhausen in the black Mercedes S500 took less than half an hour. Petar looked out through the tinted windows. The snow had long ago melted in the old town of some 34,000 residents. Its Renaissance-era buildings, town squares and cobblestone paths made this capital of the eponymous Swiss canton a warm and cozy place for C3's researchers to live.

The last few kilometers, first on *Radenstraße* out of town, then onto *Rotelstraße*, and finally on an unnamed dirt road took another 15 minutes as the Mercedes slowly wound its way through the narrow roads that snaked around the Rhine. Finally, they approached the secluded C3 facility.

This was the first time Ben had been to Schaffhausen, let alone the secret C3 lab. He observed the 14-foot iron fence, topped with razor-sharp darts. Numerous thin wires ran at one-foot intervals in parallel around the circumference of the fence, creating a crosshatch with the fence's unusually thick vertical poles that were densely spaced every few inches. Ben also noticed that the bottom of the fence appeared to extend deep into the gravel, rather than end a few inches aboveground, as would be more typical. Ben knew the thin wires were sensors for an alarm system and that the fence had been built to make it extremely difficult for an intruder to climb above or burrow below.

Ben also noticed that the trees on both sides of the fence had been cut back so that no branch came within three feet on the outside or six feet on the inside. Further observation revealed that the grounds were topped off by a thick layer of loose gravel, presumably to ensure that anyone who moved around the property could not do so silently. The former asylum itself was shielded by thick foliage, though it was obvious that the solidly constructed brown brick building had been built in the first part of the 20th century. Tudor in style, it appeared to be about 15,000 square feet in size.

As the car reached the gate, the driver rolled down his window and Petar could hear the muffled hum of exhaust fans. An unarmed security officer asked for their identification. After briefly returning to a small guardhouse where he checked their passports against pictures he called up on his computer, he waived the car through, directing them to park alongside the main building.

The driver continued on a few hundred feet. As they got closer, they realized the building was larger than it appeared from the road, probably 20,000 square feet, or even more, including its basement. They pulled up to a reserved parking spot just to the left of the main entrance. The driver remained in the car, while Ben and Petar exited.

Before they even reached the door, a man Petar recognized as the manager of the facility rushed out to greet them. Herr Doktor

Andreas Bauer was dressed in his white lab coat. He was 55, balding, and about 30 pounds overweight.

"Welcome, welcome," he smiled broadly as he extended his hand to the third-ranking officer of the C3 Group. "I have gathered everyone as you asked. But, is there anything you would like to review first? Would you like a tour?"

"Thank you, Dr. Bauer," Petar replied as he shook his hand. "Let me introduce my associate, Henry Toll," he added, referring to Ben by a name they had selected only an hour before. "I've already had the tour, but perhaps Mr. Toll would appreciate the five-minute version. Then we can get down to work. I'm afraid we have to get back to Zurich this afternoon, so we have only about an hour."

"Very well. Good to meet you Mr. Toll," Dr. Bauer said, again extending his hand. He led his guests through the main doors and into a small reception area. Ben noted the two-inch thick steel plates on the exterior doors. Just inside those doors, an armed sentry sat behind a small desk. Though well-lit, the room had no windows. It was sparsely furnished with six simple chairs and a side table stacked with recent magazines. Black and white prints of U.S. skylines and old buildings hung on the cream-colored walls. The sentry must have pressed a hidden button or lever because suddenly there was an audible click, and a hidden door opposite the sentry's desk rolled back on its tracks.

At Dr. Bauer's urging, they proceeded inside, only to discover that they had entered a room that was slightly larger than a standard elevator. Like the entry foyer, black and white prints hung on cream-colored walls. There were cameras at each end of the rectangular room, a pedestal with a telephone and nothing else. With a slight hum, the door to the lobby slid shut. Almost immediately, another door hidden at the opposite end of the small room rolled back into the wall.

"Gentlemen," Dr. Bauer said, pointing the way through the open door. As they walked inside, they entered a much larger and more expansively decorated lobby. This time, the seating area included several chairs and two sofas. Side tables and coffee tables completed the arrangement. There was a credenza along one wall with a coffee maker, sugar, powdered milk, cups, spoons and napkins. Each of the other three walls included a door, bookcases and other furniture. Except for the armed sentry sitting behind a pedestal that boasted sophisticated monitors and communication equipment, it could have been the waiting area of any prestigious corporation. Four casually dressed men and one woman were seated as they entered. The attractive 40ish woman immediately stood and came toward them.

"We will be meeting in the conference room just off to the left. I believe the others are already there. Mr. Raic, you may wish to join them for a few minutes while I show Mr. Toll around. Fraulein Huber can accompany you and see to your needs," Dr. Bauer explained.

Huber offered Petar her hand and smiled. Petar reciprocated. "Thank you, Herr Docktor. I think that's a fine suggestion. We can make some introductions while you give Mr. Toll his tour."

"Good. Mr. Toll and I will see you shortly."

Huber then walked over to the door on their left. She keyed in a code on the small pad to the door's right and the door unlocked. Pushing it open, she escorted Petar inside and to the conference room.

"Mr. Toll, would you join me please?" Dr. Bauer requested, as he walked over to one of the other doors and keyed in the appropriate code. The door unlocked, and they proceeded inside.

"Please stay with me as we move through the facility," the security-minded manager requested. "As Mr. Raic said, this will be a quick tour. On another occasion, I would be pleased to spend more time with you."

Ben and Huber spent no more than seven minutes exploring a most fascinating facility. It turned out that there were two below-ground levels and three above ground. Each floor was about 5,000 square feet, meaning the facility totaled about 25,000 square feet. The staff numbered 90, including 35 full-time researchers, statisticians, administrators, a support staff, a security team of 30, of whom six to eight were on duty at any time, 15 orderlies who worked in rotation, and a cleaning staff of six.

Although Dr. Bauer didn't realize it, Ben was already familiar with the lab's security precautions. Every employee had been carefully vetted by Opperman Security, including polygraph tests every six months. Multiple cameras with overlapping views covered every corner of the lab. The feeds were available at the security desks in the exterior and interior waiting rooms, in a small security office in the first basement, and at Opperman Security's office in Zurich. In addition to the touch-wires lining the fence, there were motion sensors throughout the grounds and inside the former asylum. Keypads guarded access to many of the doors throughout the facility, with access codes limited to those with a bona fide need. Access codes also were required to operate both elevators and to open many of the locked storage units throughout the premises.

The high security was for a reason. What the scientists were doing was both illegal and dangerous. More importantly, should the unwilling human subjects who lived out the last days, weeks or occasionally months of their pitiful lives in the cells that lined the sub-basement escape, the consequences were too awful to contemplate. These unfortunate slaves had been kidnapped right off the streets of Switzerland, Germany, Italy and France. Each one of them was a vagrant or a beggar. No one who mattered would miss them, and regardless of the outcome of the research, they would never leave the C3 lab alive.

"Let's start with the sub-basement and work our way up. We'll use the main elevator. There's also a freight elevator in the back. It is very important you stay close to me, particularly in the sub-basement."

"Understood," Ben replied.

Just a few seconds later the elevator doors opened onto another one of those small rooms to which Ben was becoming accustomed. "Axel, would you buzz us in to the living quarters, please," Dr. Bauer asked the armed guard sitting behind the ubiquitous security desk.

The guard buzzed them in, and they entered a long bright hallway. Off the hallway were a total of 10 cells, a small cafeteria, a game room, an orderlies' station and a fitness room. Ben observed that each cell included a bolted-in bed, a small desk, a chair and a television. "While they're with us, we'd like to keep them somewhat happy. If they get too depressed, it could skew the results. That's why we have a game room and an exercise facility with Nautilus equipment, but no free weights. Our 'guests' are under constant supervision. Any effort to abuse or misuse the equipment is swiftly punished."

Although there was no natural light, the bright yellows and light blues presumably helped in avoiding depression. "The lights mimic the cycle of day and night."

"Where does the food come from?" Ben asked.

"There is a kitchen on the other side of the guard's desk. We didn't want the kitchen to be located where our guests might wander in and create problems," Dr. Bauer explained. "Come, let me show you the treatment rooms."

Dr. Bauer walked to a door, punched in a code, and entered another one of the security holding rooms. "This room is just long and wide enough for two gurneys and four orderlies," he explained as he punched in a code on the far door.

"The treatment area is painted in more subdued colors. We want our guests to be as calm as possible during tests."

Ben observed five rooms. Each had a bed and a large array of monitoring equipment. "Of course, the beds have restraints so our subjects don't hurt themselves during the tests. Ok. Let's head up to the upper basement," Dr. Bauer said.

They returned to the guard's station through a different door. After a moment, the elevator arrived and they took it up one level. This time, there was no little room and no guard. "This level is to animals what the sub-basement is to humans. We have separate holding areas here for dogs, cats, rats and mice. Each section is sound-proofed so the animals don't scare each other. As in the basement, we also have separate rooms for the experiments, though we also conduct some of the animal experiments upstairs."

While quickly showing Ben around the basement, Dr. Bauer observed, "We also keep our security office on this floor." As Ben already knew, at least two armed sentries hired by Opperman Security were always on duty. They were in addition to the sentries at the main gate, main door, interior lobby and sub-basement, as well as the sentries who patrolled the property and facility on an irregular schedule. The security team was supplemented by buff orderlies who escorted the human subjects around the basement and supervised their care and feeding.

"Let's head upstairs. We'll go up to the third floor, and then end up on the ground level where we have our meeting." Dr. Bauer again keyed in the access code, and the elevator took just a few seconds to climb the three stories.

When they exited onto the third floor, at first it looked like any other research lab. About half the floor consisted of cubicles around a large lab with interior windows. A door off the elevator presumably led to the remainder of the floor.

"If you look around, you'll see the usual cubes and computers. The inside room is a typical clean room. I'll take you for a quick look." Dr. Bauer was right. The clean room included refrigerated storage with a large assortment of vials and other containers, more desks with computers, and various centrifuges, microscopes and electronic devices used to combine and separate ingredients and assess the results. The floor had obviously been decorated by whoever was responsible for the ground floor. It had the same cream color and a great many black and white prints.

"Now let me show you our most important unit." Using his access code, Dr. Bauer opened the door near the elevator. The door was essentially at one end of the length of a five-foot by 60-foot hallway. A large steel door was located in the wall opposite the door through which they entered. About 15 feet down the length of the hallway, there was a large glass window in the same wall as the steel door.

"There's a locker room in there," Bauer said, pointing to the door in the perpendicular wall. "That steel door opens into an airlock. On the other side of the airlock are two rooms, a shower and a second airlock. Then, on the other side of the inner airlock is an airtight Level 4 biohazard laboratory. We can look inside through the window."

Ben looked at the airtight lab through the large double-paned window. There, scientists in what appeared to be spacesuits were manipulating biological matter in Petri dishes.

"If what they're working on became airborne, it could make a lot of us very sick. It might even kill, though we seldom work with substances that toxic. The risk that we would ever be infected is extremely remote, however, because that glass is six inches thick and our procedures require those who venture inside to take a chemical shower in the room I just described to you before they can rejoin their colleagues," Dr. Bauer explained to Ben, who didn't look well.

"I'm relieved," was Ben's only answer.

"Don't worry Mr. Toll, you really are quite safe. Let's take a very quick look at the second and first floors," Dr. Bauer replied as he herded Ben out of the hallway, into the elevator and down to the second floor.

The second floor was essentially a copy of the third floor, but instead of the airtight lab, there was a room for animal experimentation.

"Our time is up, and we should return to the conference room," Dr. Bauer told Ben.

"I think I'd like that," he replied, still nervous about being so close to so many dangerous toxins.

As they exited the elevator on the ground floor, Dr. Bauer quickly pointed out the administrative offices, storage rooms and two conference rooms before they entered one of them to join the meeting.

"Our goal is simple, though execution may not be," Petar explained to Dr. Bauer, Fraulein Doktor Shelly Kleist, the head of epidemiology at the Schaffhausen lab, and Herr Doktor Lukas Kappel, its overall head of research. Ben had heard it all before.

"We want to tamper with one or more drugs in order to produce a widespread epidemic in America. We also have several other requirements. First, we don't want to be caught." There was nervous laughter, as Petar continued.

"Second, we want to make certain that a large enough number of the target is infected before the U.S. even knows what is happening. We don't want panic or defensive actions until we're ready.

"Third, we want to be able to reverse what we start. Should we choose, we want to provide an antidote that will stop the dying."

"Just how many do you want to kill?" Dr. Bauer asked.

"Unless we decide to stop the attack, we want to see a minimum of 150,000 die, and preferably as many as 500,000."

"You are kidding," Dr. Kleist haltingly asked. "You don't mean it," Dr. Kappel said at almost the same time. Even Dr. Bauer looked stunned.

"Doctors, I am deadly serious," Petar replied, fully intending the pun.

"Every day there are people dying in the Balkans and the Russian Federation. That must end. Each of you has worked on projects intended to kill people. What do you think you're doing to your so-called 'subjects' every day? This sudden concern with killing is beneath you," Petar stridently asserted.

"But, it's the enormity of this. Sure, I've been responsible for killing a few hundred. But, 500,000?" Dr. Kleist asked.

As Petar was about to respond, Dr. Bauer interrupted, fearful that the dissent could prove unhealthy for Drs. Kleist and Kappel— or him.

"Shelly, Lukas, I too am stunned by the enormity. But, what stuns me is the grandeur of the vision. Just think of what we would be part of. Although no one will ever know who has done this, we would prove to ourselves that we could do something no one else has ever attempted, let alone achieved. And we would be doing it for our families!"

Pavlov could not have been more effective. Every scientist at C3's secret Schaffhausen lab shared several things in common: they had emigrated from the Balkans to escape from Tito's Communist rule and the Serbians; they had lost all or most of their families to Communist or Serbian monsters; they had sworn revenge; and they were prideful and egotistical to a fault.

Drs. Kleist and Kappel visibly relaxed. So did the other three.

"If we are past the surprise, there are a number of issues we would have to address to make this plan of yours work." A much calmer Dr. Kappel directed his comments to Petar. "Above all, with so daring a goal, unless we create a biological or chemical weapon and deliver it by airplane, or perhaps with suicide bombers, it will be very difficult to succeed."

Ben joined the conversation for the first time. "That's a fair point, Lukas. For a number of reasons, however, we have decided against such an attack. Most notably, biological and chemical weapons are historically difficult to deliver or control. It would also be difficult to simultaneously deliver the number of devices that would be required to ensure that 500,000 die."

"I don't disagree, Mr. Toll. But, biochemical warfare has come a long way. And it may be the only way of getting to these numbers," Lukas rejoined.

"I'll tell you what. I won't close my mind to that idea, but why don't we talk about some other possibilities as well," Petar said.

"Sounds fair," Lukas replied, relieved that they were about to engage in a rational discussion.

More than an hour and a half later, well beyond the deadline Petar had set when they first arrived, Ben and Petar prepared to leave for the nearly hour ride back to C3's offices in Zurich. Their wide-ranging conversation had touched on numerous potential approaches to achieving the objective, as well as an ever larger number of obstacles. The biggest problem appeared to be coupling a high probability of success with a low probability of getting caught. Dr.

Bauer and his team were going to think about the alternatives. They would consult with just two or three of their colleagues, and they would begin to study the options. When the Schaffhausen scientists narrowed the choices, they would all reconvene.

Before leaving, Petar reminded the group, "Time is not on our side. Our brothers are dying in Croatia, in Bosnia and Herzegovina, and in the Russian Federation. Delay makes the enemy stronger and us weaker."

No one disagreed.

# TWELVE

U RGED ON BY lobbyists for the major pharmaceutical companies, investigators began to focus on Internet marketers and the offshore companies that were supplying them. Although C3's ownership of *antidote.com* was well hidden behind strawmen and nominees, for the first time, a C3 business became the subject of an investigation in the United States.

Because *antidote.com*'s business violated U.S. law, its profits were funneled back to the C3 Group only after being laundered first in the Cayman Islands, and then in Panama. The process was circuitous, but not really complex. For branded products such as Raphlen purchased from C3 Pharmaceuticals, *antidote.com* openly paid the list price and transferred the money to Zurich. The company also openly paid its Canadian employees and a Canadian management company that helped run the web site. From there, nothing else was as it appeared.

*Antidote.com* paid its suppliers in India and China by wire transfer to numbered accounts in the Cayman Islands. If anyone checked, the accounts were held by trading firms registered to a local trust company. That trust company never divulged its clients. But, even if it did, all that could be discovered was that the accounts were established by a lawyer in Mexico. The lawyer received a small fee for his efforts, and did not even know the name of his client. Once the money reached the Cayman Islands account, which changed every few weeks, it was immediately wired to a numbered account in the Isle of Man. Those accounts were in the names of two or three local trust companies. Those companies were as circumspect as their Cayman Islands cousins. But, if anyone broke their security, all they would discover would be some lawyers in Chile. They too had no idea who had paid them to establish the irrevocable trusts in the Isle of Man.

Just as soon as the funds made it to the Isle of Man, they were transferred to a brokerage account in Hong Kong, where the funds were used to purchase stock on the Shanghai stock exchange. The stock was registered in the names of several nominees, law firms that would never reveal the identities of their clients. Those law firms then arranged loans against the stock, and the proceeds of the loans were deposited into numbered Swiss accounts. Two trust funds later, the loan proceeds were allocated, with a small portion wired to the country in which manufacturing occurred to reimburse costs and a small profit for the local owners and managers. The balance was allocated to accounts ultimately controlled by Petar Raic and Karasik Capital.

After paying all of its operating costs and the prices charged by C3 Pharmaceuticals for its name-brand drugs and other suppliers for their generic drugs, *antidote.com* usually netted a small profit. Part of that profit was reinvested, part was paid as income tax to the Canadian government, part to its so-called owners (John and Harriet Cowell, a retired couple living in Winnipeg who had owned one of the mail order businesses with which C3 had done business years earlier), and the balance donated to charities in the United States and Canada, earning *antidote.com* excellent publicity and goodwill. If only those charities knew how many people had been made sicker or even died to fund those paltry contributions.

It was a long and fairly expensive road between *antidote.com* and the profits deposited into Karasik Capital's accounts. Still, Karasik Capital netted more than $30 million in 2002 and that didn't even count the huge profits earned by C3 Pharmaceuticals for its name brands. All of that money was used to fund the Karasik Commission's terrorist operations in the Balkans and elsewhere.

It had been almost six months since Ben and Petar had visited the secret C3 facility just outside of Schaffhausen. In that time, Dr. Bauer and his colleagues had narrowed the alternatives. There had been many phone calls with Petar and the man they knew as "Mr. Toll." Until today, however, they had not been ready to reconvene.

Once again, a black Mercedes S500 whisked Ben and Petar to the former asylum that now housed C3's most secret research facility. After clearing the ID check at the main gate, they parked just outside the entrance. A slightly less rotund Dr. Bauer escorted them in through the double lobby.

"You're looking good, Herr Doktor," Ben told him.

"Ja. My wife tells me I eat too much. It's important to remain healthy in this business." The irony wasn't lost on Ben. He wondered if it had been intentional.

Fraulein Huber was again present to escort them to the conference room. When she offered them coffee or tea, Petar chose coffee and Ben opted for tea. Shelly Kleist and Lukas Kappel were there, along with three others from the lab, two men and a woman. After introducing them, Dr. Bauer explained, "These are our three top chemists. There is no way we could even attempt a project of this scope without them. I wanted them to participate in this meeting so they can hear your needs directly, and respond to any questions you might have."

"Good. Dr. Bauer, what have you concluded?" Petar inquired.

"Lukas, why don't you explain?"

"Thank you, Dr. Bauer," Dr. Kappel began his presentation as if he were in a meeting with the management of C3 Pharmaceuticals, rather than members of the covert Karasik Commission.

"We have considered the objectives: an attack that is undertaken sooner is preferable to one that is undertaken later; the attack should kill at least 150,000 Americans and preferably more than 500,000, unless we decide otherwise; it should be possible to stop the attack once it is already underway; it should have a very high probability of success; and, we should not be caught.

"After looking at a broad range of alternatives, including biological and chemical weapons, contaminating America's water, food, or drugs, we have concluded that the best alternative is the one you selected—contaminating the drug supply.

"When considering different means of contaminating the drug supply, we, of course, started with the most simple—adding a toxin to existing products, particularly liquids or timed release capsules. We know that is easy to do. Indeed, we have done it many times in the past. The problem is that such tampering is easy to detect."

Petar interrupted with a question. "What if we modify the drug before it's packaged, so there is no external evidence—not even a pinprick in a capsule?"

"That's the right question, Mr. Raic. But there are two aspects to our concern about detection. The first is detection as a result of a routine physical inspection that may even be unrelated to the attack. Your question deals with that risk. I agree, we can eliminate that risk.

"The second risk relates to a situation I was about to explain. That risk comes from the fact that to kill 500,000 Americans, we would have to tamper with millions of pills or tablets. Even if we use a toxin that kills in just one dose, we can't be sure where any particular pill or tablet will end up. If we tamper with 50 tablets and they end up in the same bottle, we will kill one person, not 50. If the poison is fast acting, the hospitals or the CDC will quickly figure out the source of the poison and they'll stop it. Sure, the first wave of the attack may kill hundreds or even thousands before that happens, but you'll never get to 500,000."

"Lukas, 'we'll' never get to 500,000. Remember, we're in this together," Ben pointed out.

"You're right Mr. Toll. I apologize. And the reason *we'll* never get to 500,000 if the poison is fast acting, is that once the CDC or FBI or whoever analyzes the drug, they'll immediately know what's in it. That's the second detection risk."

"What if the poison is slow acting?" Petar asked.

"Let's go through that one. If the toxin is slow acting, more people will die before anyone knows what's happening. That gets us to two 'buts.' The first is that I'm not sure we can develop a slow-acting poison that would work in just one dose. That means we need to cumulate small amounts of a toxin in multiple doses. Second, I can't imagine an approach that is so slow acting that we can infect 100,000 Americans, let alone 500,000 Americans before the government figures out the common denominator, titrates the drugs and finds the toxin."

"So, what are you suggesting?" Petar asked, curious about where this was heading.

"Now that's the half-million-person question. We've come up with an approach we think can work. Before suggesting it to you, we did some experiments here in the lab. We didn't want to propose a theoretical approach that we couldn't actually achieve. That's why Eva, Leon and Philipp are here," Dr. Kappel said referring to the three chemists attending the meeting. "They're the ones who ran these experiments."

Eva jumped in. "As you may know, many diseases are treated not with a single drug, but with a 'cocktail' that consists of multiple drugs. The best-known example of this is AIDS. But, it's also true for many other conditions. Our thesis was that we could modify one of the drugs in the cocktail so that it was not toxic on its own, but it became toxic when it interacted with another drug in the cocktail."

"If this worked," Dr. Kappel excitedly explained, "It would greatly diminish the odds of detection and complicate the CDC's ability to create meaningful regression analyses. Many patients might take one drug in the cocktail without the other. Other patients might combine the drugs, but if they don't use the adulterated version nothing will happen. Anyone who uses the trigger drug by itself won't get sick. Finally, even if the trigger drug is analyzed, the authorities might find a modification, but it wouldn't be lethal. If we do this right, the modification should be completely inert, meaning it wouldn't harm a fly unless combined with the other drug!"

"I can see why you're excited," Ben said.

"I get it," Petar agreed. "Now what about the experiments?"

"We tried many different combinations," Shelly Kleist, the head of epidemiology explained. "We wanted to keep it simple, so we ignored all cocktails exceeding two drugs. We focused on cocktails for most common conditions so we would get to 500,000 victims within a few months. Finally, and here's the toughest part, we wanted drugs that once modified would interact in a slow-acting way. No matter how we approach this, it's clear that avoiding detection means sticking to slow-acting toxins."

Eva jumped back in. "We spent most of our time on cocktails where C3 makes one of the two drugs. We realize that for the actual implementation we'd rather not use a C3 drug, but we know those the best and it made it easier during this preliminary screen to refine our choices. If you tell us to go forward, we'll look beyond C3's products.

"Anyway, after some trial-and-error, we tried modifying Emarin. That drug helps fight heart disease. It's always mixed with another drug, and there are many choices for the second drug. We modeled a modified Emarin that includes a particular antigen we have come across with a variety of beta-blockers. We concluded that with the right modification, the Emarin would cause an allergic reaction to the beta-blockers. Our modeling showed that would kill after about 30 days of usage."

Leon spoke for the first time. "What was just so exciting is that an analysis of the adulterated Emarin only reveals that it has an extra ingredient that is totally benign."

"Yet, the interaction with any beta-blocker is a surefire killer," Eva said.

"When we injected the modified cocktail into human subjects, none died before 20 days and all died within 40 days. With a placebo, or an unmodified combination, no one died," Philipp explained, finally joining the discussion as well.

"In short," Dr. Kappel summarized, "the modified Emarin killed slowly and when analyzed revealed nothing that could explain the deaths!"

Ben and Petar exchanged glances. They knew the Schaffhausen chemists were on to something. "My only concern is that this Emarin seems to have a very limited use. If I understand the cocktail, our victims would have to already suffer from heart disease," Peter observed.

"You're absolutely correct," Dr. Bauer said. "But, our purpose today wasn't to recommend any particular cocktail or drugs. We wanted to review the pros and cons of several approaches. We believe we've come up with a particularly novel approach. It's so novel that we didn't want to even mention it until we proved that it could work. We think we've done that. If you authorize us to proceed, the next step is to find the right cocktail.

"What's the right cocktail?" Ben asked.

"The optimal cocktail involves no C3 patents. Both drugs should be out of their FDA exclusive windows so that patients are able to purchase the generic versions. We can always manufacture the generic versions in India or China and then sell them on our web site or even through other web sites and regular pharmacy distribution. Finally, the cocktail should be used to treat a much less critical and widespread health problem than is true of the Emarin," Dr. Bauer answered.

"That makes sense to me," Petar said.

"Good. We have some food coming in. Why don't we take a few minutes, and then resume. We want to walk you through more detail on the approaches we rejected and we'd like to show you some reports on the Emarin experiments. Even though we're not recommending Emarin, when you look at the reports I think you'll agree we're on the right track.

"I already agree. However, Mr. Toll and I set aside today to listen. So, I'm ok with that schedule if he is."

"I'm at your disposal. I just want everyone here to know that what you seem to have accomplished is very impressive," Ben added.

During the break Ben and Petar stepped outside and called Mel on his secure cellular. Mel had a strong understanding of the relevant issues because of his hands-on supervision of MDB Pharmaceuticals.

"Let's be a little cautious here until we review the work papers. However, if the underlying results are consistent with the headlines, we may be looking at a home run," Mel told them.

A few minutes later, Dr. Bauer asked if they wanted to resume. Their answer was a resounding "yes!"

# THIRTEEN

**O**NCE THEY HAD approval from Petar to proceed, the scientists in Schaffhausen methodically began to screen the diseases and conditions that were typically treated with cocktails of two or three drugs. They screened for conditions that were prevalent in large segments of the population, particularly those, like influenza or the common cold, that did not discriminate based on race, age or medical condition.

Shelly Kleist directed the screening, which took about a month. Then, they eliminated drug cocktails that required newer, branded drugs. The goal was to find combinations that used generics. The branded drugs were no more difficult to copy than the generics. They preferred the generics because they were easier to distribute and their source would be masked by the large volume of counterfeit generic drugs originating from so many different manufacturers. Enforcement activity was also weaker, since pharmaceutical companies were particularly vigilant about trademark infringement.

After another month, they had narrowed the choices to six: pneumonia, ulcers, staph infections, herpes, asthma and diabetes. Each of the conditions was widespread and attacked people of all ages. Other conditions were also widespread, but they were concentrated in the elderly, treated with many drugs at the same time, or generally treated with newer, branded drugs that were not yet legally available in generic form.

Once the screening process had winnowed the field, Leon, Philipp and Eva began to look at the drug combinations that were most popular. They determined, for example, that asthma was typically treated with a combination of an inhaled steroid and a beta-agonist, while diabetics were often prescribed some combination of sulfonylureas, meglitinides, biguanides, thiazolidinediones, and alpha-glucosidase inhibitors.

The most difficult task was to determine those combinations that could be rendered lethal by altering one of the drugs in the combination (the "trigger drug"), while that drug by itself would not be lethal. That analysis began with day-long conferences in which the team discussed the possibilities based on their extensive experience.

Then, Eva or Leon would model the proposed modifications on their computers. For weeks, they sat at their desks modeling one approach after another.

"We don't have enough computing power to proceed this way," Shelly Kleist reported to Dr. Bauer. "We need a supercomputer with at least a 250 on the n=100 LINPACK Benchmark." The LINPACK Benchmark was a widely used means of measuring high-performance computers. The benchmark included several measurements in addition to the n=100 scale and was based on the computer's ability to solve a dense system of linear equations.

"Even with prices rapidly declining, we're talking about a $100,000 computer, maybe more," Dr. Bauer replied. "Let me look into it."

"Ok, but without it this project is going to take a lot longer."

Within three weeks, the lab took delivery of a Fujitsu supercomputer that met all of their requirements. With it, Eva and Leon were able to accelerate their modeling. Within another month, they were ready to create the adulterated drugs that would be tested on live subjects.

"What's so damn difficult about this is that we have to mate the toxin to each pair. We can't use the same ingredients twice," Philipp sighed.

"Indeed. If we don't get some more help, this is going to take all year. We have to just keep going," Leon responded, as he carefully isolated one of the toxins and slowly moved it into the advanced centrifuge that would combine it with the acyclovir used to treat herpes. Once combined, they would inject it and probenecid into rats to see if the rats developed the debilitating illness they predicted. If the results were positive, they would move on to dogs, and eventually human subjects.

The process was repeated time and again for many months, with many different drugs and for each of the illnesses.


"So far, there is one problem or another with each of the combinations. We have eliminated ulcers and herpes, but we're still working on the other conditions," Dr. Bauer explained by phone to Petar. Petar frequently checked in and had visited once again to get an update from the entire team.


By fall, they had eliminated combinations for asthma and diabetes, leaving only staph infections and pneumonia. "The problem with staph infections is that the trigger drug that works best in the lab studies is a C3 drug. The problem with diabetes is that there are so many different combinations that it may be difficult to get to 500,000 victims. We also have some doubts about our ability to solve the stability issue in the pneumonia trigger drug long enough to get even close." Dr. Kleist was summarizing results for Dr. Bauer before requesting permission to move on to a second wave of human subjects.

"Well, nothing's perfect. I think you should proceed with additional human testing for both the staph and diabetes. We may get lucky."

The human studies were similar to the animal studies, but the incubation period for illness was often longer. Each day, orderlies brought five subjects into the treatment rooms. There, Eva, Philipp or Leon administered the drugs as they would be used by a patient in the outside world. Once each day, a nurse drew the subject's blood. Urine and stool samples were also taken for examination. An orderly checked each subject's temperature and heart rate at least twice a day. In between being poked and examined, the subjects rested in their beds, watched TV, played poker, checkers or chess in the game room, or worked out until they became ill.

As the subject became ill, he or she was confined to bed. In some instances, they tried to prolong the subject's life, going so far as to hook up the patient to oxygen, or a respirator, and providing the same care as might be available in any hospital. Sometimes the subject recovered. If so, the subject was put through yet another battery of tests. For some of those who recovered, the whole process started over again. For others, recovery was short-lived. The subject would be hooked up to an intravenous drip and administered the same lethal mix used for executions by many states—sodium thiopental to put the subject to sleep, and then pancuronium bromide and potassium chloride to kill.

Whatever the outcome, once the subject was dead, a physician on C3's staff performed a complete autopsy. The results were then analyzed to help refine the next generation of the toxin, or to help rule out a particular approach. After the autopsy, the bodies were cremated and the ashes taken to several local dumps where they were rapidly absorbed by the trash and nature.

By the end of 2003, the scientists near Schaffhausen were well along in their research and the Karasik Commission was creating a plan to infiltrate tainted drugs into the American medical system to deliberately kill tens of thousands of Americans.

# FOURTEEN

**W**HILE THE YEAR 2001 began as a year of change in Yugoslavia, it ended as a year of change for the entire world. On September 11, 2001, 19 suicide bombers hijacked four passenger jets filled with fuel and 266 passengers. They successfully flew two jets originating in Boston into the twin towers of the World Trade Center killing 2,752 occupants and visitors, and one originating in Washington, D.C. into the Pentagon, killing another 125. They abandoned their efforts to hit the White House or Capitol with the fourth hijacked jet, United Air Flight 93, originating in Newark. Defeated by its unarmed passengers, they crashed the jet into a Pennsylvania field. Including the passengers and crew, some 3,000 perished in less than two hours. With these attacks, the United States moved to a war footing.

As troops mobilized for Operation Enduring Freedom to destroy the Taliban and al-Qaeda in Afghanistan, U.S. intelligence and law enforcement agencies re-assessed their roles and their deployments. On September 4, 2001, former U.S. Attorney Robert S. Mueller had been sworn in as FBI Director with a specific mandate to enhance FBI foreign counterintelligence analysis and security in the wake of the damage done by former Special Agent and convicted spy Robert Hanssen. Within days, the September 11 terrorist attacks on New York and Washington changed everything. On October 26, 2001, President George W. Bush signed into law the U.S. Patriot Act, which granted new powers to address the threat of terrorism. Then, on May 29, 2002, the Attorney General issued investigative guidelines to assist the Bureau's efforts to protect the American people against future terrorist attacks.

To support the Bureau's change in mission, Director Mueller reorganized the FBI to closely focus on prevention of terrorist attacks, counter foreign intelligence operations against the U.S., and address cybercrime-based attacks and other high-technology crimes. All this was in addition to its traditional charge to investigate public corruption, organized crime, white-collar crime, and major violent crime. The Bureau also strengthened its support for other law enforcement agencies, in an effort to end the parochialism that had prevented the FBI, CIA, FAA and other agencies from sharing information.

Thousands of agents were re-assigned to the Counterterrorism Division. Barry Weiner was one of those agents.

Weiner was a rarity in so many ways. A handsome 36 years of age in September 2001, he was born in Shanghai. When he was still an infant, his mother, Jing, moved to New York where she married Lou Weiner, an accountant from the Bronx. The family moved to Syosset, Long Island. Jing and Barry converted to Judiasm. Yes, Barry Weiner was a Chinese Jew. After graduating from Hofstra University in Long Island with a major in economics, Weiner attended Fordham Law. Upon graduation in 1994, he joined the FBI. After a year of training, Special Agent Weiner was assigned to the New York office where his first investigations focused on financial crimes, including money laundering. After a few years, he made quite the name for himself and was transferred to the FBI's headquarters in Washington, D.C. Once there, Weiner handled a range of nonviolent crimes.

Initially, like nearly everyone else in the Bureau, Weiner was charged with investigating just what happened to permit the worst attack ever on the U.S. mainland. As answers started to develop, members of the task force were given more specialized tasks. At first, Barry was assigned to a special Interpol liaison unit. Then, in mid-2004, he was re-assigned to investigate funding sources for terrorists.

Weiner had not outgrown the thrill of being part of the same organization that had tracked down Al Capone, John Dillinger, nuclear spies Julius and Ethel Rosenberg, and Unabomber Theodore Kaczynski. In the best tradition of the FBI, he immersed himself in understanding and tracking the funding that had permitted al-Qaeda to down four jets, destroy over $1 billion of real estate in Washington and New York, and kill nearly 3,000 innocent Americans and foreigners from more than 25 nations, as well as 19 suicide hijackers. In time, he began to understand the funding that could support future al-Qaeda operations.

The FBI now had to prevent crimes from occurring. With the scope of the threat, it was not sufficient to simply track down and incarcerate offenders after the fact. As part of his education, Weiner studied the results of FBI and CIA investigations, as well as studies and investigations undertaken by other law enforcement agencies, universities and corporations. Soon after beginning his new assignment, he became interested in reports being issued by the FDA about on-line pharmacies and the importation into the United States of drugs that did not meet FDA standards.

Though Weiner at first considered the problem of on-line pharmacies to be an issue for the FDA, the more he learned about the unregulated web sites, and their shadowy networks of owners and suppliers, the more concerned he became that these web sites not only provided a means for the funding of terrorist activities, but posed a direct threat of terrorist action. For the next six months, however, Weiner had more pressing matters.

At about the same time Barry Weiner was assigned to the Counterterrorism Division, 27-year-old Francine Pye joined the FDA investigative unit. About a year later, she was assigned to a high-profile task force investigating on-line drug sales in the United States. While the FBI was concerned with terrorism, the FDA was concerned with controlling America's health care system.

Theoretically, the FDA's only concern was with drug safety, though many critics believed the FDA was slow to approve new drugs in order to create a safety net around major pharmaceutical companies. By erecting barriers that were both difficult and expensive to surmount for those wishing to sell innovative medicines in the United States, the FDA helped keep prices of existing medications high, and increased the power of those already in the Club. These same critics noted the revolving door that seemed to exist between FDA lawyers and staff and the large drug companies and their law firms and lobbying groups. It was Washington at its best—policy by self-interest.

Francine had grown up in Atlanta, not really that far from the Washington office she would occupy when she went to work for the FDA. The daughter of noted philosopher Thomas Pye, she was smart, slim and fit. She had a seductive Southern drawl and a strong commitment to public service. After graduating from Atlanta's most privileged private school, Pace Academy, Francine attended Columbia's Barnard College, the last of the so-called Seven Sisters all-women's colleges. After graduating in the top 10% of the Class of '96, she spent two years as a junior account executive in New York at J. Walter Thompson, one of the world's oldest and largest advertising agencies, with accounts such as American Express and General Foods. Then, she returned to Morningside Heights for her Columbia MBA. True to her convictions, instead of pursuing a career in advertising, her next stop was the FDA, where she joined its investigative arm.

In mid-2004, 30-year-old Francine Pye was intent on protecting Americans. While her bosses might have had mixed motives, Francine did not. She began by poring through financial records subpoenaed by the FDA and transcripts of interviews conducted by the FDA and other investigatory agencies. Francine was going to figure out who really owned these rogue on-line drug stores and the sources of their drugs, so that the FDA could close them down and put their owners in jail. This was an important assignment, and she intended to do it right.

# FIFTEEN

"THANK YOU DR. BAUER, your team has done a magnificent job." Petar Raic, chief operations officer of the C3 Group, had just completed a meeting in London with Dr. Bauer. After an exhaustive study of hundreds of different combinations that took the lives of countless animals and 60 human subjects, they had their answer.

"I'm only sorry it took so long. In the end, our problem was that we didn't want to artificially accelerate the incubation period for fear that it would alter the results. We often had to wait two or three months to watch the pathology run its course. The good news is that we have found an approach that is sufficiently slow acting that 100,000 or more may be infected and some may even die before anyone knows that anything is wrong."

"Herr Doktor, you have earned your pay. More importantly, you will make an immense difference for our brothers. They and I thank you."

A few weeks later, the Karasik Commission gathered on a hot, humid August morning for a meeting in Ken's apartment at the Lanesborough. His security team had swept the Royal Suite for listening devices. Once satisfied, they set up emitters intended to block both directional microphones and laser-listening devices. Finally, the team closed the drapes and set a small gray box to emit a constant high-frequency sound. Though not audible to the human ear, if any listening device somehow penetrated the other safeguards, only a high-pitched squeal would be heard. While Ken waited in his suite, the other four arrived separately.

Petar and Stuart King, both of whom lived in London, openly visited as chief operations officer of the C3 Group, and a reporter for the *Times of London*, respectively.

Ben Opperman flew in from Paris and booked a room at the Lanesborough. Once inside, he had no trouble climbing a few flights of stairs to Karasik's extravagant suite. Mel Bottner flew in on his private jet. He was a regular at the Dorchester, located two blocks away on Park Lane, just beyond the Hilton. Bottner was too well known in London for any pretense. So he openly dined at the Lanesborough for breakfast, and then just disappeared, ending up in Ken's suite.

The purpose of the meeting was to review the many activities being undertaken by the Karasik Commission. Not surprisingly, Ken first wanted to discuss progress on his bold scheme to humble the United States through the deadliest terrorist attack yet conceived. As he repeatedly told his colleagues on the Karasik Commission, "The Slavs will finally prove to the United States what the Arabs could not. Then we will earn respect."

Though Ken intended to make a statement to the United States and the world about the hundreds of millions of Eastern European Muslims who were being oppressed by the Russian Federation and ignored by the West, his principal goal was a non-denominational one involving Serbia. He reiterated to his four colleagues, "We must stop the threat posed by Ivan Maslac, and force the United States to surrender Milosevic and protect Slavs from these Serbian hoodlums."

Though Maslac had not yet become the threat that he would pose 18 months later when the Karasik Commission gathered on Ken's houseboat the day after Thanksgiving, he was a growing nuisance. His repeated attacks on Bosnian towns and villages were reminiscent of the worst of Milosevic. Ken added, "The United States has done nothing. Now it will pay for its indifference and ultimately do what should be done—the right thing."

Ben reported, "To quickly update each of you on our status. As you know, we have been exploring for some time the possibility of distributing lethal drugs through *antidote.com* and other web sites. Early on we rejected the possibility of simply poisoning the drugs because of the risk of early detection."

Ben casually poured himself a glass of wine and continued. "We next looked at the possibility of combining two drugs in the attack. Though obviously more complicated, we thought this would minimize the risk of detection. Specifically, we have been working on a strategy under which an inert agent would be added to one drug. That inert agent would be activated by a second drug. The interaction would then produce the desired results. For this to work, we needed to identify two drugs that are often prescribed together. We appear to be making progress on this approach."

Petar added: "This will not be inexpensive, but we think we can modify nermycin so that when it interacts with cyprofaxin, the patient will develop symptoms similar to acute pneumonia. We believe that about half of those patients will die."

Ken asked Petar to explain the choice of drugs.

"Nermycin-X is a C3 Pharmaceuticals product that helps treat viral infections. Several of our competitors now manufacture and sell generic versions of nermycin. In fact, *antidote.com* itself now carries two generics, one we manufactured in the very same plant in India that manufactures Nermycin-X. The other is made by a competitor."

"Cyprofaxin is the active ingredient in a series of drugs used to treat bacterial infections. Though the manufacturers of cyprofaxin have repeatedly advised against it, many patients with staph infections or other infections of indeterminate cause have been ordering Nermycin-X or one of the generics and mixing it with cyprofaxin in an effort to simultaneously treat both viral and bacterial causes of their infections."

Ben jumped back in. "The whole point is that each year hundreds of thousands of Americans develop infections of uncertain origin. Many of these patients are already combining Nermycin-X or one of the generics with cyprofaxin. If the interaction of the two drugs led to more serious side effects, then we could expect widespread illness and deaths."

In this case, C3's medical team believed the interaction of the tainted nermycin and the cyprofaxin would cause an illness with symptoms almost indistinguishable from pneumonia.

"One of the beauties of our plan is how hard it will be to detect given the usual outbreaks of pneumonia. Each year between two and four million people in the United States develop pneumonia, with about 1.2 million hospitalizations. The mortality rate is from 10% to 25% of those hospitalized, which should mask our attack. As a result, it is very unlikely that the Centers for Disease Control or any other agency will identify the incremental hospitalizations or deaths," Petar explained.

"We've been through this before. Why are we using a C3 product?" Ken asked.

"Ken, we've tried all the alternatives. Not one comes close. Most importantly, we couldn't find any other drug we could manipulate with the same potential stability, lethality and likelihood of avoiding detection," Mel answered, exasperated that they were again revisiting this subject.

"I'm not pleased that Nermycin-X is a C3 product. But, the plan is to use only the generic forms. Lots of companies sell that. We just can't find an alternative, unless you want to scrap the idea altogether," Ben added, somewhat testily.

"I'm still concerned, but we've been down this road before and I'll just have to live with it. We better make sure no one confuses the generic with Nermycin-X," Ken resignedly conceded before moving on to the next topic.

"What if we get what we want?" Ken asked.

"I hope that's not just theoretical. I suppose we could issue a medical alert bulletin through *antidote.com* or one of our other distributors warning of an unexpected side effect involving the generic versions of our drug and suggesting remedies. Most hospitals would be able to treat patients suffering from the interaction, and from then on, the adverse consequences should be contained," Ben responded.

"What about timing?" Ken asked.

"We still have some more testing to do before we can proceed," Petar responded.

"The goal is to pass inspections and to avoid any immediate understanding of what is happening," added Ben. "It is very important that the ingredient we add to nermycin be undetectable and inert until combined with cyprofaxin."

"Which means...?" Ken looked at Petar.

"Which means at least another three to six months of development is needed in the lab, and then at least another few months of testing is needed before we commence manufacturing," Petar replied.

"That sounds like another year," Ken said, asking "What about distribution?"

"We assume that we will use generic nermycin combined with a forced shortage of C3's Nermycin-X. That way we can supply multiple distributors and deny any involvement. We'll supply cyprofaxin whether or not the FDA exclusive window ends," Petar answered.

"Bottom line," Ken asserted, "it seems that if this idea will work, and we don't yet know that for sure, it could be 18 months before we're fully underway. Am I missing something?"

For the first time Mel Bottner joined the discussion. Like C3, MDB had a pharmaceuticals division in Zurich and, like Ken, Mel had long ago given up on basing his pharmaceuticals business around legally selling medicines in the United States. "The only thing you may be missing is that there doesn't seem to be any viable alternative that meets all of your criteria for the attack: stealth, targets must include normally healthy people of all ages, illnesses must not occur until at least a few weeks after the use of modified products begin, and the effect must be reversible if we choose to inform the authorities of the antidote. This plan may put us a few months behind schedule, but it greatly increases the potential for success, while largely eliminating our risk of being caught."

"Estimated casualties?" Ken clinically inquired.

"One minute," Ben said. Ben and Mel had a brief discussion. When they concluded, Mel responded: "If we can get the dosage just right, manufacture enough tablets, and expand our distribution to include multiple points of entry into the United States, and if the incidence of staph infection next year is standard, then we are looking at upwards of 500,000 potential casualties before anyone might possibly figure out what is going on."

"That's a lot of ifs," Ben growled.

"This is uncharted territory and in truth there are a lot of ifs," Mel responded. "Frankly, there are a lot more ifs…if we don't get caught, if the inert ingredients remain inert, if nermycin and cyprofaxin remain popular, and particularly if they remain a popular 'cocktail,' and if we don't change our minds."

Ken looked directly at Mel and slowly but clearly stated: "There is no 'if' about our intentions. If you, or anyone here, have any doubts or qualms about what we are doing, then you or they should leave right now."

No one stirred, and no one left.

"Good," Ken said. "Now let's talk about just how long it would take someone to develop symptoms and any treatments that might be available."

Mel took that one. "The usual course of treatment for staph and similar infections is from five to eight days, with a repeat course if the first fails. That means the interaction has to work within five days to ensure maximum damage, or eight at the outside, unless we want to rely on adulterated products for a higher-than-average percentage of repeat treatments."

"We don't," Ken said.

"We have assumed that. However, if we gear toward infecting a high percentage of the population of those taking a five-day course, we run the risk of early detection, and it may be very difficult to bring a rapid end to the effects once we get what we want. Consequently, we are recommending a goal of 90% plus infection for those with eight-day courses, and 30% infection for those with five-day courses. We estimate that more than 50,000 Americans will become infected within a month after we begin sales, and perhaps as many as 150,000 Americans. Since it may take a while before anyone figures out what is occurring, and the incidence of infection will be much higher for those who need a second course, we could reach 500,000 or more within a few months. We estimate that unless the American government agrees to our demands, at least 10% and perhaps 50% of those cases will be fatal.

"My only concern is getting enough of the modified nermycin into the hands of patients before the Centers for Disease Control get wise. It is imperative that we ramp up production of the generic substitutes and flood all of the unlicensed sites, not just *antidote.com*."

"Perfect!" the typically terse Karasik responded.

"And let's not forget that the sale of 500,000 courses of nermycin—more than five million tablets—should pump over $10 million into C3," Petar interjected.

"That may be true," Stuart began, "but, we will have to close down the manufacturing facilities involved and I recommend that we take no chances and put the funds someplace that can never tie the sales back to C3."

"I agree. We're going to have to write off that $10 million. I want some recommendations as to where it can do us the most good, but we must assume the FBI or CIA will track it down, so it can't ever go through any of our usual dupes," Ken declared.

"Now, where do we stand with the Interpol investigations?" Karasik asked Ben.

"As each of you knows, our activities over the last eight or so years have attracted the attention of police authorities in several nations. To date, no investigation has reached any of the Commission's members, or even our usual operatives. However, there are reports of some concern to us. First, we are hearing some indication that Interpol has finally put enough of the pieces together to detect a pattern as it relates to our activities in the Balkans, some of our more extreme measures regarding energy and pharmaceuticals, and some of our efforts to influence government action. It does not appear that they yet understand the pattern, but it bears watching.

"Second," Ben continued, "Ken has told me that his sources are picking up rather disquieting reports that someone may have leaked some information to the FBI. At this time, we can't tell if this potential informant did so intentionally, or whether someone was overheard. Fortunately, so far, we see no connection being made between the FBI and the Interpol analysis."

Stuart interrupted. "Ken, who is this source?" Ken tersely replied, "A reliable one." Stuart knew that was all he would get out of Ken, so he let the subject drop and Ben continued.

"The third report of some moment comes from within C3 itself. It appears that the FBI and FDA only just missed catching *antidote.com* in one of their recent sweeps. We are going to have to be careful, particularly as we prepare for our action next summer."

"Thank you, Ben. Now, what about Maslac?"

"It appears that Maslac is making every effort to take over where Milosevic left off," Petar explained. "Though the level of violence has clearly abated over the last year, we are very concerned that this respite will not last." Petar continued, shaking his head, "This isn't your typical war. The atrocities and barbaric torture and killings are beyond the pale." Ben dipped his head in agreement.

"Remember how the imam died when we were kids?" Ken nodded in horror. "Well," Petar continued, "if you can imagine, it's even more evil. To give you an example, Serb terrorists invade a house and force the family to tie their father or grandfather to a stake. One of his children is ordered to pour gasoline over him and they make his wife strike the match. Then they force the family to gather in a circle around the burning body to sing and dance. If their performances aren't enthusiastic enough, they are shot on the spot as a 'lesson' to others."

No one spoke a word for what seemed the longest silence.

"The U.S. isn't doing one damn thing about Maslac," Petar uttered in total disbelief.

"Yes, I know. The United States never does anything for our brothers. That is why we are proceeding with our little operation," Karasik said, more determined than ever. "Why don't we take a short break for lunch, and then go forward with the rest of our agenda," he added so matter of factly, it could have been a board meeting of one of C3's totally legal U.S. companies.

As the men who made up the Karasik Commission broke for lunch, they continued the discussion of its secret Project Sky and the on-going FBI investigation of Karasik and the C3 Group. Given the direct involvement of MDB Pharmaceuticals in the plan, Mel's views had particular weight.

Like Karasik, Bottner was a billionaire and the one man on the Karasik Commission who had once been Karasik's boss. Unlike Karasik, Bottner's money was inherited. Still, he had acquitted himself in Ken's eyes when he rejected his family's wishes and joined the Peace Corps.

Bottner's first stop in the Peace Corps was Cambodia. He expected poverty, malnutrition and excessive force from the U.S. military. But he wasn't prepared to see Pol Pot and his Khmer Rouge wage war on their own people, massacring hundreds of thousands just because they were from the wrong tribe or the wrong town. More and more, Bottner found himself understanding, and even identifying, with the special forces and CIA operatives who weren't supposed to be in Cambodia, but were nonetheless there, and in significant numbers.

When Bottner returned from Cambodia just as Saigon was falling to the North, he no longer naively saw the world as black and white. The vast new gray of his consciousness was confusing. Using those same family contacts he had eschewed two years earlier, he obtained a political appointment at the State Department. For the first two years, he was stuck in Washington writing mind-numbing papers on strategic alternatives for one unimportant country after another. Then, in 1977, he was assigned to the U.S. embassy in Italy as a junior attaché. His job was to keep track of the Left-wing groups that were increasingly based in Italy. He not only kept tabs on Italian "affiliates" of Marxist groups like the Red Brigades and the Beider-Meinhoff gang, but he also reported on the Slavic community and its growing use of violence.

Although it was neither expected, nor even wise, Bottner often went into the field. He was visiting a local bar one night when three men walked in. They obviously didn't see him. As they indulged in beer and shots of shljivovica, they talked about Tito and Yugoslavia and how they were going to make things right for their families. His curiosity piqued, Bottner listened intently as the men discussed a planned attack on a radio station in Dubrovnik. Finally, one of the men noticed him.

As he began to shout at Bottner, a scruffy looking brown haired man came in. Though only about 20, the new man seemed to be in charge. When two of the older men threatened him, the young man intervened. He asked Bottner to explain. Panicked, Bottner told him the truth—that he was an attaché at the American Embassy in Rome and his job included reporting back on efforts being made to topple Tito. Satisfied that Bottner did not pose a threat, he was permitted to leave and asked to report back exactly what he had heard.

Shortly after that incident, Bottner was transferred to the embassy in Belgrade, Yugoslavia. There, he witnessed first-hand the atrocities inflicted on the Slavs by Tito's Communist regime. The random arrests, torture and rapes made the enforced poverty seem almost normal.

Life is filled with inexplicable coincidences. More than 15 years later during a planning session for the Raphlen operation, Mel thought he recognized one of the participants. Once Mel realized that Petar was indeed that same brown-haired young man who had saved his life in that Rome bar, he warmly embraced him and thanked him for his life. The irony was not lost on either of them that by saving Mel, Petar had done more for the Slavs than anything else he had done to that date. Through back channels, MDB had become one of the biggest defenders of Muslims in the Balkans, and Mel was now critical to the success of the operation that would come to be known as "Project Sky."

After a few depressing and frustrating years in Yugoslavia, Mel decided that diplomacy was not for him. He knew that there was much more he could and should be doing to make the world a better place. While he figured out how to do so, he finally agreed to spend some time in the family business.

His father immediately appointed his nearly 31-year-old son MDB's vice president of strategic planning. In that capacity, Mel was responsible for creating the game plan for MDB's global growth.

When Mel hired Ken, he set in motion the events that fundamentally changed his life.

# Sixteen

THE YEAR 2001 had also been an important year for the pharmaceutical industry in the United States. Just the year before, the industry had suffered an unaccustomed defeat when President Clinton signed into law the Medicine Equity and Drug Safety Act of 2000. That law opened the door for Canadian and other foreign drug manufacturers to enter the U.S. market. But, there was a catch. The U.S. Secretary of Health and Human Services first had to certify that implementation would not compromise the safety of U.S. pharmaceuticals.

Avoiding that certification was the job of people like William Bowne. Born at the top of the baby boom in 1950, Yale-educated, a graduate of Annapolis, and a former Marine officer who served in Vietnam during the final year of the U.S. withdrawal from that devastated country, Bowne had devoted the last 25 years to PharmCorp, his wife and their two children. In that order.

PharmCorp was just one of the manufacturers and distributors of pharmaceuticals. It wasn't even the biggest. Yet, its revenues in 2004 topped $50 billion. Its *profit after taxes* exceeded $12 billion—more than the entire *revenues* of the C3 Group. More than 125,000 employees in over 75 countries developed, manufactured, and marketed prescription medicines and consumer healthcare products worldwide. Its drugs ranged from treatments for cardiovascular and metabolic diseases, central nervous system disorders, arthritis, pain, infectious and respiratory diseases, to cancer, eye disease and allergies.

Its consumer products included medications for oral care, colds, flus, gastrointestinal health, skin care and eye care. PharmCorp sold its products around the world to health care providers, such as doctors, nurses, pharmacists, hospitals and government agencies, as well as mass marketers such as Wal Mart and Costco.

PharmCorp was incorporated in 1935. After more than 50 mergers and acquisitions, its headquarters came to rest in New York City. There, from the 50th floor of PharmCorp Tower on Park Avenue, PharmCorp's chairman and chief executive officer, David Cole, and its president, Bob Estrich, presided over a megacorporation and influenced an entire industry. Each received a salary and bonus totaling more than $10 million a year, and that was before adding the millions more each earned from stock options, deferred compensation and pension benefits. More than 30 PharmCorp employees received more than $1 million each year in salary and bonuses. William Bowne was one of them. With stock options and other benefits, his total income usually topped $3 million a year. Bowne earned every penny of that $3 million with his devotion to PharmCorp, his sweat, and the stress of one of the most difficult jobs in the company.

As executive vice president of special projects, Bowne reported directly to Cole and Estrich. He also worked closely with PharmCorp's general counsel and its head of corporate communications. PharmCorp's head of global security and its chief government lobbyist reported to Bowne. In fact, Bowne had been promoted to his current position nearly eight years earlier from his previous position as senior vice president for global security. His promotion matched his predecessor's promotion to president of PharmCorp. Like Bowne, Bob Estrich got to the top by doing what had to be done.

While Bowne's job included the day-to-day oversight of PharmCorp's global security and efforts to promote its interests with governments worldwide, the most critical aspect of Bowne's job was a creative one. Bowne devised ways of keeping PharmCorp's prices up and its competitors at bay, particularly potential new competitors who were not already in the Club. Working through industry associations and "casual" lunches or golf games with his counterparts at the other large multi-national drug companies, Bowne saw to it that governments stayed in line. In the United States that meant Congress, the President, Secretary of Health and Human Services, Food and Drug Administration and Federal Trade Commission. Cole and Estrich expected him to achieve the company's goals by whatever means necessary, just so long as they avoided being hauled before a grand jury or a congressional investigating committee to explain what had gone wrong.

Bowne loved the access to the top of American industry—the prestige that came with being at the very pinnacle of global business, the latitude his two bosses accorded him, and the $3 million a year he took home for results. What Bowne did not like was the $1 million hit his 2000 bonus took thanks to his failure to prevent the Medicine Equity and Drug Safety Act from becoming law. Bowne wasn't too happy about the rising tide of consumer resentment with the major pharmaceutical companies. He was apoplectic about efforts to encourage drug importation or to reduce the barriers for approval of new drugs. Consumers just didn't understand how important it was to keep PharmCorp's profit above $10 billion— even after it paid out hundreds of millions of dollars each year to its top executives.

At least Bowne and his counterparts had been able to slip a safety valve into the Medicine Equity and Drug Safety Act. Its worst provisions wouldn't take effect unless the Secretary of Health and

Human Services certified that it wouldn't compromise drug safety. Bowne made sure that never happened.

As 2005 approached, the pharmaceuticals industry faced an even more serious crisis. Legislation had been proposed that would, in effect, eliminate the safety valve. It was a brazen end-run around the industry and if it succeeded, PharmCorp's market capitalization would tumble by 30% or more; and the days of 80% profit margins and $10 million pay packages for executives would be gone. Even before Dave Cole and Bob Estrich called him in for a chat, William Bowne knew that he could not permit such a catastrophe to occur.

With the stakes this high, Cole and Estrich understood the response would have to be unprecedented. Press releases, covertly ghostwritten articles and novels supporting the industry's positions, free trips and even bribes wouldn't be enough this time. Billions of dollars and an entire industry were at stake. Still trim and fit at 54 years of age, Bowne would rise to the occasion.

# SEVENTEEN

"**I**'VE HAD A MONTH to learn about counterfeit drugs. Now that your vacation is finally over, I'm here to learn from the master," Barry said, a smile on this face. Weiner was meeting with Phil Oster. A regular at Barry's poker game, Oster was head of the FBI's Internet Pharmaceutical Fraud Initiative.

"I'm looking to learn everything there is to know about counterfeit drugs, terrorist attacks anywhere in the world using tainted drugs, and terrorist funding channels," Weiner explained.

The two agents were meeting in the small conference room adjacent to Oster's office on the third floor of the J. Edgar Hoover Building in Washington. There, Oster spent over an hour reviewing the threat posed by Internet drug sites. Unlike Weiner, Oster's mandate focused on counterfeit and sub-standard drugs, rather than terrorist threats. As Weiner packed up his notes, Oster shook his hand. "I'm glad to be back and always glad to help out my slower friends," Oster said, smiling. More seriously, he added, "You really need to talk to the investigators at the FDA and DEA to get the full picture. I'll give you some numbers and if it helps, I'll call ahead to grease the treads."

Barry thanked Oster, returned to his office and called the suggested contact at the FDA. After explaining what he needed, Oster's contact referred him to Special Investigator Francine Pye. Weiner again explained his purpose and asked Pye if she could fill in some additional details. Thrilled that her work could finally be reaching the right people, Pye was eager to assist.

"Mr. Weiner, I'd be happy to come by your office at your earliest convenience to discuss our findings," she graciously offered.

"That would be great, except that I'm way overworked and underpaid, so how about a meal on our employers instead?" Weiner replied, attempting to mix some pleasure with his work.

Francine was onto him, but he sounded cute. "Alright, how about lunch this week?"

"Lunch would be great," he said, "except that I can never get out of here in the middle of the day and I'd hate to stand you up. How about an early dinner right after work?"

She sighed knowing that she might have more work cut out for her than she had originally anticipated. "Very well. Dinner right after work on Thursday?"

He grinned. "I'll meet you at The Capital Grill at six o'clock sharp," he said and hung up the phone.

Francine smiled and returned to the piles of paperwork on her cluttered desk.

Francine and Barry met at The Capital Grille at the appointed time. Her sultry appearance caused Weiner's mind to wander, but what she had to say made him realize just how much work lay ahead.

She dug into her fettuccini and then into the facts. "Over the last seven years several factors, including the advent of Internet pharmacies and the globalization of the pharmaceutical market, have led to a dramatic surge in drugs being imported into the United States, especially drugs imported by mail order for personal use. These imports have overwhelmed the FDA and postal inspectors. As a result, the FDA's system of import controls is less and less tenable.

"Four years ago, the FDA testified at a Congressional hearing that approximately two million packages containing drugs were imported into the U.S. every year. We complained that the FDA simply did not have enough staff to inspect those packages. Barry, the FDA couldn't tell the subcommittee what percentage of those packages contained legitimate versus counterfeit product! We couldn't determine the country of origin or describe the conditions under which the drugs were manufactured. In short, the FDA knows very little about the millions of packages of drugs that are being imported."

After another bite of her pasta, she continued, "At the end of the day, the FDA is responsible for ensuring that Americans have safe and effective supplies of drugs…"

"Listen," Weiner cut her off not wanting to hear the public relations spiel, "given the exponential increase in the volume of drugs being imported into the U.S., the FDA's approach has to change."

"I'm well aware of that!" Francine snapped back, refusing to be patronized. "First of all, the FDA needs real data on the type and volume of drugs being imported and whether they contain legitimate product or counterfeits, or have been stored in unsafe conditions, or are subpotent or superpotent."

That wasn't enough for Weiner. "The FDA must engage in much more aggressive enforcement. And it wouldn't hurt if the FDA wasn't so clearly in the pocket of the lobbyists."

At first, Francine ignored the bait. "The FDA predicates its regulatory and enforcement actions on a risk-based assessment of threats to the drug supply." After a brief pause, she added, "And I can think of few more important or challenging tasks!"

As Weiner came up to speed, he determined that contrary to conventional wisdom, many terrorist organizations had extensive knowledge of medicine and biology.

"You know, Phil," Weiner leaned into the phone, "there's little doubt that some of the money paid to these unlicensed web sites is finding its way to terrorist groups. What do you think they do with that money? They purchase arms and mount attacks!" Special Agent Oster could hear Weiner's fist pounding the desk for emphasis.

Weiner continued, "We need additional resources to focus on that possibility, as well as the more frightening threat that a terrorist could use drugs adulterated with poisons or pathogens for mass murder—we know that terrorists have already attempted strikes with cyanide and ricin. And there are reports that Hezbollah and al-Qaeda are cooperating to build a joint chemical weapons lab."

Weiner paused at the thought of the devastation that such attacks could engender. Oster took the opportunity to shift attention back to his purview. "If you're worried about an attack on America through Internet fraud, I suggest you focus on our neighbors, Canada and Mexico. You know, Canada's refugee and immigration laws are among the most generous in the world. It's a veritable ball park for terrorists."

"I read about that," Weiner quickly retorted. "The Canadian Security Intelligence Service reports that as many as 50 terror groups may be operating there."

"And terrorists are known to have smuggled pharmaceuticals from Canada into the U.S. They could mount an attack using similar distribution methods," Oster rejoined.

Weiner's fist hit the desk, again. "That's what I've been saying!"

Oster appreciated his friend's passion, but didn't want to hear another diatribe. He decided to move swiftly south, "Mexico is no better. We know that millions of Americans flood across the border to purchase cheaper medicines. In fact, the number of pharmacies catering to U.S. visitors in Tijuana, Mexico alone has doubled over the last two years."

Weiner took a deep breath, so Oster rushed on, "The Mexican government barely monitors what its pharmaceuticals industry does. Terrorists could easily introduce poisoned drugs in these markets. If a popular medicine for heart disease, depression or pain control were laced with a poison, hundreds or even thousands of people could be killed!"

Oster paused, waiting for Weiner's response.

Barry sighed, "We've got our work cut out for us."


As he tirelessly continued his research, Weiner was becoming better informed and increasingly alarmed. He shared his concerns with Francine, who had been directed to focus on the traditional concerns about counterfeit drugs. As serious as that might have been, Barry was far more worried about the potential for a terrorist attack. He moved to the next phase of his investigation as he started to develop and track down detailed information about specific threats.

# EIGHTEEN

*L*IKE MOST MULTI-NATIONAL corporations, PharmCorp had the occasional need for outside consultants to solve problems they could not or would not solve themselves. The consultants offered expertise not available in-house. At times, the consultants also offered deniability. So long as a consultant signed the right contract and made the right promises about what it would *not* do, the consultant was free to undertake its assignment free of the corporation's constraints. That made for a nice and mutually profitable symbiotic relationship.

Over the years, William Bowne's consulting firm of choice for the most difficult assignments had always been Opperman Security. Based in Paris and with offices in London and New York, Opperman Security had never let him down. While Bowne usually worked directly with the firm's founder, Ben Opperman, he occasionally liaised with Tom Biffar, the steely-eyed and very discreet executive who managed Ben's U.S. operations. Which is precisely why he invited Tom to lunch at the Gotham Bar & Grill.

They selected a private table in the corner of the out-of-the-way Greenwich Village mainstay. Between the noise level in the restaurant and the distance to the next table, no one would overhear their conversation. Just to be certain, Bowne brought an electronic sweeper with him. The palm-sized device swept a radius of about five feet for listening devices. There were none.

They had been talking in generalities for about 20 minutes, when Bowne finally got down to business.

"Tom, let me be blunt. If this legislation passes it is an awfully steep drop down a very slippery slope. We're talking massive lay-offs and restructurings. I doubt we'd all survive."

"You really think a few Internet sites can make that much difference?" Tom asked, genuinely skeptical based on his understanding of *antidote.com* and the other web sites.

"Under the current regime, no. But, if they can sell the full range of medications at discounted prices thanks to Asian, Indian and African manufacturers, they will force us to discount as well. Our costs are much higher, and we won't be able to match their prices," Bowne responded, sticking to the well-worn script.

"Your prices or your profits, Bill?" Tom keenly asked.

"Either way, if the web sites drive down our prices the days of $200 billion company values and $30 stock prices are behind us. Not only that, but if the FDA starts approving more drugs, all of our research and development and our launch costs will be a complete write-down."

Tom thought that Bowne was finally a little closer to the truth. If the pharmaceutical companies couldn't justify their fat marketing budgets with monopolistic pricing, a lot of advertising agencies were going to be very unhappy. And, a lot of research would be moved offshore where salaries were much lower. A lot of pension funds might also see their stock portfolios drop. Either way, it wasn't Tom's problem. At least, not yet.

"What do you want us to do?" Tom asked.

"We've carefully thought this through. All our polling data shows that the one argument that resonates with consumers is fear of adulterated drugs. Even those consumers who think we're only in this for the money are afraid that if the floodgates open, America will be inundated with cheap adulterated or tainted product. That's our wedge issue," Bowne fairly observed. "The question is how we leverage that concern."

"Have you come to any conclusions?" Tom asked, intrigued.

"You bet I have. What America needs is a good honest-to-god attack by terrorists using these damn Internet sites. If a few hundred Americans die, they will do what Americans always do when the killing starts. They'll cut and run. In this case, right back to mother PharmCorp!" Bowne answered, his tone still seeming sane.

Tom was stunned. Between the Karasik Commission and PharmCorp, were these people intent on killing thousands of Americans and destroying the world's finest medical system? Karasik's plan was based on ideals and hopes for his people. The Muslims had been pushed to the edge and had to find some way of fighting back. But, all Bowne cared about was money. *It's disgusting*, Tom thought, as he started counting the fees Opperman Security would soon be receiving.

"Are you sure there's no other way?" Tom cautiously asked.

"We've already tried them. We started with testimony, full-page ads in the *New York Times,* interviews with the press, and the usual PR rubbish. We moved on to planting misleading stories in the press, secretly funding slanted studies and quietly ghostwriting Op Eds and even novels to make our point for us. In each case, our goal was to mobilize Americans to protect themselves. I guess it worked up to a point. A lot of consumers are worried. Just not enough of them. We have to ratchet this up and we have to do so now, before Congress legislates us out of business."

"What do you want us to do?"

"I want you to work with me on a plan to launch a terrorist attack on America using Canadian Internet sites. I want to be certain we don't get caught, and it would be nice if fatalities were somewhat limited," Bowne explained.

"What does 'somewhat limited' mean?"

"I don't know," Bowne said as he thought about it. "I guess I'd rather see a few hundred or a thousand die than see 10 or 20 thousand. Our goal is to scare the bejesus out of voters and Congress, not kill them off."

"Anything else?"

"I want this attack no later than the end of 2005. That's when the hearings will probably happen for this legislation. We don't want it passing."

They spent the balance of lunch having what Tom perceived as a surreal conversation. A man who was supposed to be helping to save lives was talking about using drugs to kill thousands of Americans as if it was just another cough drop promotion. Unknown to that man, he was discussing his idea with someone who right that minute was in the midst of developing a very real terrorist attack that hopefully would kill a lot more than just a few hundred Americans.

"What about our fee?" Tom asked.

"I was thinking maybe $10 million and expenses," Bowne responded.

"I was thinking maybe $100 million and expenses," Tom responded, quickly adding, "Of course, the final call is Ben's."

Bowne didn't even blink. He just nodded and stuck out his hand.

Tom had to talk to Ben. At the very least, there had to be a way for Opperman Security to get paid for the Karasik Commission's attack! The irony was delicious. So was the soufflé.

# NINETEEN

**W**HILE KEN'S RELATIONSHIP with Petar was that of brothers, and his debt of gratitude to Mel substantial, the one man whose advice Ken had come to instinctively trust had lived the most unusual life of any of the Karasik Commission's members.

The silver-haired, turquoise-eyed Ben Opperman was the epitome of old-world refinement. He exuded a sex appeal that was simply irresistible, and he was always surrounded by a bevy of appreciative beauties.

Ben was born in 1933 to a most unusual family in Chechnya. They were Jewish in a part of the Soviet Union that was predominantly Muslim. Ben learned early in life that those of faith—any faith—had to bond together against the atheistic dictates of the Communist state. When Ben was just six, Hitler unilaterally tore up Germany's non-aggression pact with Joe Stalin, and a million Nazi troops invaded the Soviet Union. After another six years and 30 million dead Soviets, peace was finally declared.

Then, Stalin decided his Jewish doctors were trying to kill him, so he killed them first. All 24 of them. Then he killed their wives and their children. Then, for good measure, he killed another five million Soviets, including quite a few of the Jews who had just escaped Hitler's Holocaust. Between Hitler and Stalin, Ben's parents, his grandparents, his two brothers and his two sisters perished. By the time he was 15, Ben was alone. That was when he heard about the State of Israel, which had been founded just the year before.

Unlike Hitler, who wanted all the Jews dead, Stalin just didn't want them around. So, if a Jew could go someplace else, Stalin didn't really care—at least some of the time. Fortunately for Ben, he chose to leave during one of those times. Ben first managed to slip across the border into Romania. From there, he caught a train into Yugoslavia. He spent about three months in Sarajevo and then Dubrovnik, just long enough to know he had to keep moving.

His next stop was Paris. Ben was not at peace there. Although Paris had always had a vibrant Jewish section, it also suffered from a great deal of anti-Semitism. While Denmark and Holland were doing their best to safeguard their Jews from Hitler, the Vichy French government turned over at least 75,000 Jews to the Nazis, all of whom were promptly deported to concentration camps and gassed. He occasionally wondered if the whole world was against him. He desperately tried to find a place to call home.

Finally, in 1949, at the age of just 16, Ben reached Israel. For the next 20 years, he built a life there. He completed high school, college and four years of military service in the Israeli army. Upon leaving the army, he started a security business. Ben and his partners, all former officers in the Israeli Defense Force, developed innovative surveillance techniques, including some truly astonishing listening devices that were ahead of their time. They also investigated businesses trying to find out about their competitors, or wives trying to find out about their husbands. In 1963, Ben married his beloved Sarah. At last, he belonged to someone and someone belonged to him. He had genuine reason to live and not just survive. By the time Syria, Egypt and Jordan tried to destroy Israel in 1967, Sarah had given him two children, a son and a daughter. His life was filled with hope and a purpose.

After the Israelis defeated the Arabs in just six days, occupying Arab land much larger than Israel itself, Ben's company expanded into providing covert assistance to clients throughout Europe. Ben's company would do anything from obtaining information to disrupting a competitor. On a few occasions, the disruption was permanent.

In 1973, the Arabs attacked on Yom Kippur, the holiest day in the Jewish calendar. The planned destruction of the Jewish State began at noon as Egyptian and Syrian military forces surged against Israeli positions on the Suez Canal in the south and the Golan Heights in the north. Rockets rained down on Israeli troops in the Golan Heights. Whether by design or utter indifference, rockets also hit Israeli settlers, including the Soviet-made missile that hit Ben's house just after his wife and children had returned from synagogue. Ben, who was still in synagogue asking for God's guidance on this Day of Atonement, never saw them again.

Beyond despair, he buried his wife and children and did what he could to help Israel defeat its enemies. Some three weeks later when the Israeli Defense Force pushed the invaders back and stood poised to take even more Arab land, the United Nations demanded a ceasefire. Three days later, after Israel occupied a further 165 square miles and threatened to annihilate Egypt's Third Army, the United States and Soviet Union forced an end to the war.

That was the end of Ben's life in Israel—he just couldn't remain. He sold out to his partners and moved to Paris. Ben wasn't exactly sure why he chose Paris, but in the 30 years since World War II, the Jewish community in Paris had become one of the most creative and vibrant in Europe. Ben still wasn't entirely comfortable there, but he wasn't necessarily uncomfortable either.

Ben started a new security business. With his wife and family dead, Ben's moral center was gone. Unlike his business in Israel, Opperman Security would focus on covert disruptions, particularly those requiring extreme measures. He sought and received assignments that few others would handle. Whether the target was a titan of business, or a government official, Ben's company became adept at removing the target. At times that meant discrediting the target with bogus but well-documented scandals or criminal charges. Other times, it meant sudden crises among key suppliers or customers. Sometimes, it meant assassination.

It was a small world among intelligence operatives in Eastern Europe. Ben's first meeting with Ken was arranged in 1992 by one of Ben's freelance operatives, Mike Mihalic, the very same agent who had befriended Peter Raic in the early '80s. Mihalic had been of use to Ben over the years, dating back to Mihalic's days in the CIA. When Mihalic left the CIA in 1987, Ben found him to be a useful resource.

Ken and Opperman met for the first time at an ultra-private club in London. Ken selected the library with its double-height mahogany shelves lined with books as much as 200 years old. The library was lit by a skylight and more than 40 table lamps. Small tables and hunter green leather chairs were arrayed throughout the large room. Some members were reading newspapers while others were drinking sherry served in the wood-paneled bar across the hall. Most were engaged in whispered conversation. Although called a library, conversation was not only permitted, it was expected.

They lowered themselves into overstuffed armchairs in a quiet corner. The smell of the rich leather was soothing to the senses. Each wore a coat and tie, as required by club rules. As they introduced themselves and the Jew and the converted Roman Catholic began learning about each other, they both knew this would become one of those rare relationships each would appreciate for a long time to come.

Those feelings had never changed, though events of the next several months would sorely test them.

# TWENTY

**R**OHIT DATAR LOOKED out at the vast manufacturing floor of more than 10,000 square meters. Some 500 workers were responsible for every aspect of manufacturing and shipping, from sorting the ingredients delivered to the facility's large loading dock, to distilling and mixing the highly sensitive ingredients in just the right proportions, to filling the capsules manufactured right in the facility or compacting the carefully mixed ingredients into tablets. The facility created most of the shrink-wrap, blister packs, containers and boxes that would hold the drugs, and packed the pills or salves into the containers. Those few containers that were not manufactured at the facility were manufactured directly across the street at another facility, also owned by RD Pharmaceuticals.

Everything that RD Pharmaceuticals manufactured could be readied to the most exacting standards and the highest quality. In reality, it had been years since C3 Pharmaceuticals had cared about RD's capabilities. With rare exception, C3 had been concerned more with the beauty of the boxes and containers, and the precision of the seal on the capsules, than it cared about the quality of the ingredients or the process of combining those ingredients into life-saving drugs. So long as the product looked world class and vaguely delivered some of the promised benefits, C3 didn't care about potency, shelf life or efficacy. The bottom line was, as long as it looked good, C3 wanted it fast and cheap.

Datar sighed. Before he had sold a controlling interest in the company he founded to a Taiwan pharmaceuticals manufacturer for a significant profit, a continuing financial interest, and the right to keep his name on the firm, Datar had been proud of what he had accomplished. Born in Bombay to an upper middle class family, Datar was educated in the American school there through high school. Then, like his banker father before him, he journeyed to the United States for college, attending the University of California at Los Angeles. In 1987, Datar was proud to become a UCLA alumnus, receiving his B.A. in economics. He worked for a year as a junior analyst at Merrill Lynch, while applying to business school. Accepted by most of the schools to which he applied, he chose to remain in Los Angeles.

In 1990, he received his MBA in logistics from UCLA's Anderson School of Management. He then returned to Merrill Lynch, this time as a full associate in the investment banking division in New York. Two years later, he transferred to Merrill Lynch's London office. While there, he focused on business expansion in India. After three years in London, Datar was promoted to vice president. His salary and bonus that year totaled $250,000—more than his father earned at the peak of his career as executive vice president of Bombay Commercial Bank.

As a vice president at Merrill Lynch, Datar worked closely with some of the largest corporations in India, as well as more modest-sized firms seeking financing for the burgeoning opportunities that were increasingly available in India. He also worked with some of the largest worldwide conglomerates, particularly those with interests in the pharmaceuticals industry—companies such as PharmCorp, Pfizer, Bristol-Myers, and C3. Datar also became involved in charitable work, including Doctors Without Borders, which helped bring medical care to disadvantaged people throughout the world. Despite his income, Datar lived frugally, saving as much as he could so that he would have the capital to achieve his dream of owning his own company in India. He told his wife, "I will accomplish what no one in my family ever could. I'm going to use American-style capitalism in India."

In 1997, after seven years at Merrill Lynch, Datar decided the time had come to return to India and begin the process of making his dreams a reality. With its attention to education and improving infrastructure, India had become an exciting place for business. More and more European and American companies were outsourcing manufacturing, software development and even telemarketing to India. With his background in international finance and his industry focus on pharmaceuticals, Datar was certain that he could build a successful company, while contributing to the prestige of India by developing and manufacturing worthy products that would help many people around the world.

Datar invested $500,000 of his own money, $2.5 million raised from friends and family, and $5 million borrowed from the Bombay Commercial Bank. He obtained promises of business from PharmCorp, C3 Pharmaceuticals and other former clients at Merrill Lynch to launch RD Pharmaceuticals in the Western city of Pune. "We will manufacture drugs for major pharmaceutical companies to the most exacting standards required by the U.S. FDA. Then we can build a research capability that will let us obtain our own patents and help cure the diseases that make life so difficult for too many," he optimistically reported to his key investors. By 2000, Datar was well on the way to achieving his dream. That year, RD's gross revenues were nearly $100 million and its profits were close to $10 million.

About 60% of RD's revenues came from its largest customer, C3 Pharmaceuticals. Most importantly, 2000 marked the first year RD had patented its own drugs. RD had begun trials and expected to commence sales outside of the United States by the end of 2001. The good news meant that while RD was growing it would require additional financing to support its research and development activities, as well as the trials and approval process for its own drugs. After seven years at Merrill Lynch, Datar was confident he could obtain the required financing.

Unfortunately, Datar's timing was not propitious. Stock markets around the world were in turmoil and private funding had almost dried up. Still, India was a growth market and Datar had strong contacts and an enviable track record. After several months, Datar thought he had the perfect deal: he sold 60% of RD Pharmaceuticals to Taiwan Pharmaceutical Investments Ltd., a company introduced by C3. Half of the $60 million paid by Taiwan Pharmaceuticals went into the company to fund its research and approvals and to expand its manufacturing facilities, and the other half went to Datar and his other investors. With any success, in just a few years the 40% interest retained by Datar, his friends and his family could be worth two or three times the $30 million they had received for the shares they sold to the C3 affiliate.

"Things couldn't be better!" he told his beautiful wife when she asked about the business that consumed so much of his time. Datar retained operating control of the company and continued to expand it. Then, in mid-2002, things changed. Datar did not understand "why," but he certainly understood "what."

First, Taiwan Pharmaceuticals advised him that it had sold its 60% controlling interest to a Panamanian company Datar had never heard of, Inversiones y Distribución Médicas de Las Producciones S.A. From then on, he was to take his instructions only from a man named Peter Fell. Though Fell claimed to be an American, he had an odd accent and Datar was quite certain that Fell was not from the United States. Fell instructed RD to slowly reduce its support for its other customers. "We will make up the volume," Fell told him. "RD is to continue manufacturing the drugs it supplies to its other customers. From now on, however, it will deliver those drugs to

Inversiones y Distribución Médicas de Las Producciones." Though Fell promised that payments would be made by that Panamanian distributor, in fact, payments were often routed through other countries and were often late.

Fell instructed Datar to "significantly reduce costs," and he specified a series of cuts in virtually all aspects of RD's operations.

"I don't understand. With these cuts, we will be unable to maintain quality standards," Datar protested.

Fell's response made Datar profoundly uncomfortable. "It doesn't matter. Just so long as you preserve the quality of C3's name-brand drugs, the quality of the other drugs is of no consequence."

Datar didn't like what was happening, but the profits were continuing to roll in, Fell never interfered in Datar's own drug development program, and even at reduced quality, the drugs being manufactured by RD remained effective, usually.

In late 2004, Fell visited Pune. After taking a tour of the plant, he sat with Datar in his office above the manufacturing floor. "We have decided to make you a very rich man," Fell began. "Last year, your profits were $15 million. This year, if trends continue, your profits could reach $20 million. Within a few years, if C3 and our principals continue to purchase products, and if your own drugs start to take off, your profits could double. On the other hand, if C3 does not renew its contract or if we choose to put our business elsewhere, RD Pharmaceuticals will fail. Your hopes of building your own brand will be lost."

Datar just stared at Fell, waiting to see where this was headed. It sure sounded like Fell was getting ready to make a very low offer for the 40% owned by Datar and his investors.

"It's simple. We are prepared to give you back the 60% of RD we now own. In return, you will enter into a manufacturing contract that gives us complete control of all aspects of manufacturing, a confidentiality agreement, and a purchase option for $1.00. If you breach the manufacturing agreement or the confidentiality agreement, we have the right to buy out all investors for just one dollar. Otherwise, for five years, you pay 75% of your profits to us as a rebate on our manufacturing contract. At the end of the five years, the rebate ends. Two years later, you are free to sell the company or do whatever else you want, so long as you don't breach the confidentiality agreement. If things go well, seven years from now you can sell the company for hundreds of millions of dollars."

Datar was stunned. Six years ago, he and his investors, most of whom were family, invested $3 million to create RD Pharmaceuticals. Just three years ago he and his investors sold 60% of RD for $30 million and the funding the company needed to expand. Now, they were being offered the chance to keep the $30 million, and get back the 60%! Not only that, but the company could continue to work on its own drug development program, originally funded by C3's Taiwan affiliate. Datar and his investors might have to give up 75% of the profits for a year or two. But by the time all the new drugs became profitable in a few years, they would keep all of the much larger profits they expected then, and if they sold the business, potentially hundreds of millions of dollars more. As things stood, they were already giving 60% of their profits to the Panamanian company; what possible difference would an extra 15% for just five years make, compared to getting back 100% ownership?

"I don't understand," Datar responded. "You already control this company, and now you wish less control, since we can develop our drug program as we wish. You already receive 60% of our profits, so all you ask is an additional 15%? There must be something else…."

"Nothing that would concern you," Fell replied.

"Yes?" Datar retorted, his look of concern belying his disbelief. "So, there is something else."

"We need to seal off part of your facility and we need the exclusive use of one of your production lines for a limited run. When the run is completed, the equipment will be destroyed. This may cost the company $1 million. However, that will affect your group by only 25% of that sum, or just $250,000. Even that cost will be reduced by your share of the profits for manufacturing this special run."

"I cannot be involved in illegal drugs," Datar said, without emotion. His calmness masked his concern that he had already become enmeshed in a scheme that involved unlawful activities. Still, he had to draw a line somewhere. If he still could.

"You have my word that no controlled substances are involved. We will be manufacturing and testing a new generation of an existing product. The improved generation includes some additional ingredients, but it's as safe as the current generation, which you already manufacture."

Datar shuddered as he tried to guess what this was about. "What is the product and what must we do?"

"We will disclose the product to you only if you accept our terms and sign the confidentiality agreement. You will find those services no different than what you already do for your existing products," Fell calmly explained.

"How can I make a decision when I do not know the risks? If I say yes, and if what you propose cannot be done, you could acquire my entire financial interest in this company for just one dollar. You would leave my investors with nothing. How could I do such a thing?" Datar asked, already knowing the answer he would receive.

"You and your investors have already made many times your investment in RD. If you choose not to proceed, RD will lose nearly all of its business. That will be the end of RD and the end of your reputation. The worst that can happen if you accept our terms is no worse for you, and probably far better. You have my word that the next generation drug we will test and manufacture here will be completely safe and hopefully very effective at treating a growing health threat." Technically, what Fell said was true.

"I will talk to my wife. We can meet again tomorrow morning," a very worried Rohit Datar told the man he now perceived as his tormentor.

The following afternoon, Peter Fell boarded his Air India flight for Agra. He had three more stops on his itinerary before he could return to London. After visiting Simla Manufacturing in Agra, he had stops in Malaysia, Myanmar (better known as Burma) and Yunnan province in China. He expected those visits to be every bit as successful as his business in Pune.

"Everything is in place," Petar reported to Mel. It was remarkable how rapidly phone service had improved throughout the world. Even with the encryption device over the handset, Mel and Petar could understand each other perfectly.

"When can we begin the next phase of tests?" Mel asked.

"If the lawyers move quickly, it will still take a few weeks to complete the contracts. Then, we have to send our teams to isolate the lines and make sure there are no security problems. Ben will take care of that. I don't know, maybe six weeks," Petar concluded.

"That should work out perfectly. There are still some issues in Zurich, and I don't think they'll be ready until at least next month.

Maybe even later than that." Mel terminated the call and dialed Paris. "We're a go once the legal clears," he said.

"Good," Ben Opperman responded. "We'll have the teams on the ground as soon as you're ready." Ben smiled at the redhead lying beside him at the Hay-Adams Hotel, just across the street from the White House. Not for the first time, Ben thanked modern technology for routing calls placed to his secure Paris line halfway around the world.

"What was that all about?" she asked. "Nothing to concern you," he said, still smiling at her. She smiled back. Neither of them was the least bit sincere.

# TWENTY ONE

"**A**RE YOU ABSOLUTELY sure?" an incredulous Ben asked.

"Absolutely," Bowne responded.

"You understand that if there is even a suspicion, the government will take PharmCorp apart, brand by brand?"

"There won't be a suspicion, that's why you're getting $100 million."

"Actually, it's going to be $150 million and we'll take care of the expenses. I can't quite see sending in a chit with supporting documentation for expense reimbursement, can you?"

"You have a point there. Do you also have a plan?" Bowne asked as coolly as if he were in a meeting of the marketing department. In a way, he was, as he arranged for hundreds or even thousands of Americans to die. Despite Ben's amorality, Bowne's cold greed still amazed him.

"Do you really want to know the plan?" Ben asked, as he reached for a napkin. Bowne, Ben and Tom Biffar were in the middle of a very casual Italian lunch at Maria's on Washington Street in Hoboken, across the Hudson River from New York City. No one knew them there, but it was just 10 minutes from midtown Manhattan. The perfect place for this discussion.

"Ben, I didn't get where I am by playing dumb. Whether I know the plan or not, if they track it back to me, I'm dead. The more I know, the safer PharmCorp's gonna be. Besides, I might even have a thought or two. It's been known to happen," the executive vice president of one of the world's largest pharmaceutical companies replied, politely putting Ben in his place.

Bowne took a sip of wine as Ben responded, "Ok. I couldn't give you all the details, even if I wanted to. There are other people involved and they wouldn't be very happy if we started sharing trade secrets."

Just as Bowne began to interrupt, Ben raised his hands. "Give me a minute here, Bill. I'll tell you what I can and we'll go from there, ok?"

Bowne nodded and Ben continued.

"All right. The goal is to use on-line drug distributors in a so-called terrorist attack. We need to bring tainted drugs into the United States. Patients need to die. At least a few hundred, though I know you'd rather keep the death toll below a million," Ben sarcastically explained as Bill made a face.

"Now let's look at some of the issues," Ben began counting them off, using the fingers of his right hand. "First, you want a terrorist attack, not a defective delivery. That means someone has to make demands. They have to actually claim credit for the attack. If they don't, the government will think it was an accident, incompetence, or even recklessness. A terrorist attack is willful and preplanned. If you want a terrorist attack, there has to be a claim of credit."

Now Ben had Bowne's attention. The PharmCorp executive nodded his agreement.

"Second, if you want to be certain that at least a few hundred people die, the tainted medicine can't be fast working. If it is, as soon as the first victims get sick, they'll track it back and stop the shipment.

"Third, when the government eventually figures out what's going on, they're going to back-track the drugs. Believe me, they will figure out where the drugs were manufactured, where the ingredients came from and who licked the labels. That means a foolproof system has to be created so they can never go beyond the manufacturer. Think of it, you have to be able to develop, manufacture and distribute this drug and pay for all these activities. Yet, you and all of your intermediaries will have to be absolute ghosts."

"You've really thought this through," Bowne remarked with genuine admiration. He would never know just how much thought had been going into the plan's creation.

"Fourth, when you make your claim of responsibility, it can either be a demand or just a claim. Either way, you have to threaten to do it again. You don't really have to, but your threat has to be credible."

Ben had only one finger remaining on his right hand and he used it.

"Finally, you have to be ready for things to go wrong. They always do. It might be a delay. Or someone refuses to go through with it. Or, maybe I get hit by a truck."

"More likely, you get stabbed with a nail file," Bowne joked, well aware of Ben's reputation with the women. Then, more seriously, "All good points. So, what do we do?"

Ben took a moment to finish off his veal cutlet, and then answered. This time he counted on his left hand.

"First of all, we need to put a lot of distance between PharmCorp and this plot. That means, no PharmCorp distributors, drugs or manufacturing sites. Second, we need a front. Preferably a real terrorist cell so the government doesn't doubt its guilt. The larger and more sophisticated, the better."

Bowne was again nodding. Tom had a small smile, as he quietly observed Ben work.

"Third, we either need a poisonous ingredient with a very delayed effect, or even better some combination of drugs that have to interact to produce the intended harm."

Bowne was getting excited. "That's genius," he said. "There's no doubt that the latter is far superior. It will allow us—I mean them—to ship product that will pass inspection. No one will ever think to test different drugs together!" Bowne observed. It was Ben's turn to smile. This was going better than he had expected.

"Ok, let's say we do it your way." Ben was done counting fingers. He took another sip of wine and affected deep thought. After a moment, he continued. "Ok, ok, we do it your way. But, that means we have to find some chemists smart enough to alter two or even three drugs. The drugs have to be part of a typical cocktail so we know patients will order all of them. And there still has to be a delay, or the Centers for Disease Control will figure it out."

"I agree with everything you've said. Do you have a group? Do you have the drugs?"

"Not so fast my friend," Ben laughed. "I have some ideas on the group. As to the drugs, you only now decided how to proceed. I need some time on that one."

Now Bowne had a small smile. He said nothing, but he knew when he was being played. Still, all he cared about was the result. He had just agreed to pay $150 million for results. If Ben already had another scheme going, Bowne was happy to piggyback onto it.

"So, what do you need?" Bowne asked.

"Right now, all I need is for you and Tom to work out the payment method. I want the two of you to stay in contact. The cliché applies here—don't call me, I'll call you. One other thing, I may need some of your chemists. Maybe not, but I can't be certain. I assume you have some top notch chemists who can be trusted?"

"I have some thoughts. If they can't be trusted, they'll be expendable," Bowne said, surprising both Ben and Tom with his steel. For the first time, Ben thought it might be a mistake to underestimate Mr. William Bowne.

Their business completed, they ordered cappuccinos and Tom ordered a cannoli. "You really do like desserts," Bowne commented, recalling the soufflé Tom had ordered the last time they had shared a meal. Tom just laughed, but he also noted Bowne's powers of observation. He too concluded that it might be a mistake to underestimate William Bowne.

"You've received several messages from an Alexa Bart," Ken's assistant informed him. It had been years since he had heard from her. They had done some business a long time ago. The last time they had been together was in London. The night would have been perfect, but for his need to be certain there were no sharp objects anywhere near the bed.

"Thanks. Email the number and I'll take care of it."

"Alexia, my dear, to what do I owe the pleasure," Ken asked his former associate.

"Oh, the pleasure has always been all mine," she coyly answered.

"Come to think of it, that's probably true. What can I do for you?"

"I'm moving back to Hillcrest Valley to care for my grandfather. I thought we might get together. I've never been inside the Bolero Road estate."

"For good reason, my dear. I don't know if the wife would really appreciate that."

"Oh Ken. We're both so much older and wiser now. I'm sure Miss Mexico and I would be terrific friends. I can look after her for you. And I promise I won't tattle."

"I have complete confidence in your discretion, dear. That has never been the problem."

"Well thank you. You see, we do get along."

"As long as we're on the same side, we get along famously. Let me think about your offer. I'll get back to you."

"Ken, my offer is sincere. I'm moving back because Grandpa is very sick. It's been so many years, I don't have any friends in Hillcrest Valley. I think I'm going to need a few."

"I'm sorry, Alexia. I didn't realize it was that serious. I'll call. I promise," he said, his tone softening just a bit.

# TWENTY TWO

**B**ARRY WEINER HAD become immersed in learning about terrorist threats to America's medical supply system. An interagency task force targeting counterfeit drugs, Operation Cyber Chase, had uncovered amateur operations in Canada and elsewhere. None of the suspects were terrorists, and none involved large multi-nationals. Basically, law enforcement had picked the low hanging fruit. Weiner's job was to take that effort to the next level.

In looking through the Interpol reports, Weiner observed a few mentions of the London-based multi-national C3 Group and its CEO, Ken Karasik. He decided to get Francine's view. He punched her speed dial and in a few seconds, they were connected.

"I want to run something by you," he said.

"Who's this?" Francine teased.

Normally, Barry would have played along, but he was focused on the information in front of him. "Francine, it's Barry. I just want to review some things with you."

She heard the tension in his voice and switched gears. "Shoot!"

"This is very odd," Weiner mused. "I'm reading some reports about C3—you know, Ken Karasik's company."

"What do they have to do with this?" Francine asked.

"Good question. That's what I want to know," Barry agreed. "Interpol is concerned with violence, including gun running and even murder. I wouldn't be surprised to learn that C3 fixed some prices, paid off the odd government official, or even stole some technology here or there. But, given Karasik's prominence and wealth, it's odd that C3 might be involved in violence, let alone terrorist activities in the Balkans. Yet that's exactly what Interpol suspects."

"Has anything been proven?"

"No, but Interpol is reasonably certain that C3 and another large multi-national, MDB Corporation, have been involved in supplying weapons in Bosnia and Croatia, and potentially in at least a half dozen assassinations."

"Assassinations?"

Barry shuffled papers. "Yes, and here's a report that a C3-owned pharmaceuticals company might have been involved in the mutilation of a chemist in Zurich."

"Mutilation? What's that about?" Francine asked, horrified yet fascinated.

"There were reports that a chemist named Carl Horst had raised questions about Raphlen, a C3 drug. Soon after, he had a skiing accident in which he lost the use of his left hand. Despite being questioned by local officials and Interpol, Horst insisted that he had no concerns about Raphlen or C3, and that his injury had been accidental."

"Well, that sounds worth investigating," Francine responded. "I'll see what we have on C3, Raphlen and Horst. You let me know if you find any more interesting tidbits."


Weiner tried to learn all he could find about C3 Pharmaceuticals. It wasn't easy. Only part of the C3 Group was public, and C3 Pharmaceuticals wasn't in that part of the Group. Thanks to the Patriot Act, Weiner accessed tax returns and other financial documents maintained by the Internal Revenue Service. However, since C3 Pharmaceuticals was a Zurich company and the C3 Group was headquartered in London, it wasn't surprising that little in the IRS records was helpful. Weiner made a note to spend some more time with the IRS documents. He also put in a request to the Justice Department to request copies of C3's tax returns from Inland Revenue in Britain.

A few days later he got a call from Lisa Fuller, an always upbeat staff lawyer at Justice. Barry had dated Lisa for a while, but it eventually petered out. After some obligatory flirting, she turned serious. "You know that C3 is Karasik's company, don't you?"

"Of course," Barry answered, "And your point?"

"My point?" Lisa asked. "My point is that Karasik is very rich, very well connected and very wired in. Are you sure you want him as an enemy?"

"I know who he is. What I want to know is what C3 Pharmaceuticals is up to. Something isn't kosher over there, and I don't like *traif*," Barry immediately replied, using the Yiddish word for unclean food. "Be careful what you wish for...." Lisa answered with her favorite warning. She promised to file the request within the next few days.

Leaving Inland Revenue in Lisa's capable hands, Barry returned to gathering information about Karasik and C3. "I need a search of all legal filings involving the C3 Group or any of its subsidiaries. And while you're at it, I need the same for Ken Karasik, MDB and Melvin Bottner III," he instructed his highly-efficient assistant, Stacie Amezcua.

Finally, he put in a call to Francine. She answered on the first ring.

"Time for some more information exchange," he told her. "That's boring," Francine chided him. "Why don't we exchange something more interesting?"

"Sounds good to me," he replied, a little too quickly. Francine had a yoga class at 7:00, so they agreed to meet for dinner at 8:30.

They met at his favorite Chinese hole-in-the-wall in Georgetown. She was in her sweats, and he was still in a suit and tie. After ordering wonton soup for two, chicken and broccoli, sweet and sour pork, and a pot of green tea, they got down to the first item on their agenda.

"I think Operation Cyber Chase is doing a great job of stopping counterfeit drugs, but I think they're missing out on the big boys. There are some very sophisticated players out there and I don't think we're anywhere near them," Barry explained.

"Talk about damning with faint praise," Francine began. "You know I agree. Although we have to stop the small guys, they're just fly-by-night operations. Gone today and replaced tomorrow. The big guys control the manufacturing and the more popular brands. When they fall, they won't be so easy to replace."

"Right," Barry agreed, ladling soup into two small bowls. "More to the point, there are four groups I'm looking at that are capable of funding and organizing the whole thing—from designing and manufacturing the drugs, to distribution to the web sites, and then sales into the U.S. I'm focused on these four because the Bureau has received disturbing reports on each one of them that raise doubts about their real motives."

Francine took a spoonful of wonton soup and listened intently as Barry continued, "You already know about C3. The other three are the Toi Group, a multi-billion dollar company based in Indonesia; Brower Limited, based in Brussels; and MDB Corporation, based in New York.

"The Toi Group has operations throughout Asia and the Middle East. Don't let the name fool you. The Toi family are devout Muslims. They are very active in all the wrong places. Jack Toi, the founder's son, is on the CIA's terrorist watch list, and there is no doubt they are involved in pharmaceuticals in Indonesia, Malaysia and Burma. They have the expertise, the money and the ideology to do us some real harm." Barry skewered a steaming piece of broccoli with his chopstick in emphasis.

"Brower Limited is also owned by Muslims, including some of the wealthiest families in Pakistan. There is no question they own some of the plants involved in making counterfeit drugs. Several of their operatives are on the CIA's watch list. They have every motive and opportunity to expand what they're doing." Barry waived his arms and the precariously mounted broccoli tipped over, as if in agreement. "I know they're guilty of simple counterfeiting, the question is whether that is all they are guilty of."

He went on, "MDB is a long shot, but something just isn't right with MDB and the C3 Group. Ken Karasik is the common denominator here. A Bosnian by birth, Karasik came to the U.S. about 25 years ago, attended Columbia and Wharton and then went to work for Mel Bottner, the guy who inherited MDB. Karasik apparently helped Bottner get a huge energy contract in the Soviet Union and then went out on his own."

Barry paused to take a sip of his now tepid tea. "As you know," he continued, "Interpol has been reporting on rumors of major bad stuff involving Karasik for more than a decade, particularly some very ugly violence involving the Balkans. Bottner shows up in more than a few of those reports. On top of all that, both C3 Pharmaceuticals and MDB hold patents on a long list of drugs in Europe, yet they seldom apply for FDA approval to market here.

"Now, here's the capper," Barry was getting excited, "Phil Oster is certain that C3's brands are streaming in through the Internet and he believes C3 has also been involved in some of the counterfeit drugs, though he can't prove it." Barry popped the limp broccoli into his mouth and finished, "Something just doesn't smell right here."

Francine had been uncharacteristically silent during Barry's long report, the product of more than six months of careful investigative work. It had been more than two months since their first lunch together. In that time, Francine had developed a strong professional respect for Barry, as well as more than a little personal interest. Though her mind had wandered to the second item on their agenda, she maintained her focus.

Francine wasn't quite as excited as Barry about Karasik and C3. "I've done some digging around on C3," she explained while finishing off her share of dinner. "They've got a few approved drugs, but they operate primarily in Europe. No record of any trouble in the U.S. Karasik may be a bad guy, but nothing you've said makes him a terrorist, certainly not here. A counterfeiter? Probably. A terrorist in the Balkans or elsewhere in Europe? Maybe. But I don't see how that adds up to terrorism in the United States. Toi and Brower sound much more promising."

"Francine, I've been going after really bad people for more than 10 years. Call it gut. Call it intuition. I just don't like the picture I'm seeing. We don't have all the pieces. Of course I could be wrong. But, I think we're onto something that we're not going to like."

"I'll tell you what," Francine said, "Let's go back to my place for some more intensive analysis and I'll see what I can get on this tomorrow." The idea seemed a good one to Barry, who promptly paid the check. Francine got behind the wheel of her silver BMW 325i and headed home. As planned, Barry got into his black Z3 and followed. Unknown to both of them, as they left the restaurant, just down the block a man in a tan Toyota quietly took his car out of idle, slipped into traffic, and became the third car in their little caravan.

When Barry and Francine arrived at her apartment, they parked on the street. As they walked into the lobby arm-in-arm, the tan Toyota found a space directly across from the building. The driver turned off the engine, adjusted the directional microphone, and readied himself for a long night.

# TWENTY THREE

**W**ASHINGTON, D.C. WAS blanketed with snow, and more was on the way. This didn't prevent the media from coming to a press conference called by the Drug Enforcement Administration to tout the latest successes in their war on untested and substandard drugs being sold via the Internet. DEA Administrator Karen Tandy announced the results of Operation Cyber Chase, a year-long Organized Crime Drug Enforcement Task Force joint investigation involving the Justice Department, DEA and FDA that targeted international Internet pharmaceutical traffickers operating in the United States, India, Asia, Europe and Caribbean. These e-traffickers distributed drugs worldwide using "rogue" Internet pharmacies.

"Over the past 48 hours there were 20 arrests in eight U.S. cities and four foreign countries. Domestically, arrests occurred in Philadelphia, Pennsylvania; Fort Lauderdale and Sarasota, Florida; Abilene and Tyler, Texas; New York, New York; Greenville, South Carolina; and Rochester, New York. Internationally, arrests occurred in Costa Rica and in New Delhi, Agra and Bombay, India," Tandy advised the gathered reporters.

Francine Pye was glued to C-SPAN in her FDA office as she watched the unfolding news conference with special interest.

Francine got an earful. "Operation Cyber Chase targeted major pharmaceutical drug traffickers who allegedly shipped Schedule II-V pharmaceutical controlled substances including narcotics, amphetamines, and anabolic steroids directly to buyers of all ages without the medical examination by a physician required by U.S. law. These e-traffickers used more than 200 web sites to illicitly distribute pharmaceutical controlled substances."

Without emotion, Tandy continued, "For too long the Internet has been an open medicine cabinet with cyber drug dealers illegally doling out a vast array of narcotics, amphetamines, and steroids. In this first major international enforcement action against on-line rogue pharmacies and their sources of supply, we've logged these traffickers off the Internet."

Or so she said. Barry Weiner was also paying very close attention to the C-SPAN report from his desk at FBI headquarters. He understood how much of this press conference was puffery, as everyone there pursued his own agenda. He also knew just how much work lay ahead. As the agencies basked in their latest successes, not a word was said about the most profound threat—terrorism.

John Walters, Director of National Drug Control Policy, took the podium. "Prescription drugs help millions of Americans every day, but their misuse is becoming a serious problem, abetted by drug traffickers who are using the Internet in an attempt to subvert our medical prescription system. E-traffickers are now the target of law enforcement action," he threatened, "while we continue to ensure proper access to needed medications."

"You can assure nothing of the kind," Weiner muttered back at the television set, wondering whether they would even mention the gray market favored by the major pharmaceutical companies, or whether they would challenge only the little guys.

Walters then sought and dished out praise, "I would like to thank and applaud the agencies and offices involved in this investigation as their efforts truly make America safer."

Weiner made a note to call Francine. Then he looked up again and continued to watch.

Walters was putting the problem into perspective. "In the last two years, these criminal organizations distributed approximately 2.5 million doses of Schedule II-V pharmaceutical controlled substances, including Vicodin, anabolic steroids and amphetamines per month."

FBI Director Robert Mueller next stepped up to speak, "The FBI remains committed to investigating the illegal sale of pharmaceuticals over the Internet. The FBI's Internet Pharmaceutical Fraud Initiative is working with the Drug Enforcement Administration, and other federal, state, local and international law enforcement partners to combat this crime and dismantle the responsible criminal enterprises."

Mueller warned, "Illegal pharmaceuticals pose a great risk to the health and welfare of the American public. These drugs are being manufactured overseas in unregulated facilities, smuggled into the United States in an uncontrolled environment, and distributed without oversight of a licensed physician or pharmacist."

While the Internet Pharmaceutical Fraud Initiative was focused on the sale of counterfeit or substandard drugs, Weiner was more fearful of a deliberate attack that could kill hundreds of thousands or perhaps millions of Americans. Mueller had tasked Weiner to focus on that risk, as well as the use of Internet sites to fund terrorist activity. Weiner knew that he had to deliver results.

Michael Garcia, Assistant Secretary of Immigration and Customs Enforcements, was getting his moment in the spotlight: "This investigation dismantled a major source of illicit pharmaceuticals that posed a significant public health threat. Closing down these illegal Internet drug pipelines is essential to protecting consumers of pharmaceuticals."

Weiner took his pen and drew several hard, bold lines beneath his note to 'Call Francine' as the press conference came to an end.

"The combined efforts of law enforcement agencies in an investigation of this magnitude produce a formidable force against narcotics trafficking and money laundering. Individuals and businesses utilizing the Internet to sell pharmaceuticals are bound by the same laws and regulations that apply to the corner drug store," said Nancy Jardini, Chief of IRS Criminal Investigation. "The link between where the money comes from, who gets it, when it is received, and where it is stored or deposited, can provide evidence that a crime was committed. Finding and connecting those links is what the IRS brings to this cooperative effort."

Ben Opperman laughed out loud as he listened to the press conference from his St. Regis hotel suite on Manhattan's Fifth Avenue. He shook his head, "Amateurs!" Ben reached for his cell phone to call Tom Biffar. While he was in town, he could meet with PharmCorp's William Bowne to maintain client relations and to finalize plans for the multi-national's "terrorist attack."

Petar Raic, watching from London, just smiled. In just over a year, the Karasik Commission would make all these substandard and counterfeit drugs seem like candy. Silently, he also congratulated himself that not a single C3 company had been implicated in the far-reaching sting. Emboldened by that success, he placed a call to Irfan Pradeep. After describing what had just occurred, Raic gave Pradeep new instructions, "Step up Far East manufacturing operations to sop up the business that will now become available. As long as any of the web sites still operate, someone has to fill the demand, and it might as well be us."

Ben completed his call to Tom and poured himself a bourbon. He didn't appear to have a care in the world.

Francine's phone rang. "Hello?" she said in her usual seductive way.

"Wanna run away with me?" Weiner said.

"Sure," she replied. "Where to?"

"How about an early dinner at The Capital Grille, say six o'clock?"

"That would be great," she replied. "Who are you?"

Weiner laughed. "Francine, I hope your body holds out longer than your memory."

"I'll be there," she quipped.

In Hillcrest Valley, Alexa turned off C-SPAN. It had been a world ago, but she always kept herself informed. You just never knew when it might come in handy.

She looked at the time. It was time to go, she had a 3:00 appointment with her new friend Nely.

# Twenty Four

"**T**HIS IS A PLEASANT surprise," William Bowne said as he met Ben at a bench in Bryant Park on West 42nd Street and Avenue of the Americas, just behind the New York Public Library. It was a clear and comfortable 44°, though both Ben and Bowne wore Burberry overcoats. Ben saw the irony. "We look like spies out of *Casablanca*. Very low key!"

"You've heard of hiding in plain sight?" Bowne asked, cool as ever.

"Indeed. We haven't spoken in a while and I thought I'd give you a progress report and answer any questions Tom hasn't been able to answer," Ben said, now all business.

As the two got up from the bench and started to stroll around the small park, Ben continued. "I'm sure you're very pleased with yourself over this Operation Cyber Chase. You've certainly got the FBI and DEA doing your dirty work for you."

Bowne grinned.

"Anyway, this crackdown isn't going to make the attack any easier. While none of our assets were identified, some of them have some peripheral involvement in the subject. If law enforcement gets too close it may delay things."

174

"I understand. Is there something you're asking me to do?" Bowne inquired.

"No. Even if you could intercede, it would be a mistake. It would expose you to a risk that you don't need."

"I appreciate that. But, let me be certain about what you are telling me, my friend. Are you warning me the price might go up? Or are you warning me that we might miss our schedule? Or, is it something else?"

"I'm certainly not asking for a raise. As to delay, I suppose that is possible, though unlikely. I don't think I have a specific message. So, I will accept 'something else,'" Ben vaguely replied.

"Now I'm confused, what does that mean?" Bowne gruffly asked.

"Calm down, Bill. There are no hidden messages. Since we started on this assignment we have made terrific progress. We are still several months away from the attack and a lot could happen in that period. We've been down this path before. At least one thing has happened—the government is cracking down. While that may be exactly what you wanted, like many things in life there can be unintended consequences. All I'm doing is giving you an update. Think of it as the risk section of one of those prospectuses you guys are always filing."

Still suspicious, Bowne tried again. "As of now, is there anything occurring that leads you to believe that we will not be able to launch this attack on time, on budget, and with the intended results?"

Ben and Bowne were about the same height, though Bowne was much broader and much more fit. Still, when Ben wanted to convey strength he could. This was one of those times. He stopped, turned toward Bowne and slowly responded. "We seem to have a credibility problem here. I don't work with clients who don't trust me. It's been my experience that when trust is lost, the consequences are often fatal. I do not intend to die for PharmCorp. So let's be very clear. I know my assignment. We have agreed the price and the terms of the engagement. When and if I conclude that I cannot perform, I'll tell you. Until then, if you prefer we suspend any interaction or updates, I am happy to comply... Well?"

This time, Ben had him. Bowne observed Ben and yet again reminded himself of just how tough and clever Ben could be. He had started with a warning, and now he was challenging Bowne to disregard the warning. "Ok, Ben. We'll see how things go. I have complete confidence in you. Let's play this one out."

"I should know more in about 90 days. If things go well, we will be ahead of schedule. If not, I might need your chemists. Either way, I think you'll be pleased with the attack. Once it happens, I suspect you'll get Congress to keep out competition until long after you're promoted, cashed out and retired."

"Perfect," Bowne tersely replied.

"Good. Now, how's the wife and kids?" Ben asked, the purpose of his meeting having been fully accomplished.

# TWENTY FIVE

**P**ETAR RAIC DREADED the call he was about to place, but there was no choice. They were going to fall at least six months behind schedule and there was nothing he could do about it. The nermycin was too unstable. In the lab, where every particular could be measured precisely and all fail-safes employed, it worked. But, in the field, whether India, Burma or China, the results were very different.

Even when their top team was put on the case, it simply could not meet the standards necessary to execute the plan. Perhaps it was too many years of degrading the performance at these plants to the point that they no longer knew how to meet the highest standards. Perhaps it was the low quality of ingredients they had grown accustomed to ordering for their drugs. Perhaps the chemists in Zurich just weren't as smart as they thought they were. Whatever the cause, the result was the same. They had to either find a new formula that would remain inert and stable for at least six months—while the drugs were shipped around the world and until they were used by patients—or they had to find another plan.

Petar was also concerned about the increased attention being given to counterfeit drugs by U.S. law enforcement agencies. Just a month ago, DEA Administrator Karen Tandy had held her press conference to announce the results of Operation Cyber Chase.

Although *antidote.com* and C3 had escaped unscathed, 20 arrests, including arrests in New Delhi and Bombay hit close to home. Any further delay only increased the risk that some law enforcement agency would start looking their way.

Petar pressed the 13 digits that always found Karasik, routed through a tortuous maze of repeaters. The pattern of the repeaters changed each month, but for the last several months the sequence started with the international dialing code, followed by "66," the country code for Thailand. Within seconds, Ken's slightly electronic-sounding voice answered, as he always did, with a simple "Yes." Petar made his report. "Very well," Ken answered in his usual terse fashion, "Given the delay, let's carefully consider the situation with Maslac. We have to do more." Then he added, "One more thing, the FBI is about to begin a preliminary investigation of C3. Be ready." With that, Ken terminated the connection.

Petar always marveled at Ken's sources of information. Now, he reached right into the heart of America's law enforcement community to learn what the FBI was going to do, even before it had done anything. As a first step in their defense, Petar advised each of the Commission's other members. Then, he called Eric Jacobs, the C3 Group's general counsel and told him to be prepared.

Karasik had induced Jacobs to leave McDermott, Knowlson and Jacobs, a 1,000-lawyer firm with offices on three continents, by offering him a compensation package that exceeded $6 million a year, offices in New York and London, a staff of 200 lawyers and stock options worth over $50 million. Petar once asked Ken, "Why the hell are you paying him so much?"

Ken laughed knowing that Jacobs helped him avoid liabilities worth at least five times what he was paid. "I like him and I want him to be rich," was his simple response. Ken was very careful to keep the work of the Karasik Commission away from Jacobs, an observant Jew, who would not have remained if he had known the truth.

Jacobs immediately prepared a memorandum for all of C3's worldwide companies reminding them of their confidentiality obligations and the dangers of discussing C3 business with outsiders, including family and friends. The memorandum did not mention the FBI. At Petar's request, Jacobs also pressed his rather considerable contacts into service to learn what was happening with the investigations in Europe. For the time being, they did not seek additional information about the FBI. While it would come as no surprise that Karasik knew of the European investigations, they didn't want to telegraph their ability to reach into the U.S. Justice Department.

# TWENTY SIX

**M**ORE THAN THREE years had passed since the attack that would change the way America looked at itself. American troops had smashed into al-Qaeda, the Taliban and Sadaam Hussein's Baath Party in Afghanistan and Iraq. Old friends like France were barely on speaking terms with the United States, while former enemies like Libya and Pakistan had joined the fight against terrorism. Nowhere were the changes more profound than in the U.S. law enforcement and intelligence communities.

In the largest reorganization of the federal government since the creation of the Department of Defense in 1949, Congress created the Department of Homeland Security in late 2002, and consolidated within it more than 180,000 federal employees and their 22 separate agencies, including the U.S. Customs Service, the Immigration and Naturalization Service, Federal Emergency Management Agency, Secret Service and Coast Guard.

Though the FBI remained part of the Justice Department, in June 2002, the FBI began its broadest reorganization and reprioritization since World War II, among other things, creating a new Directorate of Intelligence. For a time, the Bureau assigned nearly a quarter of its 28,000 agents to combat terrorism. Bolstered by the Patriot Act, which eliminated most of the legislative barriers to sharing information, the FBI also opened a real and open dialogue with the CIA and other law enforcement agencies.

Although Barry Weiner was just one of the thousands of agents assigned to the new Directorate of Intelligence, he was one of a much smaller number of agents tasked with uncovering sources of funding for terrorists groups. In that effort, Weiner had the assistance of his fellow agents as well as other law enforcement agencies. For example, in 2002, the U.S. Customs Service deployed a supercomputer previously used to track drug trafficking to analyze patterns in terror funding. U.S. Customs, the FBI and other government agencies also created an interagency task force called Operation Green Quest to "identify, disrupt, and dismantle" sources of terrorist funding.

On July 22, 2004, the National Commission on Terrorist Attacks Upon the United States, better known as the September 11 Commission, had issued its report. In its report, the Commission's 10 bipartisan members concluded that the United States had been woefully unprepared for the attack on September 11. Although the Commission specifically praised many hardworking government employees, not least of whom were New York's valiant firefighters and police officers, the September 11 Commission also found a disturbing lack of cooperation and candor among law enforcement agencies, particularly the FBI and CIA. To be fair, federal law had prohibited those agencies from sharing information, or from sharing information with the Justice Department. In the wake of September 11, 2001, that changed with the almost immediate passage of the USA Patriot Act, signed into law by President George W. Bush just six weeks after the attack.

That was not all that changed. Just one month before the September 11 Commission issued its report, George Tenet, the CIA's embattled director, resigned. Six months later in December 2004, both houses of Congress voted overwhelmingly to approve a landmark restructuring of the nation's intelligence community. President Bush promptly signed the bill into law thus implementing the major recommendations of the September 11 Commission, including creation of a National Intelligence Director to force cooperation among the Central Intelligence Agency and 14 other intelligence agencies. At first, only the FBI would retain its independence from the National Intelligence Director, secure in its historical niche within the Justice Department.

Then, beginning with a March 2005 report issued by yet another Presidential commission, that too changed. Under pressure from the White House, in June 2005, the Bureau agreed to permit John Negroponte, the new National Intelligence Director, to help select its intelligence director. That agreement marked the first time the Bureau permitted an outsider to play a role in its personnel decisions.

Despite the massive reorganization, Weiner was the only FBI special agent tasked full-time with considering a terrorist attack on the United States through the pharmaceutical distribution system, though he received support in that effort from the FBI's Internet Pharmaceutical Fraud Initiative and from additional resources on an "as needed" basis.

After almost a year of investigating America's medical supply system, Weiner was very concerned. He and Francine were sipping wine at a small bistro near Barry's apartment. "It's frustrating," he said, "although it's received only minimal attention in the press or in Congress, the risk of a terrorist attack involving drug importation is very real."

"You're right," Francine observed, swirling her wine. "The counterfeiters are selling pills filled with starch and sugar. It wouldn't be difficult for terrorists to make lethal drugs that look like the real thing. They already forge nearly every type of documentation, including false labels, packaging, seals and certificates. It's scary." Barry squeezed her hand. Francine uncurled her fingers from the wine stem and squeezed back, as they moved on to more personal matters.

Weiner's investigation into Toi, Brower, C3 and MDB was gaining momentum. Lisa Fuller had been able to get some of the requested documents from Inland Revenue, and Weiner had been able to obtain two full-time agents to assist in his inquiries. In addition to the four original targets, Weiner had since identified three others—a Muslim-owned trading company based in Jakarta, a Saudi-financed food and drug company based in Riyadh, and Ramadorai Group based in New Delhi.

Francine had been particularly helpful, supplying not only the FDA's information on drugs imported from these companies, but also information on suspected ties to shady manufacturers and legitimate European- and Asian-based drug companies. Francine had also been helpful in other ways, but those were only of indirect benefit to the investigation.

Weiner was reviewing internal Bureau reports when he almost jumped out of his chair. In January, a confidential source had phoned an agent in Phil Oster's unit to warn that C3 had been selling counterfeit drugs into the United States through the Internet. Weiner immediately contacted the agent, Dave Williams. Williams had little to add to the report.

"Look, a woman phoned the unit. She said she had heard about us in reports after the DEA press conference a few weeks earlier. She asked for the head of the unit. Of course, they transferred her to me since I was special agent on duty that day. She wouldn't give me her name."

Weiner barked at Williams. "Did you attempt to trace the call?"

"Of course not. As I recall, the caller ID identified the phone she was calling from as a pay phone on a street corner in the District."

"Did you try to locate any surveillance coverage?" Weiner asked, not expecting to like the answer.

"Barry, come on. We get calls like this all the time."

Barry knew Williams was right. Nonetheless, he immediately assigned a member of his team to track down any remaining surveillance tapes. Unsurprisingly, his agent rapidly discovered that all of the coverage had been overwritten weeks earlier.

All calls to the duty agents were recorded. Once Barry identified the call from Williams' log, he had no problem obtaining the recording. The woman sounded like she was probably in her 30s. She sounded white and educated, almost as though she had grown up in a European country, or spent a lot of time there when she was young. Of course, she might have been disguising her voice and the truth might be completely different.

The speaker was direct and to the point. "I read about the Fraud Initiative after the December press conference. I have come into possession of some disquieting information about a plot to sell counterfeit drugs in the United States. At first, I let it go, but with what I'm hearing… I don't know the details, but I'm certain that C3, or people associated with C3, are either already selling counterfeit drugs or intending to do so." That was it. She knew nothing more. She promised to call Williams again at any time of the day or night if she learned anything further.

Barry resisted the urge to choke Williams for withholding the phone call until he had, by chance, seen the report. But, in fairness to Williams, the report had nothing to do with terrorism or threats of harm. Rather, it seemed to be a standard Internet fraud, which fell squarely within Oster's unit. The hell with it! Everyone in Oster's unit knew that Barry was investigating C3, and now they had lost their chance to track the woman through surveillance tapes of the area where she had placed her phone call.

As soon as he was done with Williams, Barry called Francine, filled her in, and made a date for dinner that evening at their favorite Italian restaurant. Then, he returned to his office to write a more complete report on what he had learned. He forwarded that report to the other agents on his task force, Bureau management, and liaisons at the other agencies. Feeling as though he was finally making progress, Barry headed out to meet Francine.

He never noticed the man in the tan Toyota who followed him from the FBI's underground parking lot, straight to Mario's, and then parked outside of Francine's apartment with his directional microphone positioned just right.

The distinguished-looking silver-haired man in his mid-50s sat behind his antique mahogany desk. His spacious corner office had a magnificent panaormic view of the Washington Monument, Ellipse and the White House. He scanned the report from Barry Weiner, before moving on to the next task in his always overcrowded day.

He located the blue Request for Approval and marked his consent. When signed by his boss, it would authorize the FBI to execute an operation against a suspected al-Qaeda cell in California.

"Sharon, would you walk that over to the Attorney General? Before you leave, get me Secretary Chertoff."

On February 15, 2005, Michael Chertoff had replaced Tom Ridge, the first Secretary of Homeland Security. Chertoff had been the President's second choice to succeed Ridge. His first, Bernard

Kerik, had imploded amidst charges that he had employed illegal aliens and used his position as New York City Police Commissioner for personal gain. While Chertoff had come in for a large dose of criticism for his failures in providing relief after Hurricane Katrina, like many others after September 11, Chertoff's principal mission was to combat terrorism.

As his assistant dialed Chertoff's number, he again gazed at the report from Weiner. There was no doubt that Weiner was going to be trouble.

# TWENTY SEVEN

"**B**EN, YOU HAVE to get us some help here," Petar Raic yelled into his cell phone. Petar was in New York to coordinate the efforts in India, Burma and China. They were behind schedule and still had no solution to the problem with nermycin. By now, they had probably infected two dozen unwitting subjects with lethal combinations of doctored nermycin and the lower quality cyprofaxin they expected to distribute alongside it. Though it all worked fine in the laboratory, they were having one hell of a time maintaining stability in the field trials. Petar was even thinking of giving up, something he seldom considered, and almost never did.

In the meantime, that son-of-a-bitch Milosevic was running rings around the War Tribunal in The Hague, Maslac was killing hundreds of innocent Bosnians as the world just stood by and shrugged its collective shoulders, and the United States did nothing. The United States never even mentioned Muslims unless the Arabs were killing Americans or threatening to do so.

At least Stuart King was making some progress on the political end. The Karasik Commission's very secret but very potent weapon had written three articles for the *Times* calling attention to what was happening in the Balkans. He had also ghost written an article for the *Economist* and arranged meetings and gratuities for a number of influential members of the European Parliament. Clearly,

King's efforts were making a difference in attitudes. Just as clearly, it would not be enough, on its own. The good news was that King's efforts were not in a vacuum. Petar and Mel had organized additional arms shipments to the paramilitaries throughout the Balkan's fractured regions. On a more direct front, Mike Mihalic had visited the former Yugoslavia twice. Each time an important Maslac lieutenant had suffered an unexpected accident. Unfortunately, neither time had Maslac been anywhere in the line of fire.

The sad reality, however, was that none of this would help unless the United States stepped forward to do what it should have done in the first place.

Which was precisely why their plan was so important. The United States would be given a choice. Turn Milosevic and Maslac over to the Slavs for trial, or Americans die. Provide real security safeguards for Slavs in the Balkans and oppressed minorities in the Russian Federation, or even more Americans would die. Their demands were completely within America's power to implement. If America acted quickly, fatalities could be limited. If not, the death toll could easily reach into the hundreds of thousands before the Americans could figure out what was happening, let alone how to stop it.

"What do you need?" Ben asked Petar.

"We need some top chemists out in the field to work with the C3 chemists. We need it now before this Operation Cyber thing comes too close."

Ben thought about it for about 30 seconds. Then he made his decision.

"I know where to get some of the best guys in the world. I can probably have them ready within a few weeks. Where do I send them?"

"Pune, to RD Pharmaceuticals," Petar answered. "They have the best facilities and the best people. If we can't get it to work there, it isn't working anywhere."

"Ok."

"Good, Tom or I will be in touch with the details," Petar said gratefully, "Thank you, my friend." With that, Ben disconnected his cell phone. He had an important appointment with a redhead.

Special Agent Dave Williams received a call from his confidential informant. Again she refused to identify herself. This time, she warned that *antidote.com* was part of the scheme. She was in a hurry and no, she could not speak to Barry Weiner this time. Next time, however, she would call him. Even as Williams spoke to the mystery woman, he was tracking the number from which she called to a pay phone in New York's Grand Central Station. He immediately alerted the New York City police.

By the time the woman hung up, police were already scanning their monitors to find the woman, and to take her into custody, if possible. After a few minutes, they concluded that she had left the immediate area. They identified the camera that had the best view of the phone she had been using. They found the right time index and viewed the digital recording. They saw a woman in sunglasses and a scarf. None of her hair was visible. They couldn't see her eyes. And, even in the summer heat, she wore a long overcoat that disguised her weight. They did the best they could and decided the woman was between 5'5"-5'7", 125-135 pounds.

After four years with the FDA, Francine was promoted to lead a task force within the FDA's Counterfeit Drug Working Group. Although formed to confront the problem of counterfeit drugs, under Francine's prodding, the Working Group was increasingly concerned with terrorism. With her promotion, Francine was able to coordinate more closely with Barry's efforts. Together, they began to backtrack the sources of the drugs available on the Internet or through mail order.

"We've got them!" Kelly Harpin shouted. "We've got them!" The 26-year-old analyst rushed into Francine's office to tell her the good news. "I've tracked those three web sites to Toi. There's no escaping it; Toi owns those sites, lock, stock and URLs."

"That's great," Francine told her, proud that the FDA had beaten the Bureau on this one. She immediately called Barry.

"We've found them. It's only a matter of a week or so and we'll be able to track many of the drugs sold on their web sites right to the manufacturers in China and Thailand. You wait, we'll prove Toi owns those as well."

Just one week later, Francine was good to her word. With Kelly's help, they established that Toi owned two manufacturers and had a lien on the third. Three weeks later, a federal grand jury handed up indictments against Toi, its CEO, 10 U.S.-based distribution executives who worked with Toi and eight of its distribution executives in Canada, Malaysia and Thailand. Although many of those indicted were beyond reach of the U.S. judicial system, Toi had significant assets in the United States. Lisa Fuller froze all of them.

As Francine's team worked with Barry and Phil Oster's unit to bear down on Toi, Barry began to put *antidote.com* under a microscope. Two of his agents, Gary Landau and Chris Calandra worked overtime. Just after July 4, Landau announced, "It's the Cowells. John and Harriet Cowell. They're listed as the ultimate owners, at least legally. I have their address in Winnipeg."

Based on Landau's work, Barry arranged for the Royal Canadian Mounted Police to question the Cowells, the couple who were the recorded owners of *antidote.com*. Both of them denied any knowledge of C3, other than as a vendor for some of their name brand drugs, and took full responsibility for any breach of U.S. law.

Calandra was no slouch either. By poring through available records, he established that *antidote.com* carried an unusually high percentage of name brand drugs from C3 Pharmaceuticals in Zurich. "That's not all," Calandra reported. "With just a few exceptions, they pay for all of their orders by transferring funds to the Cayman Islands. We all know what that means. One thing that doesn't make sense is that they pay C3 in the open, by direct transfer, even though the resale of C3's drugs into the United States is illegal. If they have something to hide, why do that?"

"Maybe it's to protect C3, not *antidote.com*," Weiner speculated. "C3 would argue that it breaks no laws and has nothing to hide."

When Calandra tried to track the money deposited with the Cayman bank, he was stonewalled at every turn. "We're getting nowhere," he finally admitted after three weeks of fruitless efforts.

Weiner contacted C3 Pharmaceuticals in Zurich. He was referred to a lawyer. That lawyer was not very forthcoming. Weiner turned to his boss, Richard Goldstein, an Assistant Director, and to Lisa Fuller for ideas. "The best pressure points will be through C3 in London and Ken Karasik in Hillcrest Valley," Goldstein advised. Lisa and Barry agreed. Calls were made. Within a few days, the IRS was taking a much closer look at Karasik's returns and a senior Justice Department lawyer in New York was arranging to meet with Eric Jacobs.

Ken was unusually irritable. "Despite our best efforts in the Balkans, Maslac is continuing to gain strength," he told Petar. Their plan to infiltrate U.S. medical supplies with an adulterated cocktail of nermycin and cyprofaxin was on interminable hold, like a shuttle launch that could never start its final countdown. The FBI was stepping up its investigation of C3 and the IRS was beginning an investigation. Even Interpol had become unusually active in the last few months. Then there was the problem of the leak. He hoped it wasn't Nely; but, whoever it was, he would have to deal with it decisively before any real harm was done. Though he knew what was happening, he seemed powerless to stop it. Even his Trojan horse, the secret sixth member of the Karasik Commission, seemed able only to report on events—not shape them.

It was time for a meeting of the Karasik Commission. Maybe, for the first time, he would include all six members: Petar, Ben, Stuart, Mel, himself, and even Jason. He thought about it and decided that until he was certain about the leak he could not expose Jason to the risk. He set the meeting for the following week in New York. Because of all the attention, however, they wouldn't meet at his apartment. Instead, once they were in the general vicinity, each of them would take public transportation to Madison Square Garden. They would meet there during a concert, part of Cher's never-ending good-bye tour.


"So far, he's taken care of everything. This is the first time he's asked for our help," Bowne explained to his boss. Bob Estrich, PharmCorp's president and chief operating officer, was sitting across from Bowne in the "secure room" just down the hall from their offices on the 50th floor of PharmCorp's New York office tower.

They used the secure room when they wanted to be absolutely sure no one would hear them. It was really a room within a room. Short bridges ran from the hallway door to an inner bubble. There was no natural light, and the most sophisticated electronic jammers ran 24 hours a day inside the bubble, with another set of state-of-the-art devices operating between the bubble and the outer walls. In addition, sensing devices were always turned on and frequently recalibrated. The secure room had been in use for three years now and there was no record that anyone had ever been able to eavesdrop on the sensitive conversations that occurred within.

"We've committed to $150 million. While that's not a lot of money, it isn't pocket change either. Laundering that much cash and transferring it to Opperman's accounts has required some very clever acrobatics," Estrich commented.

Bowne began to speak, but Estrich interrupted. "Bill, I'm not second-guessing you on this. Dave and I are completely on board," Estrich conceded, referring to PharmCorp's CEO, David Cole. "We've both told you that and we've given you everything you've asked for. But, now you want to expose us directly. You're asking me to assign PharmCorp chemists to create toxic drugs?"

"That's not entirely correct, Bob. I'm asking you to assign two chemists from our Guadalajara R&D facility—two chemists who are already up to their eyeballs in black ops—to help complete a manipulation that is nearly complete."

"That last point is a fine distinction without a difference. But, I'll grant you that these guys could burn us now and they certainly have no compunction about killing," Estrich replied, as he carefully weighed what was at stake. His $15 million each year of base, bonus and perks won.

"Bob, I know you understand what's involved. Hell, I learned how to do this from you! What I can promise you is that when the job is complete, there will be no risk of exposure."

"I'll hold you to that, Bill. Zero risk. Zero tolerance."

# TWENTY EIGHT

ON JULY 6, 2005, London was chosen as the site of the 2012 Summer Olympics. The next day, the United Kingdom hosted the first full day of the G8 summit in Gleneagles, Scotland. That same day, beginning at just before 9:00 in the morning local time, a series of four bombs exploded on three London Underground trains and a London bus. The well-coordinated blasts struck during morning rush hour, killing 56 people, including the four suspected bombers, and injuring 700.

Then, just two weeks later, a second series of four explosions took place on the London Underground and a London bus. However, this time only the detonators exploded; there was only one injury and no fatalities.

"This is ridiculous," Stuart King muttered. His grin, however, told a different story. King was actually enjoying the irony of the Karasik Commission using a Cher concert to throw off potential surveillance and to make eavesdropping almost impossible. Each of them had arrived in New York on their own. They stayed at their usual hotels. About an hour before the scheduled start of the concert, they had each simply disappeared into New York's vast subway system, re-appearing at one entrance or another of the 20,000 seat indoor arena, by far the most famous such venue in the world.

As it turned out, only Karasik was being followed, but the maneuver worked. Ken lost the FBI agent who had been assigned to him well before reaching his destination at Madison Square Garden's Terrace Restaurant. It wouldn't be as noisy as the arena, but until the main act began, it would be crowded with fans from throughout the metropolitan area. They would seem neither conspicuous nor out of place, and they intended to complete their meeting by the time the show began. Each of them had tickets, and some of them would probably stay for the entertainment. Indeed, Christine would join Ken in their fifth row seats as soon as the meeting adjourned. She was flattered that Ken indulged her and "dated" her openly—or so it seemed—and he was confident that in return she would reveal all she had learned from her trusting cousin, Barry Weiner.

"We have a number of problems and we have to take concrete action to solve these problems," Ken began. "First of all, things are not going well in the Balkans. Maslac is continuing to gain support, the attacks on our friends are increasing, and Milosevic will never pay for his crimes. Neither Europe nor the United States are taking our plight seriously. In fact, they'd rather be rid of us," Ken turned red, before regaining his composure and continuing.

"Second, our grand response is way behind schedule. It is absolutely essential that we proceed no later than Thanksgiving. That means shipment of the adulterated products must commence by mid-September at the latest. Not to put too fine a point on it, that means we must be in production by September. Finally, the FBI, IRS, Interpol and a number of police agencies have escalated their investigations, and this leak is not helping matters."

It was difficult to hear Ken over the crowd, but each of those present understood the intensity of his tone. For once, Petar had some good news. "With Ben's help, we have identified chemists with experience in solving stability problems. With any luck, we will meet your schedule."

Petar and Ben weren't as upbeat about the situation in the Balkans.

"We are already doing just about everything feasible. With European peacekeepers on the ground, there are limits to our capabilities," Ben said. Karasik knew his most trusted advisor was right, but it was nonetheless frustrating. Petar put the bottom line in military terms: "If we could do more in theater, we wouldn't need the rear guard action. But, we are at our limit. In fact, we are devoting so many resources of late to the Balkans that it is eating into our profits and diverting us from controlling some of our less savory business partners."

"I understand. But we have a duty much greater than business," Ken reminded Petar. "If we can't pull off the operation, we have only bad choices and our brothers will pay the price," the Bosnian émigré added.

"That wasn't my point," Petar irritably replied. "No one knows more than I the importance of what we are doing. Our last hope is with Ben's chemists."

"If our chemists do their job, we should be ready to launch Project Sky by Thanksgiving," Ben advised them, referring to the name they had given to their project. The name "Sky" was a corruption of *Hrvatska,* Croatia's name in their native language.

"When you look at the worldwide publicity generated by the London bombings, I can only imagine the reaction to what we are doing," Stuart said, adding, "I can assure you that when hundreds or thousands start to die, President Bush and the European Union will find the morality they seem to have misplaced."

They spent the next 45 minutes discussing the investigations and the leak. Finally, Ken relented. "I don't like it, but I will agree to surveillance on Nely under two conditions. First, the surveillance must be discreet, and second, it must be cut off as soon as possible."

Ken was saddened that he couldn't trust Nely, but he had a duty to his colleagues and their mission.

Stuart, Ben and Petar agreed to use their sources to uncover whatever information they could locate on the investigation. "Petar, I want you to advise Eric Jacobs to stonewall. You and Ben should determine who might be open to pressure. It's time to bring this investigation to a close," Ken instructed. Although it was very unlikely the investigation would ever topple them, the legal defense was about to become expensive, and the extra-legal defense potentially even more so.

"One last thing," Ken said, "I don't want any problems with *antidote.com*."

"I understand," Petar replied.

As the sounds of *Song for the Lonely* could be heard from the arena, the Terrace Restaurant was emptying out. Ken headed to meet Christine, while Stuart met one of his many girlfriends. Petar and Mel chose to leave. Ben had what he termed a "hot date." As he left the restaurant, he headed to his seat. Just before Ken lost sight of him, he saw the still dapper Parisian put his arm around a very attractive redhead. There might have been something vaguely familiar about Ben's date, but Ken wasn't certain and forgot about it by the time he found Christine and Cher launched into *Half Breed*. As a foreigner in his own country, Ken thought he understood what she meant.

Greg Schoenfeld introduced himself to Eric Jacobs. Schoenfeld was 42, a graduate of Harvard College and Columbia Law School, and the second-ranking attorney in the Justice Department's prestigious New York office. That Greg Schoenfeld would personally meet with Eric Jacobs showed just how much attention this matter was now getting at Justice. It was not welcome news.

Jacobs was gracious as usual. He asked Schoenfeld if he would like some tea or coffee. When Schoenfeld chose coffee, Jacobs personally walked Schoenfeld to the little kitchen near his office and made the coffee for him. Then, Jacobs, 15 years Schoenfeld's senior, spent some time discussing with him fond memories of Columbia Law School and how little it had changed over the years. Next, they talked about the many judges they both knew. Finally, after about 45 minutes, Schoenfeld steered the conversation to the subject at hand.

"We need to know about C3 Pharmaceuticals. We need to understand its ownership structure, the products it manufactures and distributes, and its association with on-line pharmacies. In short, we need to know everything about C3's activities with respect to drug sales in the United States," Schoenfeld summarized in his to-the-point manner.

"May I ask why?" Jacobs deferentially responded.

"Because we have received reports from numerous sources that C3 may be involved in manufacturing or distributing counterfeit drugs," Schoenfeld told him, omitting the additional concerns created by the Interpol reports.

"C3 Pharmaceuticals does not operate in the United States. It is a Swiss corporation. It has no personnel, no facilities, no investments and no direct sales in the United States," Jacobs explained in his most reasonable tone.

"Yes, I understand that is your position. On the other hand, the C3 Group's principal shareholder is a U.S. citizen who lives and works in the United States, as do you, Mr. Jacobs. Moreover, even if everything you say is true, the question may well be its indirect sales."

"Touché, Mr. Schoenfeld. But, as you must know, corporations exist as separate legal entities, and it is a very circuitous route from a Swiss corporation to a shareholder who may live in the U.S.

As to me, I think we both know that is irrelevant, though your threat is duly noted."

"Mr. Jacobs, my visit is a courtesy. A courtesy to you, given your important contributions to the bar, and a courtesy to Mr. Karasik, given his many contributions to worthy causes here and abroad. But, I must warn you that the Justice Department is not easily put off. If I leave empty handed, subpoenas will not be long in coming."

"Then, I must thank you for your courtesy and a delightful visit. I expect we will be hearing from you shortly," Eric Jacobs retorted, his great skill hiding a deep fear that much of what the government suspected might be true.

# TWENTY NINE

JULY-AUGUST 2005
PUNE, INDIA

*I*T TOOK AN EXHAUSTING 26 hours for "Jim" and "Ron" to fly from PharmCorp's special research facility in Guadalajara to Mumbai, formerly known as Bombay. First they flew for four hours on Mexicana De Aviacion to Chicago. After a three-hour layover, they boarded Air India Flight 122 for the 18-hour flight to Mumbai. When they arrived it was nearly 2:00 in the morning.

Mike Mihalic was there to meet them. "I'm sure you've been fully briefed, but I want to emphasize the importance of secrecy and speed," Mihalic told them.

"We've done this before," Jim responded, seemingly annoyed by the warning. "We understand secrecy and we really don't care what your purpose is. As to speed, do you think we want to spend one more day in this god-forsaken place than we have to? We want to get in, do our jobs, go home, and get paid," he stridently added.

"Amen to that," Ron echoed his colleague.

Mihalic smiled. "Just so we're on the same page. I'll drop you off at the hotel for a little rest. You'll be picked up at 9:00 am and taken to the plant where I'll introduce you to the team. From that point, the length of your stay here is entirely in your hands."

"Sounds about right to me," Jim said as he settled back in the SUV for the hour's drive to the hotel near RD Pharmaceuticals.

The next morning, the SUV was right on time and so were Jim and Ron. Each wore jeans and a loose-fitting shirt and carried a state-of-the-art laptop. Within 10 minutes, they were deposited at RD, where Mihalic again met them. After shaking hands, he took them in to meet the C3 chemists.

"Jim, Ron, say hello to Steve, Shane and Beth. You guys are going to work together until you get this right. I'm told that Jim and Ron are the best there is. Steve, Shane and Beth have taken us damn close to completion. We're all hoping you can get us the rest of the way," Mihalic explained. Of course, none of the names were real and no one would discuss where they were from or why they were there. Not even Mihalic knew that Steve, Shane and Beth were really Leon, Philipp and Eva, or who Jim and Ron really were. Ben had arranged for them to help solve the problem and that was good enough.

"Any questions?" Mihalic asked.

"When do we get to work?" Jim volunteered.

"Right now," Mihalic replied, thinking they had a real hot dog on their hands. He just hoped the guy was as good as he obviously thought he was.

The social niceties behind them, Mihalic escorted the PharmCorp scientists to the lab.


The lab was actually a specially constructed section of RD's manufacturing facility. Local crews contracted by Opperman Security had built a wall along the entire south end of the plant. The solid three-inch-thick wall cut off all sound and access from the rest of the plant. Then, they divided the section they had sealed off into storage areas, offices, bathrooms, a large laboratory, and a series of small soundproofed windowless rooms with steel doors along a single hallway. Access to that hallway required passing through double steel-plated doors. A security keypad and a small reception station stood guard over that wing of the new facility within a facility at RD.

Once construction was completed, state-of-the art equipment had been moved into the lab, and bunks had been permanently bolted to the walls in the small rooms. Keypads were added to both exterior doors, one at the southeast and the other at the southwest end of the new section, as well as to interior doors throughout the new section. Cameras had been placed throughout the facility with a real-time feed to a security service located about a mile away.

When Leon, Philipp and Eva had first arrived two weeks earlier to continue the work they had begun in Schaffhausen, they had been assigned access codes for the southeast entrance, the lab and the storage rooms. Only Mihalic and the small team of armed guards had the codes for the other doors. After sundown that same day, a truck had pulled up to the southwest door. Three men and two women had been offloaded and carefully placed into the small rooms. These five hapless beggars had been selected as the next subjects in the effort to stabilize the nermycin. When necessary, they would be supplemented or replaced by new arrivals. There was an endless supply of beggars in India, and the restricted wing could house up to 12 involuntary guests at a time.

When Jim and Ron arrived, Mihalic showed them around. They noted the state-of-the art computers, and the right mix of microcentrifuges, autoclaves, evaporators and a polytron generator. They also saw the small airtight chamber into which toxins could be placed through an airlock built into the side of the chamber. Once in the chamber, the toxins could be manipulated remotely by using mechanical arms that were controlled with a computer and a joystick. Alternatively, the chemists could work directly with the substances by placing their arms into sleeves that were built into the chamber. Each sleeve ended in a glove. Implements could be passed into the chamber through the same airlock used to insert substances. There were two sets of sleeves, so up to two chemists could work at the same time. Though it normally would be too crowded, in theory a third chemist could assist by using the mechanical arms. In effect, the chamber was a portable version of the much larger biohazard chamber at the C3 lab in Schaffhausen.

Mihalic also showed them the small prison, the holding area for the animals, and the treatment rooms in which the animal and human experiments would take place.

"Pretty standard," Jim observed. He didn't need to point out that PharmCorp's Guadalajara lab was very much like the one in Schaffhausen. Mexico was a superb source of human subjects who would never be missed.

After he completed the tour, Mihalic gave them access codes to the southeast door and labs.

"Any more questions?" Mihalic asked.

Ron nonchalantly asked, "What do we do when we want to dispose of one of the subjects?"

"You tell him," Mike pointed to John, a buff 30ish man who had been observing the group. "He'll take care of it. He'll also be responsible for ensuring that no one else here gets in the way."

It was Jim's turn. "What's to keep the RD personnel from bothering us?"

"We've been here for over a month. In that time, it's become very apparent to the employees that they are not welcome. I don't think you'll have a problem. But if you do, John's your man."

"Anything else?"

Surprisingly, there was not.

"Ok. There's a lot of work ahead of you. Why don't you spend some time in the lab coming up to speed. If you need anything we don't have, tell John. It may take a day or two, but we'll get it."

They all headed into the lab. Ron looked around the pristine cutting-edge, high-tech facility. Several large computer monitors blinked while banks of glass vials, refrigerated cases and testing equipment sat across from them on glistening steel tables.

As it turned out, they spent nearly two months and needed more than 30 subjects before they solved the problem. Their process was similar to that used in Schaffhausen to find the right combination. They would slightly alter the formulation, both the precise nature of the toxin and the amount of the toxin. Then, they would subject it to heat and humidity that emulated up to six months of shelf life before use. Finally, they would administer the drugs to the animals and the human subjects.

When Mike Mihalic reported to the Karasik Commission that in order to solve the stability problem they'd had to reduce the toxicity of the nermycin, no one objected. "Not only will the final formulation be nearly impossible to detect, even after patients start getting sick, but our circuitous distribution plans will make it impossible for anyone to backtrack the problem to C3," Mihalic told Mel and Stuart via conference call.

Ever the pessimist, Stuart told Mihalic, "I wouldn't want to bet my life on that."

"Oh, but you have. And so have I," Mel countered.

"What about the antidote? I still hope the U.S. buckles," Stuart observed.

"I think we're all in agreement. It's the result we're after. I'm sure Ken and Petar would be just as happy to avoid killing thousands of civilians—if we can get our way without doing so," Mel agreed.

"I guess the pressure is now on me to generate the media coverage and lobbying efforts that either make this unnecessary, or grease the way for success," Stuart mused.

"There's no one better qualified than you. You've done it for us before. I'm not optimistic that you'll move this mountain, but you have about five months left to try," Mel told him.

"And God help us and America if I fail," the lapsed Anglican replied.

Stuart King was the Karasik Commission's secret weapon. With his family relations, prestige as a top columnist for the *Times of London,* access to the highest-ranking officials throughout Europe, and utter lack of morals, King was the perfect influencer. Time and again, he had succeeded at changing policies and practices for the benefit of the Karasik Commission and C3. Though he had become very rich in the process, his appetite for danger and intrigue only grew.

King was born on July 4, 1962 in London, just three years after his soon-to-be world-renowned aunt first took a seat in Parliament. He had never been a particularly good student, nor a particularly well behaved one. He was much more concerned with what the girls thought of him than the grades he received from his teachers. Once Aunt Margaret became Britain's Prime Minister, he relished telling the headmaster and his teachers exactly where to go.

Nonetheless, Stuart followed his favorite aunt to Oxford, where in his spare time he earned a degree in psychology. Using his family's contacts, he then secured a position as a foreign journalist for the *Times of London,* a position he thought of as rather dashing. His first posting, however, was strife-torn Yugoslavia, just two years after Tito's death. The posting did little for his social life, and the demands of sending in daily reports required real work, something Stuart eschewed whenever possible. Still, despite his insouciance, Stuart began to understand what was happening to Yugoslavia's minorities. To his chagrin, it troubled him that the Serbs could massacre their neighbors with such savagery.

After a year in Eastern Europe, Stuart's postings took him to Rome, Paris, and ultimately the United States. In 1991, the now seasoned journalist was asked to interview Ken Karasik, the young tycoon who flew below the radar, about his growing global businesses. The two met at the Four Seasons, one of the premiere power spots in New York. Its stark, contemporary design and fine food made it a favorite of the New York elite—the icons of media, publishing and finance who dictated national and even international trends from their offices on the East Side, their apartments in Manhattan, and their weekend retreats in the Hamptons.

It was a meeting of opposites. Karasik, 33, born in Bosnia, graduate of Columbia and Wharton, intense entrepreneur extraordinâire was already worth more than $250 million, and Stuart King, 29, scion of an influential British family and a rakish journalist for the most prestigious British newspaper. They could not have been more different. And that is precisely what Karasik saw in Stuart. An entrée to political connections that would prove extremely valuable. In turn, Stuart saw in Ken exactly what Ken wanted him to see—access to money and to a dangerous side that Ken kept hidden from most.

Their next encounter was almost a year later. Ken knew that as a journalist for one of the world's leading newspapers and a nephew to the former prime minister, Stuart could be an invaluable asset. By the time their second dinner was over, Stuart was on board.

He had agreed to subtly alter stories he was writing about the Balkans and to see what he could do politically. In return, Stuart received useful information from Ken for his newspaper and access to another party circuit. Surprisingly, it also made Stuart feel useful to be doing something about the atrocities he had first witnessed almost a decade earlier.

Over the next few years, the relationship between Ken and Stuart became more complex. Stuart increasingly ignored his journalistic ethics to help Ken, not only as it related to the Balkans, but also on issues important to Ken's business interests in Europe. Each article helped Ken achieve an important business or political objective.

The more Stuart understood what he was a part of, the more eager he was to help. And help he did. He used his contacts to influence the British government at critical moments in 2000 and 2001, when action was finally taken against Milosevic. His efforts also helped ease the way for Ken's many companies to do business in the United Kingdom, the Common Market and later, the European Union into which it evolved. In return, Stuart was taken into Ken's confidence and helped plan some of the more extreme actions undertaken by Raic, Opperman and Bottner.

While he affected inattentiveness, his contributions proved anything but.

# THIRTY

**B**ACK IN HIS LONDON office, Petar punched in the 13-digit code. After Karasik's perfunctory answer, Petar advised, "It's a go at all five facilities."

Within a few days, tainted nermycin and substandard cyprofaxin were readied for shipment from facilities in India, China, Malaysia and Myanmar.

After nearly two months in Pune, Jim and Ron had been back at PharmCorp's Mexican R&D facility in Guadalajara for about three weeks. While in Pune, they had been able to tweak the engineering so the tainted nermycin would remain stable for up to six months. It had been an interesting problem and they enjoyed solving it. That people might die wasn't their concern. Getting paid was.

"Have you heard anything yet?" Jim asked Ron, talking about their overdue bonuses.

"Nah. I'll give it another few days, but then I'm gonna start making some waves," Ron replied.

The two colleagues headed out to the parking lot. They both had beautiful beachfront houses. A half-million-a-year went far in Mexico.

Jim located his brand new silver 2006 Mercedes SLC55 AMG. A cool $140,000. He keyed the remote and the locks opened. Within seconds he was in the car listening to the 5.4 liter V8 roar. He loved that sound and he loved the ride that would take him home in under half an hour. He waved to Ron and headed out of the lot.

At about the same time, Ron slid into his blue 2005 Aston Martin DB9 coupe. At more than $180,000, it was the most expensive thing Ron had ever owned. He constantly washed the car and he sent it in for check-up every month. It was his baby. As he pulled out of the lot, his V12 made quite a statement. Just the right statement for Luisa, his date for the evening.

Jim never made it home and Ron never met Luisa that night. About 10 minutes after they left the parking lot two explosions ripped through the hot Guadalajara night. Jim and Ron were killed instantly and $320,000 of sports cars turned to junk.

"We're proceeding with distribution," Bowne reported to Estrich and Cole. The three of them were having lunch in the PharmCorp executive dining room on the 42$^{nd}$ floor of PharmCorp Tower in New York City. The rich wood paneling, leather chairs and food were more like a five-star restaurant than any employee cafeteria. It was one of the perks they were fighting to preserve.

"And that little problem?" Estrich asked, taking a sip of water as the waiter placed his braised duck in front of him.

Bowne eyed his 14-oz steak and responded, "It's been solved."

David Cole, PharmCorp's chairman and chief executive officer, absorbed the conversation, quietly eating the Cobb salad he had selected. Then, he did what he did so well—he took control, "Good! Now, let's talk about our lobbying efforts. We've got to make certain that Congress and the American people understand the dangers of imported and reimported drugs. God knows there are counterfeiters everywhere and the risk of terrorist attack is almost too awful to contemplate. But, if something goes wrong, we have to make certain the industry is at the forefront of 'solving' the problem."

Taking the cue, Estrich added, "There are bills in front of Congress to make it easier for foreigners to sell drugs here. Those bills are bad for the American public. It's our job to make certain they know that."

"They will. Soon enough, they will," Bowne slowly said in an almost singsong voice.

They all chuckled as they continued their dinner and started planning the lobbying effort to come.


It had taken Barry Weiner almost 18 months to get to this point, but thanks to their mysterious informant and disturbing reports from Interpol and police agencies in Switzerland and India, there was now broad interest in learning more about C3 and Ken Karasik. With the Toi announcement out of the way, Francine turned her task force's attention to C3, MDB, Ken Karasik and Mel Bottner. By the beginning of September, the FBI, Justice Department and Interpol also were investigating.

"There are too many inconsistencies," Weiner told Francine by phone. "I want to revisit *antidote.com*'s connections to C3 Pharmaceuticals in Zurich."

After saying good-bye to Francine, Weiner called in Chris Calandra, the agent who had uncovered *antidote.com*'s Cayman Island accounts. "You have to intensify your efforts to track funds into and out of *antidote.com*. I know the difficulties, but I want to prove the connection with C3."

"You know the problem. I've had no luck so far. The Cayman banks are not cooperating and their government just turns a blind eye. We may be at a dead end," Calandra demurred.

"Chris, you're just going to have to find a way," Barry said, ending the discussion.

Canadian authorities were unusually cooperative in arranging for an FBI Special Agent and an FDA investigator to interview the Cowells, the Winnipeg couple who supposedly owned *antidote.com*. Bright and early one morning, Barry and Francine boarded Air Canada Flight 5963, leaving out of Dulles at 7:59 am for Chicago's O'Hare Airport. At O'Hare, they transferred to Air Canada Flight 4560, arriving in Winnipeg at 12:13 pm. Both flights were about two-thirds full, and uneventful. When they arrived at Winnipeg, they stopped briefly to eat lunch, and then waited for an officer of the Royal Canadian Mounted Police who had agreed to meet them at 1:00 pm for the 20-minute ride to the modest home in which the owners of *antidote.com* lived.

As they pulled up, Francine commented, "This is a very nice neighborhood and the homes are obviously well cared for, but the people who own *antidote.com* should be living in a much nicer place. Either they don't care about money, or they aren't the real owners." Barry agreed. RCMP Constable O'Brien knocked on the door. They waited a moment, and when there was no answer, O'Brien knocked again. "I told them yesterday that we would be here between 1:30 and 2:00," O'Brien remarked as he rubbed his chin. "Let me take a look around back," he added.

A moment later, O'Brien returned. "I think you need to see this," he said. They all walked around to the back of the small but comfortable house. When they got there, O'Brien pointed to the rear door, which was ajar. "Don't touch anything," he said. Barry was getting a bad feeling about this. A moment later, they all had a bad feeling, particularly Francine who had never before seen a dead body. Her first two were particularly gruesome. John and Harriet Cowell were slumped backwards in their easy chairs. Their throats had been slashed from ear to ear. Still crimson-colored blood was coagulating on their laps.

As O'Brien called for the medical examiner and crime scene investigators, Barry punched some numbers on his cell phone and asked his assistant to cancel their hotel reservations and make arrangements for their immediate return to Washington.

The Cowells couldn't have been dead more than a few hours. "This isn't a coincidence. Someone knew we were coming. Obviously, they didn't think this interview was a good thing," Barry told Francine.

"Most drug counterfeiters avoid violence, "Francine observed.

"I know. But we're dealing with murderers. This is something much worse than mere counterfeiting," Barry answered as they got into Constable O'Brien's car. They all returned to the airport with a renewed sense of urgency.

# THIRTY ONE

**A**S ADULTERATED NERMYCIN and subpotent cyprofaxin rolled off the production lines in India, Malaysia, Myanmar and China, a certain Panamanian distributor contacted many of the least reputable Internet web sites, particularly those willing to fill orders without requiring a prescription. C3 reduced shipments of Nermycin-X, forcing customers to select the generic alternatives. Meanwhile, Inversiones y Distribución Médicas de Las Producciones offered special deals on nermycin and cyprofaxin. The goal was to "sell in" the equivalent of at least 500,000 courses of both drugs by early January, so the tainted product would start shipping to end users in November.

"At least one thing is going far better than we had hoped," Bowne reported to Cole and Estrich. "As you know, the attack will be in the guise of treating staph infections. Many doctors prescribe a cocktail of drugs in the cyprofaxin and nermycin families. With the tainted product, once the drugs interact somewhere between 10% and 30% of those receiving treatment will ultimately get sick. Because we've experienced an outbreak of staph infections this year, that means a much quicker sell-in."

"What's the pathology?" Cole asked. Bowne, Cole, Estrich and Bowne's deputy Max Linville were in the secure room on the 50$^{th}$ floor of PharmCorp Tower. Linville had been brought into their covert group when Ben asked for help. The request necessitated Ben's explaining the nature of the attack to Bowne. Ben kept secret the identity of the terrorist cell that would undertake the attack, though Bowne had his suspicions. Bowne had used Linville to coordinate with the R&D facility in Pune.

Linville was a small ferret-faced man who had spent the last nine years at PharmCorp as Bowne's deputy. Before that, he had been involved for more than 20 years in special projects for one large multi-national after another.

"As patients ingest the nermycin and the cyprofaxin, the inert toxin in the nermycin is activated. In those most susceptible, a five-day treatment might trigger pneumonia-like symptoms within as little as a week to 10 days. In other instances, even eight or 10 days of the drugs might not lead to disease, or only minor symptoms, easily confused with a cold. To some degree it depends on whether the patient selects a full-strength cyprofaxin or the weaker product the 'consultants' intend to offer," Bowne explained.

"In fact," Linville added, "If they purchase the subpotent product, more than half of the patients will require two complete courses to get their staph infections under control. That's perfect, because the tainted nermycin will be more than twice as dangerous when taken for two courses of treatment."

Bowne continued. "The incubation period for most patients who develop the 'pneumonia' is 20 to 30 days. Our guys predict that 10% of those taking a five-day course of treatment with the nermycin and 30% of those with eight-day courses will get sick. Based on the number of doses that will be manufactured and the elevated level of staph infections, our guys estimate that from 5,000 to 10,000 patients will become infected. The estimate for fatalities is 5% to 10%, so we are looking at 250 to 1,000 deaths. By the way, the fatality estimate has been reduced because our guys had to reduce the lethality of the latent toxin when they were in Pune."

"That's acceptable," Cole answered. "When do shipments start?"

"We're looking at later this month. The first illnesses should occur just after Thanksgiving," Bowne answered.

"And the claim of responsibility?" Estrich asked.

"To be honest, I'm a little vague on that. As I understand it, the claim will come in December or January when all of the product has been purchased and used by patients," Bowne answered, for the first time showing some weakness in his grasp of the plan.

"Bill, we're not paying $150 million to guess at the denouement. By the time we next speak, I expect to know what we're getting for our money," Cole pointedly observed.


Ben had told Bowne that only a very limited number of adulterated nermycin tablets would be manufactured. In fact, the Karasik Commission intended to manufacture almost 20 times that number and to continue selling the tainted product until their supplies were exhausted. At least 25,000 patients would be infected within six weeks after sales began and depending upon how many Americans purchased the weaker cyprofaxin there could be 100,000 victims in that time. With a morbidity rate of 5% to 10%, that still translated to more than 10,000 deaths within the first two months of sales. The risk of death was particularly high for the young and the old as well as those with compromised immune systems, though most normally healthy adults would probably survive the pneumonia that resulted from the interaction between cyprofaxin and the tainted nermycin.

Ben had also failed to share two very important items of information with his PharmCorp client: there was an antidote for the nermycin, and the antidote, Abcyclene, was manufactured by a European subsidiary of PharmCorp. Ben reasoned that it was unnecessary for PharmCorp to know there was an antidote, and besides, they had never asked.

Ben realized that Bowne would have been very unhappy to learn that the secret antidote was a drug owned by PharmCorp. That news could point a finger directly at the pharmaceutical giant. Some cynics might then even assert that PharmCorp had created the incident just to sell more Abcyclene.

"There's no accounting for the wild theories some people might leap to," Ben told Tom when he explained why PharmCorp would be less than pleased to learn about the antidote.


When Barry Weiner and Francine Pye returned from Winnipeg, their new urgency was obvious. Wiener immediately contacted Lisa Fuller. There was no time for their usual flirting. "People have already died, Lisa. You've got to get us complete cooperation from the IRS and Inland Revenue. And this stonewalling in the Caymans and Switzerland has to end. If we don't track the money, we're never going to prove our case. There are at least two dead and I'm telling you there are going to be a lot more dead if we don't act."

Lisa had never seen Weiner be so strong. "I'll do my best, "she said. "But don't expect miracles, especially in the Caymans and Switzerland." Despite her superb efforts, her admonition proved to be prophetic.

"The IRS is on board, and believe it or not, we also got Inland Revenue to cooperate. But, no luck in the Caymans or with Swiss banking officials," Lisa reported to Barry.

"Not good enough," was all the thanks she got. Assisted by Calandra, she continued her efforts.

By the end of the week, the IRS and the Financial Crimes division of the FBI started poring over Karasik's and C3's financial records. The following Monday, Greg Schoenfeld issued a broad subpoena that required the C3 Group to divulge everything about its activities involving pharmaceuticals and the allegations in Europe.

A week later, Lisa finally reported a small crack in the Swiss wall of secrecy. "This is as good as it's going to get," an exhausted Lisa reported. "The Swiss just won't force their banks to share financial information with the FBI—but, they've agreed to issue requests for information to both C3 Pharmaceuticals' and MDB Pharmaceuticals' Zurich offices. They aren't promising to tell us what they find, but they aren't telling us they won't."

"That's great Lisa. I owe you one," an enthusiastic Barry told her.

"You owe me a lot more than one," Lisa answered before taking another call.

# THIRTY TWO

**C**3 FOUGHT BACK. Eric Jacobs filed motions to quash Schoenfeld's subpoenas. His papers called the investigation "nothing more than transparent harassment." Jacobs argued that if any crimes had been committed, they were outside of the United States and beyond U.S. jurisdiction.

C3 and MDB also fought back through their friends in government. The two companies, with combined sales in the tens of billions of dollars, made it clear that the continuing investigations would jeopardize important energy contracts that were vital to the United States and several European nations. Petar Raic, chief operations officer of the entire C3 Group, personally visited with the Finance Minister in Switzerland to point out just how many jobs and how much investment was at risk. The reception was surprisingly warm given the investigation underway.

PharmCorp just stood aside. When Cathy Lee, Bowne's chief lobbyist in Washington, reported rumors of an FBI investigation of C3 and MDB, Bowne instructed her to "find out what you can, but take no action." Bowne wondered whether the investigation had anything to do with Opperman. He would not be surprised if it did.

As he told Estrich the following day, "If there's a connection, we don't want the attack to be derailed. Of course, once it's over, it wouldn't be a bad thing if the FBI closed them down—two fewer competitors for us to worry about."

"Keep me apprised," was Estrich's only response as he headed to the PharmCorp fitness center for his daily game of squash.

By early November, the first shipments of tainted nermycin and substandard cyprofaxin were reaching U.S. patients eager to treat their staph infections. In some cases, one course of treatment (about five days of both drugs) was sufficient to treat the infection, but in many other instances, it took two courses. At times, the cyprofaxin was so dilute that even a second course was insufficient. Given the poor quality of the drugs delivered by the Canadian web sites, many of those who purchased the knock-offs remained sick longer than was necessary.

As shipments began, Ken, Mel and Petar again gathered in New York. Ben was unavailable.

"Let's walk through the timeline one last time," Ken requested.

"Based on current shipments, more than 150,000 Americans could be infected by February," Petar explained. "But, given the incubation period, only a few thousand are expected to get sick by the end of January, and perhaps 25,000 by the end of February. Just a month later, the number of those infected could grow to 150,000."

"Of course, deaths would lag. Large-scale deaths probably won't begin until March, with a sizeable death toll by April or May," Mel pointed out.

"Or, if America complies, we'll tell them about Abcyclene, and fewer than 500 might die. It's up to them," Ken responded.

"If we don't tell them about Abcyclene, it will take at least until June or July to figure out the cause and identify a treatment. By then 50,000 will be dead, and perhaps many more. It's a lot less than we had hoped for, but that's almost as many deaths as America suffered in Vietnam," Mel added.

"Let's hope that doesn't need to happen," Ken replied.

By the middle of November, *antidote.com* and more than a dozen other web sites were busy filling orders for cyprofaxin and nermycin.

As Thanksgiving rolled around, a few cases of apparent pneumonia were beginning to appear among the very young and the very old. All would have been perfect for the Karasik Commission, but for Weiner's investigation, and the growing death toll in the Balkans. Maslac's attack that week on a Tuzla police station had exterminated 108 Slavs, and instilled fear throughout the region. That "but" was by no means inconsequential.

Ken usually looked forward to Thanksgiving in Hillcrest Valley. This year would be different. He had invited Ben, Stuart, Petar and Mel to the Bolero Road estate for the Thanksgiving celebration. There was some peril in having them all together in a somewhat public way, particularly Ben, who had no known association with C3. Ken thought about it. The other guests would consist of his closest business associates, Nely's personal friends, and Alexa. His wife and Alexa had become very close. He didn't yet know if he approved.

Given all that was happening, it was worth the risk for Ben to attend. He had to get the entire group together. Ken concluded that Project Sky was in danger, and finding a solution to that problem was far more important than the extremely limited risk of exposure.

A few days later the Karasik Commission met on Ken's houseboat near Hillcrest Valley. The endgame was in sight. Too many sacrifices had been made to permit Barry Weiner or anyone else to interfere in their plans. As expected, Mel, Ben, Petar and Stuart had developed recommendations to stop Weiner and ensure the success of Project Sky. That success would once and for all free the Balkans of men like Ivan Maslac. Ken considered the plan, made a few adjustments and smiled.

It would take another several weeks before all was ready. But, when that happened, Ken was very certain the United States would play its role perfectly. The Karasik Commission would win, as it always did.

# THIRTY THREE

"**I** NEED YOU TO intervene," Karasik told the distinguished-looking man sitting next to him. The two seldom met, but this was not the time for half measures. Karasik had flown to Washington, D.C., where he managed to elude the team the FBI had assigned to observe him by unexpectedly hurrying into the Metro at L'Enfant Plaza and boarding the Green Line. Karasik rode the subway for some 19 minutes, emerging at the Branch Avenue Metro Station in Suitland, Maryland eight miles away.

At about the same time Karasik entered the L'Enfant Plaza station, a man headed out of the Justice Department, passed the FBI's J. Edgar Hoover Building, and entered the Archives Metro Station. There, he also boarded the Green Line headed for Suitland.

When Karasik left the train at the Branch Avenue Station, he observed an elegantly-attired man leaving the forward car. They ignored each other and as pre-arranged, the men headed, separately, to the coffee shop a block away from the station. Only when both were certain they were not being followed did they take seats together in the back. They each ordered a cup of coffee. When the waitress left, Karasik told Jason Waters that he would have to intervene. The Deputy Attorney General of the United States wasn't pleased.

"Ten years ago when I agreed to work with you, it was our understanding that you would never operate in the United States.

We agreed that if you kept your activities in Europe and Asia, I could protect you. And, I have."

What Waters said was true. At 55, Waters was another example of the American dream. Jason Waters was born in 1950 in Bihac, Bosnia. He was fortunate to immigrate to the United States in 1970 when the 20-year-old, then known as Anton Karasik, joined his grandfather Tomislav for the dangerous journey out of Yugoslavia. He entered the United States as Jason Waters, the name on his forged papers, and never again used his birth name. Like Ken, the newly-minted Jason Waters converted to Catholicism. Waters had embraced his conversion, marrying a devout Catholic and sending his three children to St. Mary's for their education. In his heart, however, Waters never forgot who he was: a very lucky man from a region the Western world simply chose to forget.

After receiving a degree in history from New York University and a law degree from Yale, he clerked for the Second Circuit Court of Appeals. Then, after just five years as an associate with the prestigious New York law firm of White & Cromwell, he was elected a partner. He left when he was appointed the U.S. Attorney for the Southern District of New York, a job he held for 'four years before being named Deputy Director of the FBI. By the time he met with his cousin in the coffee shop in Suitland, Waters was completing his third year as the second most powerful person in the Justice Department, behind only the Attorney General.

"Yes, but we also agreed that circumstances had changed," Karasik replied.

"No. You started selling drugs into the United States at a time when nothing had changed. Nothing—except your greed. Still, I stood by you. And, I stood by you with this ridiculous Project Sky. Your mother was my aunt. Your brother was my cousin. I also lost family and friends to Milosevic and Maslac. But, you are going too far." Waters looked pained as he spoke almost in a whisper.

"No! What we are doing now is the right thing and you know it. We believed in America and it betrayed us. It has ignored our families and tens of thousands died. Srebrenica was 10 years ago. Still, Mladic and Karadzic are free. They pay lip service, but it's as if we never existed. We have tried to be patient. There is no alternative!"

The cousins continued their argument for almost 20 minutes. It was an argument they'd had before. Finally, as always happened, Waters gave in. Still, he was uncertain about how to intervene. "The investigation is gaining momentum. This informer has given credibility to charges that would otherwise be dismissed. The FBI doesn't know who she is. You've got to find her and silence her. Beyond that, I transferred the lawyer who was helping Weiner. I also managed to sidetrack her requests to Swiss banking officials and the Cayman Islands. Those requests will go nowhere, which should keep the money trail a secret."

"Even if they got through to the Caymans or Switzerland, they would never be able to track the funds," Karasik said. "Nonetheless, I appreciate what you have done. Anything that slows them down will give us the extra time we need to cover our tracks and achieve success."

"I will do whatever I can, my cousin," Waters said.

With that, the only surviving Karasiks departed, each heading out of Suitland, Maryland by different means.

# THIRTY FOUR

"**I** BELIEVE KARASIK IS dirty and that he is behind *antidote.com* and half a dozen other sites. With the feedback we have received from Europe, I am also convinced that he and Mel Bottner are planning something really big. We have to take action now." Barry Weiner was presenting the information he had developed to senior management of the FBI and Justice Department.

"We have credible evidence that Karasik has been involved in bribery and extortion involving at least three foreign governments, extensive gun running and possibly even assassinations in Serbia, as well as counterfeit drugs. We are getting reports of large-scale shipments into Canada and the U.S. of several drugs, including nermycin, which was developed by Karasik's company. Something is definitely happening. We should immediately freeze Karasik's assets under the Patriot Act," Weiner anxiously demanded.

Lisa Fuller was not in attendance. As Waters had informed Ken the previous day, the energetic and supportive lawyer had been re-assigned.

"Let's take it easy," Waters said. "You and Ms. Pye have done terrific work. The indictments against Toi and the impending indictments against Brower are clearly in the nation's best interests. But, I am not convinced on your case against Karasik. He has done a lot for the United States. Not only do his companies create employment for thousands of Americans, but he has been instrumental in securing energy contracts, and in developing new chemicals and new processes. His charitable contributions are legend. Against all that, you seem to have mere speculation. And, even if what you allege is true, most of these so-called crimes don't involve the United States."

"I am inclined to agree," FBI Assistant Director Richard Goldstein opined. "I want to echo Jason's views as to Toi and Brower. However, I am most concerned about taking actions based solely on unsubstantiated rumors in Europe. As to the drugs, if this involved terrorism I would back you 100%, but the Patriot Act was not designed to fight violations of FDA rules."

Weiner was exasperated. He probably had them convinced that Karasik was involved in counterfeit drugs. And, while that was a crime, it just didn't rise to the level of a terrorist attack. He decided to try once more.

"At least permit me to obtain wiretaps. Let's not forget about our informer. From what she tells us, whether you want to call it terrorism or just plain murder, C3 is up to its neck in selling bad medicine to good Americans."

"I'll tell you what, Barry," Goldstein began, "I'm taking a few days of vacation with my family. Why don't you continue your investigation without any wiretaps. Karasik or someone at C3 may be dirty, but I am not convinced that it's terrorism. If you and your girlfriend can change my mind, I'll revisit this next week, when I return. Thank you, gentlemen."

With that, Goldstein adjourned the meeting and Barry reluctantly returned to his office, calling for Landau and Calandra to join him.

"We got shot down. You guys have done terrific work, but we just have to keep digging until even Goldstein and Waters have to listen."

"Don't worry, Barry, we're not giving up," Calandra responded. While Landau looked a little down, he nodded his agreement.

Barry next called Francine to tell her about the meeting. "I convinced Goldstein that someone at C3 is dirty. But it's not enough."

"I'm supposed to be looking for counterfeiters not terrorists. Maybe that's all Karasik is. Then again, maybe you're right," Francine said.

"Ken Karasik is planning a terrible attack on the United States and I am going to do my best to stop him," Barry resolutely replied.

"Then I'll be right there with you," Francine earnestly assured him.

# THIRTY FIVE

*I*T HAD BEEN raining for days but the sun came out on Saturday morning. External forces no longer affected Alexa's outlook on life. All of the hopes and dreams that she had shared with Grandpa were over. Simply vanished, in an instant. Just a few days after the New Year began, Nedeljko "Nicolas" Bartanovic was laid to rest in a simple grave at Green Acres in Paradise Cove. Only Alexa, Marcus and Nely were in attendance. A local priest presided over the service where a simple Mass was said without Communion. A single arrangement of two dozen Casablanca lilies in a bed of lime green leaves lay on top of the mahogany casket.

The body was lowered into the ground. The priest handed Alexa a small silver shovel and a bucket of dirt to throw over the casket. She was horrified when the dry dirt hit the wood. It seemed a final insult. She emptied the bucket into the grave as tears rolled down her cheeks. Silently, she said good-bye.


Grandpa's house no longer felt like home to her. She would give it a reasonable amount of time and then move elsewhere. That elsewhere was a world of possibilities, but it was not a decision she could make that day or that week. Instead, she phoned Nely to thank her for attending Grandpa's funeral.

Nely said the right things, but Alexa heard something in her voice that seemed odd. "Is everything alright?" she asked.

"Everything is just fine!" Nely replied, as she always did, no matter what was happening.

Alexa paused. "I'll be there in 10 minutes," she said, despite her grief.

When Alexa arrived at Nely's house, Nely looked terrible. They walked over to the cozy, overstuffed sitting room off of the kitchen. The bay windows looked onto the estate's beautiful gardens.

"Thanks for coming. I know this isn't a good day for you," Nely started.

"That's alright. What's wrong?"

"Alexa, I just don't know what to do. This morning Ken and his lawyers flew to Switzerland without any warning, and then I found this." Nely pulled a crumpled sheet of paper from her hand-bag. She flattened it out and slid the wrinkled page across the coffee table to Alexa. Alexa picked it up and began to read. It was a faxed copy of a small article that had run the day before in a Swiss newspaper. The article briefly described the investigation of C3 and Ken Karasik.

With the first tears that Alexa ever saw in Nely's eyes, she whispered, "They're going to blow this up. Soon, it will be in news-papers all over the world."

Alexa froze. The last paragraph included a brief list of the prod-ucts manufactured by C3 Pharmaceuticals, including Raphlen and Nermycin-X! Alexa instantly thought about the note she had found in Grandpa's belongings. Things fell into place for her. She thought she might know more than she had ever wanted to know. And, while she still didn't know everything, she knew far more than Nely.

Alexa wanted to leave, to digest this new information. But, with almost superhuman effort she retained her composure. Before deciding what to do next, she had to learn everything Nely knew. And then, she had to get away to think things through.

Despite Alexa's best efforts, Nely saw her reaction. But, as usual, Nely misunderstood. She thought Alexa was reacting out of concern for her, rather than out of sheer hatred and horror that her beloved Grandpa Nico had been murdered by *her friend,* Ken Karasik. To Nely, Alexa was a dear and trusted friend. Someone who was a little better educated and a little more traveled than the rest of her girlfriends, but certainly not someone who knew *anything,* let alone *more* than she did about the secret life of Ken Karasik.

Alexa collected her thoughts. "Look, we need to keep our wits about ourselves right now and deal with one issue at a time, ok?" Alexa reasoned with her. Nely was all too eager for any sense of direction.

"First of all, unless you talk to anyone and there's a leak, no one in New Mexico, let alone Hillcrest Valley, will ever find out about this," Alexa explained. "This is an international news item that will be buried in the financial pages here in the U.S. Lucky for us, our friends won't see this." She got a wan smile out of Nely.

"I'll call a clipping service I know. They'll get you copies of any other articles that run, anywhere in the world. Second, I'll place some calls to some people I know who may tell us something more of Ken's fate. Third, you need to place all of your valuables in a secret location that no one can get to. You need to pack and be prepared to go to a safe place—just in case. You may need to get out of the country, but by no means set foot in any European Union country. Do you understand?"

"Not really. But I'll do as you say," Nely replied, barely comprehending the stream of instructions.

"Good. The fact is this will probably blow over," Alexa said, thinking that Grandpa's death and Ken's role in it would never blow over as far as she was concerned.

"How long have we been the best of friends now?" Nely asked.

"Over a year," Alexa replied, wondering where this was headed.

. "You know you're like a sister to me, and with the passing of your grandfather, and no family except for Marcus, I know how you must feel."

*You have no clue!* Alexa thought of the woman with at least 10,000 immediate relations, growing angry that she was here consoling Nely, when Nely should be consoling her.

Almost as if she read Alexa's mind, Nely said "Although I've heard a lot about your grandfather over the years, you never talk about your parents. Tell me about them."

Alexa lay down on the plush sofa. Without much thought, she said, "I was born Alexia Maria Horst. When grandpa adopted me, I legally became Alexa Bart. I am the only daughter of Hans Horst. Do you know who Dr. Horst was?" she asked.

"No," Nely replied, intrigued.

"Well, most everyone in the scientific world does. He was a very important scientist—a biochemist."

"Really?" Nely said, astonished that Alexa might have come from such a gene pool.

"Um-hm," Alexa grumbled. "Unfortunately, he was conscripted by the *Stasi* to work on top secret weapons for the East Germans. My father knew that it was going to be impossible for him to flee the Communist regime—or even remain alive—if he didn't did do exactly as he was told. He wanted to secure my future should things not go as planned."

Alexa glanced archly at Nely. *She's hooked.*

"My grandparents never evolved with the changing times. When my mother was 13 years old, her father—my real grandfather—told her that she would be marrying my father. My grandfather had written to a bachelor friend, Mr. Hans Horst by name, and told him that he could have her if he wanted her—that is, after certain preliminaries had been arranged."

"Nico did that?" Nely asked, confused.

"No. Nico was really my uncle, but he raised me ever since I came to America. As far as I'm concerned, he was everything to me! I never knew my mother's father," Alexa adamantly answered.

"I understand about Nico, truly," Nely compassionately replied. "But, I don't understand what happened. Your real grandfather sold your mother?"

"This Hans Horst had been at my mother's residence on a visit several months before. Apparently, he had noticed her. He then intimated that if my grandfather wished to get rid of her, it could be brought about. She did not recall him, as her father had many important visitors," Alexa continued.

Nely looked horrified. Alexa held back a grin.

Alexa couldn't help herself. Nely knew nothing about the prohibition of religious freedoms in East Germany. "Just a few weeks later," Alexa said, "they were married by a bishop, with two priests and four altar boys to assist."

Nely was sobbing.

"I was born the following year. My parents died when I was eight years old," Alexa said somberly. "I was sent to live in Switzerland with my Uncle Carl and Aunt Maria. After a while, I was sent to the U.S. and my uncle—my Grandpa Nico—adopted me," she explained, this time telling the truth.

"Oh, I'm sorry. I'm so, so sorry," Nely got up and moved aimlessly about. "This is all so depressing right now."

Alexa was enjoying Nely's horror, as she did her best to hide the most profound hatred she had ever experienced. Now she knew not only that Ken Karasik was responsible for what happened to her Uncle Carl, but that he had also killed Grandpa Nico! What kind of monster was this man, this so-called friend, the husband of her best friend.

Still sobbing, Nely couldn't bear to hear any more, so she changed the subject. "Listen, with all of this going on, I almost forgot to tell you something. Next Friday, Faisal Ayoub is coming here to dinner from London."

Alexa quickly sat up. "You know Faisal Ayoub?"

"No. But he knows of some of my philanthropic work. So he contacted me to see if we could work together. He's coming on Friday. Obviously, I will do a dinner in his honor. Be sure to be here, ok?"

"Nely, are you sure about this?" Alexa inquired, satisfied that a very big fish would soon be on her hook.

"There you go being *negative* again!" Nely said, back in her element.


Friday evening, the staff was putting the finishing touches on the dinner party in honor of Faisal Ayoub. The dinner was to be held in the huge dining room where long tables with mint green linens and white Ecuadorian roses had been placed. Outside the large windows, high torches burned with bright flames and elaborate ice sculptures decorated the lawn.

Faisal arrived promptly at the appointed hour, strolling in from the guesthouse across the way. Nely greeted him warmly. They kissed on both cheeks. "I'm so happy that you had a day to relax and enjoy yourself in Hillcrest Valley," she told him.

Faisal was about to respond, when he became distracted. "Oh, my," he gasped.

"What's the matter?" Nely asked.

"Who is that lovely creature?" he inquired, gesturing to an attractive redhead standing among a group of other guests at the far end of the foyer.

Nely turned around. "Oh, her? That's Alexa. A friend of mine. You'll meet her a little later at dinner. I don't want to bother her...her grandfather died a few days ago."

"I'm so sorry," he replied.

*All was going according to plan.* Faisal was quite pleased with himself.

As more guests arrived, Faisal spoke with several of Ken's business associates, while Alexa continued to busy herself conversing with the locals. About half an hour later, Nely finally introduced Faisal and Alexa. The two exchanged polite pleasantries.

"I'll leave the two of you to get acquainted," Nely said. "Please excuse me for a moment."

Faisal and Alexa inspected each other.

"How is life treating you?" Faisal asked.

"I can't complain," Alexa spoke softly as she sipped Pellegrino.

"How clever you are," he remarked.

"You're not so dumb yourself," she answered.

"How is your Uncle?"

She ignored him.

"I would like to talk with you in private," he said.

"About what?"

"Did you think that settling in Hillcrest Valley would make you anonymous?"

"I don't know what you're talking about," Alexa cut him off. "I know it's only January, but I'm looking forward to spring," she observed, a complete non-sequitor.

"It seems that there is no such thing as spring," he said. "It is only the old season coming back." Their eyes briefly met. Faisal continued, "All the people in our lives, have they not been around before?"

"Surely they are the same creatures that populated the earth in days gone by," she replied, refusing to indulge his agenda.

"They are busy about the same things. They chase after the same trifles. They commit the same mistakes and blunders, as men have always done," he led her on.

"Different places, different times, it matters little," she spoke.

"Ah, but you are wrong," he said. "For time and place are often masters of fate. We both should know that…"

Alexa held her own. She studied him obliquely. He looked directly at her. "You have a face like a Benedictine monk," she blurted right out. "A wit that never lags. A generous heart when it suits you. And a tongue that runs like an Alpine cascade."

Faisal laughed, amused. And then continued to break her down in code, "A razor with which you cannot shave may have better metal in it than one with a perfect edge. It's just that one has been sharpened and the other not. And I am very sure that the men who succeed the best do not necessarily know the most; fate has simply put an edge on them—that's all." He paused. Alexa listened intently.

"As you are well aware, my dear, a good kick may start a stone rolling, when otherwise it rests on the mountain side for generations."

Alexa put her glass down sharply and walked away. He followed her.

She turned abruptly. "Why did you come here?"

"I saw you in London. What was I to conclude?" he said.

"Where did you see me?"

"In my store, where you wished me to see you, Alexia."

He grabbed her arm and then eased up. "Alexia...the sweet voiced, the mild, the sympathetic, the elegant, the gracious Alexia. You are favored by the gods with beauty and far-reaching intellect. And above all, you know the gold of silence. So I can only wonder—why?"

She pulled away. "You can never gain peace by striving for it like fury!" He spoke after her. She grinned inwardly, that he should make a comment like that of all people.

Nevertheless, he disturbed her.

Moments later, he caught up with her in the living room. "By doing what you have done, we end up with a lot of enemies...and here you are, in the middle of it," he said.

Alexa was not amused. "Strong people are not so defined by their loving friends as by their rabid enemies."

Faisal looked around the decadent digs. "But, persecution does have its compensation."

She knew what he meant. "Unfortunately, one's decline begins when one's prosperity commences," she volunteered. "Prosperous men are never wise and seldom good. Watch out when everyone starts to speak well of you!"

"I have no fears about that any time soon!" Faisal laughed.

But he pressed on, "How did you do it Alexia? Did you play the sympathy card?"

"I thought you said that I was clever. Sympathy is your game, sir."

"Alexia, Alexia," he crooned. "It took a thorn-crowned, bleeding Christ to win the adoration of the world. Only the souls who have suffered are well loved. And you weren't going to let all of your suffering go to waste."

"I do not live for the approval of others…" she corrected him.

Sarcastically, he went on, "I see that you still possess that firm reticence as to the supreme secrets of your life, and your steadfast loyalty to that which you believe is truth." He paused, "I tell you, it must forever command the affectionate admiration of those who prize integrity of mind, who hold fast to the divinity of love and believe in the things unseen which are eternal."

Alexa knew she was being insulted. "Life is a stern business, Mr. Ayoub, and this earth journey is warfare."

"How would your father feel if he knew?" He cut to the chase now.

"Knew what, Mr. Ayoub?" she forcefully inquired.

A bell rang and the butler summoned the guests to dinner, ending their duel, for the moment.


After dinner, a local orchestra played as the guests danced in the parlor and the main foyer. The beautiful double-height rooms had been decorated with special lighting, large candles, and flowers of every variety.

"Excuse me, sir. May I please cut in?" Faisal asked Lyle Cooper, a local developer who was waltzing with Alexa. The gentleman stepped aside and Faisal wasted no time. As they slowly danced, he resumed as though there had been no break in their conversation. "I can understand why you did what you did," he said. "But what I don't understand is *why* Karasik?"

"It's such a beautiful night," Alexa said dreamily. "There are no nights in London quite as beautiful as this, am I right?"

"Look, I'll be the first to admit that it's not fair, what happened to your father. He was a brilliant man. It's also not fair what happened to your Uncle. And it's certainly not fair what happened to you. But such is the world we live in, my dear child. It's not designed to be fair." He tried all angles, "Look at what's happening all around—one leader is deposed because he did nothing, and his successor gets an assassin's bullet because he did too much."

Alexa played along, "Certain men must be put out and others put in!"

"Your father was determined to save you even as he could not save himself. His gift was his mind and your inheritance was his greatest discovery. The Germans could not steal that from him."

Alexa hummed to the *Blue Danube Waltz* as they glided some space away from the nucleus of the party.

"Alexia," he continued virtually exasperated, "you could have done anything you wanted with his technology, so why did you sell out to Karasik?" he finally demanded to know.

With what she now knew about Karasik, she wondered the same thing. But, she would not give Faisal the satisfaction of being right. She continued to dance, seemingly oblivious to his chatter.

"Alexia, it is not too late. I know that you are a shrewd woman...you can still make an even greater fortune and a noble difference. I can help you! Together, we can become a force for the better," he offered adamantly.

"Knowing what I know," she began seriously, watching an earnest expression cross Faisal's face, "I think there is a lot of good dessert left in the kitchen. Some of that coconut torte would be divine!"

Faisal sighed in frustration as Alexa spun out of his arms and dashed toward the front door.

Alexa requested her shawl and handbag from the butler and headed out the door.

"Is she leaving?" Faisal asked Nely.

"Looks that way," she replied. They looked out the window as Alexa got into her Mini Cooper and headed away. "I thought she was having fun. I don't always understand that girl," Nely added.

Faisal laughed. "Yes, she is a very clever girl. Very clever…"

Nely looked at him, shrugged her shoulders, and steered him out onto the dance floor.

# THIRTY SIX

**A**FTER ALMOST SIX months of surveillance uncovered nothing unusual about Nely, at least not any more unusual than would be expected given her idiosyncrasies and, in Ben's view, somewhat extravagant tastes, Ben was inclined to end the surveillance. Ken had never been happy with the thought that his wife was a suspect, and would no doubt be pleased to end the unwelcome intrusion into his personal life. And yet, they were no closer to finding the source of the leaks to the FBI. With Project Sky already in progress, and the time rapidly approaching for their demands to be made, Ben was loath to lose any opportunity to find their Judas. After careful thought, he decided to continue the surveillance just a little longer.

"Ben, I'm not happy. The hearings will soon start and not one word has been publicized. There's nothing in the press, and more importantly, there've been no terrorist threats or claims. What are you doing to me?" William Bowne said over the secure line he had established after demanding that Tom Biffar arrange for this call.

"Bill, you have to calm down. Everything is on schedule. Tainted nermycin is shipping, our intelligence shows us that people are getting sick and at least 50 to 100 have already died. Yet, no warnings anywhere. It's perfect."

"What the fuck do you mean perfect? Where's the fucking terrorist claim?" Bowne responded in language making clear his exasperation.

"Bill, that's not necessary," the unflappable operative replied. "I know we're a couple of weeks behind, but we agreed that at least 250 deaths had to occur before an announcement. It does us no good if the FDA or DEA close down our shipments, or the CDC develops a cure. Just give it another couple of weeks."

"What do you mean close down shipments? By now, all of the tainted medicine should have been sold. The attack should be just about over. And why does it do us no good for a couple of hundred Americans to die. That's just the point we wanted to make!"

"Look, Bill, there are other people involved. A terrorist attack is not an advertising campaign. You don't just buy the media, or pull the ads if you're not happy. There are a lot of very dangerous people I have to keep happy."

"You mean your friends Karasik and Bottner?" Bowne asked.

Ben snapped back, "What are you talking about?"

"What do you think. We're PharmCorp. We have our sources. I know the FBI is investigating C3 and MDB. I can put two and two together."

"Well this time you put two and two together and got 12. I suggest you keep your theories to yourself. If you try connecting too many dots you can get caught in the web."

"Are you now threatening me, Ben?"

"Whoa. Slow down. I'm not threatening anyone. I think you're getting nervous. I know you're under pressure, but it just doesn't do either of us any good to start throwing darts, particularly on this project. Just let it be another few weeks and I assure you the outcome will be well worth the wait."

"You haven't answered my question about why shipments are continuing," Bowne answered, unaccustomed to backing down.

"Shipments are continuing because yours is not the only agenda. To make this work, I've had to balance the agendas. The total shipments may be somewhat greater than your preference, but it won't change the outcome."

"The hell it won't. A lot more people are going to die."

"It's a little late to be getting a conscience, isn't it, Bill?"

"Fuck you. If this falls apart, you're going down with it. I'll talk to you in two weeks, and I better hear some good news."

After disconnecting, Ben stared out of the window of his Paris office. Then, he pressed the speed dial for Tom Biffar.

"Tom, we might have a problem. Bowne is smart. He's figured out that the shipments are larger than he expected. He's upset about the delay in the terrorist demand, and he suspects Ken's and Mel's involvement. We may have to sever our ties."

"Do you think he passed on his concerns and suspicions to anyone else?" Tom asked.

"I don't know. Next time you talk to him, sniff around."

When Bowne hung up, he looked across his desk at Max Linville.

"Ok, you heard what's going on. Let's get some teams ready to move. Start tracking Opperman and while you're at it, let's keep an eye on Biffar. Meantime, let's step up security over here. I wouldn't want to wager on whether they'd try a pre-emptive strike, especially if things are as big a mess as they might be."

Linville looked concerned. He was, not only for what Opperman might do, but also for what Estrich and Cole would do when they found out. Linville was a tough character who knew how to take care of himself. But, compared to Opperman, Bowne or Estrich, he was a minnow.

Alexa was restless and tired. The old house was the last place she wanted to be—ever again. She felt drained. The time was coming to move on.

Her cell phone rang. She recognized the caller's ID and on the last ring, she picked up, "Yes."

"That's the right answer," the male voice said.

Tired, she chuckled nevertheless.

"What are you doing?" he asked.

"Nothing," she replied.

He understood her anguish even though he rarely heard anything but optimism and wicked wit from her. "Listen, I miss you," he said sincerely. "How about you get on a plane tomorrow and we meet in New York?"

Alexa never acted without purpose, but today would be different. Without thinking or hesitation, she simply said, "Ok. I'd love to see you."

This pleased her lover; he was genuinely fond of Alexa. The two shared a history that creates a lifelong bond between man and woman, regardless of their destiny or the eventual outcome of their relationship. "Cleo will make the arrangements and I'll have Gerry pick you up at the airport," he said.

Just past 6:00 the following evening, Alexa landed at La Guardia's American Airlines terminal. Having lost nearly 10 pounds following Nico's death, she looked unusually lean in her black cashmere turtleneck and jeans tucked into a pair of black suede stiletto boots. Her lush red hair was full and curly and now past her shoulders in length.

Gerry, the always reliable chauffeur, met her as she passed through security. His dedication and discretion were unsurpassed.

The drive from the airport into Manhattan was a painless half hour. Alexa rarely stayed at his lavish apartment at Trump Tower. On occasion, she settled into the posh apartment she had purchased some years ago on Fifth Avenue and 78$^{th}$ Street. The eleventh floor residence had magnificent views of Fifth Avenue. Undoubtedly, she would be using the apartment more often, now that her time in Hillcrest Valley was drawing to a close.

This time, Alexa preferred to blend in and checked into her favorite hotel instead—the St. Regis. It was a stone's throw from the Trump Tower and within strolling distance of all of her favorite boutiques. This was going to be a vital transition time, a turning point, and Alexa was determined to figure out the next course of her life. *Who knows?* She thought to herself. She might even settle down, get married and raise a family.

As Alexa relaxed in her opulent suite, she slipped into the hotel's cozy bathrobe and began to draw a hot bath in the sunken tub. He would not arrive until tomorrow, and God knew Alexa needed a restful and dream-filled night. Fortunately, she slept for nine hours and awoke refreshed. She spent the day visiting some old friends and updating her wardrobe to her new weight, before returning to the hotel to get ready for dinner.

At 6:55 there was a knock on Alexa's door. She rushed to open it only to encounter dozens of roses in delicate shades of pastel pink. Standing right behind the massive bouquet was the only person she wanted to see right now. He placed the flowers on the table and hugged her passionately. As always, he seemed to have her under his spell. She kissed him longingly and they just wouldn't end their embrace.

"I would rather we not go anywhere," he whispered in her ear, "but let me guess, you're hungry, right?"

"You guessed it!" Alexa replied.

"C'mon, let's feed you," he said in total resignation.

Alexa loved Manhattan in the winter. Le Cirque 2000 offered the best food, even if she wasn't too crazy about its retro 50s décor. He would do anything to please her. Their favorite table in the corner by the street window was ready and waiting. The wine was already chilled and on the table. A special cabbage soup that the chef had just created and a silver bowl of caviar with blinis was brought out immediately upon their arrival as the couple looked over the menu.

"What have you been up to?" Alexa opened up the conversation innocently enough.

She had never seen him look so concerned. "We're facing some real challenges," he said, sounding tired. "There seems to be a leak. The authorities just have way too much information and they're closing in. I may also have gone too far on some related business." After a long pause, he simply said, "It doesn't look good."

She looked at him lovingly and placed her hand on his knee. "I'm so sorry you're going through all of this," she spoke softly.

He kissed her on the forehead and took her hand. "I know, honey, I know."

He hesitated, but went forward anyway. "I don't know how to say this, but we even suspect it may be one of us on the inside."

In an instant, Alexa died a thousand deaths. "One of us?" she said jokingly as if the thought was utterly absurd.

"Well, not you, of course. No one knows about you," he replied and then continued, as he lightly massaged her arm. "Nely is suspected."

Alexa was able to breathe again. "You can't be serious."

"It's serious enough that Ken has authorized surveillance 24/7," he confirmed.

"Since when?" Alexa asked.

"Since mid-October."

A million thoughts rushed through her head. *What do they have on me? What did I say to Nely? Thank God Grandpa has occupied so much of my time! Is it just a matter of time before they watch me too? Is it happening already?*

"Well, it's a waste of time, I say. None of your loyal band is a Judas!" she said lightly, quickly switching gears as if none of it mattered in the least bit.

As he placed their order, she lovingly snuggled next to him.

After a passion-filled night in her suite, he had work to do. He let himself out after a final body check as she remained dreamily in bed. He blew a kiss from the door before pulling it shut behind him.


Alexa quickly dressed. After heading out of the hotel, she turned east and kept walking until she reached Third Avenue. Then she headed uptown. When she reached 72$^{nd}$ Street, she located a pay phone. Using a prepaid calling card she had purchased for cash some weeks earlier, she placed an international call.

After a series of short rings, a British-accented voice answered. "This is Miss Bart calling for Mr. Ayoub. Will you tell him I'm on the line, please?" she instructed.

The man hesitated only briefly. Only the most important of his boss's colleagues had this number. "One moment please," he said most graciously.

In less than 30 seconds, Faisal Ayoub was on the phone. "Yes?" he said with great anticipation.

"I am in New York," she said, "I can be in London tomorrow."

A surge of hope filled Faisal as he stood even taller. "I'll wait to hear from you," he said.

She disconnected the call. Then, she walked about two blocks, found another phone, and using cash, made a reservation to London for the following day in the name of Alexia Horst.

# THIRTY SEVEN

SOUTH CHICAGO WAS a permanent shade of dingy gray. The foul smell offended with every breath. The only ray of sunshine in Fatima's life was the bright spirit of her seven-year-old daughter Sheila. Fatima and Sheila had integrated themselves nicely into the Italian neighborhood on Princeton Street. She even sent her lively and inquisitive child to the St. Jerome Catholic School down the street, although they were of the Muslim faith.

Five days a week, Fatima got on the city bus and put in long and hard hours cleaning office buildings on Lake Shore Drive—a world away in privilege and lifestyle. On weekends she worked as a maid in the wealthy homes of Glencoe. The hope and dream that sustained her was that one day, her only child would rise above her meager circumstances. There was every indication that she would at least have a fighting chance.

When the second grader got a rash and experienced a slight rise in temperature, the school nurse told Fatima to take Sheila to a doctor and that he would probably prescribe an antibiotic. Fatima was concerned not only for her daughter but also about taking time off from work, which was seriously frowned upon by her supervisor.

Later that evening, she expressed her concerns to her next-door neighbor Sofia, a secretary at St. Jerome's parish. Sofia put

Fatima's mind at ease and told her that she could get antibiotics without a prescription on the Internet. When Fatima said that she wasn't so sure about this, Sofia told her that it was no different than booking a flight herself instead of calling a travel agent, "You save a lot of time and hassle." Fatima thanked her neighbor. She logged onto *antidote.com* with her Visa card.

Two days later, Sheila's cyprofaxin and nermycin arrived and within another week, the child was feeling much better. The fever disappeared almost immediately, and the rash was nearly gone. After another few days, the rash cleared up completely. Two weeks later, when she received an emergency call from the school nurse, Fatima left work immediately to bring Sheila to the hospital. Within hours, Sheila was on a powerful antibiotic drip, fighting a severe pneumonia.


About 350 miles away in St. Paul, 13-year-old Johnny Rodriguez took a fall after doing wheelies on his bicycle on Rosemont Street following choir practice at St. Gertrude's. Johnny knew his wheels as well as any teenager, but boys will be boys and Johnny outdid himself on this occasion. His grandmother took him to see Dr. Rollinger to clean up his cuts and bruises. Dr. Rollinger lectured the boy on safety, but Johnny insisted that he lost control when he felt a little weak and dizzy. Dracula Rollinger, as he was known to his patients for routinely requesting over-the-top lab work, ordered a series of blood tests. Johnny had contracted a staph infection somewhere and Dr. Rollinger wrote out a prescription for antibiotics. He told Johnny's grandmother to keep an eye on him and then reassured her that a healthy and fit live wire like Johnny would make a complete recovery.

Later that evening, when Jonny's mother came home from her job at the hair salon, she boiled a great big chicken and made a clear broth for Johnny to "sweat out the bug." She also went on the

Internet to order the antibiotics prescribed by Dr. Rollinger. The next day, the cyprofaxin and nermycin arrived by FedEx.

Within a week, Johnny was back to his old tricks and goofing off with the kids from Hale, a nearby school. The next week, he was enjoying a Coca-Cola and Hostess Sno Balls at Ron Beamer's house—something his mother would *never* permit at home—when Johnny collapsed on Mrs. Beamer's kitchen floor. Scared out of her wits, she immediately called 911 and then attempted to locate Johnny's mother.

By the time the paramedics arrived, Johnny had turned blue and appeared to have lost consciousness. They performed emergency procedures, placed an oxygen mask on his face, laid him out on a stretcher, turned on the siren and rushed him to Columbus hospital. Although the sudden onset of pneumonia was not unusual, it was very rare that a 13-year-old would die within a week, never responding in any way to the most powerful antibiotics that were available.

The investigation had been slow going, despite a team that had swelled to almost 10 investigators, including Barry Weiner, Gary Landau, Chris Calandra, two special agents from Phil Oster's Internet Pharmaceutical Fraud Initiative, an IRS investigator, Francine Pye, Kelly Harpin and another of Francine's best investigators, as well as support from Interpol, Swiss authorities, the RCMP and the U.S. attorney's office in New York.

"We're no closer to tying Karasik or Mel Bottner directly to any illegal activities, past or future. On the other hand, it's now beyond challenge that *antidote.com* has been selling counterfeit drugs. There's little doubt that at least some officers of the C3 Group were involved in the creation of *antidote.com* and that some of its products have come from a manufacturer in Pune, India with ties to

C3," Weiner explained to Oster. Weiner had stepped into Oster's tasteful office to discuss progress on the investigation.

"Bottom line Phil, we now have certain evidence that *antidote.com* is breaking the law. The time has come to close it down. Since we're not yet charging terrorism, that's probably in your jurisdiction, not mine," Weiner added.

"I agree. We have a compelling case in two areas. First, there is no doubt that *antidote.com* has been selling brand name drugs that are approved for sale in Europe and elsewhere, but not by the FDA. Second, the lot numbers on a considerable number of *antidote.com*'s other drugs are fakes. I'm going to recommend prosecution. Justice should have *antidote.com* closed within the month."

"It's sad, catching the chum and not the shark, but I appreciate your support," Barry said. "I know Francine will also be pleased. Her people did a terrific job tracking those lot numbers. Now, I have to focus on these rumors we keep hearing that something big is going down. I still think Ken Karasik is behind this and my gut tells me it's going to get worse before it gets better."

"What about the funds flow?" Phil asked.

"No joy there—yet. The Caymans and the Isle of Man are nothing more than money launderers. The damn governments there make millions coddling the worst scum, and wrap their garbage in language about personal freedoms, efficient banking, and estate planning," Barry fumed.

"On top of being stonewalled in the Caymans, Isle of Man and Switzerland, even Justice seems to be dragging its heels on this one. That Waters is a piece of work," Barry added, his ire rising.

"Barry, let's take this one step at a time. Within the month, *antidote.com* will be off-line. You're making progress on the ties to

C3, and maybe Karasik. It's only a matter of time before you uncover whatever is going on."

"I sure hope so. I sure hope we uncover whatever is happening before a lot of people die."

"They're going to close *antidote.com* and he's getting closer to C3," Christine Liu told Ken, referring to her cousin, Barry Weiner. At the time, they were lying in bed in Ken's suite at the Eden Au Lac Hotel in Zurich, watching Wolf Blitzer grill the latest hapless politician. Journalist Tom Friedman was next. He was going to again describe the many benefits of manufacturing in India. Ken agreed.

David Salzman was concerned. There seemed to be an uptick in deaths from pneumonia. The increase was small. So small, in fact, that most observers would not have noticed it. David Salzman was not the same as most observers. After receiving his B.S. in microbiology from the University of Michigan, the Chicago native decided that what he really enjoyed was math. He went on to the University of California at Berkeley, where four years later he received a PhD in applied mathematics. That was 10 years ago. From the day he graduated, he worked in Atlanta at the Centers for Disease Control and Prevention, where he now led the center responsible for pathological physiology—the origination, development and outcome of diseases.

The CDC was one of the 13 major operating components of the Department of Health and Human Services. Since its founding in 1946 to help control malaria, the CDC had been at the forefront of public health efforts to prevent and control infectious and chronic diseases. With its headquarters in Atlanta and facilities throughout the United States and many countries around the world, the CDC was often viewed as the first line of defense against public health crises.

Salzman prided himself on seeing trends before anyone else could, before they were even really trends. That is what Salzman saw in the reports. He decided to make a few calls and to review related data. In particular, he wanted to understand any potential increase in instances of pneumonia, or reports of any new strains. The key to preventing a problem like this from becoming a crisis was early detection, and then prompt prophylactic action. Salzman wasn't going to waste any time. Pneumonia was a dangerous illness, particularly in the middle of the winter.

"Our tracking studies suggest that the mortality rate is still low. We are guessing somewhere between 50 and 75 deaths. Based on orders at some of the web sites we control, we selected 100 cases for intensive follow-up. Of that number, about 20 became sick enough to require hospitalization. Fortunately, three of those patients were admitted to hospitals where we have influence: St. Joseph's in New Mexico, Western Memorial in St. Louis and City Memorial in Sacramento."

Max Linville continued his report to Dave Cole, Bob Estrich and William Bowne. The four were participating in a brief conference in the secure room on the executive floor of PharmCorp Tower in New York.

"Of the 20 who required hospitalization, three died, in line with our projections for fatalities. One of those who died did so at one of our facilities. Nicolas Nedeljko Bartanovic, 72, died at St. Joseph's. His case was a little strange. Apparently, he was recovering and was about to be discharged, when he suddenly died. Our guy at St. Joseph's is Harlan Pullman, the hospital's president. He's been on the payroll for several years. Thanks to him, St. Joseph's purchased over $10 million of our drugs, and has helped us conduct a number of unregulated studies. I've asked one of our cutouts to get a full report from him."

"What's the big deal?" Cole asked.

"Maybe nothing. But, any unexpected pathology may suggest a misjudgment or a mistake. With this much at risk, we should be particularly careful," Bowne answered for his deputy."

"So, let's send someone out there," Estrich instructed.

"Bill, before we adjourn, I want to remind you how unhappy I am that the terrorists have not yet issued a claim or a demand. I trust you are also looking into that?" Cole injected.

"Absolutely," was Bowne's only response. After Cole and Estrich left, Bowne turned to Linville. "What's the status on Opperman and Biffar?"

"We have round-the-clock teams on both of them. If you decide to eliminate them, we're ready."

"Good. In the meantime, why don't you send Biffar to look into this situation at St. Joseph's. He's visited with Pullman in the past and he's best positioned to get to the bottom of it."

"Ok. Should we pull our coverage off him while he's out of town?" Linville asked, concerned that it would be difficult to watch Biffar while he was traveling and more aware of his surroundings.

"Sure. Oh, when you talk to Biffar let him know that he has complete discretion on the disposition of this matter."

With the meeting over, Bowne returned to his office down the hall and Linville headed for the elevator. He had to get to his office on the 20th floor so he could make some calls.


At about the time the PharmCorp executives were meeting in their secure bubble, Ken, Petar, Mel and Ben were participating in a teleconference on protected lines.

"The death toll is behind our projections," Petar explained. "Perhaps we should wait another few weeks before issuing our demands?"

"I agree," Mel said. Ben echoed that conclusion.

"What has been the fallout from the article?" Ben asked, referring to the Swiss newspaper article about Ken that had made Nely so hysterical.

"Fortunately, very little so far," Ken responded. Stuart has helped limit the damage in Europe and no one has picked up the story in the United States. Our bigger problem is the investigation itself. My sources indicate that the investigation is moving at full speed, and *antidote.com* is likely a goner."

"Should we close it down?" Petar asked.

"No. But we should make sure that except for the legal sales from C3 Pharmaceuticals, we are as far away from that problem as possible," Ken responded.

"Any fallout in Canada from the Cowells' deaths?" Mel asked.

"None," Ben responded. "It was clean. Thanks to Ken's tip, we were in and out before Weiner arrived." Neither Ben nor the others on the call knew that Ken actually had two sources on Barry and Francine's trip. It never hurt to cover your risks, even when one of your sources is Deputy Attorney General of the United States.

"What about the leak?" Mel asked.

"So far, nothing," Ben responded. "Nely seems clean, and at this point we're stumped."

"It's been a while since our problem lady has phoned the FBI," Karasik added. "Ben, let's end the surveillance on Nely."

"Ken, if you don't mind, could we let it run another few weeks. It's looking like Nely isn't involved, but until our Judas contacts the FBI again, we can't be sure," Ben said.

"Alright, another two weeks, but that's it."

Special Agent Dave Williams answered the outside line. "I'm ready to talk to Weiner," the by now familiar voice said. "Hold and I'll transfer you. Ok?" Williams asked his confidential informant. "I'll hold," she said. As Williams started a trace, he phoned Weiner on his other line. "It's her," Williams said. "She wants to talk to you."

"Transfer her," Barry replied. "I assume you're tracing the call," he added.

"Of course," Williams responded as he continued the trace.

Barry pressed the blinking button and for the first time he was connected to the woman who had given so much impetus to the investigation. "Special Agent Weiner here, with whom am I speaking?" he asked in a businesslike tone.

"Special Agent Weiner, this is your ticket to fame and a promotion," the voice responded. "I know you're tracing this call and so we have less than a minute. People are going to start dying. I read the article. Forget Karasik. He's being misled. Look at Petar Raic. He's the one directing this. It's going to get very ugly, very soon."

"What do you mean? How do you know this?" Barry asked, very concerned about the woman's one-minute deadline.

"What difference does it make? Your target is Petar Raic. You're moving in the right direction, but you need to re-focus. Gotta go."

"Wait. How do I find you?" Barry asked.

"You don't. Have a good day Special Agent Weiner." With that, she broke the connection just as Barry's assistant, Stacie Amezcua, rushed in with a note from Dave Williams. The trace showed the caller was at a pay phone on 53$^{rd}$ Street and Avenue of the Americas in Manhattan. Agents were already closing in.

Barry didn't expect their caller to be there by the time agents arrived. At least this time they should be able to find her picture from the surveillance cameras that ringed the area. Between NYPD, Rockefeller Center security, area banks and high-end retailers, Barry was certain they would finally be able to learn more about their mysterious source. He also wondered about the latest information. The caller's insistence that Karasik was not involved and the new target intrigued him. It also concerned him. *What were the caller's motives? Was she motivated by concern, or, just possibly, was she a plant? Or, had Karasik learned of this traitor and turned her for his own advantage?*

"What about Raic?" Barry asked Special Agent Gary Landau.

"We have a long dossier on him. Born in Bosnia. Muslim. In the '70s and '80s he was a top anti-Communist terrorist in Yugoslavia, based in Italy. He immigrated here in 1981, attended City University of New York and then enlisted in the army where he was in special ops. He's now chief operations officer of Karasik's C3 Group, based in London," Landau reported.

"It's hard to believe that Raic would be running a rogue operation within C3, though I guess anything's possible. And, he fits the profile. Thanks Gary."

As Barry pondered the meaning of the call and Landau's report, Dave Williams called. "We lost her."

"No surprise there," Barry responded.

"We're canvassing the area for video. I'll let you know as soon as we find anything," Williams advised him.

"Thanks." Barry disconnected the call and yelled out to Stacie to get the team ready for a meeting. He wasn't going to give up on Karasik, but they were sure going to put Raic under a microscope.

After making her reservation for London, Alexa took a walk. When she calmed down, she reached for her cell, and speed dialed Ben's cell phone. When Ben answered, she sadly told him that she had just learned that one of her dearest friends was losing her battle with breast cancer. She had only a few days to live, and Alexa had to fly to London to be with her. Alexa was just devastated. He understood. Feeling her pain tormented him. He promised her that he would be there for her. She began to cry. His kindness simply overwhelmed her. She hung up the phone, her face turned dead serious and she stared ahead.

By 5:30 am the following morning, Alexa was boarding a non-stop Virgin Air flight to London. She checked no luggage, and produced her computer-printed boarding pass and her Swiss passport for identification before settling into her first class seat. The male passengers perked up at the sight of the attractive redhead.

That evening, London time, Alexa took a black cab to the Dorchester Hotel. She checked into the magnificent Oliver Messel Suite that looked across the soft green swaths of Hyde Park, and placed a call to New York. Ben was eager to hear from her. He advised her to take a sleeping pill and get a good night's rest before facing the next day.

"Great advice," she told him. "I'll instruct the front desk not to put any calls through so that I can try to sleep. I'll call you tomorrow." She paused briefly and added, "I love you." He automatically replied in kind.

Instead of resting, Alexa jumped into the shower. She quickly dressed in black pants, a white silk shirt and her long overcoat. She slipped on a pair of black leather gloves and lifted her sable collar to protect her from the vicious chill on this drizzling night. The concierge had arranged for a prepaid cell phone prior to her arrival. She picked it up on her way out and got into another taxi. She instructed the driver to cruise around Knightsbridge until she informed him otherwise. Then she dialed a long series of numbers. Faisal answered immediately. "Where?" was all she said.

"St. James's Club," he replied. "Mr. Weiss will direct you. You are to ask him, 'Do you think there is going to be a blizzard tonight?'" She hung up.

"7-8 Park Place," Alexa instructed the driver.

The razor-sharp wind made her teeth chatter and she physically shook from the cold when she arrived at St. James's Club. Once inside, she looked around, spotting a refined gentleman who stood apart. They looked at each other but he offered no sense of familiarity. Nevertheless, she approached him and smiled, "Do you think there is going to be a blizzard tonight?" The man's expression did not change as he answered, "This way, Madam."

She followed him onto a private elevator and into a suite of richly decorated rooms in bold reds and vibrant jewel tones. "Please make yourself comfortable," he said before exiting the suite and closing the door behind him. She raised an eyebrow and removed her coat. The dining table had a tray of assorted breads and cheese, a fruit bowl, Evian water and Cristal champagne. She casually picked up a huge red strawberry and took a bite.

Alexa was oddly calm considering the situation. Ten minutes later, the doorknob turned. Faisal let himself in and greeted Alexa with a formal handshake and kiss on the cheek—three times, in the Muslim tradition.

He turned on the television for background noise and took a seat at the table. She sat across from him. "Looks like Karasik is going down…" he began.

"It will never happen," she said most confidently.

"It will, Alexia. It will," he said.

"He'll take a beating, that's for sure, but he's just too damn smart...he covered all of his tracks."

"Not this time," Faisal persisted.

"Oh, there will be fall guys, don't get me wrong," she added, "but Karasik has more lives than Morris the Cat."

"Are you one of the fall guys?" Faisal asked calmly.

She went quiet. "I don't know," she uttered with complete vulnerability.

"What do you have left?" He got down to business.

"It's in a safe deposit box, under a numbered account, in a Swiss bank," she said in a low monotone. "There is a copy buried in a concrete container at a location only I know. I buried it myself by digging long and deep when I was 12 years old. I didn't trust anyone."

"We're going to be very rich," Faisal said almost whispering.

"We're already very rich, Mr. Ayoub," she said to his face.

"Never rich enough," he informed her.

She understood. And he waited. "Opperman needs to go," she began. "If you can take care of him without a trace, the key to my inheritance is yours."

"With that key, I will make you wealthy enough to rival the Queen!" Faisal said confidently. He rose, extended his hand and announced, "We have a deal."

"We have a deal," she replied quietly in return.


Alexa left St. James's Club and headed back to the Dorchester. Images of her childhood played themselves over and over in her head. The first emotion she learned was fear. The first skill she acquired was survival. She could never stop looking over her shoulder or take the slightest incident for granted. She trusted no one, and from time to time, she viewed the image in the mirror with a reasonable amount of suspicion.

Some of what she had told Nely was true.

When her father was taken by the Communists, Alexia was a child of eight. She remembered trembling in the corner of the kitchen with its primitive stove that was used for warmth and for cooking. Black kettles and wooden spoons hung from the low ceiling. She shook from cold and fear in her flannel pajamas that sported little airplanes. They were a gift from her father. Her mother remained stoic with superhuman strength until the *Stasi* marched her father down the cobblestone street and into a waiting army jeep. An officer remained behind and told her mother that her husband had betrayed the State.

"My husband would do nothing of the kind," she replied defiantly. The officer walked over to Alexia and stroked her curly head. The child froze in horror and her mother held her breath. When he marched out at last, her mother fell to the floor, weeping. A few of the neighbors arrived and attempted to console her to no avail. No one thought to console the mortified child in the corner. All seemed to assume that little Alexia was just too young to comprehend what was happening.

Four months and 17 days later, her beloved and heartbroken mother collapsed to her death. Previously, a trusted elderly woman in the neighborhood had been given specific instructions and information. She notified Carl Horst and informed him of his niece's fate. Carl was able to make arrangements to take Alexia out of East Germany. He sent Maria to collect the child and bring her to Zurich. While they waited for Carl to complete the arrangements, the elderly woman took Alexia into her care. She presented Alexia with a large manila envelope. "You must keep this and guard this as if your life depends on it," the woman told her sternly. Alexia had witnessed life and death and comprehended all too well the literal seriousness of the kind woman's unmistakable instructions.

Two days later, Aunt Maria arrived. Alexa left her childhood behind with very little. The kindly neighbor gave her a colorful sack with a long shoulder strap. It served as her only luggage. She filled it with the envelope, a few scanty garments, the pearl brooch her mother had worn every day, a loaf of white bread, and a treasured puffed rice bar that her second grade teacher gave her for good luck. Her teacher cried in the school's doorway. She hugged the little girl and told her that she had a special destiny and had to make good for all of them.

Many years later, she had sold some of the formulas in that envelope to Ken Karasik, and still others to Faisal Ayoub. Those formulas had been used by Ken to create pharmaceuticals for C3 and by Ayoub to create weapons for causes Alexa never wanted to know. Both paid her well, and both would continue to pay for the contents of that manila envelope.

Alexa was beyond tears. With each injustice, she became more determined and powerful. Her so-called lover had been part of the conspiracy that took Grandpa Nico from her. This time, the enemy would pay. Ben Opperman would die.

# THIRTY EIGHT

**B**ABY KENAN HAD been acting up for a couple of days. That afternoon, his nanny, Carol Craige, noticed that the baby had a rash. When she took his temperature it was 101 degrees. She immediately informed Nely.

Nely asked Carol to take his temperature again. Alarmed to learn that it was up to 102 degrees, Nely asked her to keep an eye on him. "I have a dinner to attend, but I'll be back in a few hours. If there's a problem call Dr. Rose Taylor."

Kenan was crying non-stop. When Carol couldn't locate Dr. Taylor, she tried to reach Nely on her cell phone, without luck. Finally, Carol and Isabella decided that they would take the baby to the Paradise Cove Memorial emergency room. Carol carefully placed baby Kenan into the car seat in Isabella's Toyota. Then she got in and they headed for the hospital.

The baby would not stop crying. Carol paced the emergency room lobby while Isabella tried to comfort him. After nearly an hour, Kenan was finally called and placed into an examining room. Right across the hall, a resident had pulled a sheet over a young man's head and somberly walked out of the room, closing the door behind him.

The resident professionally examined the baby and ordered blood work. After the attending physician on duty reviewed the results, he concluded it was a mild staph infection, gave the baby a dose of antibiotics and wrote out prescriptions for two additional antibiotics.

"Let's get out of here," Isabella said to Carol as she wrapped up the baby. "Why don't I drop you at the drugstore so you can fill the prescriptions," Isabella asked.

"Oh, that's not necessary," Carol replied. "We gotta get you modernized, Isabella. Now you can get prescriptions on-line and delivered to your door the next day!" the know-it-all proclaimed, apparently unaware that the pharmacy would have delivered the prescriptions that very night.

"I can't keep up with all the changes in the world," Isabella muttered in her usual complaining tone.

The baby had finally fallen asleep. Isabella took him to the nursery as Carol went to the study, logged on and punched in *antidote.com*. She ordered the two drugs the doctor had prescribed. Both medicines arrived the following day.


"Something's not right," David Salzman explained to Suzy Liebig.

"The incidence of pneumonia is rising, particularly among the young. Both hospitalization and morbidity rates are up." Salzman knew that 10% of all adult hospitalizations and 20% of all newborn and infant mortality deaths in the United States were due to pneumonia. But, those results were regional and the current season had been a mild one.

"It's rare for children between five and 12 to be hospitalized with pneumonia, particularly in warmer parts of the country, and even rarer for them to die," Liebig agreed.

"Nonetheless, 50 children under 12 have died from pneumonia in warmer parts of the country alone since Thanksgiving. Death rates may also be up among adults," Salzman told his new deputy director.

Liebig had recently joined his team from the FDA, where she had been a researcher involved in reviewing the trial results on which the FDA relied when determining whether to approve the sale of drugs in the United States. Its decisions, and hence Liebig's recommendations, were worth billions of dollars to the pharmaceutical industry and were the nation's principal defense against ineffective or dangerous medicines. Salzman had considerable confidence in Liebig's judgment.

"I want you to take a look at this data. Get whatever else you need to put it in context. Tell me what you think. Is something going on or am I seeing shadows?" Salzman asked Liebig.

"What do you think is going on?" Liebig asked. The 35-year-old biologist was dressed in her usual lab whites, although she looked more like a model than a scientist. Salzman thought, not for the first time, that he might stand a chance with her, though he would never act on that thought.

"I'd rather not color your thinking. I want a fresh set of eyes. You're the best I have. Take a look and get back to me whenever you can, as long as it's by tomorrow," Salzman said with a smile.

"Will do," Liebig answered, wondering whether Salzman was flirting with her. As she left, Salzman's gaze remained on her until she was out of sight. Salzman sighed, and returned to the data. *Something wasn't right.*


Eric Jacobs got off the phone with Greg Schoenfeld. The senior prosecutor was pressing hard for an interview with Petar Raic.

Jacobs knew that sooner or later Schoenfeld would win this round. Raic was a U.S. citizen. His responsibilities included all C3 Group companies, both in the United States and elsewhere. He even had a second office in C3's North American headquarters. Jacobs could probably fight a subpoena for a few weeks, or even a few months, but that would only make things worse in the end.

"Petar, you're going to have to make the time for this," Jacobs explained to the reluctant chief operations officer on a transatlantic call.

"What are the consequences of putting this off?" Petar asked the seasoned litigator.

"If it would help matters, you know I would fight. But, it will only make us look bad. Not just to Justice, but to a jury or a judge if this goes that far. In planning our defense, I have to do my best to avoid an indictment, but I also have to plan for the worst-case scenario," Jacobs counseled C3's third-ranking executive.

"Which is?" Petar asked for probably the twentieth time in 45 days.

"As I have explained," Jacobs patiently reiterated, "There is a risk that the C3 Group or any of its parts could be criminally indicted. There is also a risk that all or any of its officers, or anyone else implicated in unlawful behavior could be indicted as well as, or instead of, C3. For individuals that could mean fines and jail time. This is very, very serious, Petar."

"How does voluntarily coming in for this interview help matters?"

"It signals strength. Your refusal to submit will be seen as an admission of wrongdoing, no matter what a judge instructs a jury. Further, it will enrage the Justice Department. If you think Justice is being difficult, you haven't seen anything compared to what will happen if Justice thinks we're jerking them around. You need to do this and you need to do this in the next two weeks. There are no alternatives," Jacobs bluntly advised him.

Petar hoped that two weeks would give them enough time, but he wasn't certain.

# THIRTY NINE

**R**OHIT DATAR HAD never been so relieved. The special production line was being dismantled. Within a few days it would be gone, replaced by new equipment. The last of the product was being packed into containers for shipping. In a week, all tangible evidence of RD Pharmaceuticals' role in this scheme would be gone. Datar didn't know what it was all about and he certainly didn't want to know. He had done as Peter Fell had asked him to do. Now, it was up to Fell to deliver. Fell had promised Datar that he and his family would get back complete ownership of RD Pharmaceuticals. All he had to do for the next five years was fulfill normal orders from C3 Pharmaceuticals and some of his other customers. He could focus on RD's proprietary drug development efforts.

Hopefully, the new drugs being developed by RD would make this all worthwhile. Datar believed those drugs would make life better for many millions of people. The success of RD Pharmaceuticals would be a symbol of India's transition from a mere manufacturer of parts to the very forefront of biotechnology.

Datar was not proud of his role in whatever nefarious scheme Fell had orchestrated. Nor was he proud of what RD Pharmaceutical had become—a chop shop for substandard pharmaceuticals. He might have to live with that for another few years, but then he would have the rest of his life to make up for it.

There were times when a price had to be paid to achieve good. Datar thought about the many terrible things that had been done by those who believed the end justified the means. He piously concluded that he did not fit into their category.

"We've shut down in Pune, Agra, Malaysia and Myanmar," Petar reported by secure cell to Mel and Ben. Mel was overseeing the efforts from Zurich, where he was visiting Ken, and participated from his room at the Eden Au Lac Hotel. Ben was in his office in Paris, and Petar was in Kunming, capital of Yunnan province in China. "Given the late start here, it may be another week or two before we can close down in China. I'll know more after my meeting."

"Where do we stand on shipments?" Mel asked.

"It will be at least another week in India, Malaysia and Myanmar before the last of the products are packed and shipped. It could then be up to a month before that product reaches the Canadian web sites. Basically, that means sell-through will continue until April or May, giving us a full six months, or more, of sales," Petar explained.

"So far, deaths are below 100. If the American government does not acquiesce, we are looking at tens of thousands or even hundreds of thousands of deaths by this summer. The numbers should start growing rapidly in about a month, and then peak this summer. Deaths could easily continue straight through next fall, depending upon how quickly products are ordered and used," Ben added.

Mel responded, "I'll update Ken. He'll be pleased."

"Petar, Weiner has turned his sights on you. You must get to New York as soon as you can," Mel added.

"If things go right, I'll be able to leave tomorrow," Petar replied without fear, ending the call.

Kunming was a beautiful place. Its history of more than 2,400 years owed its importance to the fact that Kunming was the gateway to the celebrated Silk Road that facilitated trade with Tibet, Sichuan, Burma and India. A few months earlier, Petar might have stopped to enjoy one of the most magical cities in China. Now, thanks to the FBI and a traitor in their own organization, they were in a race to prevent their plan from unraveling. If the government learned that people were being infected too soon, they might prevent the distribution of cyprofaxin and nermycin before enough Americans were infected to give the Karasik Commission the leverage it needed. That was why they had waited so long to make their demands. That was why they still had to wait.

It did little good to kill a couple of hundred Americans unless there was a credible threat that tens of thousands would die. While the Karasik Commission did not believe the substandard cyprofaxin or tainted nermycin would be detected, or the cause of the sudden rise in deaths from pneumonia traced back to those drugs, they could not be certain. If they prematurely made their demands, there was a possibility that the CDC would find the victims and trace the cause back to cyprofaxin and nermycin before so many were infected that the government would be unable to ignore the Karasik Commission's threats. The risk was remote, but not so remote as to be acceptable. Once the number infected was in the tens of thousands, it would be too late to avoid many thousands of deaths even if the CDC figured out the cause.

To Americans, the deaths of 168 Americans in Oklahoma City was a national tragedy and the deaths of 3,000 in New York and Washington almost beyond endurance. How would America handle the deaths of 10,000 or 50,000, or perhaps even more. Fifty-eight thousand Americans died in Vietnam, and the country never recovered. Project Sky would be even more deadly, and far more efficient.

To achieve their goal, more than 200,000 Americans had to order the cocktail of cyprofaxin and nermycin from the web sites that had purchased their counterfeit products from a certain Panamanian distributor or its subdistributors. The math had been computed over and over again. Originally, they thought they would need no more than 60 to 90 days of sales. Once the toxicity of the nermycin had been reduced to solve their production problems, that period increased by at least 30 days and maybe longer. That was why they were so carefully monitoring the effects of the tainted drugs. They needed to know precisely when their plan had crossed the point of no return. Then, unless they disclosed that Abcyclene could stop the illness, no medical genius was going to avoid mass death.

It was amazing how sophisticated killing had become, especially when the killer wanted the ability to put the toothpaste back in the tube long after the tube had been squeezed dry.

"Mr. Fell, an honor as always to have you with us," Jack Huang proclaimed.

"Thank you, Mr. Huang. My time is limited, but there are some problems here that need sorting out," Peter Fell né Petar Raic responded.

"There seem to be rather serious production deficiencies here. When you and I made our little arrangement, I had expected this plant to produce more than six million tablets. Instead, production is at just two million tablets, and nearly a quarter of those were defective. What little is of use to us is still sitting on the dock. Not one tablet has shipped out of China. If I didn't like you so much, I might think this was on purpose."

Huang looked at Fell in abject terror. He had a wife, a child and elderly parents to support on both sides of the family. Huang had started Golden Manufacturing because he wanted to build financial security for himself and his family, and because he wanted to contribute to China's re-entry into the global community. But, how could he do that if the medicines his plant manufactured didn't work, or even worse, killed people? Jack Huang didn't quite understand what Mr. Fell was up to, but he knew the plan did not include curing sick people.

Huang had been at the University of Texas in Austin when the students challenged the government at Tiananmen Square in June 1989. Like many other Chinese students then attending college in the United States, Huang chose to remain in America. He worked as a chemist at a number of leading U.S. companies. As China began to liberalize its economic policies, introduce limited democracy at the provincial level, and even permit some freedom of speech, like many of his fellow Chinese émigrés, Huang returned to his homeland.

Many of the "returnees" of his generation wanted to "do good and do well in China." His generation was much more idealistic than the younger Chinese who came to America in the late 1990s. The returnees had witnessed the disasters of the Cultural Revolution and experienced the benefits of China's first steps toward a free society, including being given the precious opportunity to study advanced sciences in America, an opportunity their talented parents and older brothers and sisters did not have. Huang shared these aspirations. Like many other returnees his age, Huang had a strong sense of social responsibility and a mission. He wanted to have a positive impact on Chinese society and the Chinese people who had endured so many disasters with great patience and diligence, while also doing well by participating in China's economic boom.

With capital he had saved and loans and investments from friends, he founded Golden Manufacturing in 2002. Two years later, the company became profitable by supplying high-quality pharmaceuticals to Asian and European drug companies.

Just a year ago, Peter Fell approached Huang with an offer he couldn't refuse. Huang agreed to effectively turn over one-quarter of his production capacity to Fell for up to six months. In return, Fell agreed to a series of substantial payments, most of which would become due only over a three-year period after the project was complete and only if Huang kept his part of the bargain, including confidentiality. As part of the deal, a company in Shanghai that Huang had never heard of obtained a security interest in Huang's equipment. If Huang breached the deal, the Shanghai company would foreclose, and Huang would lose everything.

Things too good to be true usually are. When one of Huang's executives overheard Fell talking on his cell phone in Croatian, a language he understood well enough since he had once worked in Sarajevo for another Chinese company, Huang learned the truth. He resolved that very day not to cooperate.

"I don't know what to say, Mr. Fell. Your team has had direct responsibility for all of the special production. All we have done is arrange for shipment. We cannot control what the Customs Office does. You knew this risk when you selected us."

Petar knew a lie when he heard one. "I am going to give you one more opportunity to tell me the truth and to arrange to ship the million-and-a-half tablets that have been manufactured. You have already forfeited your right to additional payments. This is your only chance to avoid more dire consequences," Petar told him, his gaze penetrating to Huang's inner core.

"Neither my people nor I had any role in manufacturing the tablets. If there is a problem, then I suggest you speak with your own people. As to the shipping problems, I will do my best, but I cannot promise what the Customs Office will do."

Petar knew this was pointless. Fortunately, he had foreseen this problem when Golden Manufacturing failed to meet its quota.

Production at the other facilities had been boosted. By the time they closed down production in India, Malaysia and Myanmar, they had made up all but about 500,000 tablets. Based on their projections, that would equate to about 1,000 fewer deaths—an acceptable loss.

Petar agreed to meet Huang that evening for a report on progress with the Customs Office. Relieved that Fell's reaction had not been worse, Huang made a few perfunctory calls, knowing that would be insufficient to resolve the problem. He reported his efforts to Fell that evening. Fell expressed his disappointment, but told Huang that he would be leaving China the next day. The two parted without shaking hands. Fell left first in a rented car. After paying the bill, Huang departed in his Audi.

Huang was calming down as he headed home. True, the Shanghai company might try to foreclose, but Huang could always contest the foreclosure. If need be, he would start again.

Traffic was fairly light, though Huang passed a number of cars and trucks. As he rounded the last corner before the block on which he lived, he noticed a large truck headed his way on the other side of the road. At the last moment, the truck swerved directly into his lane. A few seconds later Huang was flung back, his neck snapping in the impact as the two vehicles smashed into each other at a combined speed of nearly 100 miles per hour. He was dead by the time Petar Raic removed his harness and helmet, delicately climbed down from the truck, lifted the small motorcycle secreted in one of the truck's rear compartments, and sped away, being careful to stay well within the speed limit.

Suzy Liebig had carefully reviewed the data Salzman supplied. Though she might not have noticed anything amiss if Salzman had not asked her to review the data, she too saw an unusual level of morbidity from pneumonia among the young in parts of the country that should not have been experiencing such results. She wasn't entirely certain that the numbers were beyond the usual vagaries of medical conditions, and she didn't think there was anything odd in any other group. Suzy needed a few days more than the one day Salzman had allotted. It was time well used. She was able to obtain another week's data on deaths from pneumonia, as well as other statistical series. She also made a few phone calls to hospitals in Los Angeles, Denver and Houston. When she had completed her analysis, she reported to Salzman.

"I need to start with some caveats," the capable scientist informed Salzman. "As you probably know, pneumonia is the sixth leading cause of death in the United States. It could be caused by bacteria or viruses. Outbreaks usually occur between January and April. Death is not uncommon among those hospitalized.

"Now, despite the foregoing, and the fact that there is no strong evidence nationwide of higher-than-normal admissions or deaths attributable to pneumonia, I believe that a re-examination of the data on a regional basis and by age and economic status produces discomforting data. Though I'm not certain, I think something out of the ordinary is going on. At the very least, healthy children are being admitted in warmer parts of the country with a new and very resistant strain of pneumonia. While most appear to be recovering, the morbidity rate is high, if not quite alarming."

Salzman interrupted. He'd heard exactly what he'd both feared and expected to hear.

"I'd like some additional analysis of what's going on, Suzy."

"Will do."

"Suzy, please try to expedite that analysis," Salzman said before he moved on the next stack of papers on his very crowded desk.

# FORTY

**B**ARRY WEINER WAS incredibly proud of his team. Despite lack of support from so many quarters, they were just days away from an order closing down *antidote.com* and they would soon be able to prove ties among *antidote.com*, a manufacturing facility in India, and the C3 Group. Though they had found nothing connecting Ken Karasik to these activities, they had found plenty to tie in Petar Raic. And, if they could flip Raic, they would get Karasik.

"Raic is no lightweight. With his background, he may be prepared to go to the wall for Karasik. Literally. If C3's drugs have killed and we can pin that on Raic, we can go for the death penalty," Barry explained to Francine between munches of his burger. They had stopped in at T.G.I. Friday's on Pennsylvania Avenue at the end of another long day. After quickly downing a burger, fries and beer, or in Francine's case, a cheeseburger and a beer, they headed for his place. For a change, the man in the tan Toyota had the night off, and they were alone. In the morning, the man would check the tapes to see if any relevant information had been recorded by the extremely small but powerful listening devices he had secreted in Barry's apartment.

Suzy Liebig issued a request for information to hospitals nationwide. She wanted information about any unusual or new developments regarding pneumonia, particularly involving children. Hospitals had 72 hours in which to respond.

"They know about the special deals on cyprofaxin and nermycin," the man currently known as Paul Little reported to his boss, Tom Biffar, the U.S. manager of Opperman Security. "They know that at least half a dozen of the Canadian sites have been selling the drugs. They haven't figured out any motive, but given the obvious connection between nermycin and C3 Pharmaceuticals, they see it as likely significant. It also sounds like they will be ready to move against *antidote.com* as early as this week," he added.

"The subject is in his apartment," Pierre Aubenas reported via his secure cell phone. Aubenas had walked a few blocks away before filing his report, just to make certain that his call wasn't picked up on any scanners protecting Opperman's apartment. His partner had remained behind to maintain their discreet surveillance. Though it changed from day to day, today they were gardeners, carefully maintaining the small gardens in front of the townhouses that dotted the street where Opperman resided in Paris.

"Anything unusual?" Linville asked him.

"Nothing," Aubenas responded.

"Ok. Stand by. Be prepared for additional instructions within the next few days. Make sure that you or Michel are available at all times, regardless of who else may be on duty."

"Understood," Aubenas disconnected and sauntered back to the Rue Branly, just across from the Eiffel Tower.

Biffar thanked Little for his report and ended the call on the secure line. Since it was lunchtime, Little headed back outside, got into his tan Toyota and headed to a quick lunch.

Harlan Pullman was nervous. When the man he knew only as "Tim" demanded an immediate meeting, it could not be anything good. Pullman had no choice. He had been paid more than $1 million over the last few years for services rendered to Tim and others who had preceded him. In return, Pullman had agreed that St. Joseph's would purchase a disproportionate share of its drugs from PharmCorp. Pullman had also agreed to use some of PharmCorp's unlicensed drugs in controlled studies on patients who mistakenly thought they were helping the FDA approval process. Most recently, Pullman had even agreed to track the progress of a number of patients admitted with pneumonia-like symptoms.

As it turned out, all of those patients had recovered. All, that is, except one. That damn Michael O'Donnell. Pullman had made the mistake of telling Dr. O'Donnell about the tracking study, and in particular the analysis of nermycin. The fool had babbled on about what he was doing while he was with that old man, Nico Bart. O'Donnell thought Bart was unconscious and wouldn't hear anything he said. What medical school did that man graduate from? So-called unconscious patients often have an awareness of what is going on around them. And then, to add insult to injury, the fool left a note about nermycin that Bart's granddaughter found. What choice did he have? Bart had lived a full life. At age 72, and after months of various illnesses, who would ever find out what had really happened?

Pullman continued to wait for Tim at a Starbucks coffee shop in Hillcrest Valley. Last week, one of Tim's minions had asked Pullman about Bart. Why? What would make them care, or even notice? But, they did notice. They were curious about how Bart had dramatically improved and then suddenly died. You would think they were the damn FDA, not some hoodlums from God knows where!

Tim sat down next to Pullman. "I want you to start at the beginning. I want a full report on Nicolas Nedeljko Bartanovic. Do not leave out anything," Tim told Pullman.

As president of St. Joseph's for the last 10 years, Pullman was not used to being spoken to as though he was a junior analyst. Though he seethed at the treatment, he knew he had no choice. He told Tim everything, being careful not to leave out any details, except one. When he got to the part about how O'Donnell had messed up, he omitted the fact that when O'Donnell had come to him in a panic, Pullman decided that Nico had to die. Though it was Pullman, not O'Donnell who decided that a lethal dose of medications should be administered to Nico, Pullman only reported on what O'Donnell had done to kill Nico, and not who had made the decision.

Tim took no notes and remained expressionless throughout the report, asking a question here or there to clear up a detail. When Pullman was done, Tim had a few final questions.

"O'Donnell took this action on his own? He never consulted with you in advance?"

"That's right," Pullman answered. "O'Donnell called me worried that the granddaughter might learn something. I told him to calm down; that we would figure out what to do. Instead of waiting, O'Donnell killed Bart."

"Bart?" Tim inquired, puzzled.

"I mean Bartanovic. His legal name was Bartanovic, but he often used just Bart."

"What did you do when O'Donnell told you what he had done?"

"Other than scream at him, you mean? Nothing. There was nothing I could do. Well, nothing except arrange for the body to be moved to the morgue as quickly as possible and to make sure there would be no autopsy. The last part was easy, with someone of this age and pathology an autopsy is the exception. Since the granddaughter, Alexa, didn't demand an autopsy, he was buried without one."

"What's the granddaughter's full name? Has she followed up on what she learned?"

"She just goes by Bart, Alexa Bart. No, I don't think she's figured out anything. She certainly has not been in contact with O'Donnell or me."

"One last question. Why did you lie to us about what happened?" Tim asked.

Pullman started to sweat again. "I don't have a good answer. I guess I was just afraid to tell you how we had messed up. I know it was O'Donnell's fault, but I was afraid you would blame me. I'm sorry. It will never happen again."

"I agree. It won't," Tim enigmatically replied just before leaving the coffee shop.


The next day, residents of Hillcrest Valley were shocked to learn their safe haven was no longer so safe. In a town that had never had even a single murder, at least none that they knew of, there were two in just one night. Harlan Pullman, president of St. Joseph's Hospital, and Dr. Michael O'Donnell, the chief attending physician at its Marlowe Neurological Center, were found dead. Each had been shot in the head at point blank range. Pullman was found slumped over the wheel of his late model S-class Mercedes in the driveway of his three-million-dollar home. O'Donnell was discovered the same night sprawled on the steps leading to his front door. Neither had been robbed. No one had heard a thing. No one had seen a thing. Police Chief Lee Stucker was not pleased. His perfect record had been destroyed, twice in one night.

Tim handed his tickets to a United Airlines flight attendant at the gate in Santa Fe. "Thank you, Mr. Biffar. Have a pleasant flight. You will change planes in Denver and then you are booked straight through New York." Tom Biffar thanked her and boarded the flight. He would report to Ben and Linville when he returned to New York.

"The evidence is conclusive," Ron Craig, an analyst on Suzy's staff, reported. "More than 200 hospitals responded to our request for information. Every one of them reported an unusual new strain of antibiotic-resistant pneumonia. Here's what's really interesting. Twenty of the hospitals reported that after further examination, their physicians aren't even sure if the illness *is* pneumonia, though the symptoms closely parallel classic bacterial pneumonia."

"Are you sure about that?" Suzy inquired.

"Absolutely. We called several of the hospitals. The general symptoms are the same as pneumonia—chest pain, fever, shaking, chills, shortness of breath, and both rapid breathing and heartbeat. Hospitals reported that many of these patients are experiencing high fever, a rapid heart rate, low blood pressure, bluish skin and mental confusion. While each of these symptoms also occurs with pneumonia, the hospitals believe that the duration and severity of the symptoms are atypical."

"This isn't good," Suzy mused, the understatement masking her growing concern. "Get me the data, I have to see Salzman," she instructed.

About half an hour later, Ron and Suzy were sitting in David Salzman's office, explaining the situation.

"Hospitals are particularly concerned that an unusually large number of patients are not responding to the usual protocols. While 200,000 Americans die each year from pneumonia, most of them respond to treatment to some degree. It's just that their response is too weak, or their hospitalization too late for the treatment to be effective. By contrast, with this new outbreak, hospitals are reporting that the usual treatments seem to be completely ineffective for most of those who died," Suzy reported, quickly summarizing the research and the additional phone calls her staff had made.

"What about Legionnaire's disease?" Salzman asked. First diagnosed in 1976, Legionnaire's disease was caused by the organism *Legionella pneumophila*, and was acquired by breathing droplets of contaminated water. At first, neither physicians nor the CDC had been able to identify Legionnaire's disease, which led to a very high mortality rate. Eventually the CDC concluded that Legionella was not passed on from person to person, but that it might be much more common than once thought. Some experts even believed the organism caused up to half of all pneumonia cases.

"I don't think so. Most of these hospitals know how to recognize Legionnaire's disease," Suzy replied.

"Let's put out an alert to all hospitals. I'll get you some additional staff. We need to know what's really happening. If we act quickly we just might avoid a panic." Though Salzman had only been a resident in 1976, he remembered well the widespread panic caused by Legionnaire's disease. It was his job to avoid a re-occurrence. "Make sure to focus on detailed histories for each of the patients who died," Salzman added.

Francine ordered the tuna salad and Suzy ordered liver and onions. Ever since Suzy had left the FDA for the comparatively academic life at the CDC, the two friends had lunch or dinner at least twice a month. Sometimes Francine flew down to Atlanta. More often, Suzy combined lunch or dinner with a business trip to Washington. They usually talked about men, clothes and work.

"He's kind of cute, if more than a little nerdy," Francine confessed to Suzy, who wanted to know all about Barry Weiner. They laughed. "It's wonderful to have the same goals," Francine added.

Suzy reported to Francine on her latest activities, not to mention David Salzman's latest ticks and averted glances. "You know, if he would just ask me out, I'd probably say yes," Suzy admitted. They had another laugh.

They turned more serious as Suzy told Francine about her strong suspicions that a new resistant form of pneumonia was threatening a significant increase in the death rate for the disease, particularly among children. "David thinks it's also affecting adults and seniors, but I'm not so sure," Suzy commented.

"Either way, I sure hope you get to the bottom of it," Francine replied, before they went on to discuss the hot-selling new diet book, "Body Transformation."

# FORTY ONE

KENAN WAS A happy, high-energy baby. He had recovered nicely from his staph infection, but now he was running a fever. Nely instructed Carol to make a doctor's appointment for the following day.


"I guarantee the demand will be made within two weeks," Tom Biffar told William Bowne. They were sitting on Bowne's favorite bench in Bryant Park. "The death toll is just short of where our friends need it to be. We've been pushing them to accelerate their plans, but there's only so far we can go."

"Tom, I am under intense pressure. That means you are under intense pressure. If anything more goes wrong, you and Ben are going to rue the day you took PharmCorp's $150 million. I know I sound melodramatic, but I'm hoping that I have made myself clear," Bowne told him, again losing his usual calm.

"Crystal, Bill. Crystal," Tom succinctly answered.


About an hour before Petar Raic's deposition was scheduled to begin in New York, Weiner received another call from his unknown informant. After instructing his assistant, Stacie, to trace the call, he answered.

"This is Special Agent Weiner."

"Ben Opperman," she replied, and then immediately hung up.

A few minutes later, Stacie came in with the results of the trace. "The call originated at a phone box in central London. We have an address."

"Gary," he yelled out to Special Agent Gary Landau, "Get the Scotland Yard liaison on the phone. Stacie has the address of the call-box used by our informant. Let's see what we can get." Although British MI5 and Scotland Yard maintained an extensive network of video surveillance throughout London, Barry knew it would be at least several hours before he could obtain any useful information on their caller.

"Will do," Landau replied, even as he started dialing the Scotland Yard liaison, who was located right in the FBI's own head-quarters building, a few floors away.

"Stacie, get Nate in here," Barry next instructed his assistant, referring to Nate Siegel, the latest addition to his growing staff. In less than a minute, Nate was in Barry's office.

"I want you to find out everything you can about Ben Opperman. You have 30 minutes."

"Seriously?" Nate asked.

"You now have 29 minutes," Barry answered, wanting the information before Greg Schoenfeld walked into the C3 offices for Raic's deposition.

Just 27 minutes later, Siegel reported that Opperman was a 72-year-old Jew, who had been born in the Soviet Union, moved to

Israel, and then to Paris. His family had been killed during the Yom Kippur War and since then he had run a security firm of dubious ethics. Weiner immediately called Schoenfeld with the information.

They sat around a conference table on the 63$^{rd}$ floor of C3's New York office tower. Petar Raic, Eric Jacobs and two lawyers from Jacobs' staff appeared to be in uniform—each wearing a white starched shirt with monograms and engraved silver cuff links, a red and gold Zegna tie, and a dark blue Zegna suit. Schoenfeld and the mid-level staff lawyer he brought with him each wore blue button down shirts and striped ties. Schoenfeld dressed in a conservative blue pinstripe suit, while his colleague wore a tan suit. A technician who would videotape the deposition looked sloppy in his distressed jeans and oversized polo shirt. The only woman present was the court reporter, who wore a proper gray pinstripe suit and white blouse. All had worn overcoats given the time of year and the two-inch layer of white powder covering the streets from the latest snowfall.

"I want to thank you for voluntarily appearing," Schoenfeld began the proceedings, which were being both videotaped and transcribed. "Is there any reason you cannot give accurate and complete testimony today?" he asked Petar.

Petar was the only person present who would appear on camera, which was tightly focused on him from the middle of his chest. The light used to illuminate the conference room glared off his forehead and his lip occasionally quivered. In his nearly 25 years as a killer and an executive for the C3 Group, Petar had never before been deposed. His life was based on keeping secrets, not telling the truth under penalty of perjury to an experienced U.S. attorney in New York City.

"Before Mr. Raic answers that question, I want to remind you of the ground rules for this voluntary appearance by Mr. Raic. Mr.

Raic does not have to answer any question I direct him not to answer. He has the right to a break whenever he wants one, and he may consult privately with me at any time. Finally, the total time allotted to this questioning will be one hour," Jacobs stated for the record. Though he would not appear on camera, his words were being recorded for the video and the transcript. It was very important that if things went poorly, Jacobs could later point to the fact that Petar's appearance had been voluntary.

Things went poorly almost from the start.

"Mr. Raic, would you answer the question, please," Schoenfeld said.

"Could you repeat the question?" Petar asked.

"Of course, is there any reason you cannot give accurate and complete testimony today?" Schoenfeld replied.

"No. I mean yes, I can testify today," Petar stammered.

"Good. What do you know about *antidote.com*?"

"I don't know what you mean," Petar replied.

"You have never heard of *antidote.com*, Mr. Raic?"

"No."

"You are under oath, Mr. Raic. Let me ask you once again. Have you ever heard of *antidote.com*?"

"No."

"Very well. Have you ever heard of Taiwan Pharmaceutical Investments Ltd.?"

"No."

"Have you ever heard of RD Pharmaceuticals?"

"No," a shaken Petar Raic answered, shocked that they knew anything about Taiwan Pharmaceuticals, let alone RD. Taiwan Pharmaceuticals had never been owned by the C3 Group, though it had been indirectly funded by Karasik Capital to acquire drug manufacturers in Asia, including 60% of RD Pharmaceuticals. Taiwan Pharmaceuticals eventually transferred that 60% interest to a very secret company in Panama, Inversiones y Distribución Médicas de Las Producciones S.A.

"What about Inversiones y Distribución Médicas de Las Producciones S.A," Schoenfeld pressed.

"No." Petar's head began to spin. Perhaps a dozen people in the entire world knew about Inversiones y Distribución Médicas de Las Producciones. How could this be?

"Mr. Raic, do you know a Ben Opperman?" Schoenfeld politely inquired.

"Who?" Petar replied, totally stunned. *How could they possibly know about Ben? What else did they know?* And then it hit him, it was the leak. *Whoever she was, the government knew everything. The Judas must have told them everything. My God, how would they be able to proceed? How would he protect Ken? How would he protect Project Sky?*

"Mr. Raic, please answer the question. Do you know a Ben Opperman?"

"I don't know him. I need a break. I need to talk to my lawyer," Petar was perspiring as he removed his microphone and practically dragged Eric Jacobs out of the conference room.

Once in the hallway, Petar told Eric that he had to end the deposition. "They know things they couldn't possibly know," Petar told his lawyer. "I need to talk to Ken. Something is very wrong."

Now it was Jacobs' turn to be concerned. "Are you telling me that you have been lying under oath? Do you actually know this Ben Opperman? Do you know the companies he was asking about?"

"Look, I can't talk about these things. Not to you and certainly not to him!" Petar jabbed his finger in Schoenfeld's direction, regaining some of his usual cockiness. "You're just going to have to get a postponement. I'm leaving." With that, Petar walked to the elevator, and left.

All of the lawyers in the conference room saw exactly what happened through the glass walls of the conference room that looked out onto the main hallway at the C3 Group's North American headquarters. When Jacobs returned to the conference room there wasn't much left to say. They all knew that the deposition had not gone well for Petar, or for the C3 Group.

Baby Kenan was turning blue. He vomited and he was having difficulty breathing. This time, even Nely suspected that this wasn't normal. "Give him another one of those antibiotics that worked before and I'll take him to see Dr. Taylor in the morning," Nely instructed as she walked into her bedroom for the night.

The following morning, Kenan looked worse. Nely sent Carol to take Kenan to the emergency room at St. Joseph's and instructed Isabella to look after the girls. She told them she would leave for the hospital as soon as she finished dressing. This time, Kenan was seen after just a few minutes, diagnosed with pneumonia, and immediately admitted to the children's unit of the hospital.

An hour later, Nely arrived. She swept into the hospital, nervously talking into her cell phone, "Alexa, I just don't know what's wrong with the baby…" A hospital worker reminded her to turn the phone off inside the hospital. With the staff still on edge over the unsolved murders of President Pullman and Dr. O'Donnell, the worker immediately notified security when Nely was slow to react. As the portly guard moved in her direction, she finally put the phone away.

"I'm Mrs. Nely Karasik," she informed the receptionist. "My son was brought in here this morning. Where may I find him please?"

The receptionist reviewed her monitor and said, "He's been admitted. He's in room 314."

When Nely walked in, a nurse was moving the baby onto a gurney. "Where are you taking him?" she asked the nurse, suddenly concerned that Kenan could be seriously ill.

"The doctor has just ordered him moved to the intensive care unit," she replied.

"Intensive care!" Nely shouted, now extremely concerned. "Oh my God, what is going on with him?"

"He has acute pneumonia, Mrs. Karasik," the nurse said, "we need to monitor him very closely."

They headed for the ICU, where nurses hovered around the baby. First, they moved him to a crib. Then, one nurse inserted an intravenous line and attached a saline solution that would soon be filled with life-saving drugs, while another hooked him up to a device that would monitor his vital signs. The monitor showed his vitals were weak—and getting weaker.

Barry Weiner was elated. Raic might just as well have admitted everything by his act in New York. Slowly but surely his team was putting the pieces together. Weiner's team had indeed done an impressive job. Raic was right that the government knew everything, or just about everything. But, he was wrong in assuming that the informant had been the source of most of the questions being asked by Greg Schoenfeld at the deposition. The source of most of that information had been good old-fashioned detective work, aided by subpoenas and police forces around the world.

Once the Cowells were murdered, the FBI had ripped apart *antidote.com's* records, and with the assistance of the Royal Canadian Mounted Police, they found and reviewed practically every legal and financial record ever created by the Cowells or *antidote.com*. The connection to C3 Pharmaceuticals wasn't even a secret—meaning Petar Raic wasn't a very smart liar. He easily could have admitted to knowing about *antidote.com* without giving away anything away.

Raic's very own signature appeared on the wire transfer instructions that funded *antidote.com* back in 2000. In fact, for the first few months C3 openly operated the web site through one of its indirect subsidiaries. It was only when *antidote.com* began to sell unlicensed drugs that the web site was supposedly sold to the Cowells. Raic had no reason to hide his role in *antidote.com's* formation. It had to be something else.

"I don't know the whole story, but I know that *antidote.com* and at least half a dozen other web sites are purchasing large quantities of counterfeit pharmaceuticals from a series of distributors. In turn, those distributors receive their products from Inversiones y Distribución Médicas de Las Producciones S.A., a Panamanian company," Barry explained to his boss, Assistant Director Richard Goldstein.

"It took a while, but finally the Caymans gave Calandra just enough banking information to establish that the ultimate distributor is this Panamanian company. We still don't know who owns it, but the banking records show that Inversiones purchased its products from at least a dozen different manufacturers all over the world," Barry added.

"Barry, you've done a fabulous job. I still don't know if this is terrorism, but there's no doubt these are some seriously bad players, either way."

Weiner, Goldstein, Calandra and Landau were meeting in the small conference room near Barry's office. By the time Goldstein had come down at 8:30 the morning after the deposition for a quick update, the entire team had already been at work for at least an hour.

"By the way," Goldstein asked, "Any progress identifying the informant?"

"Unfortunately, no. Our analysis of pictures from Rockefeller Center has been a dead end," Barry admitted. "On the other hand, we know a lot more about *antidote.com*. Chris, why don't you tell the Director what you've learned?" Barry said, giving Calandra an opportunity to interact with Goldstein.

"We have learned quite a bit. For example, we know that *antidote.com*'s largest supplier was RD Pharmaceuticals in Pune, India. We haven't found out much about RD yet, but in running all of the relevant names through government databases around the world, we found something very interesting in Taiwan," Special Agent Chris Calandra reported in his first meeting ever with the Assistant Director.

Taiwan's existence depends upon China's continuing belief that the United States Navy would intervene should China seek to forcibly re-unite with that island-nation. The *quid pro quo* for U.S. support has long been favorable economic arrangements for U.S. businesses and efficient and complete cooperation with U.S. intelligence agencies and the FBI. Fortunately, Taiwan maintains comprehensive and highly computerized records for corporate transactions that occur there.

"Thanks to cooperation from the Taiwan tax authority, we found a 2002 tax return that recorded the sale of a controlling interest in RD Pharmaceuticals from a Taiwanese company, Taiwan Pharmaceuticals, to the Inversiones company," Calandra explained, justifiably proud of his work.

"I'm still not sure of the ultimate meaning of this information. But, we're getting there. We need to interview people at Inversiones, Taiwan Pharmaceuticals and RD Pharmaceuticals," Barry said.

"You've got it," Goldstein interjected. "Just get me a budget and a travel request as quickly as possible."

"Thanks boss," Barry replied, glad that Goldstein had made the unannounced visit.

They were finally making progress. The discovery of Inversiones y Distribución Médicas de Las Producciones S.A was important for another reason. For weeks Francine and her investigators at the FDA had detected a large increase in shipments to many of the Canadian web sites from an unidentified source. Now they knew the source and they were starting to review the records to determine just what had been shipped, and where. More than ever, Barry was convinced this was no ordinary counterfeiting operation.

Barry sat down to write a report on the day's events. The report would be distributed to the entire team, as well as those participating in the investigation at the FBI, IRS, FDA and Justice, including Jason Waters.

Viktor Dzogan had fully recovered from the gunshot he suffered in the attack in Tuzla. This time, the strike would be even more deadly.

Their routine was familiar. They left their base in two jeeps. Two experienced killers sat in the front seats. As usual, they wore military-style fatigues, but without rank or unit insignia. Their M3 .45 caliber automatic weapons and assault vests were stacked in the rear. Each assault vest was packed with five magazines—150 messengers of death—and six antipersonnel fragmentation grenades. The target would have no defense.

They had no problem entering Bosnia and Herzegovina and within half an hour they approached the beautiful spa town of Srebrenica, infamous for more than 7,000 Muslims slaughtered right under NATO's watchful eyes just over 10 years earlier. They pulled off to the side of the road for a final weapons check and to suit up in their assault vests. Within two minutes they were ready to kill. Dzogan turned to his three colleagues and gave the "go" signal.

With that, the four Serbians sped into Srebrenica. They came to a stop at the red brick elementary school. There were two entrances, both facing the school's front plaza. Quickly, Dzogan and Jovan Tesla took position at one entrance and Slavisa Popovic and Srecko Andric took position at the other. As soon as they were in place, Dzogan again signaled. They burst inside. First, they targeted the guards, two old men who likely were unarmed. Dzogan cut one down with a three-shot burst to the head. Just a split second later, Popovic located the other and killed him with two shots to the chest.

At the first sound of gunfire, two adults, probably teachers, ran to see what was happening. Popovic and Andric killed them before they could find out. Students began screaming and against all logic, ran into the hallways. Switching to fully automatic, their large .45 caliber bullets tore through skin and bone, taking countless young lives in just seconds. The smell of cordite and the stench of death were overpowering. Pandemonium erupted as the students finally began running for cover. It was too late.

The unit split up, with each man selecting a classroom. Using two-shot bursts to conserve ammunition and fragmentation grenades in classrooms filled with children, they systematically exterminated the Slav students. Razor-sharp slivers from their grenades indiscriminately sliced into arms, legs, throats and heads, and the panicked cries and moans became even worse. The toll of dead and wounded mounted.

By then the melee was in full eruption, with screams everywhere. Students and teachers were jumping from windows, and shouts could be heard from nearby residences. The four continued to fire into the defenseless students for nearly a minute. Then, Dzogan took out a whistle and blew three short blasts. With that, the four Serbian terrorists withdrew, careful not to slip on the once polished floors now slick with the blood of helpless children.

They returned to their jeeps and headed out of Bosnian territory. In less than four minutes, 130 students, eight teachers, the principal and the security guards were dead and another 70 students were seriously wounded.

Stuart King immediately went to work, using the tragedy to generate press around the world. For once, the editorials were swift and the condemnation strong.

Ken called Nely on her cell. When there was no answer, he left a message and called her at home. She wasn't in, so he asked for Isabella. She told him that baby Kenan was in the hospital, and had been there since yesterday. Furious that he had not been contacted immediately, he phoned the hospital. Nely came to the phone at the nurse's station, sobbing. "Ken, sweetheart, I just didn't want to worry you," she wept, before breaking down completely.

"Alright, alright," he replied, "don't cry now…we'll get our baby the best doctors and he'll recover," he reassured his wife, who eventually calmed down.

As the days wore on, Kenan remained critical and showed no signs of improvement. Ken hired a special case manager to review his condition and make recommendations. Three days later he read the report, which included the following: "On January 13, 2006 at 9:07 pm nanny Carol Craige purchased a 10-day supply of cyprofaxin and a 10-day supply of nermycin from *antidote.com*. Kenan Karasik responded to one five-day course of the antibiotics and administration of the drugs was discontinued at that time."

Ken immediately knew what was happening and he was horrified. He placed an emergency call to Ben. "I need the Abcyclene and I need it now!" he demanded. Ben made a phone call at once. That very evening, a physician employed by C3 flew to Hillcrest Valley with the Abcyclene.

For the first time in Ken's life, he was unable to focus. With the potential loss of his only son hanging over his head, he chain smoked Cuban cigars and gritted his teeth. He agonized and analyzed. And he prayed for help. First, to his Lord and Saviour, Jesus Christ. Then, he did something he hadn't done in more than 30 years. He got down on his knees, faced Mecca and prayed to Allah.

And then, the *other* unthinkable happened.

Though his cousin had not been very successful in slowing the investigation, Waters had been able to get copies of grainy surveillance stills distilled from the video cameras that had caught the mysterious informant during her call to Barry Weiner from New York's Rockefeller Center. So far, the FBI had not been able to identify the woman. Ken realized that this woman, whoever she was, had to have a connection to the members of the Karasik Commission. He intended to carefully examine the pictures. If he failed to recognize the woman, he would pass the photos on to Ben and the others.

Ken poured over the grainy photographs. He viewed frame after frame of the originals, as well as special digitally-enhanced copies. He smoked and he viewed. Most of the pictures showed a woman so covered up by sunglasses, a scarf and a long overcoat that they were useless. When a bit of ash fell onto one of the shots in front of him, he quickly brushed it away. Then he looked a little closer. He got up, walked over to a lamp and placed the photograph directly beneath the light bulb. Then he walked over to the window and looked against the sunlight. Although he still couldn't see her, there was something about her posture and the way she swept her hair out of the way that was familiar. He knew who she was.

He opened his cell phone and placed his second call of the day to Ben. When he told Ben that he was almost certain Alexa was their leak, Ben laughed. "Ken, with all the added pressure you're under with the baby, I'm going to forgive you for your paranoia. But, you're my friend. So tomorrow morning, I'll find Mihalic or Biffar and have them look into it."

"Ben, you should take this seriously," Karasik responded, shocked at the brush off.

"I'll take care of it. I promise."

After returning his cell phone to his pocket, he again looked at the photos. He thought about Ben and Alexa dancing together at the Thanksgiving party, and it dawned on him. Could this be the same woman who had seemed so familiar at the Cher concert in New York? He would give Ben until the morning, but if Ben didn't come around, he would resolve this himself.

Petar had been wandering the streets of Manhattan all day. He had to figure out what was happening. Only the members of the Karasik Commission knew everything. It was inconceivable one of them was the leak. Yet, who else would know so many details? Could it be Mike Mihalic? Or, perhaps one of Ben's people? Could it be Nely? Nely certainly knew Ben and of his association with Ken and the others around him. But, how would Nely know about

Inversiones, or Taiwan Pharmaceuticals, or RD? How would she even know about *antidote.com,* though it was possible Ken had talked openly about the web site when it was first established. Even if he assumed that Nely wasn't quite the bump on the log that she appeared to be, why would Ken tell her so much? No, Ken was never home, it couldn't be.

Could the FBI have figured this out on its own? Ken's usually impeccable sources hadn't warned him, or Petar would surely have known about it. It didn't make sense. And who could he call? Each and every member of the Karasik Commission was suspect. He couldn't count on any of them. Petar decided to sleep on it before deciding what to do next.

Ben shook his head as he poured himself another scotch. He picked up a report Tom Biffar had written for him on the mess at St. Joseph's. Too bad Tom had to kill Pullman and the doctor, but unreliable operatives were just too damn risky. He was about to start the report, when the phone rang. It was Alexa, still at the Dorchester in London. "Hello darling," he said to her sweetly. "Ben!" she squealed in utter delight. He just loved it that she was always so enthusiastic when they spoke. "How are you, honey?" he asked.

"Ben, I am so grateful to you for insisting that I come and see Lucy. I'm so glad I was here for the funeral. I suppose it's time to go home—if I knew where that was—maybe I'll come visit you in Paris," she said, still upset about Nico's death. He tried to console her. Alexa stopped for a moment, "You know Ben, we all have to meet our maker sooner or later. None of us is getting out of this racket alive."

"I know, honey," he replied. "I'm glad you had a chance to see your friend one last time." Then he added, "I miss you. I want you to take your time but I sure can't wait for you to be back here with me."

"Just close your eyes and imagine me there, Ben," she said dreamily. "You'll feel my presence almost instantly."

"You just might be the one to rein in this old bachelor," he said, as he laughed merrily.

About an hour later, Ben started reading Tom's report. None of it was very interesting until he got to a sentence he just couldn't believe. Nicolas Nedeljko Bartanovic was also known as one Nico Bart. His granddaughter was Alexa Bart. It didn't make sense! *Or did it? Could Ken be right? My God... am I to blame for the leak?*

A few moments later, there was a knock on the door. A private messenger held a large manila envelope. "Mr. Opperman?" the uniformed messenger asked. "Yes," he replied. "It's a special delivery for you, sir." Then he quickly shifted his left hand, which had been hidden by the envelope, to reveal the silencer on a 9-mm gun. Before Ben could take a breath, a single shot to the head sent him flying backwards onto the floor.

Within an hour, Max Linville woke Bowne. "I just got the report from our men in Paris. Opperman's dead."

At about the same time Bowne received his call, Alexa's cell phone rang. It was Faisal. "The Frenchman has departed," he said.

Petar Raic returned to his hotel room at the Four Seasons, but he couldn't sleep. Finally, he decided to call Ben. Petar had to warn him that the government knew about him. He reached for his secure cell phone and punched in the number that always found Ben wherever he was. It rang several times and then went to voicemail. Petar left a one-word message that was their code for an emergency. The few times he had left a similar message over the last 10 years, Ben had always returned the call within an hour. Petar finally fell asleep at 4:00 in the morning. He still hadn't heard from Ben. When he awoke at 10:00 the next morning, he again tried Ben's number. There was no response.

Something was clearly very wrong.

Ken left for London. He realized that if Alexa had been clever enough to pull this off, killing her was not going to solve their problem. It was time for a candid discussion.

# PART III

*"But if the wicked, turning away from the wickedness he has committed, does what is right and just, he shall preserve his life; since he has turned away from all the sins he has committed, he shall surely live, he shall not die."*

Ezekiel 18:28

# FORTY TWO

ALEXA'S CELL PHONE rang as she lay down for a massage at the Dorchester's spa. She wasn't expecting Faisal. She wasn't expecting anyone. She pressed the button to answer the call but said nothing.

"Alexa, this is Ken," she heard.

"To what do I owe the pleasure of this call?" she asked, amused.

"Ben is dead."

"I'll send flowers," she replied, not in the least bit broken hearted. "Two dozen Casablanca lilies should do." *Same arrangement as Grandpa's*, she thought.

"Alexa, a meeting would be mutually productive."

"I'm on vacation."

"Alexa, we need to discuss the situation before more people get hurt."

"There's nobody in my world left to hurt, Ken."

"The choice of what happens next is yours."

"Are you threatening me?" she asked confidently.

"I'm at the Lanesborough. Where can we meet?"

She thought for a moment. "Harrods Food Halls. In front of the butcher shop at noon tomorrow."

"C'mon Alexa, that's ridiculous!" he protested. "It's a jungle there…"

"That's right," she said calmly. "It's a jungle where you'll have your killers and I'll have mine. Ciao, mi amore." With that, she hung up the phone and succumbed to Omar's strong thumbs.

Ken dialed Petar's secure cell phone.

"I'm in London. There are some things you have to know. Ben is dead. Baby Kenan is ill. He's been infected by Project Sky."

Petar was stunned. "What happened? How?" referring to both Ben and Kenan.

"Ben was shot in the head in his apartment. We don't know yet know who did it. Mike is on top of it. As to Kenan, the staff ordered drugs from one of our web sites. Petar, just hours before he was murdered, I called Ben to arrange for Abcyclene to be flown to Hillcrest Valley. I've checked. Ben acted immediately… We'll find who did this."

It was ironic, even as Ben lay dead with a bullet in his brain, the Abcyclene he arranged for was arriving in Hillcrest Valley to save Kenan's life.

"My friend, one favor. Please follow up to make certain there is no problem with the antidote."

"Of course, Ken. I'll go personally," Petar softly replied.

"Thank you, but there's so much going on that you should send someone else—someone you can trust."

"Ken, my deposition was a mess. The government lawyers seemed to know everything. They knew about our distributors, our manufacturers and *antidote.com*. They even know about Ben, not that it will hurt him now," Petar became sad, before continuing. "Whoever is leaking information must be one of us. I don't see any alternative."

Ken listened quietly. He did not reveal to Petar that he knew Alexa was the informant, and Ben himself unwittingly the leak.

"These are troubling times. We have to remain strong. Work with Eric. Get someone over to Hillcrest Valley. And don't worry, we're going to win!" Ken solemnly told him.

"I know. With all that's happening, we should accelerate our plans," Petar suggested.

"We will. Once we know baby Kenan is out of danger, we will move into the final phase. I'll be back in the U.S. within a week. We'll discuss it then.

"Oh, Petar, one last thing," Ken began, "the time has come to eliminate our Mr. Weiner. Please ask Tom to handle this personally."

It was very unusual for Ken to directly give such an order. Petar knew Ken was tired and upset. "I don't think that's a very good idea. I'd be happy to see Weiner dead, but killing him won't end the investigation. In fact, it might incite the FBI and have just the opposite effect. Why don't you sleep on this and make a decision tomorrow? In the meantime, I'll get hold of Tom and ask him to stand by in Washington. Maybe Tom can even undertake some scouting," Petar explained, hoping that Ken would change his mind.

"Ok, I'll think about it overnight. Just make sure Tom is ready to move," Ken conceded, sounding exhausted.

"Thanks. I'll assign Paul Little to look after Kenan."

"Thank you, my friend. Now let's make sure Ben's life wasn't wasted. Let's make a difference," Ken said before terminating the call.

Petar called Tom and headed off to find Eric Jacobs. He did not look forward to their next meeting.

The following day at high noon in London, Alexa strolled into the Harrods Food Halls attired in her trademark black turtleneck, perfectly fitting blue jeans and black suede Gucci stiletto boots. A long solid black sable hung from her shoulders and her hands were placed inside the jeans' pockets. She looked like any other upper crust lady about town on such a fine day.

Ken arrived with Mike Mihalic. He spotted Alexa nibbling on a piece of white chocolate she had picked up from the confections bar. "Would you like a bite?" she offered as he approached her.

"No, thank you," he said. "Can we just go somewhere where we can sit down and talk?" he asked, sounding frustrated.

"I think better on my feet," she replied as she placed her arm in his and they slowly strolled past the shoppers like any other caring couple. Mike trailed a few feet behind. Alexa winked at him. It would not have surprised Ken or Mike to know that Faisal was carefully monitoring them on Harrods' security system, while three plain-clothes members of his security team lingered nearby. It also would not have surprised Alexa or Faisal to know that half a dozen armed members of Mihalic security team were among the crowd and another half dozen armed members of the team were nearby. Their job was to protect Ken, and if he so instructed by pre-arranged signal, kill Alexa.

"I'm not here to screw you," he insisted.

"Mr. Karasik!" she said dramatically. "You'd screw a lamp post if it suited you."

"I've never underestimated you," he began diplomatically.

She threw her head back and laughed seductively. "Now you're hurting my feelings, Ken. Why, to be underestimated is one of the best qualities one can possess."

"I'm not going to ask you why, because I know why," he went on. "But what will it take to end this path of destruction you're on and bring you back on board?"

"To rearrange the deck chairs on the Titanic, Ken? I'm not interested in the job."

"Alexia, if I go down, how long do you think before it's all over for you, too?" he threatened.

She chuckled. "I'm no longer in business with you, Ken Karasik. Don't think I haven't made arrangements for the truth to find its way to the FBI should something untoward happen to me." After a pause, she added, "You're not unlike King Harrod of Egypt. When he ordered all boys under the age of two to be killed in order to destroy Christ, his own son got butchered in the process."

This filled Karasik with rage. If they had been anywhere else, he would have killed her with his bare hands. "How is the little fellow doing anyway?" she inquired casually.

"We don't know," he answered, struggling to control himself. "I'm going to put the genie back in the bottle, Alexia. No more innocent people are going to die."

"Kenan Anton Joseph Karasik III! You impress me with your newfound conscience," she said mockingly. "Have you been going to therapy? Have you found religion?" Despite her bravado, Alexa knew that if Karasik wanted her dead, she would be dead, threats of tell-alls to the FBI, or not. There was a reason she had led the FBI toward Raic and away from Ken. As much as she enjoyed causing him pain, in the end she very much wanted to live.

"Alexia, I'm willing to trade, within limits. I do not intend to remain in London past this weekend. I suggest you consider your options and formulate a proposal before I leave. If I leave before we have an arrangement, the decisions will be mine alone."

"You have nothing I want."

"I have your life," he countered.

"Perhaps," she parried, "but I have no heirs to miss me. You do," she threatened. He ignored her.

"Oh, and Alexia, dear, I certainly hope that you had nothing to do with Ben's death. He was very important to me and I don't expect his killer will die very easily. On the other hand, if we have a deal, I will respect it so long as you do. Am I clear?"

"Transparent," she responded, a small crack showing in her insouciance.

"Do let me know if we have anything further to discuss. I prefer a business solution. But there will be a solution, Alexia." With that, Ken and Mike headed for the street. Only a few members of the security detail left with them. The others remained in place. They were to stay very close to Alexa and report back to Mike. Beyond that, their instructions were to be ready. No detail was provided on just what it was for which they were to be prepared.

As Ken and Mike headed for Brompton Road, Alexa wandered around the Food Halls. She stocked up on her favorite chocolates. She knew that Ken's men would report her every move back to him. Appearing to be lost in oblivion at the Food Halls should confuse them.

Clutching her Harrods green plastic bags, she hailed a taxi and headed back to the Dorchester. Once inside her suite, there was no one with whom to discuss her predicament, nor many options to consider. She was financially secure but personally vulnerable, a position she would never permit herself to be in again.

Although she had set up a masterful maze to protect herself—as clever as any Karasik ever created—she simply did not have his vast resources at her disposal. Alexa knew that she could become a formidable enemy by joining forces with Faisal and his allies in Saudi Arabia. But, did she really want to do business with them? How powerful could she become as a Karasik insider?

It was like a replay of Operation Cyber Chase. On January 31, 2006, as Washington, D.C. was again blanketed with snow, agents of the Organized Crime Drug Enforcement Task Force closed down *antidote.com* and four other Canadian web sites that had been selling counterfeit drugs. There were 10 arrests in three foreign countries: Canada, India and Costa Rica. Those arrested either operated the web sites or distributed product for the web sites.

It was just the tip of the iceberg. Barry Weiner's task force was gathering evidence that likely would lead to additional arrests in the United States, India, Malaysia, Switzerland and Panama. At least 10 more web sites were implicated. The big targets remained Ken Karasik and Mel Bottner. So far they had eluded the net. There was still time.

An overachiever named Lauren Alexander had enrolled at Northern Arizona University in Flagstaff for its famed "journalism camp." She was the most naturally gifted and hardest working writer there. It wouldn't hurt her career that she was downright gorgeous.

On Tuesday, Lauren and her best friend Miriam, drove to visit Miriam's grandparents who had retired in Scottsdale. By the time they had arrived at Gainey Ranch, Lauren wasn't feeling well. Miriam complained to her grandparents that Lauren had arrived at NAU with the sniffles and had been burning the candle at both ends. By nightfall, Lauren was burning up with a 102.6 temperature. Miriam got Lauren into her grandparents' Lexus and drove her to Scottsdale Healthcare Hospital at Osborn. She was seen right away.

"That's what I get from flying with people who don't have the good sense to stay at home when they're sick," the germophobic Lauren mumbled upon entering the emergency room. Yesterday, Lauren had been honored with the comical albeit prestigious "Balls of Steel" award from her fellow journalism campers. Within a few days she would be clinging to life on a respirator, as her pneumonia-like symptoms became life threatening.

In Beverly Hills, the strikingly beautiful and socially promi-nent widow of the late movie mogul, Henry Yodleman, felt a pres-sure in her chest. Since her husband had died less than a year ago, Susan's stress-related ailments were nothing unexpected. But this time her distress persisted. She phoned Dr. Digney. He convinced her to come down for blood work and general labs. "Better safe than sorry," he told her.

Less than 24 hours later, Susan Yodleman learned that she had picked up a staph infection somewhere. The nurse phoned in some prescriptions at the pharmacy on the first floor. On her way home, Susan picked up cyprofaxin, and a number of other drugs. When her daughter Jackie called to check in, Susan told her about the staph infection. Jackie went on the Internet to learn about staph infections. She found a web site that promised much quick-er relief when cyprofaxin was mixed with nermycin, so she ordered a 10-day supply.

The next day, Jackie brought the nermycin to her mom's house. Although Susan was already taking the drugs her doctor prescribed, she agreed to also take the nermycin.


The data was pouring in to the CDC.

"There's no doubt that this new 'pneumonia' is somehow associated with staph infections. Though most of those being admitted for pneumonia report no staph infections, far too many of the most serious cases report a staph infection occurring within the previous two months. The statistical association is particularly noticeable among those who have died since December," Suzy Liebig reported to David Salzman.

"We may know part of 'what.' We need to know 'why.' Let's focus on why staph infections are leading to this pseudo-pneumonia. And, while we're at it, let's find out what this so-called pneumonia really is and why it's so resistant to the usual protocols," Salzman instructed her.

"Anything else?" Suzy asked, her quizzical look suggesting that she thought the assignment was already more than sufficient.

"I know it's a tall order. But a lot of sick people are depending on us. Just let me know what I can do to help," Salzman replied, his dedication to his job once again coming to the fore.


"Stuart, we owe you. Your articles have changed the dialogue, worldwide," Ken told Stuart on his secure cell, after the two had discussed Petar's deposition in New York and progress in finding Ben's killer.

The Serbian atrocities at the school in Srebrenica had reminded the world of Bosnia's precarious position. King's articles and phone calls had whipped the story into front page news throughout Europe and the United States. Where the attack on a police station in Tuzla barely registered on the international consciousness, the death of innocent children was entirely different. Everywhere, there were demands for action. Even the U.S. Secretary of State demanded that Ivan Maslac and Viktor Dzogan be brought to justice. At the headquarters of the European Union's peacekeeping forces, orders were issued to find them. For once, public opinion was obtaining action.

Suzy Liebig punched in Francine's number. "I have to make a quick trip to Washington, are you free for dinner on Monday?" she asked her friend.

"Of course. Anything special?"

"Well, I thought it might be nice to finally meet Barry," Suzy responded in a child-like voice.

"If I can convince him to join us, he'll be there!"

"Good, how about Monday at 7:00 at Morton's?"

"Done," Francine said before they exchanged good-byes and hung up.

# FORTY THREE

**W**HEN TOM BIFFAR landed at Washington's Dulles airport on Friday morning, he found numerous messages
waiting for him on the voicemail of the secure service he used,
including two messages each from Petar and Mike Mihalic. Tom's
first call was to Mike. He punched in the 13-digit code, but instead
of being patched through, he received a fast busy signal. Though
unusual, it had happened before, so he waited a moment and tried
the call again, with the same result.

Giving up for the moment, Tom tried Petar's private number.
This time he got through. "I have some bad news," Petar began,
"Ben is dead." Without giving Tom any time to consider the impli-
cations, Petar continued.

"My deposition was a mess. It's clear the U.S. government is
better informed about Project Sky than we had thought. Ken is insti-
tuting protective measures, while assessing the next steps. For one,
we all have new numbers—take these down." Petar quickly rattled
off sets of 13-digit numbers, then abruptly added, "Stake out
Weiner. Ken may want him taken out."

"That's not a good idea," Tom replied.

"I know. I have made that case to Ken. But, until he changes
his mind, I would do as he asks."

Tom always traveled with only carry-on luggage, so he wasted no time in getting through customs. Before boarding a taxi for the hour ride into Washington, he called Mike. Mihalic was able to fill in some additional details about Ben.

"We know that a messenger bluffed his way in by claiming he had a delivery. He killed Ben with a single silenced shot to the head from a Glock 9mm automatic. We also know that Ben suspected he was under surveillance."

"How?" Tom asked.

"That's what he told Georges," Mihalic explained, referring to Ben's deputy in the Paris office.

"Anything else?" Tom asked, immediately concerned that the assailant could have been sent by PharmCorp.

"No, not yet. Tom, do you have any ideas? Odds are that it was one of your clients."

"I need to think about it. There are several possibilities, but none that jump ahead of the others," Tom lied to Mike. "Still, give me a day or two and I may be able to narrow your search."

"Good. We're going to catch these bastards. I can assure you of that. By the way, there's a conference call set for tomorrow at 2:00 pm Eastern time. Secure lines. I need you on the call."

"Who will be on the call?"

"Don't worry about it. One last thing," Mike said, "Petar asked me to forward the surveillance reports on Barry Weiner. Where do you want them?"

"Just email them to the usual address," Tom responded.

Tom got in the taxi line. When his turn came, he asked the taxi to drop him at the Sheraton at 1201 K Street, NW. Once he got out of the cab, he entered the hotel and continued walking until he reached the side exit. Then, he left the Sheraton, turned right, and headed on for another 10 minutes until he reached the small apartment he kept in Washington. Tom remained there only long enough to shower, shave and change his clothes. He downloaded and read the report on Weiner, taking note of Weiner's address, habits and girlfriend. Then he put on a sweater and a warm overcoat and headed back out to begin his surveillance.

"Bill, this is falling apart. You have one week, then this isn't going to be yours to fix," Estrich told Bowne. They were sitting, alone, in the secure bubble.

"Bob, I know you're disappointed in the timing. But, the reality is that product has been shipped, people are dying and all that remains is the claim to create panic. The hearings haven't even started yet. There's plenty of time to make our case," Bowne said with more conviction than he felt.

"That may be, but we don't give bonuses around here for dumb luck. The hearings should have started last month. If that had happened, we—you would have blown the $150 million. Speaking of which, what kind of deals are you making now? Don't we usually pay for performance?" Estrich asked sarcastically.

"We've got to stay calm. Our goal is well within sight," Bowne said, realizing that he was sounding more like Ben with each breath, and not any more credible. "I'm not any happier with the delay than you. We gambled big, but so far we're still in the game. More important, no one knows about our role. We hear all these rumors about C3 and MDB. Not one about us."

"That makes me feel real good. You haven't destroyed the company, so I should be happy. Damn it Bill, Dave and I have to justify this $150 million to the executive committee. You think it was easy to get them behind this scheme in the first place? Sure, they signed off on it, but that was when only a few hundred people were going to die. Now, we have the worst of all worlds, God knows how many will die, and no claim of responsibility."

"I get it Bob, I really do."

"I hope so Bill. In another week it will be out of my hands."


Tom obtained the frequencies for the listening devices Paul Little had installed in Weiner's apartment. Thanks to voice activation and advances in battery technology, the devices were still active. After carefully checking to make certain that no one was around, Tom expertly picked the simple lock on the door to Barry's apartment and walked inside. Quickly, he walked through the apartment, learning its layout and the location of its furnishings. Tom conducted no search of Barry's papers. Little had already done that. Besides, almost as the fictional Goldfinger had once remarked to James Bond, Tom didn't want information from Barry Weiner. If so directed by Ken, he would want nothing more than Weiner's death. After completing his tour, Tom relocked the door, and left. His next stop was across the street from the FBI, from where he could follow Weiner when he left for the day.

# FORTY FOUR

FEBRUARY 4, 2006
WASHINGTON, D.C., ATLANTA, NEW YORK
PARADISE COVE, LONDON

**B**ARRY WEINER WAS perplexed. He was in the office on a Saturday so that he could review the preliminary medical examiner's report on Ben Opperman. That report showed that by the time Greg Schoenfeld questioned Raic, Opperman was already dead. The old man had been shot in the head the night before Petar's deposition. As usual, the Paris police were not very helpful when it came to U.S. security interests. Barry expected no more than the bare facts. Here, even the bare facts suggested either that their informant had an agenda, or that there was discord in the C3 camp. Alternatively, who knew how many enemies this Opperman had? Maybe it was a coincidence, but Barry didn't think so.

"For the last three months Inversiones has been heavily discounting its sales. Francine's staff has gone over the materials we obtained from the RCMP's search of *antidote.com*. Ten different drugs are involved in the 'promotion,' ranging from analgesics to AIDS medications to cyprofaxin. The offer also includes generics for two FDA-approved C3 drugs, Nermycin-X and Tamsuloren," Barry explained to Richard Goldstein. He had just phoned the Assistant Director to update him.

"That so-called promotion is a red flag," Goldstein observed. "You've got my approval to expand the investigation. Pick four agents and two accountants. Get into the field and visit with the distributors and manufacturers in Panama, India, Malaysia and China."

"Thanks boss. That's what we need to nail these guys."

"What's going on at the FDA?" Goldstein asked.

"Given their core expertise, Francine's team is trying to determine whether there's a pattern to the drugs in the promotion. If so, perhaps we have more than mere counterfeiting going on," Barry explained. He was certain that something more was going on.

"And Phil's team?" Goldstein asked, already aware that with the cooperation of officials in Canada and Costa Rica, Phil Oster had been able to sequester the warehouses used by *antidote.com* and the other web sites shut down by the FBI.

"My guess is that within a few days our labs will begin examining the drugs. I've asked the lab to give priority to the 10 drugs distributed by Inversiones, particularly nermycin, Tamsuloren and any other products we trace to C3."

"By the way, the new Justice Department lawyer is seeking access in Canada to all of *antidote.com*'s records. After talking to the Ministry in Ottawa, she's sure we'll get it," Barry explained to Goldstein.

"Good work. Convey my thanks to your team and to Francine. I'll see you Monday," Goldstein said, before heading outside for a softball game with his two sons.

If Barry had been part of Phil Oster's Internet Pharmaceutical Fraud Initiative, he would have been on cloud nine. With a lot of help from very capable investigators at the FBI, FDA and elsewhere, they had broken the back of a major counterfeit drug ring. But, Barry was not part of the Internet Pharmaceutical Fraud Initiative. He was part of the Directorate of Intelligence, tasked with preventing a terrorist attack on the United States. Barry was very certain that he was on his way to achieving that goal, even though no proof of a terrorist motive had yet come to the fore.

The CDC was also working that weekend. David Salzman had summoned Suzy Liebig and her team to review the apparent new strain of pneumonia. "Deaths meeting the criteria now total 250 and there are at least several thousand hospitalizations that do or may also meet the criteria," Ron Craig reported to the assembled group. "The core criteria are: (1) the patient exhibits symptoms consistent with pneumonia; (2) the patient does not respond at all, or responds insufficiently to customary treatment protocols; (3) the patient has no prior history of pneumonia; (4) the patient has no other illnesses that typically predict pneumonia; and (5) records show the patient has been treated for a staph infection within the last three months," Craig explained.

"The number of hospitalizations and the number of deaths are clearly growing, and the rate of increase appears also to be on the rise. That is extremely unusual. We are also beginning to see sufficient evidence that I now agree with David that this event is not limited to the young," Suzy said as sweetly as she could. She looked over to see Salzman's reaction to her concession. She was not disappointed, as his face visibly reddened at the compliment.

"Have we found any commonalities in the staph infections or the causality?" Salzman asked.

"No," Ron and Suzy answered almost in unison. "That's what's so confusing about this," Suzy added.

"Have we come at this from the other end? By that I mean, have we gone back to look at the population that contracted staph infections during the relevant period and assessed whether there is anything in that population that would predict who develops this pneumonia, and who does not?" Salzman quizzed the team.

"We are starting to do that," Suzy responded. "We need at least another week to isolate all the factors involved. At this very preliminary stage, we have not found predictive attributes of the staph infections, but it is too early to rule that out."

"Ladies and gentlemen, we are approaching a crisis. The good news is that we have caught whatever is occurring before there have been many fatalities. We all know the bad news. Each one of you has to think outside the box. We need to figure this out." With that, Salzman adjourned the meeting. Though he didn't show it, he was worried.

The conference call began promptly at 2:00 pm Eastern time for Petar in New York and Tom Biffar in Washington, and 7:00 pm in London, where Mike was staying with Ken, who had not yet left for the U.S. Surprisingly, Ken himself also participated, which he seldom did when Tom was involved. In fact, the usually taciturn Karasik spoke non-stop for nearly five minutes.

"Project Sky is in trouble. Ben is dead and Petar is facing the full weight of the U.S. Justice Department," Ken solemnly began.

"Based on the medical data, we should delay our demands for at least another two weeks, and maybe three. As each of you knows, events are moving too quickly to permit us that luxury. The FBI has closed down about half of the web sites selling our products. Distribution to the remaining web sites has been disrupted. It is only a matter of days or a week at the most before the FBI closes down the remaining sites."

Ken continued, drawing on information he had obtained just that day from his cousin, Jason Waters, and his mistress, Christine Liu. "The FBI does not have any understanding of what we are doing. However, even in his ineptitude, Weiner is getting uncomfortably close. Absent some very bad luck, it will take another few weeks for them to figure it all out. At that point, there still will be little they can do without the antidote. Nonetheless, within a few weeks, at the outside, we can expect all sales of cyprofaxin and nermycin to be suspended and we can also expect announcements asking the public to return whatever unused product they have.

"We have to make our demands by next week. Even though the FBI will figure out what we are doing just days later, more than 25,000 Americans could still die without the antidote. That should be enough to compel compliance with our demands."

Suddenly intense, Ken demanded, "The United States must end its silence. It must support our brothers. The time for talk about freedom is over. Either the United States government will hand over Milosevic and Maslac, or its people will die.

"Finally," Ken continued one of the longest speeches he had ever made to the Karasik Commission, "We need to start covering our tracks right now. Petar and Mike have been briefed."

Petar started to ask a question when Mike interrupted and informed the group that Ken had left the room.

Based on his previous briefing with Ken, however, Petar knew exactly what was expected of him. As a devout Muslim he believed that Allah protected those who could not protect themselves, whether they were Muslims, Christians or Jews. Petar would see this through to the end no matter where that took him. He asked Mike to carry out the mission previously described to him. He asked Tom to complete his assignment in Washington and then travel to Panama City using one of his aliases as soon as he could. His instructions would be waiting there.

Once the call was over, Petar headed out to a pre-arranged appointment with Eric Jacobs. Tom headed back to Weiner's apartment. He had an assignment and some thinking to do about Ben's death.

As Alexa sat in her room at the Dorchester, she thought about the gems. Neither the IRS nor any law enforcement agency knew about the diamonds or the emeralds. Alexa could hear Nely's voice echo in her head: "My husband is a great humanitarian. Heads of state and important people often ask him to help their country. He is such a kind man that many times he never even took money for all of his hard work." *No, he just took the gems and the oil.*

"Consider this your come-to-Jesus call," Bowne told Tom via secure cell phone. "Your boss is gone, but you have more than $100 million of our money and I expect you to deliver what your boss promised," he added.

"I'm looking into everything. The attack is already underway and an announcement is less than a week away. Everything is working out," Tom replied, not at all confident that anything was working out for PharmCorp, Opperman Security, the Karasik Commission, or Tom Biffar.

"I'm not feeling that way, Tom. There's not a whole lot I can do about it right now, but with the old man gone, you're in the hot seat. It's time to step up," Bowne snarled.

"Just what was your role in that?" Tom bluntly inquired.

"It's irrelevant. That's in the past. You should be concerned with what's in the present, and the future. We'll talk again tomorrow, Tom."

Bowne disconnected the call and Tom just sighed. He had to complete his current assignment. Then he had to figure out Opperman Security's financials and what to do if Ken did not make his demand on the new schedule. If Ken again delayed the plan it would not be a good thing for anyone.

Eric Jacobs always worked on the weekend. It was still only late afternoon in New York when Petar arrived at Eric's office.

The prestigious lawyer had been blunt during their last contentious meeting, when he tore into Petar. "Your behavior is utterly unacceptable. I will not abide it. If you ever again lie to me, even once and even a little, I will invoke the provisions of my contract that permit me to resign with full pay. Are we clear?"

Petar had apologized profusely. "I've never been in a deposition before. I didn't know what to expect. I need your help," he pleaded.

Finally, Jacobs had relented, on condition that Petar tell him the truth. That was why they had scheduled this meeting.

"Eric, the truth is that I have been operating behind Ken's back. I saw a business opportunity involving counterfeit drugs and I took it. I didn't steal from Ken. Not one cent. All of the profits have gone right into the C3 accounts. I never made a dime. I was getting such terrific returns on our money. I knew Ken would be pleased with the returns, and he was. Aside from that, I got nothing for myself." Petar just kept rambling on. "I am very sorry... I just didn't expect anyone to get hurt... I didn't think anyone had. It was just a business deal, and now it's obviously gone wrong."

"Petar, you do understand that by using C3's money and putting the profits in C3's accounts you've exposed all of us to potential liability? You understand that it looks as though the corporation was involved in the plot?" Eric asked the nearly broken man before him.

"Not really," Petar replied. "When I did it, I thought that by keeping Ken, Steve Maier and you out of it, I was protecting not only them and you, but also C3. How could C3 be liable if its CEO, president and general counsel are in the dark?"

"For the third time, Petar, as chief operations officer of the entire group, your involvement alone is sufficient to subject the C3 Group and Karasik Capital to criminal liability. Equally important, it must be extremely difficult for the government to believe that Ken is not involved."

That last one hit home. Petar would never knowingly do something that placed Ken in any danger.

Jacobs forcefully continued, "It's just not credible that you alone created *antidote.com*, Taiwan Pharmaceutical Investments Ltd., and that Inversiones company. How am I supposed to make the government believe otherwise?" Eric wasn't sure he believed it, no matter how strongly Petar was willing to take full and complete responsibility.

Getting nowhere, Jacobs moved on. "What about Ben Opperman?"

"He's a security consultant I used to do business with. I haven't seen him in years. I just froze when his name came up," Petar explained.

"Petar, I'm sorry. You're going to have to step down from your positions in the public companies. I'll have to talk to Ken about the private companies. You're going to need your own attorney. I can recommend some excellent criminal defense lawyers. I have to focus on how to avoid C3 becoming the next Enron." Jacobs was also thinking about how to ensure that his severance agreement would be enforceable, even if C3 failed. He would not have wanted to know what Petar was thinking.

Just a short while later, though the time was much later at night in London, Alexa's cell phone rang. A Mr. Weiss was on the line. He would be making a special delivery, if she was alone. "I'll order room service," she informed him.

An hour later, her late dinner arrived. Red cabbage soup, steak and raw onions. Heavy fare at such a late hour, but Alexa needed protein power more than ever. When the waiter left, she removed everything from the delivery cart and placed the items on the nearest dresser. Then she lifted the tablecloth and removed an envelope. Inside, a brief note scrawled on a small piece of paper read: "Business plan will follow." *So, Faisal was claiming not only knowledge of Ben's death, but credit. How convenient and probably true.*

As the time approached midnight in London, she picked up her cell phone and dialed yet again. Ken answered on the second ring.

"I'd hate to have you leave on an empty stomach," Alexa said to him. "After all, you came all this way just to see me, so why don't we have lunch tomorrow at noon at Daphne's?"

"I'll see you then," he replied and disconnected.

Tom had been waiting for Barry to return home for almost four hours. Finally, he saw Barry's black Z3 approach the underground parking lot. The gate opened, and the car disappeared into the garage. Tom wasn't sure if Barry was alone, but he would know as soon as Barry entered his apartment and any conversation was picked up by the listening devices planted there.

Ten minutes later, Tom had his answer. Barry was alone, but only for a while. Francine would be coming over within the hour.

Tom headed across the street. When he reached the front door of the building, he quickly picked the lock and entered the lobby. He knew Barry lived on the third floor. Instead of taking the elevator, Tom sought the fire stairs he had located during his visit the previous day. While climbing the stairs, he screwed a 6.5-inch noise suppressor to the barrel of his specially threaded 9mm Glock automatic. The extra six ounces barely affected the gun's balance. When he reached the third floor, he gently pushed open the door to the hallway. When he was certain that no one was in the hallway, he walked to Barry's door. The listening devices told him that Barry was in his bedroom, watching television. Tom carefully picked the lock, for the second time, and entered Barry's apartment.

Francine was headed home from the gym when she got Barry's call. Though she told him that she would stick to her plan, as soon as she got off the phone she changed her mind. She decided to head straight for Barry's place. She could shower and change there before they went out for dinner. Since Barry's place was a mere three blocks from her gym, this was a far better plan she thought as she congratulated herself for saving so much time.

As usual, she parked on the street. As she approached the door, it was closing behind someone who had just gone inside. By sprinting up the steps, she was able to grab the door before it closed. She entered as the previous visitor disappeared into a stairwell. Having had enough exercise for the day, Francine pushed the elevator button. After about half a minute, the doors opened. She walked inside and pressed the button for the third floor.

Tom stopped for a moment. Hearing nothing except the television in Barry's bedroom, he proceeded to the hallway just outside the room. Inside, Barry was putting on a fresh pair of pants. Tom rounded the corner, raised his gun to a level firing position and prepared to enter.

Suddenly, Tom and Barry heard the loudest blood-curdling scream either had ever experienced, followed by shouts of, "GUN! GUN!!! GUN!!!" As Tom pivoted to see Francine standing in the doorway, Barry leapt from the bedroom and tackled him. Tom's gun was knocked from his hand, but he immediately regained his composure and hit Barry full force in the head. Barry staggered back and Tom scrambled to get the gun. Just before he got there, Francine kicked the weapon across the room.

Tom lashed out at Francine, knocking her off balance. By then, Barry had recovered and had again rushed at Tom. This time, Tom was prepared. He fended Barry off with a vicious kick to the groin. Barry moved back at just the last minute, dissipating the force of the kick. At the same time, Francine grabbed a candlestick and swung it at Tom. She swung wide, and Tom responded with a punch to Francine's head.

With all the noise they were making, neighbors were alerted. Two called 911. Caleb Beck, a Capitol policeman who lived down the hall, reached for his gun and cautiously headed to investigate.

Tom realized that this was getting out of control. In an apartment house in Washington, D.C. likely to be full of law enforcement professionals, a strategic retreat was warranted. The last thing Karasik needed was for Tom to be arrested or killed.

Francine crawled up to a dresser and picked up the lamp. But Tom saw it coming. He again swung at Francine, solidly connecting with her head. This time, she collapsed unconscious. He heard doors opening in the hallway as Barry lunged at him. Tom swung at Barry, pushing him back. Quickly, he ran out of the apartment, leaving his untraceable gun on the floor. As he darted into the hallway, he heard shouts of, "Stop! Police!" He just kept going, disappearing down the staircase. Fortunately, the policeman who had shouted at him did not pursue. When Tom reached the landing, he heard sirens approaching. He dashed out of the building and left the area before additional police arrived.

Once Tom had jumped into the stairwell, Beck retraced his steps and headed for Weiner's apartment. He entered the apartment with his gun drawn, ready for a second intruder. Weiner was bent over Francine, checking her pulse. "Caleb, thanks. He was alone," he said. "Would you help me get an ambulance? She's been knocked out cold. I don't think it's too serious." As Caleb looked at the mess, he begged to disagree.

# FORTY FIVE

**N**OON IN LONDON was only 7:00 am in New York and Washington. Alexa always found it exhilarating to have that head start on the United States.

The modern Italian restaurant in South Kensington had always been a favorite of Alexa's. She arrived early and took a seat in the brick dining room. She asked for a cup of chamomile tea and felt calmed by Daphne's atmosphere with its rustic charm. She looked onto the garden—glass-roofed, light-dappled and scattered with citrus trees and olive plants. This sunshine trap echoed the blue skies of its faraway inheritance.

Several couples were already at the restaurant by the time Alexa arrived. She assumed at least a few were Ken's security team, though she didn't know which ones. Promptly at noon, Mike and a man unknown to Alexa took a seat near the entry as Ken walked over to Alexa's table near the fireplace. "Tea?" he mocked her a bit. "I don't know about you, but I could use a good drink."

She smiled kindly and handled her cup delicately. Alexa decided to take a gentle, non-accusatory approach, "Look," she began, "I know that none of us started out to hurt anyone. We're all victims of circumstance and sometimes we get caught up in things we live to regret." Ken was quite relaxed—on the surface anyway.

She took a sip of tea. The waitress brought the breadbasket and left the menus. "My father suffered a horrible fate, as did my mother and virtually everyone I ever cared about. I've gotten to a point where I no longer feel, Ken," she said, playing for sympathy. "My father left me a treasure and I guess that you can say I used it for evil," she said, taking the blame away from Ken and placing it on herself. At least that's the impression she wanted him to walk away with.

"None of us can be certain about what the future holds," he played along.

"We've both come too far and can still do great things if we can get back on course. Ken, if you'll just stop producing bad medicine, I can make this investigation go away."

"How could you possibly do that? And how can I trust you?" he asked, aware that they had already closed down all manufacturing operations and that soon all traces to C3 in general, and to Ken in particular, would be gone.

"I can continue to feed the FBI information. This time, the information can point them in the wrong direction. You can monitor my every move," she offered, a possible second meaning in her smile.

"That's a start," he replied, disregarding the second meaning. "But, I don't know how you unring this bell."

"You do know that I have already protected you. I know you have your sources. Check them. You'll learn that I have directed the FBI elsewhere."

Ken already knew that Alexa had pointed Weiner toward Petar Raic, an egregious offense he intended to use to his advantage. Ken also knew that Alexa had phoned Weiner just a few days ago to point him toward Ben Opperman. He did not know whether Alexa had been responsible for Ben's death, though he certainly suspected it. At the least, Alexa likely knew who had murdered Ben.

"What else do you want?" Ken asked.

"I want my diamonds and emeralds in the Cayman vault converted to cash."

He raised an eyebrow. That amounted to nearly $50 million. A nice chunk of change.

"Why would you need that kind of money?"

"Security for a rainy day," she replied mischievously as she placed an order for arugula salad and grilled salmon.

"Are you expecting a flood?"

"Just a legitimate business and a bit of charity."

"What kind of business?"

"Oh, I don't know," she sighed. "Maybe I'll make a dent in Mr. Murdoch's empire," she said with a seductive and infectious laugh. Ken was amused. He grinned as he ordered the prime rib.


After 45 minutes of banter, serious discussion, and negotiations, they reached an understanding. The U.S. government had already closed down *antidote.com*. He agreed to end production of tainted drugs, without specifying which ones. He made no agreement on counterfeit drugs, and she really didn't care about those. She also had no way of knowing that all production of tainted drugs had ended weeks ago.

"Alexia dear, I'll make this even easier. There are many more convenient ways I can earn money, so I will sell off C3 Pharmaceuticals. It's time to move on," he said sincerely. Given the on-going U.S. crackdown and the unfair advantage enjoyed by the major drug companies, C3 Pharmaceuticals would soon become much less profitable. Ken knew he could make a lot more money selling C3 Pharmaceuticals at the top of the market, rather than compete in rigged and regulated markets.

"In return, I expect every copy of every document you have on me, my family, C3 and anyone else now or ever associated with me. I also expect you to turn over to me ownership of the formulas for the C3 Pharmaceutical products from which you have been earning royalties. I think $50 million is enough to compensate you. That, and your life, of course," Ken said.

"Oh, now you've gone and ruined the moment," Alexa said. "Still, I accept your gracious offer," she added.

"Who knows," he went on, "maybe I'll even join forces with you and together we can topple Murdoch. Oh, and Alexia, remember, our deal is for all copies."

He raised his glass. She raised her teacup. He proposed a toast, "Here's to my freedom and your future success."

"Cheers!" they each spoke simultaneously.

The last swallow of her tea had the sweet taste of honey that had settled on the bottom. Ken's scotch increased his appetite. He would get dessert later.


It was not the first time Tom had been unable to complete an assignment. It was, however, the first time his failure was attributable to a 110-pound candlestick-wielding female MBA. Embarrassed though he was, Tom reported back to Petar. "I'm absolutely certain that neither Weiner nor Pye have any idea who I am. Neither is going to be able to track me."

Petar was secretly relieved. Maybe the aborted effort would dissuade Ken from a second effort? If not, Weiner would be on his guard, but Petar knew that next time Tom would plan the assassination more than an hour in advance, and Weiner would be his.

"Petar, we have to talk about something else," Tom said hesitantly.

"Sure. What's up?"

"I don't know how to tell you this, but I have to. I may know who killed Ben and it may affect Project Sky."

"What are you talking about?" Petar asked, suddenly on guard.

"I might as well just tell you. About 18 months, ago PharmCorp hired Opperman Security to undertake a terrorist attack that would show the weakness of our medical distribution system. Ben basically convinced them to piggyback on what we were already doing, although he never told them that's what he was doing and he never gave them any information about who we, I guess you, were." Tom paused and took a deep breath.

"Go on," Petar tersely instructed.

"I will. I just needed a moment. This isn't easy. Anyway, the only time Ben had to tell them anything was when we were having trouble making the nermycin work. Ben convinced this guy William Bowne, who ran this project for them, to send us his best chemists. Those were the guys Mike met with in Pune. They really saved the project," Tom said, sounding a little more weasely than he intended.

"They never knew who they were working with and PharmCorp had them killed as soon as they returned to Guadalajara. Everything was going smoothly until December. First, PharmCorp figured out the attack was going to be a lot bigger than they had intended. They were expecting maybe a thousand deaths, not 100,000 deaths. Then, we had to delay our demands. Public demands from a terrorist group are critical to them. Basically, they paid us to kill people so they could get good PR out of it for some legislation they're opposing."

"What else?" Petar asked, as he thought about how one of his closest friends had used them, even if it turned out that Ben's selfishness had saved the project.

"Two things. Bowne has basically figured out the C3 involvement through their sources in Washington. They know all about the investigation and they put two and two together. Second, last month, Bowne threatened to kill Ben if we didn't make our demands public by now. He even put a tail on me, though they disappeared when I started traveling. Now Ben's dead."

"What were you paid for this job?" Petar asked.

"$120 million, with $30 million still due," Tom honestly explained.

"When and what was your last contact with PharmCorp?"

"Bowne called me yesterday. He implied responsibility for Ben's death and threatened that I would be next if the terrorists didn't issue a public claim or demand."

"Is that it?"

"I swear to you. That's everything. Neither Ben nor I ever would have done anything to hurt you, Ken, C3 or Project Sky. And we didn't. In fact, the PharmCorp chemists were the key to the whole thing. Now Ben's dead and they're the most logical cause."

"Do you know for a fact they killed Ben?"

"No. Bowne only implied it."

"Who else is involved at PharmCorp other than this Bowne?"

"I know Mike spoke to a Max Linville when they arranged for the chemists to go to Pune. Other than Linville, I don't know. Ben might have, but I don't."

"Tom, I'm not going to sugarcoat this. I'm astonished. I need to talk to Ken and I can't make any promises to you about where this is going to end up. We've known each other for 10 years, and I don't know if we're going to survive this. For now, just do your job—and you better let me know the minute you hear anything from anyone at PharmCorp. Are we clear?"

"Very. I understand. But, you have my word that I have never misled you or failed to do an assignment or compromised C3 in any way. You know that Opperman Security has many other clients. Ken and C3 have always come first, second and third," Tom told Petar, basically pleading for his life.

Using Ken's new phone number, Petar reported to him both the failure and the much more disturbing information he had just learned.

Ken was in a surprisingly good mood, despite the bad news.

"On Weiner, I've decided that you were right. Leave him alone," Ken finally agreed.

"On Ben. I'm sorry I didn't tell you, Petar, but I knew about the deal with PharmCorp. Every last penny of that contract was going into our efforts against the Serbs and the Russians. I guess Ben never told Tom that we knew," Ken said, a twinge of sadness in his voice, before adding, "I didn't realize this Bowne was putting so much pressure on Ben or Tom. I'll ask Mike to look into it. If Bowne had anything to do with Ben's death, he'll be next, I promise you. Meantime, Tom's a good kid. It couldn't have been easy for him to talk to you—."

"How could you keep this from me?" Petar interrupted, stunned for the second time in just a few minutes.

"Petar, I'm sorry. It had no effect on Project Sky, except to help it. At least, that's what I thought. Maybe it got Ben killed. Look, we'll issue our demands next week. Mike and Tom should focus on the loose ends and you need to focus on what is happening in New York and Washington. When I get back we'll sit down and talk about this," Ken told him.

"I'll make sure Project Sky succeeds. But, this can't happen again. What about the leak?" Petar asked.

Ken was emphatic. "Don't worry about the leak. It has been sealed."

Petar was now more confused than ever. *This wasn't like Ken. Despite what Ken said, had Ben been the leak? Had Ken killed their partner? Was that even possible?*


As soon as Ken got off the phone with Petar, he called Mike Mihalic. "You need to talk to Tom Biffar about Ben's involvement with PharmCorp. It may have gotten him killed. If it did, one of their top people is going to pay the price."

"We'd usually use Opperman's guys to follow up something like this," Mike pointed out.

"This time use someone else. They don't need to know what we're up to, or what PharmCorp is up to. They only have to figure out if PharmCorp was tailing Ben, whether the watchers were there the night Ben died, and who at PharmCorp pulls the strings on something like this."

"I'll get someone on this right away," Mike promised.


The *Sunday Times of London* included a lengthy front page exposé on Serbian atrocities, with particular emphasis on Ivan

Maslac and Europe's failure to protect the Slavs throughout the Balkans. The article detailed years of atrocities, culminating in the attack on the Srebrenica school that killed 130 students, eight teachers, the principal and volunteer security force. The irony of what had happened in Srebrinica just 10 years earlier was inescapable. World leaders had no choice. The article quoted many leading political figures in England and on the Continent who spoke passionately about the need to do something to stop the carnage. Officials of the European Union Force, which had replaced the former Task Force Eagle Stabilization Force and NATO at the end of 2004, were quoted on their renewed efforts to track down Maslac and stop the killing.

The article ran over 10,000 words, one of the longest articles published by the *Times* in a long time. Its author, Stuart King, was widely applauded for his in-depth report. Within a few days, the article or extensive excerpts from the article appeared in over 600 newspapers throughout Europe and the United States. By the time the Sunday morning news programs were broadcast in the United States, more than 12 hours had passed since King's article was published. Both ABC's *This Week* and NBC's *Meet the Press* included extensive reports on the situation in the Balkans. The following weekend, *Newsweek's* cover story would be about deteriorating conditions in the Balkans, including a call for strong international action to protect the embattled region.

King's article also traced the parallels to the plight of oppressed minorities, particularly Muslims, in the Russian Federation.

Francine had spent the night in the hospital for observation. On Sunday morning, Barry came to pick her up. "If you ever want to leave the easy life at the FDA, I think there's a place for you at the Bureau. The wrestling team is always looking for a few good women," Barry kidded Francine. Though she had a headache to end all headaches, Francine was otherwise fine. "Special Agent Pye reporting for duty, Sir!" she announced. Both were very pleased that neither of them had been badly hurt and they celebrated by taking the rest of the day off, together.

"I had absolutely no involvement in, or knowledge of *antidote.com*, Taiwan Pharmaceutical Investments Ltd., Inversiones y Distribución Médicas de Las Producciones, RD Pharmaceuticals, or Petar's scheme," Ken promised his attorney, Eric Jacobs. Even though it was Sunday, Eric had initiated the call because he had to know how to proceed. He couldn't make those decisions without input from Ken. Now, Ken was saying all the right things. The problem was that Eric didn't believe him.

"What about Ben Opperman?"

"I know the name. I'm not sure, but I think we may have met once or twice, many years ago."

"Have you seen or spoken to him lately?" Eric prodded.

"No. I have no idea what he may be up to."

"How did you meet?"

After pausing to think about it, Ken answered "I can't swear to this, but I think that just after Petar started with us, he introduced me to Ben as a possible security consultant."

"Has C3 ever hired him as a consultant, or otherwise?"

"This is actually kinda fun," Ken said, before responding. "To the best of my knowledge, neither I nor C3 has ever hired Ben Opperman."

"Ken, this isn't a game. It's really important that you tell me the complete truth," Jacobs admonished his boss, very much aware of the special resignation clause in his contract.

Ken knew precisely where his general counsel was headed. "That's insulting. I have told you nothing but the truth, always," Ken bristled. "I simply have no knowledge of any counterfeit drug scheme."

"Good. I have suspended Petar from the public companies. I recommend that Petar be terminated by both the public and private companies. You must distance yourself from what Petar has done and we have to come clean with the Justice Department. If we do not, we could well become the next Enron or Arthur Andersen," Eric advised Ken, ending the interrogation and reverting to advisor.

"I know. I agree," Ken said. "Terminate Petar. Then call Justice and tell them we will provide any books and records we have. Let's work out a settlement."

"What about severance pay?" Eric asked.

"None. Petar has been well paid. He has fundamentally breached his trust with me, in the process exposing all of us to great liability. He has plenty of money. I am sure he can afford the best lawyers. We have a greater duty to our employees and investors worldwide. I have never been this close to someone who has taken advantage of me in this way. It is very depressing." Ken sounded very sincere. Maybe he really had no knowledge or involvement?

"You realize that to settle this we may have to agree to a fine, or to dispose of some of our pharmaceutical businesses," the lawyer counseled his client.

"We will do what we have to do to put this chapter behind us," Ken replied.

Baby Kenan responded well to the Abcyclene. Within a few days he was greatly improved. Since the doctors at St. Joseph's had no idea that Kenan was being given Abcyclene, they were amazed at his progress.

With his business in Washington concluded, Tom Biffar headed to Dulles where, as Tim Whittle, a software salesman from Austin, he boarded Taca flight 353 to San Salvador. There, he switched planes and after a three-hour delay, arrived early that morning at his destination—Panama City. He was pleased to be far away from PharmCorp.

# FORTY SIX

ARLY MONDAY MORNING, Ken and most of his security
detail headed out to Gatwick where they boarded his
Gulfstream V for their return to Washington. He would be there to
confront any inquiries, see first hand the results when terrorists
demanded that America stand up for the Balkans, and make arrangements with Tom to retaliate for Ben's assassination.

Mike would soon be arriving in India, and the remainder of
Ken's security detail stayed behind to keep an eye on Alexa. Ken suspected that she might well be the real culprit in Ben's death. He
trusted her about as much as he liked garlic in his food. Ken was
allergic to garlic.


Ken left on a beautiful day. The temperature was a comfortable
7 Celsius (45 Fahrenheit). A few hours later, Alexa headed back to
Harrods. "Does that woman do anything else besides shop?" one of
the C3 security officers tailing Alexa asked of his partner.

Once at Harrods, she discreetly notified the head of Faisal's
personal security detail and was ushered to his private office. "Mr.
Ayoub, lovely to see you, sir," she greeted him as she would a dear
old friend. He was equally pleased.

"I did not expect you today," he said pleasantly surprised. "I assume you got my message."

"I certainly did," she said. "How do you intend to proceed?"

"GC Weiss," he replied. "Weiss has been my most capable resource to date. I'd stake my life on his word. Anyway, he came to me with some very exciting news. A major pharmaceutical outfit capable of mass producing product for the global market has just been privately put up for sale," he salivated. "By the end of the day tomorrow, we will be making a secret bid to buy the company. It looks very good. Then, we can implement our latest discoveries," he said with a wink and a nod. "The drugs will be available to consumers before you know it." After a pause, he added, "We are going to be very, very rich."

"And what will you do with your added wealth, Mr. Ayoub?" Alexa asked, a bit tongue-in-cheek.

"Please Alexa. You must call me Faisal! We are business partners and friends, now." Then he proceeded, "You know the old expression: If you can't beat 'em, join 'em?"

"Yes," she replied waiting to see where this was headed.

"I will begin by buying a newspaper group and then I will expand into television stations and perhaps a network."

"Well, sir, the media sure could use a bit more diversity these days," she said as she rose to leave. "I apologize for my unannounced visit."

"You are always welcome, Alexia. You will be hearing from me soon."

With that, she headed for the door behind a security guard who led her downstairs. "What's on sale?" she asked him.

Just before heading to Washington, Suzy Liebig reviewed the results of the weekend's work with David Salzman. "So far, no clear correlations have been developed between the staph infections and the pneumonia-like symptoms. On the other hand, we are now fairly certain that the pneumonia-like symptoms are not, in fact, the result of pneumonia. Examinations over the weekend suggest that some of the patients have a condition with a very similar pathology, but that varies in discernable ways from pneumonia. That means the causality might differ, as well."

"Good work," Salzman replied. "Let's start carefully questioning patients as to the nature of their staph infections, their treatments, and any other symptoms we might not have considered," he directed. Suzy promptly communicated the instructions to her team, and promised to check in during the afternoon.

Tom Biffar landed at Tocumen International Airport in Panama City, and immediately cleared customs. He hailed a taxi for the 30-minute ride downtown. Once there, he used his secure cell phone to obtain instructions.

After a day off with Francine, Barry was back at work bright and early Monday morning. Metro was looking into the attack. The fact that the intruder's gun had a silencer virtually ruled out burglary as a motive. Neither Barry nor Francine had gotten a very good look at the assailant. It had been too fast. Both agreed to look through mug books later that week, though no one was very optimistic they would get anywhere.

"Barry, I want you to be careful for a while. Until we get some idea of what this was about, we have to assume that someone wants you dead." FBI Assistant Director Richard Goldstein had come down to Barry's office to express his concern. "I know you can take care of yourself, but there's no point in taking unnecessary risks."

"Thanks, Richard. I can't think of who would be out to get me, though in our line of work I suppose it's an occupational risk," Barry responded.

"I like your attitude, but I like having you around even more. Be careful, for me?" With that, Richard and Barry shook hands and Richard returned to his spacious office on the fourth floor.

Barry had no idea who was out to get him. Over the years, he had worked on several cases that had left some rather unsavory characters in jail. He thought about the death last week of Ben Opperman and wondered if there was a connection. Then he returned to the phone where he was coordinating arrangements for the FBI to visit Taiwan Pharmaceutical Investments Ltd., Inversiones, and RD Pharmaceuticals.

It was the fourth time they were meeting in Eric Jacobs' office. This would probably be the last. Petar surrendered his company credit cards and security access cards to Eric. He filled out some papers, and after more than 10 years with Karasik Capital and the C3 Group, Petar Raic was formally unemployed. Jacobs was under instructions to approach Greg Schoenfeld at Justice with what he knew.

"As a friend, I strongly advise you to retain counsel. I can't predict what Schoenfeld's next step will be, but there's every possibility that he may seek a warrant for your arrest. You need to be prepared," Jacobs advised Petar, truly concerned for his fate.

"How long do I have?" Petar asked, realizing he sounded like a patient on one of those medical programs on TV.

"I have made an appointment to see Schoenfeld this afternoon. I plan to brief him and invite his staff to review our files. Depending upon what else he knows, they could be after you as early as tomorrow, or this could extend over many weeks. There's really no way to know," Jacobs explained.

They shook hands and wished each other well as Petar headed down the elevator for the last time.

As Suzy Liebig headed to meet Francine and, she hoped, Barry, she checked in with Ron Craig to see if anyone had developed any leads on the staph infection or any behaviors associated with it. Craig was excited. "We're not certain yet, but we think we're seeing one factor recur to a statistically significant level—."

"Yes, yes, get to the punch line!" Suzy exploded.

"Nermycin," Craig responded.

"What?" Suzy asked.

"Nermycin. Most of the patients whose records we have reviewed and who fit the criteria treated their staph infections with nermycin," Craig explained.

"What else do you have?" Suzy asked her eager analyst.

"Not a whole lot. Most of these patients also took other drugs, which is not uncommon when a staph infection is involved. Some of those we think fit the criteria do not appear to have taken nermycin at all. So far, we have only reviewed a fraction of the records," Craig replied.

"Listen, you have done some very good work here. Stay with it. As you review additional records the pattern may become clearer. While you're at it, see if some of the patients have any unused nermycin. Let's get it down to the lab for testing," Suzy instructed.

"Let David Salzman know what you've found. I have a dinner now. I'll catch an early flight back tomorrow, and I'll be in by late morning," she said before she ended the call.


It was Monday evening local time by the time Mike arrived in Pune, after a change of airplanes in Mumbai. While on the ground in Mumbai he had checked with the team he had assigned to look into Ben's death. They were still completing their work and asked for additional time. When Mike arrived in Pune, he called them again. He immediately phoned Ken with what he had learned.

"There was at least one hit team and perhaps two in Paris the night of Ben's death. There were also at least another two teams of watchers. Georges was right about that. From there, it gets murky. Through a source on the *Sureté* we tracked back through cell phone usage. There's no doubt PharmCorp knew about Ben's death immediately after it happened. That doesn't prove they did it, but it's very damning."

"Any indication of who else might have been involved?"

"We know Ben's been seeing someone the last few months. We don't know who she is, and there's been no sign of her since Ben's death hit the papers. That alone is odd. We can't discount this mystery woman."

Ken gave nothing away about his fear that Alexa had been seeing Ben, and that she might have been the cause of his death, instead asking, "What do we have on PharmCorp?"

"Basically, what we know comes from Tom and C3 Pharmaceuticals. The top guys are Dave Cole and Bob Estrich. Cole's the CEO. The point person on this project is William Bowne and his deputy, Max Linville. I've spoken to Linville. We don't know who else is involved, but we know for a fact that Bowne and Linville are. We also know that someone authorized $150 million. Finally, we know that Estrich was promoted from Bowne's job."

"So, Bowne's the hatchet man?"

"I suppose. Or Estrich. It's hard to tell."

"Let me think about this. But, the way it looks to me right now, Tom is the one person who can get close to Bowne, though there's probably very little security around any of these guys. We either take down Cole, or we take out Bowne to send a message. Either way, I'm not letting Ben's death go unpunished."


It was still only 8:30 am in Panama City when Mike arrived in Mumbai, halfway around the world. Tom phoned Mike's office, where the security chief's deputy provided him with detailed instructions about the assignment and the Opperman Security operatives he would meet. Tom was pleased to learn he would be joined by Ernesto and Jose, two of the firm's most experienced Central American operatives.

The local team had developed precise information on the targets' whereabouts and patterns. It would be easy. None of them had any security. It wasn't even clear to Tom that his presence was needed. Ernesto and Jose were very experienced, their plan completely sound, and the objective undefended. With little effort and no mistakes, they would complete the assignment before the day was over.

Indeed, by 7:30 that evening, Tom boarded a flight for the 40-hour sojourn from Panama City to Kuala Lumpur, Malaysia. Using his identification as Tim Whittle, he began with a flight from Panama City to New York on Copa - Compania Panamena, arriving on schedule at 1:43 in the morning. Since the next leg of his journey didn't begin for almost 12 hours, Tom headed to an apartment in Queens maintained by Opperman Security. Although Ben's death would probably mean the eventual dissolution of the firm, for now Tom himself was responsible for its operations, and he would remain in charge at least until Project Sky was complete. Then, his future, if any, was up to Ken Karasik.

Francine had been eager for Suzy to meet Barry. Their relationship was coming along nicely and it was time to get her friend's assessment of the very special agent. First to arrive at Morton's steakhouse on Prospect Street was the ever-punctual Francine. Bundled in a thick purple sweater over a pair of heavy wool pants that were tucked into her no-nonsense winter boots, she removed the long overcoat as she was seated at one of Morton's spacious tables. She ordered a pot of hot green tea.

Suzy Liebig was only minutes behind. She was startled to see the bruise on Francine's face. "What the hell happened to you?" she asked, bewildered.

"Oh, a break-in, a shoot-out, a knock-em-out, drag-em-down fistfight," Francine said sarcastically just as Barry stumbled in. The waitress approached and Francine, famished after her workout, ordered while Suzy and Weiner engaged in small talk.

"I'll start with the spinach salad," Francine began, "and then I'll have the filet mignon with steamed asparagus and sautéed wild mushrooms." Suzy operated best on low fuel and ordered a Caesar salad with plain grilled salmon. Barry decided that a Maine lobster was a welcome splurge and he went for it.

"How did you two meet?" Suzy asked Barry, wanting to get his side of the story.

"The FBI and FDA needed to join forces on a particular case and Francine came highly recommended to me," he explained. "Shortly after we met," he continued, tongue-in-cheek, "she began stalking me." They all burst into laughter. "I chased her until I let her catch me," he added.

"Enough about us! What has kept you so busy, Suzy?" Francine asked.

"It's that strange pneumonia I've told you about. We're positive now that it is a very aggressive illness that's a lot like pneumonia, but isn't really pneumonia, and that it has something to do with staph infections."

"No idea what's causing this pseudo pneumonia?" Barry asked.

"One of my guys thinks it may have something to do with one of the drugs some of the patients used to fight the staph infection, but it's premature to know for sure," Suzy answered.

"How would a drug cause pneumonia?" Francine asked.

"It shouldn't. Even if it's not working properly it might make someone ill, but not with these symptoms," Suzy replied.

"Which drug?" Barry asked, viewing the discussion as part of his education on drug efficacy and side effects.

"It's ironic. The drug isn't even very popular. I guess when we know more, we'll be kicking this over to the FDA anyway. It's called nermycin."

Barry and Francine looked as though they had been electrocuted. They practically jumped out of their seats as they yelled in unison, "Nermycin?!"

"You've heard of it?" Suzy asked, surprised by their vehement reaction.

"Heard of it! We're analyzing a whole shipment of it right now. Do you know where these patients got their nermycin?" Barry asked.

"No. Why is the FBI involved in this?" Suzy inquired, still confused.

"Why? You want to know why? Because I think someone has purposely tampered with the nermycin to make people sick. I think we may have uncovered the iceberg that has been lying submerged just below the surface. Not only that, but I think we just got a whole lot closer to nailing one of the worst terrorists we've ever seen," Barry responded.

Suzy turned to Francine, "What's he talking about?"

As Francine started from the beginning, Barry was already on his cell phone alerting his team to be in the office at 8:00 am sharp the next morning for an all-hands meeting. Then he called the lab to make certain that they continued testing the nermycin overnight. Finally, he called Phil Oster and filled him in. By the time he was done, Suzy was on her cell phone updating David Salzman and giving new instructions to Ron Craig, while Francine also called her team.

The three of them were so frantic that others in the restaurant wondered about the two beautiful women and the handsome man who managed to completely ignore each other as they made call after call on their cell phones. When they were done, Barry paid the bill, declaring, "If ever there was a time the Bureau should be picking up the tab, this is it!"

# FORTY SEVEN

TOM ARRIVED AT the safe apartment in Queens at about 3:30 in the morning. He destroyed all papers bearing Whittle's name. He would never use that identity again. For the next leg of his journey, Tom selected three sets of identity papers that had been previously prepared for his use. He unpacked, picked out the clothes he would need, and repacked. He then lay down for about six hours of sleep, before heading back to John F. Kennedy International Airport for a grueling 14-hour flight on Korean Air to Seoul. At least he was flying in Business Class.

Promptly at 8:00 am, Barry Weiner's team assembled in the conference room. Barry reported what he had learned about the nermycin. "It's now clear to me that somehow Karasik or Raic, or both, have manufactured tainted nermycin and they have used it to infect a lot of people. I don't yet know how, and I sure as hell don't know why. Your job is to help me answer those questions.

"Nate, I need you to head down to the CDC in Atlanta to work with them in reviewing the records of those who have been infected. I don't expect you to figure out something they don't already know, but I'm not taking any chances," Barry explained.

Next, Barry assigned an agent to head over to the FBI lab to do everything possible to accelerate the testing of the nermycin seized in the raid on *antidote.com*. "I want you to make sure the results are compared to the tests being run by the CDC on the nermycin they obtained from patients. I also want you to make sure the other drugs seized in the raids in Costa Rica are tested on an expedited basis."

Finally, Barry assigned Guy Landau, Craig Calandra and two other agents to assemble teams to locate and tail Karasik, Raic and Mel Bottner. "We keep focusing on Karasik, but let's not forget the connections to Bottner. I don't trust any of them," Weiner told his senior agents.

After the meeting, Barry phoned Richard Goldstein. He wanted his boss to expedite the travel plans for the agents and analysts who would be auditing Taiwan Pharmaceutical Investments Ltd., Inversiones y Distribución Médicas de Las Producciones, and RD Pharmaceuticals.

He then phoned the Justice Department staff attorney who had replaced Lisa Fuller. Nina Kaufman was a no-nonsense lawyer who demanded a lot of backup before taking action. This time, Nina was convinced. "I'll do my best to get cooperation in the Caymans, Isle of Man and Switzerland. I'll also revisit wiretaps on Karasik and Raic." Barry thanked her and called Greg Schoenfeld in New York. The division chief was expecting Eric Jacobs later that day. He would call Barry as soon as he knew more.

Suzy Liebig arrived back in Atlanta about 11:00 am. She headed straight for her office. When she arrived, a lot of very tired men and women were hard at work.

"We've combed through hundreds of records. There is just no doubt that the unifying thread among these patients is nermycin,"

Ron Craig reported. Beyond that, nothing else seems special or out of place."

"When will the lab have results on the nermycin?" Suzy asked.

"Later today," Craig responded.

Francine had alerted her boss, Bob Treiger, that there might be an emergency involving nermycin. Treiger called David Salzman at the CDC and Goldstein at the FBI. Subject to the results of the testing being done at the CDC and the FBI, he was prepared to recommend a nationwide alert be issued on the FDA's web site, and to the media, hospitals and physicians warning them of the dangers. He also authorized Francine to assist the Justice Department to prepare criminal complaints against the web sites and so-called John Doe defendants.

In the former Yugoslavia, European Union troops received a tip on the whereabouts of Ivan Maslac. In the past, they would have ignored the tip. Now, in the wake of Maslac's savagery and world condemnation, U.S. and EUFOR troops prepared to move.

This time, Eric Jacobs met with Greg Schoenfeld at the U.S. Attorney's offices at One St. Andrew's Plaza near Foley Square in lower Manhattan. "I regret to inform you that one of our most trusted employees and an officer of one of our foreign subsidiaries has engaged in behavior I can only describe as shocking," Jacobs began. Over the next hour, he laid out a complete case against Petar Raic for embezzlement and violation of half a dozen U.S. and foreign laws involving counterfeiting and fraud. He promised to cooperate fully in the investigation and acknowledged that C3 may have received profits as a result of the illegal activities. "Of course," Jacobs solemnly explained, "C3 will disgorge any profits it may have earned as a result of these unlawful activities."

"Have any of the drugs been manipulated to include toxins?" Schoenfeld asked.

"These drugs were generic counterfeits. At no time was there any tampering with our branded products. Still, we acknowledge that unknown to anyone else at C3, we were unfortunately involved in this terrible incident. I can also tell you that while these counterfeit generic drugs may not have been as efficacious as they should have been, they weren't toxic," Jacobs responded.

"I can also assure you categorically that Mr. Karasik had no involvement in Mr. Raic's scheme," Jacobs added.

As the meeting drew to a close, Jacobs told Schoenfeld, "We have terminated Raic and severed all ties with him. I have recommended that he retain separate counsel. From now on, the C3 Group is in this with the Justice Department. We have done nothing wrong and we have nothing to hide."

A clearly skeptical Schoenfeld thanked Jacobs, and promised to get back to him within a few days.

Jason Waters carefully parked his dark blue BMW 745i in the underground lot at the Fashion Center shopping mall in Pentagon City. After checking that he had not been followed, he took the escalator to the street level and exited on the west side of the building. There, he took a down escalator, extracted an electronic ticket from his wallet, walked down a flight of stairs and after a brief moment, boarded the Blue Line subway for one stop to Crystal City. There, he climbed a flight of stairs and took yet another escalator. When he reached street level, he turned southwest and headed for the Marriott.

Once in the Marriott, he located the pay phones just off the main lobby. To be certain that the call he was about to make would not be traced back to him, he paid for the call with cash rather than a calling card. He punched in 13 numbers and after a brief delay, Karasik answered, the many relays creating a slight echo.

"Not very good news, I'm afraid," Waters began. "The FBI is proceeding with the investigation. They are getting close to Project Sky and the Centers for Disease Control has detected a pattern with all these deaths. There is no doubt that someone with access to your plans has been advising them. The time has come to issue your demands and end the leaks... Permanently."

Sitting in his well-appointed office, behind his ornate desk, Ken Karasik placed the secure phone back on its cradle. The time had come. Three years of planning were over. He picked up another phone and punched in the numbers for Petar Raic.

"We are running out of time, my friend. If we do not act within the next 48 hours it may be too late. Are you ready to do what must be done?" Karasik asked his closest friend.

# FORTY EIGHT

FEBRUARY 8, 2006
NOVI SAD, KUALA LUMPUR, WASHINGTON, D.C., AGRA
ATLANTA, TAIWAN, NEW YORK

*I*T WAS A CHILLY, moonless night as more than 100 troops in full combat gear from the European Union Force, known as EUFOR, quietly moved down multiple routes through the Serbian countryside. They had departed over a five-hour period in groups of four to 12, in convoys never larger than three or four vehicles. Given the frequent military traffic on these roads and the small unit sizes in which they traveled, there was nothing unusual for any observers to notice or report.

They were supported by surveillance provided by a Predator drone operated by the CIA, and a squad of battle-hardened U.S. Special Forces experienced in capturing and killing Baath Party and al-Qaeda targets in Iraq. The squad of 12 U.S. Army Rangers came from a completely different direction and traveled in two groups so that they too would blend in with the usual traffic.

Their destination was the city of Novi Sad, capital of the Autonomous Province of Vojvodina, located on the left bank of the Danube River. The city was divided into the municipalities of Novi Sad and Petrovaradin. The latter was a mixture of sad dilapidated homes and once comfortable neighborhoods, now fallen into disrepair.

By 3:30 am, lead units infiltrated one of the nicer neighborhoods of Petrovaradin. Over the next half hour, as the build-up of troops concentrated in the northeast quadrant of Petrovaradin finally exceeded the levels that would avoid attention, they closed off a four-square-block zone around their target. Though no one challenged their exclusion zone, from then on they assumed defensive positions as though their presence was known to the enemy, while they continued to act quietly and without specific focus, in the hope that it was not.

At 3:45 am, two U.S. Army AH-64D Apache helicopters lifted off from their base outside Tuzla for the 10-minute flight to Novi Sad. As the Apaches hovered 30 seconds away, just outside of hearing, the Rangers, backed by EUFOR troops, surrounded a brown villa located in the middle of the exclusion zone.

There would be no warning; this was not a police raid in the Bronx. This was a military operation in a very dangerous part of the world.

At precisely 4:00 am, local time, while it was still pitch black, EUFOR Colonel Mark Kurta ordered the troops to advance. At first, all was silent as the Rangers entered the villa on the first floor. Then, shots rang out, as the villa's residents, already alert to the troops surrounding them, defended themselves with their M3 and M4 automatic weapons. The Rangers pulled back and returned fire with their Heckler and Koch MP5 9mm submachine guns.

As the EUFOR troops joined the fight with their M16A2 5.56mm semi-automatic rifles and M249 fully automatic machine guns, paramilitary killers suddenly appeared in defensive positions on the roofs and in bedrooms of adjoining houses. They joined in the fight, firing modern M3s and M4s, older Kalashnikov AK-47s, and rocket-launched grenades at the U.S. and EUFOR forces.

The EUFOR forces took casualties, as paramilitary snipers took positions along both sides of the street. But, this was not to be a repeat of Somalia. The EUFOR force was much larger and better positioned. The neighborhood consisted of two-story dwellings, not the larger buildings found in Mogadishu. Moreover, with the aid of the Predator, real-time information was pouring in to the EUFOR troops on the precise positions of each defender.

Kurta called in air support. Within 30 seconds, an Apache helicopter fired three Hellfire missiles, shredding a large part of the villa, and two neighboring houses. The second Apache began firing its M230 chain gun at the militia on nearby roofs, its 30mm rounds ripping jagged holes in the houses and the defenders.

The first Apache then joined in the attack on the defenders, firing rockets and then its M230 chain gun. As the locals desperately sought cover from the unbearable fire raining down on them from above and up at them from the streets, EUFOR troops used RPGs to kill Serbs taking cover inside the houses.

The Serbian defense had been based on the long-standing reluctance of U.S. and EUFOR troops to hurt or kill innocents as the price of winning a battle. They were shocked when it became clear the EUFOR troops were under orders to suppress the militia, regardless of collateral damage. As added proof of those orders, even as the defense began to die down, EUFOR troops continued to lay down a withering stream of fire into the defenders' positions.

Within 10 minutes, the firefight was over. One American had been killed and six injured. Three EUFOR troops were also dead and 14 others were injured, though none seriously. In addition to at least 30 Serbian paramilitary members who were seriously injured, 18 bodies were discovered in the rubble. Although Kurta wanted DNA tests for the record, it was clear that both Ivan Maslac and Viktor Dzogan were among the dead.

"We have a problem," Michael Pochna, the FBI's Panamanian station chief, telephoned Barry to warn him. "What is it?" Barry asked.

"Two days ago, the president, CFO and attorney for Inversiones y Distribución Médicas de Las Producciones were found dead, and both the company's and the lawyer's offices were destroyed. To top it off, the computer systems were infected with viruses and are now useless."

"Have you been there personally?" Barry inquired.

"No, not yet, but I'm very pessimistic we are going to get anything useful."

Mike Mihalic took the train from Agra, back to New Delhi. He spent the night at the Hotel Ajanta near the train station. The next morning he boarded a 7:00 am Cathay Pacific flight for Chiang Kai Shek International Airport in Taiwan. His visits to RD Pharmaceuticals in Pune and Simla Manufacturing outside of Agra had been very productive.

Rohit Datar and two of his investors had just completed a celebratory dinner at Datar's comfortable home when a furnace exploded. All three, a housekeeper and Datar's nanny were killed almost instantly. At almost the same time, an explosion rocked the offices at RD. Mysteriously, a computer virus rendered the company's financial records unreadable. Similar mishaps occurred in the computer systems at RD Pharmaceuticals' accountants and law firm.

Within a few hours, Mike and his C3 security team had erased any possibility that investigators in the United States could connect RD Pharmaceuticals to the C3 Group.

The team Mike met in Agra had already developed a similar plan for Simla Manufacturing. Once Mike had an opportunity to review the plan and scout locations, he gave the go ahead. Within six hours after arriving in Agra, four men were dead, their offices were destroyed, and another computer virus had done its work.

It had been a long few days when Mike finally boarded the Cathay Pacific flight for Taiwan. He was looking forward to some rest.

Tom was finally deplaning in Kuala Lumpur. Even before he cleared customs, he used his secure cell phone to call Mike Mihalic. They exchanged brief reports. Mike was on his way to Taiwan. Things had gone well in India.

Barry was on a conference call with David Salzman, Suzy Liebig, and Ron Craig from the CDC, Bob Treiger and Francine from the FDA, Phil Oster, and the FBI chemist who had analyzed the nermycin seized in Costa Rica. They were stumped.

"Ok, so the CDC and FBI labs agree that the nermycin has been modified, but it doesn't appear to be toxic. Indeed, as I understand it, the additional ingredients don't do anything?" Barry asked the group.

Salzman jumped in. "We must be missing something. Suzy, are you certain that the only commonality among those infected is the nermycin?"

"Well, it is the only common item the least bit out of the ordinary," she responded.

"Fine. Now, what is common that is ordinary?" Salzman inquired.

Craig took that question. "We have been over this again and again. The staph infections were all over the place. Some were serious, some mild, and the infections were of different varieties. I guess there is a commonality on treatments, but that's to be expected."

"What do you mean 'commonality of treatments'?" Treiger asked.

KENIN M. SPIVAK • JULIE CHRYSTYN

"The usual drugs," Craig replied and then provided a list of a half dozen drugs that meant nothing to Barry, except one. "Did you say 'cyprofaxin'?" Barry asked.

"Yes, that's one of the customary drugs. There's nothing unusual about that," Craig responded.

"Nothing, except of all the drugs you named it's the only one Inversiones y Distribución was shipping to all those web sites," Francine excitedly observed.

"We need to dig further into the cyprofaxin. Where did they get it? How many of the patients meeting the criteria used both cyprofaxin and nermycin? We should also get some leftover samples in for testing," Salzman instructed.

"We already have the cyprofaxin seized in Costa Rica in our lab," the FBI chemist observed. "We'll immediately begin testing, as well."

"I'm going to put out a nationwide alert on all forms of nermycin. Even though we don't know what they've done to it, the coincidence is just too great. Any change in the drug voids its approval. As of now, it is illegal to sell Nermycin-X or any other form of nermycin in the United States," Treiger announced to the group, which adjourned shortly thereafter.


Mike Mihalic met the C3 security team assigned to monitor Taiwan Pharmaceutical Investments Ltd. The small investment company had only two employees, a lawyer, and an accountant. By the end of the day, it had lost all four to gunshot wounds, their offices had been ransacked, and their computers taken. None worked on a network. Their backups consisted of discs they kept at home. Those discs were confiscated and destroyed. By midnight, Taiwan Pharmaceutical Investments ceased to exist.

361

Mike had one last stop before he could go home.

Petar Raic shook hands with his new lawyer, Steve Silbert. Raic and Silbert had already spent almost five hours reviewing the situation and expected to meet for at least another two. The fit, handsome 60-year-old had a reputation for being smart and tough, two attributes that would be sorely tested in the weeks ahead. Based on the reports from Eric Jacobs, an indictment was only days away. Raic and Silbert were considering pre-empting the process by offering to voluntarily surrender to the Justice Department in return for avoiding unpleasant scenes in the press. Unless Raic decided otherwise, Silbert would make that offer the next morning.

At the end of the day, the FDA put out a nationwide bulletin urging Americans not to use Nermycin-X or any other form of nermycin. The FDA release advised that neither Nermycin-X, manufactured for C3 Pharmaceuticals in Zurich, nor any generic versions of nermycin, were approved for sale in the United States and that recent testing had indicated that a significant number of the generic versions being imported into the United States had been adulterated with potentially toxic substances. The FDA urged Americans not to purchase any form of nermycin and not to use any form of nermycin they had on hand.

The following day, sales of all forms of nermycin virtually stopped, and C3 Pharmaceuticals in Zurich was deluged with hostile calls and emails. More ominously for Ken's net worth, the stock prices of the public companies within the C3 Group fell by 10%, or more, even though the FDA had not claimed any problems with the Nermycin-X made by C3 and C3 Pharmaceuticals wasn't even publicly traded.

While they might not yet have found a cure or a motive, Barry, Francine and the team at the CDC had stopped the attack from infecting new victims.

Barry saw the day as one of mixed results. On the one hand, the FDA had put out its advisory on nermycin, Justice would soon indict Petar Raic, and they might be getting closer to understanding what was happening with the latest news about cyprofaxin. On the other, someone was systematically destroying their evidence trail in Panama, India and now Taiwan. What could be next?

# FORTY NINE

UNITED STATES SECRETARY of State Condoleezza Rice used her regularly scheduled press conference to emphasize America's commitment to the security of the Balkans. "Recent events have emphasized that for too long the United States and our European allies have looked the other way. You may rest assured that there is a renewed commitment to the Balkans generally, and Bosnia and Herzegovina in particular. We will not permit the mistakes of the past to recur."

Secretary Rice did not mention the Muslims and other oppressed minorities who died every day seeking their freedom in the former Soviet Union.

"It's lip service, but it may be enough," a resigned Ken told Mel.

The deal was done. Petar Raic would surrender that afternoon to Greg Schoenfeld. Petar then would be freed on bail, after surrendering his passport.

Petar arranged a conference call for the remaining members of the Karasik Commission. They had to make a decision. Some 50,000 Americans were probably infected as a result of the sales of cyprofaxin and the tainted nermycin. Though only a few hundred had died so far, without treatment many more would die over the next two to three months. That was far short of the 150,000 or more they had expected to put at risk, but it was still considerable leverage.

"The questions are three," Ken began. "First, with Maslac's death and the announcements made by the United States and European governments, have we achieved our objectives? Second, if we have achieved our objectives, is there any reason to proceed tomorrow with our demands? Third, if we do not proceed, do we wish to inform the authorities about Abcyclene?"

Petar spoke first. "None of us has suffered more at the hands of the Serb savages than I have and none of us has worked harder and longer to make things right for our families than I. Little has changed for Chechnya or Azerbaijan. Still, I believe we have accomplished most of what we set out to do. We could not have done that without Stuart's beautiful articles and his tremendous assistance. Stuart, you will always be my brother.

"Now it is time to stop. We will do our brothers in Chechnya and Azerbaijan more harm than good by continuing. The press will simply view this as another Muslim attack on America. That is not what we wanted. We can still help them, but this is not the way," he concluded.

Stuart thanked Petar and then spoke simply, "We do not want to become those whom we hate. We should stop and we should let America end the deaths."

Mel was next. "We have won that which we most wanted. We will deal with Milosevic in due course. We should end this and tell the authorities about Abcyclene."

Weiner was waiting for her call. "Ben Opperman is dead," he told the mysterious informant.

"I know. He crossed Raic one too many times. They have destroyed their infrastructure. It's over, though more will die without the antidote."

"Antidote to what? What have they done?" Barry asked.

"I am running out of time. Many tens of thousands will die if you do not resolve this. It is more important than any one man, even Raic," she said, disconnecting the line.

The trace showed the call originated from an anonymous pre-paid mobile phone in Britain. Later, they would determine the mobile had been somewhere within a 10-block radius of Piccadilly Circus. There was no way to find the caller.

First the CDC lab reported in. The cyprofaxin they obtained from the dying patients had nothing wrong with it. Some of the samples were exactly what they should be, while others seemed weakened. None of the samples had been tainted in any way.

The FBI lab also reported nothing wrong with the cyprofaxin seized in Costa Rica, other than its very poor quality. There was no evidence of toxins.

"What are we missing?" was one of the most popular refrains that afternoon in Washington and Atlanta at the FBI, FDA and CDC. They all knew they were missing something and that they had to find it to prevent many more people from dying. At the CDC, David Salzman ordered Suzy's team to carefully review every last bit of data on the patients who had died, or who had been admitted to the hospital. "We know the answer is in the data. Our job is to find something that is probably so obvious, we're missing it because it is obvious," Salzman told them.

That afternoon, Petar Raic surrendered to Greg Schoenfeld. As they agreed, he turned his passport over to the Court. He was fingerprinted and booked. Within an hour he was released on $5 million bail.

A very tired Mike Mihalic boarded an 8:30 am Malaysia Airlines flight for Bangkok, arriving two hours later. He transferred to Thai Airlines for the hour flight to Chiang Rai. Once he arrived, he rented a car, driving the approximately 90 minutes to an inn on the Thai side of the border with Myanmar. There, he met with the three local operatives who had made preparations for his arrival.

After carefully reviewing their plans and the digital photographs they had taken, the three men returned to the room they shared and Mike got some very welcome rest.

That day, another 30 Americans died from the pneumonia-like illness induced by the cyprofaxin and tainted nermycin.

# FIFTY

THE FOUR MEN awoke before seven that morning. The three locals immediately left for their return to Myanmar. Mike followed an hour later, when he passed into the former Burma as an American tourist. The manufacturing facility known as Bagan Manufacturing was only 10 minutes across the border. It had no guards, no cameras, no security of any kind. Its 60 employees were paid little more than slaves.

In a repressive country that boasted one of the largest slave labor contingents in the world, the 60 overworked laborers considered themselves lucky. None of them paid any attention to the beggars and the unemployed who wandered around the factory every day. They certainly paid no attention to Mike's team. Because Mike stayed out of sight, they also paid no attention to him.

It only took about an hour to rig the factory to burn to the ground. The timers were set for that evening when the factory would be abandoned. At lunchtime, two of the local men entered the small office at the rear. They set three incendiary devices to explode at the same time as the other devices. That was more than sufficient to completely destroy the office and everything in it. By the time the lunch break was over at 2:30, Mike's two men had melted into the crowds and gone their separate ways.

Nyan Win and Kyaw Win were brothers and the two officers of Bagan Manufacturing. They lived in a small house with their sister May. It was located just half a mile from the plant. Each day, without fail, they headed home for a two-hour lunch starting at 12:30. This day, Mike and the third man, Thein Tun, were waiting for them when they arrived.

Just minutes after Nyan and Kyaw began eating the chicken and rice prepared by their sister May, Mike and Tun entered the small house through the open rear door. Each was armed with a silenced 9mm Glock. May gasped as they entered, but before she could warn her brothers, Mike shot her twice, in the head and the chest. She collapsed, knocking over the pots she had been cleaning.

The noise alerted Nyan and Kyaw, who called out to their sister and rushed in to see what was wrong. As they entered the kitchen, Mike shot Nyan and Tun shot Kyaw. The brothers died instantly, as blood oozed from multiple wounds in their chests and shoulders.

It took less than 20 seconds from the time Mike and Tun entered the house until all three Win siblings were dead. Stepping around their bodies in the cramped kitchen, Mike and Tun entered the small dining room and began their search for any Bagan Manufacturing files, ransacking the house. Within a few minutes they located the records in a cabinet in the den. They burned the records and set incendiary devices around the house to complete the job. The devices were set to go off at the same time as the devices at the plant. Then, it would take only a few minutes before the wood frame house ceased to exist. It was only 1:30 when Mike and Tun left the Win house.

They next headed for the small office where Bagan Manufacturing's accountant worked. The office was located within a quarter of a mile from the Win house. They arrived there less than five minutes later. When Mike and Tun walked inside, the accountant was

sitting with his secretary and a client. It was a virtual repeat performance. Mike and Tun shot them with their silenced Glocks. The
secretary was the last to die, and the only one who realized what was
happening. She began to scream and her scream died with her. Less
than 10 seconds after they entered the office, all three were dead.
Mike and Tun located and burned all the files involving Bagan
Manufacturing. Next, Mike attached thumb drives to both computers. They introduced viruses that destroyed the hard drives. The
computers weren't networked and there was no evidence that they
had ever been backed up.

Mike and Tun set incendiary devices. This time, however,
there was no reason for the authorities to make a connection to
Bagan Manufacturing, so the timers were set for just 30 minutes.
That was more than enough time for Mike and Tun to cross back
over into Thailand.

Two and a half hours later, Mike boarded a Thai Air flight
from Chiang Rai back to Bangkok. Shortly after arriving in
Bangkok, he boarded an 11:55 pm flight from Bangkok. With a
plane change in Tokyo, that flight would have him in Washington,
D.C. by 11 the next morning, local time, where he would catch up
with Ken. Long before Mike arrived in Washington, there was nothing left to tie C3 to any operations in Myanmar.

Tom completed his assignment in Kuala Lumpur. The
Malaysian manufacturer that supplied *antidote.com* and other web
sites no longer existed. Its president and CFO were dead and its
offices destroyed. The offices of its lawyers and accountants were in
shambles, their computer systems beyond repair. Tom returned to his
hotel. It was done—all connections between C3 and the Karasik
Commission and the manufacturers and distributors of the tainted
nermycin had been destroyed. Normally, he would be looking forward to his return. This time, he knew that one way or another, he

would have to deal with the situation at PharmCorp before it or the Karasik Commission dealt with him.

Tom headed for the airport for the long flight to Washington.

They were stumped. Each day, more and more victims were dying. If the mysterious phone caller was right, they would have to deal with Raic. Somehow, Raic and others had violated America's medical supply system through the back door. Now, hundreds and soon thousands would die from illegal medicines purchased from Canadian web sites. Though they had probably succeeded in closing down on-going sales of the tainted pharmaceuticals, they still had no idea how they worked, how to save those already infected, or why Raic had done this.

This was the worst-case scenario Weiner had always feared— a full-scale terrorist attack on the United States was underway *and no one even knew it!!* Weiner and Pye were very frustrated, but they had done their jobs, and done them well. Now, they had to continue to do so. They had to put American lives ahead of their own desires to make the terrorists pay for what they had done.

The rate at which Americans were contracting the pneumonia-like symptoms and the rate of death were increasing. Across the United States, not just the very young and the very old, but once healthy, vibrant children and young adults were becoming very ill. The numbers were still not so great that the overall incidence of pneumonia failed to mask what was happening. Nonetheless, each life taken was a special and unique individual taken down by the insidious attack. Within another few weeks, the body count would rise to the level where it became visible to hospitals throughout the nation. Then, the numerous funerals each day and the lives cut short would become a tragedy unlike any other in America's 230-year history as a nation.

With the approval of David Salzman and Bob Treiger, Richard Goldstein recommended to Jason Waters that an offer of amnesty be made to Petar Raic, conditioned on his ability to provide an antidote for whatever was happening.

Seldom had the Justice Department acted so quickly. Within an hour after Waters received the recommendation for immunity, he had approved the recommendation and faxed the approval to Greg Schoenfeld in New York. Waters' transmittal letter directed Schoenfeld to move as quickly as possible "because every hour more Americans are dying and it is incumbent upon us to save every life that can possibly be saved."

"It's amazing. You won without a fight," Steve Silbert advised Petar. "The government will grant you full and complete immunity from prosecution. In return, the only thing they want is an antidote."

Silbert forcefully added, "Notwithstanding what you told Eric Jacobs, the government doesn't see this as a simple case of tainted drugs causing harm. They see it as a deliberate terrorist attack on the United States. If you don't cooperate, they want you to know that they will seek the death penalty.

"I have no doubt they are telling the truth. If you have any ability to deliver an antidote, I strongly advise you to accept this deal," Silbert said as he looked Petar directly in the eye, trying to communicate the strength of his recommendation. "One last thing. You only have until tomorrow. After that, the Justice Department has the right to rescind the offer," Silbert added.

"Assuming, hypothetically, that what the Justice Department says is true, what good would it be to get immunity? Some crackpot with a gun would kill me before I even left the courthouse steps,"

Petar observed. Then, after a moment's pause, he instructed Silbert, "Go back to Justice. Tell them that I'm not conceding I know what they're talking about. But, if I can get them what they are seeking, I want a blanket immunity not only for me, but also for the C3 Group and anyone associated with the C3 Group."

Silbert looked at Petar like he was crazy. "You have an offer of complete immunity and you are going to turn it down unless the people who fired you get the same thing?"

"You have it. Plus, I don't want any press releases or public announcements coming anywhere near the word terrorism, or alleging any possible wrongdoing by anyone at C3," Petar added, as though he were structuring the positions for an ordinary commercial deal, rather than playing brinkmanship with his life.

"You know I'll have to discuss this with Eric Jacobs?" Silbert asked.

"Discuss it with whomever you want. It's simple, if the government believes what they're saying, their choice is to see tens of thousands of Americans die and then explain to the public that they did nothing to stop it, or save those Americans and let a few guys off the hook. To be honest, I don't see a choice, and I'm willing to bet they won't either," Petar answered, his logic impeccable.

"Just as long as you know that the stakes on this bet are your life," a resigned Silbert answered, as he reached for the phone to call Greg Schoenfeld.

"Are you crazy?" Schoenfeld shouted into the phone. Half an hour later he agreed to discuss the terms with Justice Department officials in Washington, D.C.

Silbert completed his call with Eric Jacobs. At first, Jacobs sounded astonished that the Justice Department suspected Raic and C3 of intentionally tainting the nermycin as part of some far more sinister plot to kill Americans. He asked Silbert, "Are you telling me that a man we fired just a few days ago, without any severance pay or support is putting his life on the line to shield C3 and its executives—including me?"

"That's exactly what I'm telling you," Silbert answered.

The incredulous general counsel concluded, "I can't imagine the Justice Department seriously considering these terms if they believe this is an act of terrorism. Still, I have an obligation to my client. I'll discuss this with them and get back to you as soon as I can."

"Just make sure it's by tomorrow morning, or the opportunity may be gone," an equally skeptical Steve Silbert advised his colleague.


Jacobs first reached Steve Maier, president of the C3 Group, who was as bewildered as Jacobs about these latest allegations. Maier conferenced in Karasik. "I'm surprised. I'm shocked. I have no idea what to make of this," Ken asserted. "I'll make a few calls and I'll get back to you later tonight, or tomorrow morning," Ken told them.

"Based on what Petar's lawyer told me, I doubt we have past tomorrow morning, at the latest, to make a deal," Jacobs explained.

"I understand. Just stand by until I can get some additional information," Karasik replied before disconnecting.


Ken Karasik smiled one of the broadest smiles he had ever smiled. Things were working out just as he had planned. Using an anonymous prepaid cell phone, he made a pre-arranged call to another anonymous prepaid cell phone that would be destroyed immediately after the call.

"How far can we go?" he asked.

"They're very scared about the mounting death rate. I see no reason you can't go all the way. We'll throw in a demand or two to save face, but nothing that you'll really care about," Jason Waters replied before disconnecting and throwing the prepaid cell phone into a dumpster just minutes away from being picked up by the Sanitation Department.

Weiner was apoplectic. He was convinced that Ken Karasik was behind one of the most devastating terrorist attacks in the nation's history. Though no one in the public had any idea beyond the FDA's announcement of risks involving nermycin, Weiner also was convinced that the death rate would soon be much higher than they realized. "The overall severity of pneumonia and the incubation period are disguising the true size of this attack," Weiner told Goldstein. It was one thing to give Raic a pass, but all of C3 and Karasik? That was too much for the veteran agent.

As Friday began to run out, Jason Waters received recommendations from Salzman at the CDC, Treiger at the FDA, Goldstein at the FBI, and Schoenfeld, Justice's division chief in New York City.

Salzman's comments echoed Barry's concerns. "The death rate is about to grow at an accelerating rate," Salzman began. "Whatever they've done, we're only seeing the first wave of deaths now. Countless thousands are undoubtedly infected and we don't know how or who," Salzman told Waters. "Anything we can do to stop this we have to do, no matter who walks."

Treiger agreed. "This isn't about whether the FBI might possibly one day make a case against Karasik, this is about thousands who will die right now if we don't act," he insisted. Despite some misgivings, Francine also agreed.

Goldstein was on the same page, "There is no doubt that Barry, Francine, Suzy and their teams should be proud of their work. Thanks to them, we have stopped this attack before untold tens of thousands are infected. I am confident that we have a case against C3. With more hard work we may even develop a case against Karasik. But, the price of vengeance here is too great. In the circumstances, I will not object to letting Karasik off the hook, but we really should force C3 to pay a sizeable penalty for what they've done."

"What if we made them divest C3 Pharmaceuticals?" Waters suggested.

"Sure. That would suit me. Or a large fine," Goldstein replied.

"Ok, put that in your memo to me," Waters instructed.

Barry just shook his head as he listened to the conversation. He understood Goldstein's position, but Karasik was a terrorist, and he was about to get off the hook with nothing more than a slap on the wrist. With his phone on mute, Goldstein looked at Barry. "I know what you've accomplished. When all this is over, we will make Karasik pay. You have my word," the FBI Assistant Director pledged.

Schoenfeld too reluctantly agreed with immunity. They really had no choice. Every hour meant more deaths. Despite incredible work, they were losing to the terrorists.

Waters gathered the individual recommendations, and tied them together into a formal recommendation to the Attorney General. Ultimately, the President would have to sign off on any pardons. Though that process normally took weeks or even months, they had no time. Each day that went by meant more deaths. Waters called the Attorney General. He would return from

Los Angeles. They could meet at 10:00 am the next day. Since that would be a Saturday, they agreed to meet at the Attorney General's Georgetown home.

"It's over. We've lost," Bowne reported to Dave Cole and Bob Estrich late Friday evening. He had called them in for an emergency meeting in their secure bubble.

"What's happened, Bill?" Cole asked.

"After getting all the assurance that the terrorists were proceeding, we now know for certain that either Ken Karasik or his crazy Muslim lieutenant, Petar Raic, were behind this. For whatever reason, they're throwing in the towel. Our D.C. sources tell us that the Justice Department is putting the final touches on an immunity deal. In return, they get an antidote and no one ever knows."

"That doesn't sound so bad," Estrich said. "We never wanted thousands to die. From what you tell me, this may keep the death toll to just a few hundred. I'd say that's a good thing."

"The problem is that if the real terrorists never claim responsibility and the government puts a gag on the incident, no one will ever know what has happened. That would mean the entire operation was for nothing," Cole added, already distancing himself from the very real terrorist attack he had authorized, approved and funded.

"I suppose we could put out a press release," Estrich facetiously suggested.

"What did this cost us, Bill?" Cole asked.

"You know the numbers. We paid out $120 million. Our other costs were maybe a few million. Call it $125 million all in," Bowne responded.

"Let's not forget two of our best scientists," Estrich said, referring to the two deceased researchers from the Guadalajara facility.

"Does Karasik know of our involvement?" Cole asked, yet again changing the subject.

"I don't know. It's possible. Opperman obviously had some association with C3. There's no way to know what he told them."

"This isn't a very satisfying outcome, is it Bill?" Cole asked.

Bowne remained silent, knowing a rhetorical question when he heard one.

"Bill, I think you should go home now while Bob and I figure out how to clean up this mess," Cole said.

"Come on Dave, I've served this company for more than 25 years. We've always solved things together. Why should this one be any different?" Bowne pleaded with his bosses.

"I hear you. Just stay calm. Everything will be fine," Cole replied. "But, I really do want some time alone with Bob."

Bowne knew what it meant when someone suggested remaining calm. He knew what it meant when Ben had advised him to stay calm, and he knew what it meant when he had given the same advice to Dave and Bob just a few weeks earlier. Still, he had no choice.

"I'll be in my office for a while. When I leave, my cell phone will be on. Don't hesitate to call," he said as he left the secure room.

Bowne headed to his office and sat down at his desk. His Pentium 4 computer was to his left, in its custom-built Art Deco stand. After quickly keying in the password, he selected a segregated partition on his local hard drive that was never backed-up onto the PharmCorp servers. He pressed a few keys and ran the program that would irretrievably fragment the sector. Whatever happened next,

Bowne wanted to be very certain that no investigation could find a connection between PharmCorp or him and his latest project.

He sat deeply back in his cushioned leather chair as he thought about the risks he had taken and the deaths that likely would result. Each time he did the calculations, he came out the same way. It was unfortunate, but it was necessary. He was very certain that he had done the right thing.

When Bowne had left and the automatic door had resealed, Dave turned to Bob. "You know what has to be done, don't you? Soon."

He got no disagreement.

# FIFTY ONE

*I*T WAS JUST 8:00 am when Jacobs received a call from Ken Karasik. "You're going to get an offer this morning. Just listen. When you have the offer, call me."

The Attorney General signed off on Waters' recommendation. If possible, they would avoid a Presidential pardon, but the result would be the same: complete immunity from prosecution for any acts, known or unknown, undertaken by the C3 Group, or any shareholder, director, officer, employee or representative relating to nermycin, Taiwan Pharmaceutical Investments Ltd., Inversiones y Distribución Médicas de Las Producciones, or RD Pharmaceuticals. In short, a totally free pass.

In return, C3 would be required to divest of C3 Pharmaceuticals, pay a $100 million fine and agree not to again enter the pharmaceuticals business for at least 10 years. Raic would plead guilty to a single count of importing tainted drugs. He would be sentenced to a fine of $1 million and a one-year suspended sentence.

In return, they wanted an antidote and they wanted to know who was infected.

Although Waters was authorized to proceed, it would be subject to the President's approval if Waters reached a deal. The Attorney General did not want to involve the President until that time.

"We've got it!" the CDC chemist shouted to his colleagues. "It's the cyprofaxin and the nermycin together. Get Suzy."

Schoenfeld called Jacobs and Silbert. "I have an offer. I'd like to meet with both of you as soon as possible."

"How about my office at 1:00 pm?" Jacobs offered.

"That's fine," Silbert said.

"Ok, Eric's office at 1:00," Schoenfeld agreed.

Salzman, Liebig and their staff were spending another weekend in the office. They were making progress.

"David, we may have figured it out. There appears to be an interaction between the cyprofaxin and the nermycin that somehow causes this pneumonia-like illness. They're going over it again to verify. They're also going to see if the FBI guys can duplicate the results," Suzy reported to David Salzman.

"That's really good work Suzy. The hell of it is that it's only a first step. Knowing what is happening is still a long way from knowing how to stop it, or even knowing who's infected. But it's an awfully important first step," David told her, a little relief creeping into his voice.

Still, Salzman was right. Tens of thousands or even hundreds of thousands of Americans could die while the CDC worked to find a cure. The truth was that, unless and until Justice obtained an antidote, more Americans would die.

By 2:00 pm Jacobs had Karasik and Maier on a secure conference call. He explained the terms. "If we're innocent, I don't see why we should do this. Sure, we may have to pay a fine for the nermycin, but this could ruin us. More to the point, if we haven't done anything, we can't comply, since to do so we have to provide an antidote and a list that doesn't exist," Jacobs advised.

Maier was particularly concerned about their stock price. "If the market gets wind of this, the 10% drop we experienced will feel like a gain," Maier complained.

"Thank you. I've made my decision. You are to accept the Justice Department offer on the following conditions. First, there is to be absolutely no publicity about this. In fact, the FDA is to announce our complete cooperation on tracking down the tainted nermycin and our agreement to cease its manufacture. Second, the fine will be reduced to $50 million, an amount more consistent with the mistake we made. Third, it is to be clear that I will agree to sell C3 Pharmaceuticals only because we failed to detect what Petar was doing. Finally, we want two years in which to sell C3 Pharmaceuticals."

Jacobs was stunned. He saw right through Ken's denials. "Are you telling me that we did these horrible things?"

"Eric, I'm telling you that Petar must have done these things and that I want nothing to do with this problem. I will get the lists from Petar. Once this is resolved you may resign. I wish you well.

"Before you go, I want you to coordinate with Mike Mihalic to complete our part of the deal," Ken ordered Jacobs, and then he disconnected from the call.

After Maier, too, disconnected, Eric Jacobs just sat there shaking.

"It turns out that Ben and Karasik were working this PharmCorp angle together. You're getting a pass," Mike Mihalic explained to Tom. They were sitting in a coffee shop not far from the Hay-Adams Hotel. Both of them looked exhausted, but they had accomplished their assignments without a hitch.

"Ken has one more job for you. He wants Bowne taken out."

"Do you think he was responsible for Ben?"

"We don't know. Ken's also working another angle. But, either way, he wants to send a message."

"I'll get back to New York as soon as I can."

"The sooner the better."

"Good, I'll pick someone to work with me. I need one night to catch up on some sleep, and we'll be on this tomorrow or the next day, at the latest."

"This is your operation. You're the boss now, my friend."

They clasped hands. After all they'd been through, both of them were relieved that Tom was still very much on board.

As the lawyers negotiated terms, another 60 Americans died from the pneumonia-like illness.

# FIFTY TWO

*T*HE CDC AND FBI confirmed that the illnesses were caused by cyprofaxin interacting with the specially modified nermycin. From there, finding a cure was the CDC's job. After meeting most of Sunday, they agreed that task could take months, during which time tens of thousands of Americans would die.

The President of the United States signed off on the terms. All would be kept in the strictest confidence. The fine would be $50 million, including a fund for returns of unused nermycin, regardless of the form, source or manufacturer. Karasik had up to two years in which to sell C3 Pharmaceuticals. The FDA would publicly thank C3 for its assistance. Petar Raic alone would take the fall. The government irrevocably agreed that other than Petar, neither Ken Karasik nor anyone else associated with the C3 Group would bear any responsibility for Petar's acts.

Sunday afternoon, the papers were signed. Petar delivered to Eric Jacobs two envelopes. In one was a card that contained one word "Abcyclene." In the other was a comprehensive list of all those who had purchased the tainted nermycin from the Canadian web sites. The second envelope also included that information on two CDs, in two different database programs. After all, the C3 Group wanted to be as helpful as possible in assisting the CDC to track down and treat those who might be ill. Somehow, Kenan Joseph Anton Karasik IV's name was deleted from those lists.

In total, 100,000 Americans had purchased the tainted nermycin. Most of them undoubtedly also purchased cyprofaxin, whether from their local pharmacy or on-line. The government had its work cut out for it as it tracked down those 100,000 potential victims, assessed who had contracted the pneumonia-like symptoms, and prescribed Abcyclene to them to treat the illness.

The FDA put out a further alert. C3 Pharmaceuticals had been fully cooperative. There had never been a problem with Nermycin-X. Nonetheless, because C3 had developed the drug and was concerned that it could be modified by counterfeiters, it was ceasing production of Nermycin-X and would recall all product on the market. Anyone who had purchased Nermycin-X or any generic form of nermycin and had not used all of it would receive a full refund from a $50 million fund established by C3. It appeared that very few consumers who had taken nermycin had become ill. Thanks to C3, the FDA would be contacting all those who had purchased nermycin for a check-up and if necessary they would be treated with another antibiotic that should completely resolve any risk.

There was virtually no blood. No one had seen or heard anything. The NYPD Crime Scene Unit was stumped. That didn't change the outcome. William Bowne was dead and a small, very deep hole in the middle of his forehead was the immediate cause. More precisely, the 22-caliber hollow-point bullet fired from close range and lodged in Bowne's head was the cause of both the hole and Bowne's death. CSU and the detectives would continue to ask questions, but after six hours at the crime scene, they were pessimistic about finding many answers.

Strangely, despite Bowne's senior position at one of the world's largest corporations and the location of the crime scene on the 50<sup>th</sup> floor of PharmCorp Tower, just a few feet from the chairman's and president's offices, little pressure was being exerted by Bowne's employer to find those answers. The detectives didn't know it then, but like Bowne's death, PharmCorp's lack of interest was a permanent condition.

PharmCorp lost no time in naming Bowne's successor as executive vice president of special projects. Their choice was Max Linville. The payroll department processed his raise from $400,000 to $750,000. Not as much as Bowne had been making, but Bowne had been on the job almost 10 years. Linville also received 50,000 stock options and his new corporate ID card. Among other perks, the card would entitle him to eat in the executive dining room, priority reservations for the squash and tennis courts, and free membership at exclusive clubs in New York, London and Paris.

As Linville was moving from the 20<sup>th</sup> floor to his large office on the 50<sup>th</sup> floor, his new boss, Bob Estrich visited. "Max, I want to welcome you. Dave and I have every confidence we made the right choice. While Bill may have made some mistakes, both Dave and I thought very highly of him, as did the board."

"Thanks Bob. I hope I live up to your expectations."

"All we can ask of you is the same dedication and creativity we got from Bill," Estrich said.

"You know you'll have it," Max nervously replied.

"I know that, Max. I'm sure you'll be there for PharmCorp—whatever the cost."

# FIFTY THREE

IN ACCORDANCE WITH the terms of the settlement, Petar Raic was scheduled to appear in Federal Court promptly at 11:00 am. There, he would plead guilty to the importation of substandard medicine. He would pay a fine of $500,000 (reduced from the $1 million originally demanded) and receive just a three-month suspended sentence.

Petar hailed a taxi. He intended to meet his wife, who had just flown in from London, and Steve Silbert at the courthouse. Silbert had assured him the hearing would take no more than an hour. After the hearing, Petar would be forever known as the criminal responsible for importing tainted nermycin into the United States, causing hundreds to become ill, even if inadvertently. There was good reason for Petar's concern that the public might not view the penalty as proportionate to the crime.

As the taxi proceeded down the FDR Drive that ran along Manhattan's East side, a fuel tanker abruptly changed lanes just ahead of them. Though the taxi's driver slammed on his brakes, they plowed directly into the tanker at nearly 60 miles per hour. There was a terrible explosion; the tanker and the taxi erupted in flames.

Steel was hurled in all directions. Cars and trucks on both sides of the FDR pumped their brakes. Three more cars plowed into the fireball and steel crumpled as 20 cars collided in two chain reactions. In all, at least 10 died and 30 were injured. Petar and the drivers of the taxi and tanker were incinerated as the fireball superheated to more than 2,000 degrees.

When the police went to inform Mrs. Raic of the terrible accident, they couldn't find her. She had disappeared.

Christine Liu was at the Hay-Adams watching CNN when a special report interrupted. "Oh my God!" she gasped. She immediately called Ken, who was in the suite's sitting room. "It's terrible. Petar's been killed."

News footage of the fireball on the FDR Drive played non-stop on CNN and the other news channels. When Nely Gonzalez Karasik saw that Petar had died, she was sad for her husband's friend. But, her life was a good one. Baby Kenan was well and back home. After a time, she wandered into Kenan's room. Whatever the real meaning of Petar's death, it wasn't her problem.

Alexa watched a replay of the CNN story at her suite in the Dorchester. She just smiled. The close of one chapter meant the start of the next.

Ken headed for the airport to board his Gulfstream V for the eight-hour flight to Paris. He had a deal to work on. If all went well, C3 would soon be much larger.

Richard Goldstein completed briefing the Director of the FBI and the Attorney General. As the Attorney General reached for the phone to arrange time with the President, his eyes were moist. Whether his tears were for the hundreds who had died and the many hundreds who might still die, or for the fact that this had happened on his watch was unclear. About the only thing that was completely clear was that the attack had been avoidable. If America had followed through on its commitments, this would never have happened. Once again, they would act only after the horrible consequences of failure.

Hundreds had already died. Despite the President's willingness to let C3 and Karasik off the hook, hundreds more would surely die before they could be located and the antidote administered. It just didn't have to happen. Not on his watch.

"Mr. President..." the Attorney General said solemnly into the phone, as he began his tragic report.

With Petar's death and the government's silence, the story soon faded away, the many thousands who became sick and the thousands who died simply a rounding error in the statistics for pneumonia. The public was now safe and the man the public believed responsible for the tainted nermycin had paid the ultimate price.

# AFTERWORD

The origin of *The Karasik Conspiracy* is a worthy subject for an entirely separate book. Indeed, since October 2005, that story has received widespread coverage in the press, including, from among others, *The Washington Post*, *The Philadelphia Inquirer*, *New York Daily News*, *The Los Angeles Times*, and National Public Radio (NPR). Other newspapers, on-line newsletters and blogs have picked up the story. Some of the details are revealed here for the first time. Additional information is available at *www.karasikconspiracy.com*. A password may be required to access certain content on the site. If so, the password is "Conspiracy." Please see the site for details.

The story begins in approximately April 2005 when Mark Barondess,[1] a consultant for the pharmaceutical lobbying group PhRMA, approached Phoenix Books with a plan for PhRMA to fund the creation and publication of a novel about a terrorist attack against the United States utilizing counterfeit pharmaceuticals distributed via on-line Canadian pharmacies. As understood by Michael Viner, president of Phoenix Books, and Julie Chrystyn, the writer selected by Mr. Viner and approved by Mr. Barondess to write the book, the goals were to create a dialogue that would scare Americans so that we would (1) not purchase less expensive prescription

---

[1] To avoid making this a personal matter, the authors and publisher had initially declined to identify Mr. Barondess or the PhRMA marketing executive assigned to the project. When *The New York Daily News* broke the story, a spokesperson for PhRMA apparently identified Mr. Barondess, who subsequently gave interviews to the media on this project. Two weeks later, apparently relying on sources at PhRMA, *The Philadelphia Inquirer* identified the marketing executive as Valerie Volpe, PhRMA's deputy vice president for federal and state affairs.

drugs from Canadian on-line pharmacies; and (2) oppose amendments to the Medicine Equity and Drug Safety Act that would make it easier for us to purchase such drugs.

Ms. Chrystyn was given just 45 days in which to complete the assignment. The goal was to publish the book before hearings on legislation that would weaken the Medicine Equity and Drug Safety Act by eliminating the requirement that the Secretary of Health and Human Services first certify the safety of drugs imported from Canada before such importation could occur. If enacted into law, the legislation would facilitate the importation into the United States of lower-priced drugs from Canada (for a more complete discussion of the political issues involved, please see the Foreword at the beginning of this book).

Shortly thereafter, Ms. Chrystyn met with Mr. Barondess and Valerie Volpe, a PhRMA deputy vice president. Ms. Chrystyn recalls being told that it was important that the book include fluff and entertaining reading for women, while depicting the deaths of thousands of children.

As the book was being written, Mr. Barondess reviewed drafts and complimented the story and content. After the book was nearly complete, Ms. Volpe asked for a completely different story. Among other things, in conference calls with Ms. Chrystyn, Mr. Spivak, Mr. Barondess and Mr. Viner, she instructed that the terrorists be transformed into fundamentalist Arab Muslims and that their motive be greed. She did not appear to understand that the draft manuscript's description of the situation in the Balkans was historical fact (she said she thought it was fictional); she asserted that terrorists are born that way and do not evolve based on their life experiences. She wanted the book to be made extremely simple for her hoped-for female readers. Although many of the proposed changes were neither viable nor consistent with the pitch previously delivered, a compromise was reached with Ms. Volpe and Mr. Barondess on rewrites for the book.

As the manuscript was being written, the cover was designed, advertising commitments made and reviews secured. Through Mr. Barondess, payments were made to Phoenix to reimburse these costs as they were invoiced.

Mr. Spivak joined with Ms. Chrystyn to make the changes requested by Mr. Barondess and PhRMA. As each draft was delivered, Mr. Barondess communicated some approvals and some disapprovals. Increasingly, the changes requested by Ms. Volpe and Mr. Barondess conflicted.

Some weeks after the final rewrites were delivered, Mr. Barondess advised Phoenix that the project would not proceed. Whether that decision was made in whole or in part for the reason given by Mr. Barondess—that PhRMA did not like the book—or because PhRMA became concerned that it might look bad for it to be funding a novel, or for any other reason, PhRMA withdrew. Phoenix and Mr. Barondess then debated whether PhRMA would pay all or any of Phoenix's outstanding invoices as well as related financial issues. Mr. Barondess then advised Mr. Viner that Ms. Volpe would not approve any further payments. No further payments were made.

Rights in the book reverted to Ms. Chrystyn, Mr. Spivak, and ultimately Spivak Management Inc. The manuscript was rewritten into a more traditional and complex thriller without the polemics, cliché fundamentalist Muslims or fluffy "women's" content required by PhRMA. The resulting work, *The Karasik Conspiracy*, has some similarities and many differences when compared to the version written for PhRMA.

When Mr. Viner advised Mr. Barondess that Phoenix intended to publish the new book, Mr. Barondess insisted that it not include any mention of what had transpired, nor any criticism of the pharmaceuticals industry or PhRMA. Mr. Viner recalls that Mr. Barondess made it clear to him that PhRMA had a battery of lawyers and that it would not be pleased if Phoenix published such a book. Mr. Viner recalls advising Mr. Barondess that Phoenix's arrangement with PhRMA and Mr. Barondess did not prohibit it from doing so. He does not recall Mr. Barondess disagreeing.

After Mr. Viner rejected Mr. Barondess' threats or perceived threats, Mr. Barondess next tried money. He offered to pay various sums to Phoenix to resolve Phoenix's financial claims, to buy silence about his and PhRMA's involvement in the original book, and to eliminate any criticism of the pharmaceutical industry from *The Karasik Conspiracy*. Ultimately, to avert litigation, Mr. Viner indicated a willingness to compromise his financial demands by agreeing to accept a settlement of $100,000. In order to avoid the animus of PhRMA and the consequences Mr. Viner feared based on his conversations with Mr. Barondess, Mr. Viner also agreed that the marketing for *The Karasik Conspiracy* would not mention any of the events described above in this Afterword. He believed that *The Karasik Conspiracy* would otherwise be as free as any other book to endorse or admonish the pharmaceutical industry, or anyone else.

Mr. Viner thought he had a deal. He was wrong.

On August 2, 2005, Mr. Barondess sent a proposed agreement to Mr. Viner. His transmittal email stated that "all" of the provisions were material, and nothing would be negotiated. He not only insisted that Mr. Viner sign the agreement, but also that Ms. Chrystyn and Mr. Spivak do so.

As expected, that agreement settled the financial dispute between Phoenix and PhRMA for $100,000 and also prohibited Phoenix from publicly disclosing the events described in this Afterword.

It was the balance of the agreement that shocks the conscience. It granted Mr. Barondess the right to read and approve (or disapprove) the manuscript, and with extraordinary arrogance, it required that forever, none of Phoenix, Mr. Viner, Ms. Chrystyn or Mr. Spivak could "in any of their public, private, or promotional statements or writings...in any manner disparage, denigrate, demean, criticize, malign or cast in an unlawful or unethical light Barondess, the pharmaceutical industry, or PhRMA."

Neither Mr. Viner, Ms. Chrystyn nor Mr. Spivak had any interest in being dictated to for the rest of their lives by Mr. Barondess or PhRMA—certainly, none of them could ever imagine that they would be asked to *forever* refrain in their "*private* statements" on any matter and at any time from "criticiz[ing] Barondess, the pharmaceutical industry or PhRMA." [2] They refused to sign the agreement and true to his word, Mr. Barondess remained intransigent. No further money was paid to Phoenix, which remains out-of-pocket for many of the costs of the original book.

Mr. Viner, Ms. Chrystyn and Mr. Spivak can only hope that Mr. Viner misunderstood the threats he believes were made to him by Mr. Barondess, or that the public discussion of this situation will convince PhRMA and Mr. Barondess that it would be a very bad decision to follow through on those threats in full view of the public, the media, and Congress.

In October 2005, stories began to circulate about PhRMA's role in the creation of the original version of this book. *The Washington Post, New York Daily News,* Toronto's *The Globe and Mail, The Los Angeles Times, The Philadelphia Inquirer* and National

---

2   It is particularly astonishing that Mr. Barondess would expect Ms. Chrystyn or Mr. Spivak to accept any of his terms. Neither had contracts with PhRMA, neither was receiving any money from PhRMA, and absent entering into the proposed contract with PhRMA, both were as free as any other person to talk about Mr. Barondess, PhRMA and the pharmaceuticals industry.

Public Radio (NPR), among others, covered the story. *Fortune* and *Time Magazine*, among others, are preparing articles scheduled to run after this book goes to press. When reporters for these publications and NPR reached PhRMA for comment, Ken Johnson, its spokesperson, apparently acknowledged the scheme, but shifted blame. Where Phoenix and the authors had refused to personalize the situation, Mr. Johnson apparently identified Mr. Barondess as the outside consultant and in the grand tradition of Washington "spin," asserted that only Mr. Barondess and a low-level "yo yo," not PhRMA management, were responsible.

On October 20, 2005, *The Washington Post* reported that: "Johnson said some money was paid to cover research costs. He said PhRMA head Billy Tauzin 'read the riot act' to staffers involved in the project and instituted controls to prevent such a thing from happening again."

*The Washington Post* also reported that: "Johnson said the industry did not have to rely on 'pulp fiction and loony tunes' to make its case to Congress and the public. 'This absolutely was not a project that was approved or pursued by the leaders of PhRMA. This was a screwball idea,' he said."

In *The Washington Post* article, Mr. Johnson concedes that Mr. Barondess was not alone and that he worked with PhRMA staffers. Mr. Johnson also concedes that PhRMA funded the effort, though for undisclosed reasons, PhRMA funneled six-figure sums through Mr. Barondess instead of directly paying Phoenix. While Mr. Johnson seeks to minimize the financial aspects by characterizing the sums as being used only for research, Mr. Viner observes that the advances were also used to reimburse costs incurred by Phoenix for marketing and promotion, as well as the initial installment of the author's advance.

Then, in an October 21, 2005 front-page story in one of Canada's leading newspapers, *The Globe and Mail,* PhRMA honed its defense. As *The Globe and Mail* reported: "The pharmaceutical group denies its 'leadership' approved the book project but it admits that 'a rogue employee' did arrange to make payments through a consultant for the book project before it was discovered last summer and halted, according to PhRMA's senior vice-president of communications, Ken Johnson. 'We absolutely and positively did not commission the book,' he said. 'We are open and transparent about everything we did…We don't have to resort to pulp fiction.'"

*The Globe and Mail* further reported that Mr. Johnson insisted "the book project was 'a screwball idea and it was something that we would never, ever support or condone.'" He was quoted as believing that sponsoring such a project would have been "underhanded and sneaky."

As news coverage intensified, a number of contradictions emerged among Mr. Johnson's and Mr. Barondess' versions of events and the written record. In an interview broadcast by NPR on October 23, 2005, Mr. Barondess took personal responsibility for the payments to Phoenix. Here is the exchange between Mr. Barondess and Brooke Gladstone, host of NPR's *On the Media,* as detailed in the official NPR transcript of the interview:

> "BROOKE GLADSTONE: But someone from your organization was clearly in touch with this publisher and there were payments made.
>
> MARK BARONDESS: Not by PhRMA. That money was money that I paid over to them….
>
> MARK BARONDESS: I, as a consultant, paid to have a draft of this manuscript prepared."

Perhaps Mr. Barondess was unaware that Mr. Johnson had already conceded that PhRMA had funded the effort and that Mr. Barondess had been a mere conduit for PhRMA's largesse.

Moreover, an April 28, 2005 email to Mr. Barondess from Ms. Volpe, the PhRMA deputy vice president assigned to the project, lays to rest any uncertainty as to the ultimate funding source for the arrangement with Phoenix and punctures the myth advanced by PhRMA that only a single low-level staffer was involved in the project. In her email, Ms. Volpe apologized for the delay in processing a payment for Phoenix and she advised Mr. Barondess that "The check is written, it just cannot be released without the appropriate legal signoff. I will fedex the check as soon as it is released." Payment was made a few days later.

In that same NPR interview, Mr. Barondess accused Phoenix of blackmail and denied that the contract he sent to Mr. Viner would forever preclude Mr. Viner, Mr. Spivak and Ms. Chrystyn from criticizing the pharmaceutical industry. The contract, reprinted below, speaks for itself and is not in any way ambiguous.

In the NPR interview, Mr. Barondess attempted to subtly bolster PhRMA's defense that no one important had participated in the project. He explained that he had taken the idea for a novel to "a lower level individual that had the ability to agree that this is something that we could explore." Of course, PhRMA did a lot more than explore the idea; through Mr. Barondess, it commissioned a writer, reviewed cover designs, agreed on promotion plans and, according to Mr. Viner, committed to purchase 40,000 copies of the book.

Mr. Barondess told NPR that the project was killed because the book was no good (he said readers would need "Dramamine," not always a bad thing for a thriller)—and because PhRMA belatedly realized it was a mistake to finance fiction. As transcribed by NPR:

"MARK BARONDESS: A child in the fifth grade could have written better than the document that I was handed. And we thought someone might think that this was some improper conduct on the part of the pharmaceutical industry of trying to scare someone."

Mr. Barondess' assertion that the quality of the book was a cause of PhRMA's withdrawal is undercut by Mr. Johnson, who has instead asserted only that the book was not approved because higher-ranking executives of PhRMA decided the idea of PhRMA commissioning a thriller was "screwball" and "looney tunes." [3] In an interview with NPR, Mr. Johnson insisted the project was the fault of just one person, whom he referred to as a "renegade" and likened to disgraced *New York Times* reporter Jayson Blair.

By the time *The Los Angeles Times* spoke to Ken Johnson, the PhRMA spokesperson was implicitly asserting that PhRMA's involvement in the project was the result of PhRMA's structure, rather than merely the doings of a "renegade" or "rogue" staffer. In its October 27, 2005 edition, *The Los Angeles Times* reported:

"[Johnson] acknowledges that [the PhRMA marketing executive] had some 'budgetary authority,' but [he] suggests that she abused it in this instance. He says that PhRMA is evaluating Barondess' consultancy

---

3 Of course, the possibility that funding a book would be "improper conduct" is something Mr. Barondess might have thought about before initiating the project. One also has to wonder if it is Mr. Barondess' position that if the book had been better, PhRMA would have proceeded with publication. In an interview with NPR, Mr. Spivak opined that the version of the book required by PhRMA was troubled from the start. As transcribed by NPR:

"BROOKE GLADSTONE: . . .Did you think it was a pretty good book you delivered [to PhRMA], a rippin' good yarn?

KENIN SPIVAK: I thought it was what they wanted. I think what they wanted was not a terrific book. I think the book that now exists is a terrific book."

contract and is 'presently reviewing disciplinary options' for the hapless marketing exec. He also indicates that he and his boss, former Rep. W.J. 'Billy' Tauzin, who became PhRMA's president in January, know that the group has less than a sterling reputation. (The phrase he used is 'quite a lot of baggage.') One of Tauzin's goals, he says, is 'to turn the image around,' implying that the book project didn't help."

Then, an October 31, 2005 article in *The Philadelphia Inquirer* for the first time disclosed that Ms. Volpe, PhRMA's deputy vice president for federal and state affairs, was the PhRMA marketing executive who had been pilloried in the press for two weeks by Mr. Johnson. The *Inquirer* confirmed the previous reports that Ms. Volpe enjoyed budgetary authority and with evident disbelief, noted: "[Ken] Johnson said Volpe, despite her title, was a low-level employee at the group…"

At about the same time, the other shoe dropped, when PhRMA suspended Ms. Volpe, according to reliable sources. It is unclear what her offense might have been, particularly since Mr. Johnson concedes she had budgetary authority and the emails suggest that she received approval for the payments she made.

Given Mr. Johnson's vitriol about the project and its proponents, one might expect that Mr. Barondess and PhRMA would have had a parting of the ways. Yet, Mr. Barondess told NPR that he remains a PhRMA consultant. Indeed, Mr. Barondess' job may now include serving as both the proverbial sacrificial lamb and PhRMA's attack dog. If the NPR interview and subsequent news reports are any indication, Mr. Barondess seems willing to take the blame for PhRMA, mischaracterize the record and attack the authors for the quality of their book and their audacity for telling the truth.

Mr. Barondess' motive may be explained by an email he sent to Mr. Viner in August 2005. In that email, Mr. Barondess referred to PhRMA as his "most important client" and he conceded that his loss of PhRMA would be "economically devastating" to him and to his family. Perhaps Mr. Barondess' attitude is best explained in the *Inquirer* article, which reported that Mr. Barondess said of the situation: "It's a nightmare beyond nightmares."

In late October 2005, counsel for Phoenix put Mr. Barondess and PhRMA on notice that the dispute between PhRMA and Phoenix could be the subject of legal action. He advised them that no documents should be altered or destroyed. It may already be too late, as it is conceivable that documents may have been sanitized before counsel's notice was sent. In any event, Messrs. Johnson and Barondess may in the future get their stories into better alignment. Still, if there is legal action, we may yet learn the whole truth.

The situation cries out for those questions made famous during the Watergate era to be asked—and answered—what did the higher-ups at PhRMA know, and when did they know it?

The following documents consist of an excerpt from Mr. Barondess' transmittal email, and a complete copy of the proposed agreement. The reader may wish to focus on Sections 5, 6 and 9 of that agreement to understand the unconscionable positions insisted upon by Mr. Barondess. Additional documents will be posted on this book's web site, *www.karasikconspiracy.com*. As noted above, a password may be required to access certain content on the site. If so, the password is "Conspiracy." Please see the site for details.

## TRANSMITTAL EMAIL

The following is an excerpt from the email sent on August 2, 2005 by PhRMA's consultant, Mark Barondess, to Michael Viner, the president of Phoenix Books. Mr. Barondess and PhRMA are free to disclose the entire text if they believe that the editing of the email has in any way created a misleading impression as to its contents.

Michael-

I am in Chicago for the weekend. I am forwarding to you the release.... I have tried to make it as concise as possible. All of the provisions are material, and I will not accept anything less and I have no interest in negotiating its terms.... I will have funds available on Monday. I need to get the signed agreement back from you and all parties and I will then wire you the funds per the agreement. Thank you.

PROPOSED AGREEMENT

The following is the complete text of the proposed non-negotiable agreement. The reader may wish to focus on Sections 5, 6 and 9 of the contract.

{The contract begins on the next page.}

## SETTLEMENT AGREEMENT

**THIS SETTLEMENT AGREEMENT** is made as of the 15th day of August 2005, by and between Mark A. Barondess, Phoenix Publishing, Inc., Julie Chrystyn, Michael Viner, Kenin Spivak, and Pharmaceutical Manufacturers and Research of America ("PhRMA").

## W I T N E S S E T H:

**WHEREAS**, Barondess engaged Phoenix and Viner to publish a work of fiction;

**WHEREAS**, Phoenix and/or Viner engaged Chrystyn and/or Spivak to author a manuscript;

**WHEREAS**, Barondess rejected the manuscript and indicated an unwillingness to proceed with the project;

**WHEREAS**, a dispute has arisen with respect to the parties' rights and obligations arising out of the foregoing; and

**WHEREAS**, the parties desire amicably to resolve their dispute, thereby avoiding the burden and expense of legal proceedings;

**NOW, THEREFORE**, in consideration of the mutual promises contained herein, and for other good and valuable consideration, it is agreed as follows:

1.        Except as may be required to enforce its terms, each party to this Settlement Agreement covenants not to sue or assert claims of any kind against any other party to this Settlement Agreement concerning  (a) the engagement of Phoenix and Viner to publish a work of fiction, (b) the engagement of  Chrystyn and/or Spivak to author a manuscript, or (c) "The Spivak Conspiracy" or any other work based upon the general text, plot, ideas, concepts, or

characters reflected in the manuscript provided to Barondess during the summer of 2005. The matters described in the foregoing sentence shall be referred to collectively below as the "subject matter in dispute."

2.        Except as otherwise provided under this Settlement Agreement,  the parties hereby release one another, as well as their agents, assigns, officers, directors, employees, attorneys and representatives, from any and all claims, actions, causes of action, demands, rights, damages, costs, defenses, set-offs, and claims of whatsoever kind or nature, whether at law, in equity or mixed, known or unknown, that they may have arising from or related to the subject matter in dispute.

3.        The Parties hereby acknowledge and agree that the releases set forth in Paragraph 2 are general releases. They further expressly waive and assume the risk of any and all claims for damages which exist in their favor as of this date but of which they do not know or suspect to exist, whether through ignorance, oversight, error, negligence, or otherwise, and which, if known, would materially affect their decision to enter into this Agreement. The Parties further agree that they have accepted the consideration specified herein as a complete compromise of all matters between them involving disputed issues of law and fact, and each Party assumes the risk that the facts or law may be otherwise than he or it believes.

(a)        In light of the above, the Parties expressly waive any and all rights granted by California Civil Code Section 1542 (or any other analogous Federal or state law or regulation). Section 1542 reads as follows:

**A GENERAL RELEASE DOES NOT EXTEND TO CLAIMS WHICH THE CREDITOR DOES NOT KNOW OR SUSPECT TO EXIST IN HIS FAVOR AT THE TIME OF EXECUTING THE RELEASE, WHICH IF KNOWN BY HIM MUST HAVE MATERIALLY AFFECTED HIS SETTLEMENT WITH THE DEBTOR.**

(b)     The Parties acknowledge that they have bargained for the foregoing waiver of Section 1542. The Parties intend that the releases and covenant not to sue contained herein be construed as broadly as possible.

4.     Viner and Phoenix hereby agree to indemnify and hold harmless Barondess and PhRMA from any and all claims or causes of action asserted by any third party with whom either has contracted or interacted in connection with the subject matter in dispute.

5.     The parties acknowledge that Phoenix, Viner, Spivak and/or Chrystyn intend to publish The Spivak Conspiracy, or another work bearing a different title based upon the same or similar facts, plots and characters. Phoenix, Viner, Spivak, and Chrystyn each hereby agree that in any such work, whether fiction or non-fiction, and in any of their public, private, or promotional statements or writings, they shall not in any manner disparage, denigrate, demean, criticize, malign or cast in an unlawful or unethical light Barondess, the pharmaceutical industry, or PhRMA.

6.     Notwithstanding paragraph 5, above, nothing contained herein shall preclude Phoenix, Viner, Spivak and Chrystyn from utilizing in a work of fiction a fictional European pharmaceutical company, with a name bearing no resemblance to that of any existing pharmaceutical company, as part of a terrorist plot. Before publication, the final manuscript of any such work, including any foreword, flap copy, endorsement, galley, and any and all advertisements, shall be made available for review by Barondess—or, if he is unavailable, by a mutually agreeable third party—to ensure compliance with the terms of paragraph 5 and this paragraph. Confirmation of compliance, which shall be required before any such work is released for publication, shall not be unreasonably withheld. Similarly, before utilization of any promotional or advertising copy that characterizes the plot or theme of the work, such copy shall be made available for review by Barondess (or a mutually agreeable third party) to ensure

compliance with the terms of paragraph 5 and this paragraph; confirmation of compliance shall not be unreasonably withheld. (If its characterization of the plot or theme of the work does not differ materially from the jacket blurb, such copy need not be submitted for review.) In the event that the Parties are unable to agree on the issue of compliance, the arbitration provisions of paragraph 10 shall be utilized to resolve the dispute, and the parties agree to take reasonable steps to expedite the arbitration.

7.      Within two business days of receipt of copies of this Settlement Agreement executed by all other parties, Barondess shall wire to Phoenix the sum of One Hundred Thousand Dollars ($100,000.00).

8.      This Settlement Agreement and any discussions in connection therewith shall not be construed as, or deemed to be, evidence of an admission or concession by any party of liability to any other party. Except as necessary to enforce its terms, this Settlement Agreement and any discussions in connection therewith shall not be offered in evidence in any proceeding involving the subject matter in dispute.

9.      Except as otherwise required by law, Viner, Chrystyn, Spivak and Phoenix, their employees, representatives and agents shall not at any time or in any manner, either directly or indirectly, divulge, disclose or communicate in any manner whatsoever to any other person or entity (a) the existence, terms or substance of this Settlement Agreement or (b) the subject matter in dispute, regardless of how or when said information was acquired. If said parties to this Settlement Agreement believe themselves to be compelled by law to disclose the existence, terms or substance of the Settlement Agreement or the subject matter in dispute, the party shall provide notice, in writing, to all the other parties to this Settlement Agreement at least ten (10) business days in advance of the pending disclosure. The parties further agree that monetary damages are insufficient to remedy any breach of this provision and

that any party under this agreement is entitled, without objection, to an injunction by any court of competent jurisdiction to enjoin and restrain the unauthorized disclosure of any such information.

10.     Except with respect to an injunctive action of the kind set forth in paragraph 9, above, any claim relating to this Settlement Agreement shall be brought in binding arbitration proceedings to be conducted (a) by an arbitrator who is an attorney or retired judge with a minimum of ten years experience in the entertainment industry and (b) in accordance with the American Arbitration Association Rules for Commercial Arbitration. Such arbitration shall be non-appealable. The prevailing party in such arbitration shall be entitled to an award of actual damages, costs, and expenses (including all reasonable attorneys' fees) incurred in prosecuting or defending such proceeding. The prevailing party shall also be entitled to any actual costs and expenses (including all reasonable attorneys' fees) incurred in enforcing the arbitration award.

10.     (a)     This Settlement Agreement shall be governed by, and construed in accordance with, the laws of the State of California, and shall be enforceable by each of the parties hereto and their respective successors, assigns, heirs, and personal representatives.

(b)     The parties acknowledge that each of their respective counsel participated in the negotiation of this Settlement Agreement. The parties hereby agree that the wording of this Agreement shall not be construed based upon which of their respective counsel prepared this Agreement in its final form or drafted any of the provisions hereof.

(c)     This Settlement Agreement contains the entire understanding of the parties with respect to the subject matter hereof and there are no other agreements or understandings among the parties with respect to its subject matter; nor have there been any representations, express or implied, as to the subject matter herein.

       (d)      Each party further confirms that the decision to enter into this agreement is made freely, without duress of any kind.

       (e)      This Settlement Agreement may be executed simultaneously in counterparts, each of which shall be deemed to be an original.

       **IN WITNESS WHEREOF**, each of the parties has duly executed this Settlement Agreement as of the date first above written.

_____
Mark A. Barondess

_____
Pharmaceutical Research and Manufacturers
  of America
By:

_____
Michael Viner

_____
Phoenix Publishing, Inc.
By:

_____
Kenin Spivak

_____
Julie Chrystyn

# ACKNOWLEDGEMENTS

I wish to extend my most heartfelt "thank you" to Michael A. Viner, the legendary and distinguished publisher extraordinâire, for presenting me with the challenge of writing this thriller. I will be forever grateful to him for his unwavering confidence and never-ending support.

This intense process was simultaneously exhilarating and excruciating. It was also immeasurably rewarding. The final product would not have been possible without the vast talents and invaluable contribution of many dedicated professionals.

First and foremost among them is my brilliant and unstoppable manager, Kenin M. Spivak. In addition to his exceptional professional guidance, he unwittingly became not only an incredible and vigorous editor, but ultimately an indispensable collaborator.

I also thank the frightfully astute and eagle-eyed Francine Uyetake, vice president of Spivak Management Inc.; Margie Nunan, proofreader extraordinâire; Sonia Fiore, the gifted art director; SMI's Stacie Amezcua, the best multi-tasking executive assistant; Karen V. Fawcett; Sandra Skoko; and Christie Craig, Barry Weiner, Phil Oster, and Bob Pye for their input and criticism.

Finally, I am grateful to the wonderful people who have kept me on the straight and narrow, especially Suzanne Von Liebig, Cleo Cafesjian, Peter Dekom, Princess Elizabeth, Ann Graham, LuAn Mitchell-Halter, Sherry Antolic, Sonia Falcone, Dr. Mel L. Bottner, and my dear friend and mentor, Marilyn Tam.

None of the above would have been possible, however, without the life-long encouragement and support of the best brother a girl ever had—George Stankovich.

*Julie Chrystyn*
*Beverly Hills, California*

I join enthusiastically with Julie in thanking Michael Viner, C. Christie Craig, and all those at Spivak Management Inc. (particularly Francine Uyetake, Ed Lasman and Stacie Amezcua), Phoenix Books and elsewhere whose diligent efforts and insights helped make this book a reality. Without them, particularly Michael Viner, this effort would not have been possible. Francine was indispensable. Her insights and comments large and small are seen throughout the final product. Ed Lasman, Steve Maier and Christie Craig read multiple drafts, providing valuable observations at every step. Margie did a terrific job finding what the rest of us missed, and Rochelle Marie O'Gorman, Phoenix Books' new development editor, dropped everything else to make sure we got it right.

I am also grateful for the wizardry of SMI's Phil Oster and Eunice Jeong who worked with Phoenix Books' Sonia Fiore to create our striking cover. Phil and Sonia also did a terrific job developing our distinctive book design.

Of course, I thank Julie for the opportunity to fly with the eagles. It has been an amazing experience.

My friendships with Barry Weiner, Phil Oster, Bob Pye, Lisa Ragland and Linda Ragland were sorely tested by the many drafts they were asked to review. We have all benefited from their wisdom.

One of the fun things about writing fiction is the ability to name the characters. We have used the freedom to thank many of the friends and professional colleagues who supported us by naming characters after them. We even borrowed Christie's "C3" for the name of the title character's company. Lest there be any doubt, our friends (and C3) share all of the finest traits of their namesakes and none of their peccadilloes.

It is only right that for their initial support, their blunderbuss approach to their agenda, and the light this episode shines on their methods, that I also must thank the pharmaceuticals industry, its lobbyists and its consultants. Without their efforts, this book could never have existed. I commend the reader to consider the Foreword at the beginning of this book and the Afterword near its end to gain a more complete understanding of the foregoing.

*Kenin M. Spivak*
*Beverly Hills, California*